HOMEBOUND

JOHN DAVID ANDERSON

HOMEBOUND

BOOK TWO OF
THE *ICARUS* CHRONICLES

WALDEN POND PRESS
An Imprint of HarperCollinsPublishers

Walden Pond Press is an imprint of HarperCollins Publishers.

Homebound
Copyright © 2022 by John David Anderson
All rights reserved. Printed in the United States of America.
No part of this book may be used or reproduced in any manner whatsoever
without written permission except in the case of brief quotations embodied
in critical articles and reviews. For information address HarperCollins
Children's Books, a division of HarperCollins Publishers, 195 Broadway,
New York, NY 10007.
www.harpercollinschildrens.com

Library of Congress Control Number: 2022931771
ISBN 978-0-06-298600-9

Typography by David DeWitt
22 23 24 25 26   PC/LSCH   10 9 8 7 6 5 4 3 2 1
❖
First Edition

To J. B.
A genius, relative to his kind

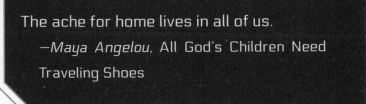

The ache for home lives in all of us.
   —*Maya Angelou*, All God's Children Need
Traveling Shoes

PROLOGUE

UNANSWERED QUESTIONS

"TAKE ME THROUGH IT ONE MORE TIME."

The poor kid looked at him, eyes burning with frustration and impatience. Or maybe just exhaustion. "The whole thing?"

"Not the whole thing. Just the part where the Djarik boarded your ship."

"The first time? Or the second?"

Salty, this one. But understandably so. Sergeant Hilliard rubbed his chin, covered in scruff. It was going on three days since he'd shaved. Four days since he'd had a hot shower. Seven since he'd had a full night's sleep. Of course as bad as he probably looked right now, the displaced teen sitting across from him looked worse. Like something a Snid sucked up and spit out. Splotched skin, bloodshot eyes, untamed hair—he looked wild. Wounded. Maybe even a little dangerous.

Hilliard couldn't blame him. He'd seen his fair share of orphans, rejects, and refugees since being stationed here, but this kid had truly been through the ringer. First he watches his father get taken away at gunpoint by the enemy. Next he's left stranded on a crippled ship in the middle of the void. Gets attacked by pirates. Then he loses his brother—though really that one was at least partly on him. Then the Djarik come *back* for him for some reason, but before they can do whatever terrible thing they've got planned, he and what's left of the ship's crew rise up and take control of the alien transport, pointing it at the closest Coalition outpost they can find, depositing this poor, skinny, beat-up teen right into Hilliard's lap.

The sergeant felt for him. Really. He was somebody's son, after all. Hilliard was a father himself; he couldn't fathom what it must feel like to have your family suddenly ripped apart like that. What he wanted was to give this poor boy a hug and a hot meal. But for now, all Hilliard could do was take his statement, get every bit of information he could. Because the kid's father was an *important* somebody.

"The first time," the sergeant clarified. "When they took your dad."

The young man nodded, then started up again. You could

tell he was just reciting at this point, like reading off a holo-prompter. He'd relived this event so many times in his head that he'd almost grown numb to it.

At least until he got to the part where his father put him in charge, asked him to look after his younger brother. Then you could see the shame printed on his cheeks. The regretful choke in his voice. Just imagine, sending your own brother away in the middle of uncharted space.

Some things seem like good ideas at the time. In moments of crisis. When there really are no good ideas.

"And the Djarik didn't say anything about what they wanted Dr. Fender for?"

The boy shook his head.

"They didn't mention anything about his research? Or EL-four eight six? Anything like that?"

"I wasn't there when they took him," the kid said. "I just know he was the only one they took."

"The first time."

"The first time."

Hilliard nodded and keyed a note into his datapad. None of his superiors bothered to tell him what this was all about, only that the kid might know something vital to the war effort, that his father was some big-shot American scientist who had been kidnapped, and that Aykari High Command had an interest in getting Dr. Calvin Fender back. Preferably before the Djarik got whatever it was they wanted out of him.

"Do you have any idea where my dad is?"

The kid stared hard at Hilliard, an intensity burning behind a pair of blue eyes, all the more striking for their bloodshot rims.

The sergeant shook his head. "We're working on it, son. My understanding is that the Coalition is making it a high priority. They want to get your father back. We all do." It wasn't just a line. Hilliard had heard stories about what the Djarik did to their prisoners: torture, interrogation, execution without trial. There was no galactic equivalent of the Geneva Convention to protect them. This war between the Djarik and the Aykari—it was brutal, and *everyone* was paying the price.

There were days he honestly wished those lanky blue-or-orange-eyed Aykari interlopers had never shown up to begin with, parking their silver ships in the Earth's atmosphere like they owned the place, dropping drills on every square inch of earth they cared to. But if it hadn't been them, it probably would have been the Scalies. Or some other alien race looking to poke holes in the planet's crust and squeeze it like a sponge, sucking out every last bit of V. That's how it was: you had something the universe wanted, they would find a way to take it. You could try to fight or you could just let them have it, but either way, it was going to cost you.

God, he was tired.

"What about my brother?" the kid asked. "Have you found

anything about him? Or the pirates that took him?"

Hilliard scrolled across his datapad's screen, bringing up all the information he had on the kid's brother. Name: Leo Fender. Age: thirteen. Human. Earthborn. Assigned as a passenger aboard the *Beagle*—a ship that was now just space dust. The family was from Colorado. A lot of ventasium in Colorado. Hilliard had gone skiing there once—before the constant avalanches made it unsafe.

That was pretty much all the info Hilliard had on the brother. But there was quite a bit about the company he was presumably keeping: several data files about the human pirate Bastian Black and his cutthroat crew, including a sizable bounty and an even bigger list of arrestable offenses. Leo Fender had picked the wrong ship to stow away on. Assuming, of course, that the kid was still with them, that the pirates hadn't sold him to a slaver or simply blasted him out of the air lock. Hilliard wasn't about to say it out loud, but the chances that someone like Black would keep ballast like that around were slim.

Unless he thought he could get something out of him. Pirates could find profit in almost anything. And if Black knew who Leo's father was . . . At the very least he could use the kid to blackmail the dad. Force him to give up secrets. Research. Anything he could turn around and sell on the black market. Hilliard couldn't think of a single thing he wouldn't do to keep his own daughter safe.

The sergeant conjured up a pathetic excuse for a smile, immediately regretted trying, and resumed his somber expression. "I'm sorry. We don't have any information about your brother, but rest assured, we are looking for him as well."

"As hard as you're looking for my father?"

Hilliard paused before answering; this kid was smart. Dr. Calvin Fender was a renowned physicist with intimate knowledge of V and the Coalition's ongoing research into its uses. Leo Fender was just a kid. One of millions who had been displaced or abandoned as a result of this war. The higher-ups made it clear that finding Dr. Fender was a priority and that all effort would be expended to do so.

The hope was that Leo would just turn up. Much like his brother had.

"We really are looking for him," Hilliard repeated. It was the best he could do.

The young man leaned across the table, fingers clinched. "Can't you tell me anything? I've answered all of your questions and you've given me nothing. You don't know where my father is. You don't know where my brother is. You won't tell me what you're doing to find them. You can't even tell me why they took my dad in the first place!"

Hilliard sighed. This kid was breaking his heart. The sergeant had already made up his mind that when this debriefing was over, he was going to go hunt down a cup of hot coffee for the both of them. Some small gesture to let this boy know that somebody out there cared, at least a little.

"Sorry, son. If there are answers to any of those questions, they're above my pay grade. Believe me, I'm only trying to help."

The kid slumped back in his chair, rolled his eyes to the ceiling. "Some help."

Hilliard decided to switch gears for a moment, maybe get the kid to refocus. "Says here you're interested in joining the Coalition Navy. That's admirable." Honestly, he could think of other words to describe it—foolhardy, impetuous, suicidal—but saying them could get him in trouble. Best not to bad-mouth the boss.

"I just want to get my family back," the kid replied. "Even if that means going out and looking for them myself."

"So what? You learn how to fly and then steal a starship and just go hunt them down?"

"If I have to," the kid said, challenging him with a stare. "If *you* won't."

Hilliard knew better than to take it personally. *You* was the Coalition. The Aykari. The whole machine. The sergeant was just a cog.

"Probably better to leave the search and rescue up to the professionals." He looked again at his notes. "Let's get back to your dad, Dr. Fender," he began, but his next question was cut off by the hiss of the door opening behind him. He turned with a scowl ready—he'd been told he could use this room for as long as he needed with no interruptions. "Excuse me, I'm sort of in the middle of some . . ."

The sergeant trailed off. Standing in the doorway was a human he didn't recognize, though admittedly he didn't know most of the personnel assigned to this outpost. She wore a Coalition uniform that looked too small, stretched over her muscular frame. A pistol sat on her hip, standard issue, but in her left hand was some other kind of device Hilliard didn't recognize—something of alien design perhaps, sticklike, pointed at one end, like an oversize stylus. His eyes gravitated up to the woman's hair—short and neon green—and back down to her eyes, which didn't even seem to acknowledge his presence. They were fixed instead on the kid sitting on the other side of the table.

"Gareth Fender?"

The boy nodded. Suddenly the sergeant's skin started to tingle, instincts from three years in the service kicking in. Something wasn't right here. According to the bars pinned to their chests, Hilliard was a higher rank, yet this woman hadn't bothered to salute. She might be in uniform, but she wasn't a soldier.

Which meant she was trouble.

The impostor kept her gaze fixed on the kid. "You're coming with me," she said. It wasn't an invitation or even a suggestion. There was no threat implied, but there was no doubt either.

Hilliard stood up, dropping his hand to his side, fingers reaching for the handle of his own weapon. "Excuse me . . . who are you? What's your name and rank? What division do you belong to?"

The woman finally looked him in the eyes and Hilliard realized a second too late just how much trouble she was. He didn't even have time to unsnap the button on the holster. The arc of blue energy spit from the tip of the unknown device, a jolt of forked lightning hitting him square in the chest, causing every muscle to seize. He hit the ground hard, feet twitching.

Sergeant Sam Hilliard's last thought before blacking out was of sitting on his deck in his backyard with his wife and daughter back on Earth. So very far from here.

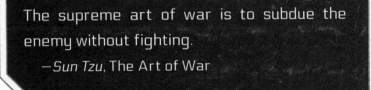

The supreme art of war is to subdue the enemy without fighting.

—*Sun Tzu*, The Art of War

FIRE AWAY

LEO FENDER COULDN'T CRY.

He tried. He stepped on his own foot, grinding the heel of one polished loafer into the toe of the other, wincing at the pain, but wincing wasn't the same as crying, and even if it was, they would still be the wrong kind of tears. Physical pain wasn't anything like what he was feeling now.

This was so much worse.

It didn't make sense. He'd cried a hundred times since that day. He'd cried himself to sleep almost every night. He teared up at the most random times: clearing the plates at dinner, putting his clean socks back in the dresser, watering the daylilies—the ones they'd planted together—along the front porch. But now, when it was called for, when everyone was surely expecting him to, he couldn't, and it made him angry at himself.

Gareth was crying. His brother's eyes had been swollen for hours, a slow but steady procession like the drip of a melting icicle, earning him no end of sympathetic pats and pouting frowns, not to mention a piece of chocolate from their neighbor Mrs. Tinsley, who insisted it would make him feel better. Not that Leo wanted anyone's sympathy or their chocolate. He just couldn't stomach the thought that someone else was hurting worse than him—or that he wasn't hurting enough. Cousins and nieces and colleagues and friends were all shedding tears. The tissue box sitting by the guest book was nearly empty. Even the sky itself was in mourning, the rain battering the stained glass windows. But Leo, dressed in his scratchy suit and clip-on tie, couldn't summon a drop. He dug his nails into his arm until they nearly broke skin. Nothing.

Even staring at the picture of her that had been placed on the altar didn't prompt the tears to come. The photo, taken the year before while they were on vacation, long hair and a wistful smile, her searching gold eyes staring across the Grand Canyon, which she was seeing for the first time. The picture, enlarged and placed on a stand, took the place of a coffin or an urn. Grace Fender had been too close to ground zero when the missile struck, practically vaporizing everything nearby. No physical remains—just a million reminders.

Leo fiddled with his watch, tempted to press the button that would summon her. That would play the video of her sitting on the porch, bringing her back to him, if only for a moment. He longed to hear her voice. *I see you there, my little lion.*

"How are you holding up?"

Leo glanced up to see his father standing in front of him, dressed in an almost identical suit to Leo's, save for the fact that his tie required a knot. His father owned a million ties. A new one every Christmas, mostly from the kids because they didn't know what else to get him. Leo shrugged. "People keep asking me that," he said.

Dr. Calvin Fender, renowned scientist, Nobel Prize winner, recent widower, and single father, settled into the pew next to his son. "Strange, isn't it? We can travel to Neptune with the snap of a finger. We can mend broken bones almost overnight. We can unlock the very secrets of the universe itself. But we can't seem to think of the right thing to say at a funeral."

"I can't cry," Leo admitted.

This time it was his dad who shrugged. "It's not a requirement."

"But don't you think I should? People will think I'm not sad."

His father shook his head. "I don't think anyone believes that. Besides, we all experience grief differently. Half of these people aren't even crying about your mother. They are crying about someone else they've lost. Or someone they are afraid to lose. Do *you* feel like you need to cry?"

"I don't know," Leo said, making shapes with his fingers, interlacing them, remembering a rhyming game she showed him once, a long time ago. *Here is the church. Here is the steeple.* "I don't want her to think I don't miss her."

His dad reached out and took both of Leo's hands in one of his own. "Well, *I* know. Believe me. I miss her just as much as you do. And *you* know. And that's really all that matters, right?"

Leo nodded, though he still wasn't so sure.

They sat for a minute more in silence, just the two of them sitting in the front row, listening to the steady drum of rain on the roof.

"I want to go home," Leo said.

"I know you do. This will be over soon. I promise."

Leo leaned into his father, eyes falling upon her picture again, staring across the giant fissure gouged deep into the earth like an open wound that would never heal.

"Hey, Leo."

His brother's voice caused Leo to sit up. He turned but couldn't spot Gareth in the crowd.

"Leo? You with us?"

He scanned the faces before him, all of them suddenly alien and unfamiliar.

"Earth to Leo?"

A finger snap.

Leo Fender shook his head and focused on the man staring back at him, the memory quickly receding. This wasn't his dad or his brother. It was a haggard face with a ragged beard and a sharp, hooked nose, so different from his father's knobby one. Scars arced above the eyebrow, along the chin.

This was the face of a pirate.

The man's hair was cropped short enough to reveal a left ear half-missing, the curved remainder an angry pink whirl of newly scabbed flesh. Leo had watched that ear get blown off by an energy bolt. Fired from the rifle of an Aykarian soldier, no less.

Because that's what you do to pirates. You shoot them. You arrest them. You hang them for treason. At least that's what Leo had always thought. But he'd been forced to rethink a lot of things lately. Especially when the Aykari started shooting at him too.

"Sorry. Got a little lost there."

"Yeah . . . well, don't freak out on me, kid. We've got work to do," Bastian Black said.

Leo's eyes readjusted to their surroundings. He'd been deep inside his own head again, somewhere far away. But now he was back. Back inside this hulking, metal, pear-shaped ship hurtling through space, staring at a man with a ratty black T-shirt asking if anyone's Got Milk.

"Seriously, ninja turtle, you okay? You look like you've just had your mind wiped by a Darvatulan brain leech."

Leo had no idea what that was, but it sounded not too far off from what he was feeling. His brain felt scrambled, like someone had scooped it out and dropped it in a blender before pouring it back in. "I'm all right," he said.

Baz put a hand on Leo's shoulder. "Definitely need to work on your lying. Time to strap in, then. We're coming out of our jump."

Leo nodded and followed the captain of the *Icarus* into the cockpit where the other members of the crew were already assembled. Katarina Corea sat in the pilot's seat, dressed in her customary black uniform, her titanium hand operating the controls while the one she'd been born with fiddled with an ugly fuzzy-blue-haired doll that Baz kept hanging from the ship's console. Skits was busy at another control panel, messing with some wiring—whether making it better or worse, Leo couldn't be sure; it probably depended on her mood. She swiveled along her bucket-like torso and smiled at Leo because she had no choice—it was her only available expression. Next to the tank-treaded robot, the four-armed Queleti was busy attacking his toe claws with some kind of industrial bolt cutter.

"Trimming your nails?" Leo asked.

"Baz told me I had to," Boo said gruffly.

"That's because when they get that long I can hear them clicking on the metal floor when you walk," Baz said. "Do you know how annoying that is? All the time. Click-click-click-click-click."

"No more annoying than you banging on the console, playing your imaginary drums constantly," Kat countered. "Besides, why would anyone take hygiene advice from you? When's the last time you cleaned your teeth?"

"I gargled some warm beer an hour ago," Baz informed her. She made a face.

Boo squeezed the handles of the bolt cutter and the tip of one claw went flying. "Incoming," he warned as the clipped nail pinged off the wall.

A week ago, if Leo had been this close to the lumbering hulk of hair and muscle that was Bo'enmaza Okardo, he would probably have peed his standard-issue Coalition khakis. But since then he'd saved the alien's life and vice versa. They'd even slept in the same bed. Not exactly what he'd envisioned three years ago when his father informed him they'd be journeying into outer space—using an alien's fur as a makeshift blanket in the bottom bunk of a pirate transport—but that's what it had come to.

The same went for all of the crew of the *Icarus*. Not long ago, Leo would have looked at them—*had* looked at them—with skin-prickling apprehension and distrust, seeing them as outlaws and traitors, the kind of people you would only be caught dead with, mostly likely because they would have killed you. But a lot had happened since he first boarded this ship. A lot that Leo still didn't understand. But he at least knew he wasn't afraid of pirates anymore.

Not these pirates, at least.

"Scootch," the captain said, forcing Kat into the copilot's seat. The first mate knew her way around the *Icarus*'s controls—she could fly just about anything—but Bastian Black had been a pilot of one kind or another since he was Leo's age. Before being captain of the *Icarus*, he'd piloted starfighters for the Coalition. And even before that, he used to fly old-fashioned airplanes.

Back on Earth. That gorgeous blue-green marble, third parking spot from the sun. Leo's home. At least the only place he'd ever called home.

A planet that, like many others rich in V, was in serious danger.

Leo conjured his father's voice in his head. *Do this for me, Leo. It could mean the world.* Those were the last words Calvin Fender said to Leo before he was taken away. The second time.

No. Not taken, Leo reminded himself. He made a choice. He could have gone with Leo or taken Leo with him, but instead he left his son in the hands of these pirates. *And now he's gone*, Leo thought. *Again.* All of them were. Mother. Father. Brother. It was just Leo. All alone.

But not exactly.

Kat spun around in her copilot's chair and fixed the captain with a hard stare. "You know, if you're wrong about this, we could be in even bigger trouble. We're already down to our last core, and the sublight engines are barely clanking along as it is. We're leaking coolant out of the starboard tank and I'm pretty sure we took some significant hull damage high-tailing it out of Halidrin. So if there are no good targets out here . . ."

"Kat, Kat, Kat," Baz muttered. "Why don't you trust me? After everything we've been through. Name one—no thr— name *five* times that I've let you down."

The first mate turned to the robot, still futzing with an electrical circuit. "Skits, access the file labeled 'History of Bastian Black's Blunders and Miscalculations, Volume One.'"

"'History of Bastian Black's Blunders and Miscalculations, Volume One' by Katarina Corea," the bot repeated.

Baz frowned. "Volume *one*?"

"I'm leaving it open for the inevitable sequel," Kat whispered as Skits started reciting from the top.

"'Number one: the time he tried to double-cross that Arzuran arms dealer by selling him a crate full of welding torches instead of actual military-grade flamethrowers.'"

"Yeah, I remember that," Baz said with a smirk. "That guy was so ticked. Never seen anyone turn *that* purple before, though he *was* sort of blue to start with."

"'Number two: the time he insisted on bringing a Zarbeast on board and it chewed through the wiring in the weapons systems and short-circuited the entire ship, leaving us all temporarily without life support.'"

"Okay . . . that wasn't smart. But you have to admit that little guy was pretty cute. With those ears? And that pudgy little snout? And that spiky tail? You know I'm a sucker for strays."

"'Blunder number three: the time he accidentally detonated a stun grenade that had been left in his pants pocket, paralyzing him for three—'"

"Okay, Skits, we get the point," Baz interrupted. "So . . . I'm human. Shoot me."

"I can name at least five entire *civilizations* that would like to," Kat countered. "Some of them have even tried."

"And failed."

Kat pointed to the captain's mangled ear.

"Hardly counts. You know what? I don't need this from you. I'm still your captain. Just bring us out of the jump at the coordinates I gave you. You'll see I'm right."

"First time for everything," Kat quipped, but Leo knew she was just giving him a hard time like she always did. There was no one Kat trusted more than Bastian Black. When she was at her lowest point, a one-armed pickpocket trapped in a mining colony, scrabbling and scraping for her very existence, Black had been the one to come along and rescue her. To take her in. To give her a family.

Leo knew a little bit about Black's history too. He'd gotten a glimpse of it secured in a box stowed beneath the captain's cot. The man who had defected from the Coalition. Turned his back on the Aykari. Stolen from his own kind. Though maybe *he* wouldn't see these as missteps. Just decisions with consequences. Or maybe just the only way to get by.

His latest adventure, though—busting into a Djarik research facility to rescue a high-profile prisoner—*that* had turned out to be a failure, though Leo couldn't blame Black for not saving his father. Not when he had the man himself to blame.

At least his father had apologized. *I'm sorry. I have to see this through.* This. Whatever the Djarik had captured him for. Whatever was on the chip Leo's father had slipped him. A way to end the war, Leo was told.

At the cost of whole planets.

"All right, ship rat. Time to buckle up," Kat said.

"And try not to blow chunks all over the cockpit again," Skits scolded.

Leo found the seat beside Boo, closing his eyes and willing himself not to throw up this time. He couldn't imagine how it could even be possible: the last thing he could remember eating was a crème-filled sponge cake that was somewhere between three and thirty years old. That, and some fake chicken he'd split with his brother, Gareth, the last time the two of them were together. What felt like eons ago, though it had only been a matter of days.

"Here we go," Kat said.

A flick of a few switches and the *Icarus* shuddered. The whole ship seemed to shrink and then expand like an accordion, and Leo felt his body doing the same, every cell seemingly turned upside down and inside out before recombobulating itself, all in less than a second. A sharp pain stabbed at the backs of his eyeballs and he felt his stomach lurch, but there really was nothing inside worth getting out. He heard his father's voice inside his head. *It's normal, Leo. No living being was meant to hurtle through space and time like this. Ventasium-based space travel breaks just about every law of physics known to humankind. It's bound to give anyone a tummy ache.*

The first time Leo had ever made a jump, he'd been holding his father's hand. All three of them threw up. Leo. Dad. Gareth. A Fender family chuck-a-thon. Eventually his father and brother got used to it—the side effects of hyperspace travel. Leo, not so much.

With the jolt and lurch, the *Icarus* reentered the void of space, and Leo found himself staring at the red disk of an unfamiliar planet. One blazing star could be seen lurking behind it, the center of whatever system they had jumped to.

"Kat, run a scan for nearby vessels," Baz ordered.

"Where are we?" Leo asked.

"SS-eight-five point four thirty-eight in the Aykarian catalog. More affectionately known as the Mirabar system. A cluster of planets renowned in this part of the galaxy for their gorgeous and exotic topography and rich biodiversity," Baz said. "At least that's what the brochures will tell you. It's a prime destination for planet hoppers. You are almost guaranteed to find at least one ship full of rich, oblivious space tourists floating out here on their yachts, eating and drinking themselves into a stupor."

"Or more than one," Kat said, pointing to a constellation of blips on the radar. "Got a prime candidate here. C-class cruiser. Not too big. Looks like a Darkashian pleasure barge. Standard shields. Nominal weapon systems. She's a baby gazelle." Kat grinned, a little mischievously.

Easy prey, Leo translated for himself.

"We have a winner," Baz said. "Jam their coms. How many black widows do we have left?"

"Two."

"Let's make it one. Hook this fish before it can swim away."

Leo suddenly felt uneasy as the realization of what was happening dawned on him. "Wait, you're *attacking* them?"

Baz turned and gave Leo a look that said, *Um . . . pirate, remember?*

"We're hitting the ship with an ion torpedo that will temporarily disable its systems so it can't jump away or try to outrun us," Kat explained. "Then we board it, relieve it of any ventasium it has, and jump away before any local authorities find out what's going on and cause trouble."

"And death to those who dare to stand in our way!" Skits

said in her mechanical chirp. So *that* was the kind of mood she was in. Leo frowned.

"Don't worry, kid," Baz said. "She's just being dramatic. If we do this right nobody gets hurt."

"And if you do it wrong?" Leo asked.

"Then *we're* usually the ones that get hurt," Kat said.

Black could obviously see the unease still in Leo's eyes. "Look. Your old man needs you to deliver that datachip to Zirkus Crayt, yeah? And, sucker that I am, I promised I would help. But the *Icarus* is running on fumes. We need fuel. And it's not like we can pull up to the next Coalition depot for a top-off—not unless we want our heads in a noose. So unless you've got a hunk of V burning a hole in your pocket . . ."

Leo shook his head. He knew Baz was right. He just didn't like it.

"All righty then," Baz said. "Kat—cue the attack music. Let's rock and roll."

Suddenly the cockpit was filled with electric guitar growls and pounding bass drums. Some really angry human started in, her voice full of gravel and sharp glass.

Hit me with your best shot.

Leo could feel the *Icarus* accelerate, zooming toward a little silver dot against the speckled black backdrop of space.

Why don't you hit me with your best shot.

"Torpedo armed."

The silver speck revealed itself to be a gleaming ship, sharp angles, sleek lines. It *looked* fast. But that wouldn't matter if it was caught by surprise.

"Fire awaaay!" Baz sang.

Leo watched as the torpedo streaked toward its target, detonating on contact, dispersing an ion charge that wove its way through the ship's hull, infiltrating all of its powered systems and temporarily shutting them down, leaving the ship paralyzed, the gazelle buckling before it could even take a step. He felt a quiver ripple down his back. It hadn't been that long ago that his own ship had been struck with torpedoes, leaving its wounded carcass stranded in space. He could still remember exactly how it felt when the Djarik boarded the *Beagle*, he and Gareth huddled in the corner of the room, waiting in the darkness for his father to come back, his brother shivering beside him, not knowing who or what was going to open the door.

Leo thought he might be sick again.

"She's stunned," Kat said.

"Then find a hatch and get us hooked. Boo, you ready to look intimidating?"

The Queleti shrugged all four arms. "Meh."

"Vicious as always."

Kat took over the controls and guided the *Icarus* to dock alongside the stricken ship while Baz gathered a couple of satchels and changed into his Jordans. Apparently flip-flops weren't the fit for a pirate raid.

"All right. Here's the plan. Kat and Boo will head to the bridge and keep the crew under control while I sneak off to the engine room and get the goods. Skits, you and Leo will stay aboard the *Icarus* and keep an eye out for incoming patrols. You tell us the moment any new ship pops up on the radar so we can skedaddle."

"In other words, wait here until you screw everything up and then come and save your sorry meat-sack hides like I always do," Skits translated.

Baz winked. "That's my girl."

Leo shook his head. He didn't like this plan. "I'm coming with you."

"Not *this* conversation again," the robot moaned. "God, Leo, would you just get over yourself already?"

Baz looked like he was thinking the same. "Listen, Leo. I know what you're going to say, and I'm not about to deny that you've handled yourself well before. But this . . . what we're about to do right here? This is pure piracy. Like walk-the-plank, ahoy-me-hearties, hang-from-the-gallows stuff. Do you really want your face on a wanted poster?"

Leo considered pointing out that he'd already had a bounty hunter after him—Baz's green-haired, gun-toting ex-girlfriend, no less. And that he was probably *still* being hunted simply because of who his father was. But those were just excuses. He had personal reasons for wanting to go on board.

"We're doing this to get V, right? Which we need to deliver the information contained on that datachip—the one my father entrusted to *me*, not you. So, pirate or not, this is my mission. And I'm coming with you."

Baz frowned. Leo hadn't known the man long, but it was long enough to know that he smiled when he thought he was about to get away with something and frowned when he knew he *wasn't* going to get his way. He'd been frowning a lot recently.

"Fine. But from now on, if you're coming along, you're going in armed. I can't have you threatening people with your asthma inhaler anymore."

The captain unholstered one of the two pistols currently riding on his hip and handed it to Leo, who took it tentatively, pinching it between his fingers like a wet sock. He waited until Baz's back was turned and then handed the pistol to Boo who turned and handed it to Kat who tucked it into the satchel slung across her shoulder.

"All right. Let's do this by the numbers. Get in. Get the goods. Get out."

Skits piped up. "And a painful and bloody death to all those who dare to hrm wrffle wrm."

Boo had placed one of his four hands over the robot's voice emitter, muffling her.

"Fine," she said, once the Queleti removed it. "*Don't* kill anybody. See if *I* care."

Leo figured it was best she was still staying on the ship.

The hatch was unguarded, just like Baz suspected it would be, and the three pirates plus Leo soon found themselves in the main corridor, looking down rows of cabins, all with their doors sealed shut.

All except for one.

Standing in that one open doorway was a species Leo had never seen before, its squished figure composed of two squat legs, two short arms, and an almost nonexistent neck supporting a triangular head that reminded Leo a little of a praying mantis's, with two antennae and a pair of bulbous red eyes sticking out of either side like oversize Christmas ornaments. The alien was holding a metal stick of some kind, brandishing it like a sword or a baseball bat, attempting, perhaps, to hold its ground against the ship's invaders.

Leo admired its bravery. He also knew the creature stood no chance.

Baz nudged Boo, who extended all four of his arms in a truly menacing fashion, stomping one foot with its newly trimmed claws. "Aaaahgh," he growled.

It didn't *sound* especially menacing, but it did the trick; the once brave Darkashi emitted a squeak through its snout, dropped its impromptu weapon, and promptly vanished behind its cabin door.

"Not bad, but your 'argh' still needs work," Kat told Boo.

"Less *ah*. More *rrrr*. Like this. Arrrrrrgh!"

Boo tried again. "Aaaarrrghh?"

Kat winced, unconvinced.

Baz pointed down the corridor. "Skits has hacked into the mainframe. She says the bridge is that way. Engine room is behind us. You two go do your thing and Leo and I will meet you back here in two shakes."

"Aye, aye, Cap'n," Kat said with a mock salute.

Leo watched as she and Boo strolled casually down the corridor, looking more like they were taking a walk through the woods than pillaging a paralyzed starship. If it wasn't for the rifle slung across Kat's shoulder—recently acquired from Zennia, Baz's bounty hunter ex-girlfriend—you might not even know they were pirates.

This wasn't exactly what Leo imagined when he pictured a boarding. His past experience with Baz had been filled with smoke and gunfire, explosions and expletives. In the span of a day Leo had found himself shot at on three separate occasions. Not to say that he was getting used to it. Only that by comparison, this seemed too easy.

Then again, if pirating was *always* dangerous and deadly, pirates would probably find some other way to make a living.

"This way," Baz said. "Stay behind me. And don't shoot unless . . . hey . . . Where's the gun?"

"Gave it to Kat," Leo admitted. "Trust me. We're all safer this way."

Baz didn't bother to argue. "In that case, stay *right* behind me."

They made their way through the ship; most of the doors they passed were sealed, and those that weren't revealed empty rooms. One was clearly a lounge of some kind. Next door sat a huge round chamber buzzing and flashing with all kinds of strange machines. "Casino," Baz said. "Or at least the Darkashi equivalent. They come here to piss all their pentars away. Sometimes they watch live video feeds of battles between the Aykari and Djarik and bet on the outcome."

Leo shook his head trying to picture this room full of stubby-legged Darkashi with drinks in hand watching one of the giant vid-screens as starships exploded and hundreds of creatures perished, all the while trading chips based on the tally of the dead. "That's terrible. Why would anyone bet on something like that?"

"We're all doing it," Baz replied. "One way or another. Most of us just don't do it while eating hors d'oeuvres."

A hundred more steps and they found themselves near the aft of the ship, staring at the door that led to the ship's engines and its faster-than-light-speed drive. Baz swiped his hand over the console. Locked. The captain pounded on the door. "Whoever is in there, open up. This is Bastian Black, terror of the galaxy. Let me in and I promise I will spare your miserable little life."

"'Terror of the galaxy?'" Leo whispered.

"Too much?" Baz wondered. "Oh well. Guess we could just try to blast our way in." But just as he unholstered his remaining pistol, a hidden speaker chimed in with a familiar voice.

"Attention passengers and crew. This is Katarina Corea, first mate of the pirate ship *Icarus*. This vessel is currently under our control. We're not here to hurt you, but we could probably live with the guilt if we did. Therefore I advise each one of you to remain behind closed doors and don't attempt anything foolish. Anyone disobeying this command will be dealt with most severely."

Leo glanced at Baz, who shook his head. He remembered what Boo had told him not long after he'd come aboard the *Icarus*: Kat was mostly talk. One of the keys to being a good pirate was letting other people's fear of you work against them.

Though fear, Leo knew, was only one way to keep people in line. There were other ways. More deceitful ways. Like convincing them that you had their best interests at heart.

"And Baz . . . ," Kat added through the speaker. "You're welcome."

There was a buzz, and the door to the engine room hissed open. Standing right there with a power wrench in his hand gawked another Darkashi, bug eyes even more bug-eyed. He took one look at Baz and swung the wrench, aiming to stave in the captain's head, but Baz easily stepped out of the way, letting the alien overswing and getting in behind him. One swift blow to the back of the Darkashi's oddly shaped noggin and the alien was down. The captain holstered his pistol and stepped over the body.

"Is he going to be all right?" Leo asked.

"He's going to wake up with a helluva headache," Baz said. "But yeah, he'll be fine."

Leo followed Baz into the engine room, much smaller than the one on the *Beagle*, and much cleaner, its surfaces gleaming. Tex—the *Beagle*'s chief engineer—never cared if the research vessel's engineering bay was clean so long as it was functioning. Leo had no idea what had happened to the big blue Eldrin with the foul mouth. The last he heard, the remaining crew—including his brother—had been brought onto a Djarik prisoner transport just before the *Beagle* was scuttled. Then that transport had just disappeared. No communication. No distress call. Just gone. Now you see them. Now you don't.

He hoped they were all okay. It pained him knowing his brother was out there somewhere. But he couldn't go looking for Gareth alone, and to even start searching required the *Icarus* to be able to get from one star to the next.

Which meant they needed more V. Couldn't do anything without it, it seemed.

And Leo was staring right at some. Next to the ship's jump

drive, in a metal storage container specially designed for holding additional cores of the precious fuel.

"Only four?" Baz said, clearly disappointed. "I thought the Darkashi were supposed to be rich." Of course four cores was infinitely more than Black found when he and his crew boarded the *Beagle*. Then, the only thing they'd come away with was Leo, hiding away in their underside storage compartment. "Better take 'em all."

Baz handed Leo the satchel, which Leo opened to reveal a row of insulated sleeves, each the perfect size to hold one core. Baz went back to the door and stared out into the corridor, leaving Leo to gather the goods.

He stood in front of the ship's supply, hesitant. This was the real reason he had insisted on coming. Four cores, plus whatever was left in their drive. Once the *Icarus* was gone, the terrorized Darkashi would want to reactivate their systems and make a jump to get away, just to be safe. Taking all four cores could very well leave them stranded out here. Leo knew what that felt like, floating in space, waiting on someone to come save you. Or finish you off.

"Come on, kid—fill the bag and let's go."

Leo quickly packed up the satchel—handling each core gentler than he knew he needed to—and then closed the storage unit. "Got 'em."

"Then let's make like shepherds and get the flock out of here." Activating the communicator on his belt, the captain hailed Kat. "Spock, this is Kirk. We've got the juice. You good?"

"All finished here. Meet you back at the air lock. And stop calling me Spock. You know I have no idea who that is."

Leo looked at the unconscious Darkashi lying in the doorway, pale green lids closed over his bulging eyes. Leo could tell he was alive by the ripple of tiny slits lining the underside of his pointed chin. "What do we do with him? Just leave him here?"

"You want to take him with us?" Baz countered. "Contrary to popular opinion I actually prefer not to take on stragglers from *every* ship I board."

Leo had to jog to keep up with Baz, the now heavy satchel banging against his side, glancing behind him with every step, waiting for an ambush of some kind. His limited experience with Baz suggested that this was about the time when something terrible should happen. Security bots swarming out from the side halls with guns ablaze or a former significant other pointing a rifle at your head. If Leo had learned anything about being a pirate it was not to let your guard down.

So he was a little surprised—though not at all disappointed—to find no platoon of armed Darkashi waiting for them by the hatch. Just Boo and Kat, the latter's bag looking not nearly as full as the one on Leo's shoulder, the former picking something out of his chest hair. "Dried gyurt," Boo said, giving it a sniff. "Or maybe snot. Can't really tell."

Doesn't say much for the gyurt, Leo thought.

"Mission accomplished?" Baz asked, nodding toward the bag slung across Kat's mechanical arm.

"More or less," she said with a shrug. "You?"

The captain glanced at Leo. The look felt loaded. "More or less," he repeated. "I told you we'd find something out here."

"Oh, I knew we'd find *something*," Kat replied. "I'm just glad it was what we were looking for, for a change."

Back on the *Icarus*, the boarding hatch sealed and ready for separation, Leo was still bewildered at how easy it had been. Not a single shot fired. No screaming sirens. No prolonged standoffs like the one he'd witnessed between Baz and Captain Saito of the *Beagle*. In and out, just like Black had promised.

Leo wondered if it was just easier for the Darkashi to give the pirates what they wanted rather than try and fight them for it. Maybe that's just how the whole universe operated: the ones with the guns took what they wanted while the ones without hid behind locked doors and waited for them to go away and leave them in peace. At least until the next guys with even bigger guns came along.

Baz took the satchel full of ventasium from Leo's shoulder and handed it to Boo, telling him to go charge up the drive before turning to Kat. "All right. Let's see what you got."

Kat dug into her bag and came up with a handful of octago-nal chips. Aykari pentars. As solid a form of galactic currency as there was in such volatile times. Leo stared at them with a sudden pang in his gut. Apparently while he and Black were pilfering the engine room, Kat and Boo were busy robbing the passengers and crew on the bridge. "I thought you said we were just going after V?"

"You know how it is, Leo," Baz remarked. "You run to the store for one thing, you come out with a cart full." He counted the chips in Kat's hand. "Six hundred? That's all those Darkashi were good for?"

"Six hundred and *this*," she said enticingly, pulling out a black cylindrical container about the size of a Queleti's fist. She handed the pentars to Baz and then carefully unscrewed the lid.

Leo couldn't see what was inside, but he could smell it. Even from ten feet away. "Is that—"

"You bet your blaster it is," Baz answered. The captain licked his lips. Leo took another big whiff.

Peanut butter.

Very few things in the galaxy smelled quite like it. Leo's mouth watered.

Kat grinned. "Apparently the Darkashi are crazy for the stuff. It's like caviar to them. I found two jars. Still full."

Leo's belly produced a different kind of pain. Before he could even tell what was happening, Baz was standing beside

Kat with his finger in the container, removing a giant glop of the stuff, admiring it as if it was melted gold or crushed diamonds. "Here there be treasure," he said with a wink.

"I know I wasn't on Earth for long as a kid," Kat said, "but shouldn't we . . . you know . . . spread it on something?"

"Waste of time," Baz said, sucking the glob from his finger. His eyes rolled back into his head. "Oh man. That may be the best thing I've ever tasted in my entire life." He dug in for another fingerful.

Kat followed suit, using her non-mechanical hand. She scooped some up and sucked her fingers, letting out a satisfied groan. "Shoot the freaking stars. Leo. You've got to try this."

She held the jar out to him. He had to admit the smell was alluring. Distinctively earthy, conjuring memories of picnics and school cafeterias. He and Gareth would sometimes carve an apple between them, dipping slices in a shared bowl of peanut butter. His mother would make peanut butter pancakes as a special treat. He started to reach for the jar but then stopped himself, swallowing hard. "That's not what we came for."

"No. But it's ours now," Kat countered, diving in for another scoop. "And if you don't hurry up and get in here there won't be any left."

Leo still hesitated. Of course the ventasium they stole—the ventasium *he* stole, because he was the one who had stuffed the cores in the bag—was worth a thousand times more than one jar of peanut butter. The difference was that Leo *needed* the V—to find Zirkus Crayt. To find Gareth. To do what he promised. This . . . this felt different somehow.

Bastian Black finished licking his fingers and stared at Leo. "Don't tell me you're taking the moral high ground over a jar of peanut butter?"

Leo didn't answer. He just stared and hoped they couldn't hear his stomach rumbling.

"What do you even know about the Darkashi we took this from?" Baz prodded.

"That they're obviously afraid of pirates," Leo said. And that they obviously had good taste.

Baz shook his head. "So you don't know that they live on a planet where basically one percent of them are part of the ruling class, and the rest are little more than slave labor. That the rich force the poor to work in factories making weapons that they can sell to the Aykari, while any leftovers get shuffled off to the Djarik at a black-market discount." Black's voice took on an edge. "So while a few privileged Darkashi prickwads are out there gallivanting around on their pleasure yachts, rubbing antennae and gorging themselves—on a food that *we* invented, by the way—the majority of their species is toiling away in factories, building guns and ships and missiles so other, even more powerful prickwads can fight to see which prickwad will rule them all and leave the rest of us wallowing in the mess they leave behind. And all of a sudden, you're worried because we helped ourselves to their buffet?"

Baz was right: Leo knew none of this. Though it didn't completely surprise him either: that the same species that would bet on the outcome of a brutal battle would supply weapons to those fighting that battle and make a tidy profit. But that didn't mean Leo had to be like them. It didn't mean he couldn't be better.

"So you're saying it's okay to steal from them just because they're rich."

Baz shrugged. "I'm saying that when I die, taking this jar of peanut butter from a bunch of stuck-up Darkashi space tourist snobs will rank pretty far down on my list of regrets. Right behind kissing Marjorie Brinner in the fourth grade even though I knew Bobby Bekerman kind of liked her. Meaning I won't regret it at all."

Sure, Leo thought. *But how does Bobby Bekerman feel?*

Leo looked again at the jar in Kat's hand. It still felt wrong, but it also smelled so good. Reluctantly he dipped one finger, brought it to his lips, took it in. He let the peanut butter sit for a moment on his tongue, a shiver coursing through him. It tasted just like he remembered. And yet he still had a little trouble getting it down.

"Here, kid," Baz said, taking the now half-empty jar from Kat and handing it to Leo. "You finish this one. Consider it your share of the bounty. I'm going to get us out of here before those bug eyes get their ship back online. Kat, stand by to detach."

Leo looked at the container with the sudden surety that he was going to eat the whole thing. He'd already crossed the line, after all, the taste lingering on his tongue making him long for more. No point turning back now.

"Oh, and Leo, one more thing."

Leo looked back at the captain, who was sucking the last of the peanut butter from between his teeth.

"I've handled a lot of the stuff, so I know what four cores of ventasium feels like. The next time I say to take all of them, I mean take *all of them*. Not *all but one of them*. Understood?"

Leo's face flushed. The captain hadn't even looked in the bag. But it didn't matter: he knew what Leo had done. He probably even knew why. But to Bastian Black it didn't make a difference. As far as he was concerned, the Darkashi could—maybe even should—be left stranded out here.

In Baz's world, it was us versus them, and the "us" didn't extend beyond the hull of his ship.

Meaning it was really just him and his crew against the rest of the universe.

Leo, for one, didn't like those odds.

But he wasn't sure what he could do to change them either.

Leo never wanted to fight, even after all that had happened.

His brother felt differently.

At least that's what Gareth said. Not immediately, when the whole world was still reeling, every human being paralyzed with shock at the horrors they'd just endured. But soon after that, when staying out of the way became all but impossible. Once the decision had been made to join the Coalition, and the governments of nearly every nation officially declared war on an entire alien species. When the factories stopped churning out cheap tablets and solar-powered hover cars and started manufacturing artificial gravity generators and incendiary grenades. Gareth had no doubt seen the posters—the same ones Leo saw on his way to school—calling out from every street corner, pointing from every digital billboard, an updated version of Uncle Sam, now a citizen of the world, begging for new recruits. *Your Planet Needs YOU!*

And the footage. You couldn't avoid the footage. Smoldering buildings. Plumes of smoke, white at first, then charcoal, like dark tentacles lashing the sky. Skyscrapers reduced to rubble. Bridges caved in, streets broken into jagged junks, toothlike hunks of pavement jutting up like stalagmites. Whole city blocks decimated, metal cars melted down to unidentifiable lumps. The carnage ran on a loop, twenty-four seven images of first-responders and volunteers sifting through the debris, looking for any sign of the living. Dozens of cities, scattered all across the globe. Everyone knew at least one person killed by the Djarik that day. The names would be etched into stone monuments and steel plaques in the weeks to come. So of course Gareth wanted to fight.

The problem was, he was only thirteen. And his father wouldn't hear of it.

There was a lot of talk in the months that followed, all of the when-I'm-old-enough variety. *When I'm old enough to join, I'm going to fly straight to Djar and drop the biggest bomb you've ever seen right on top of them, big enough to wipe out every last one of those scale-faced freaks.*

To which Dr. Fender always said, *I don't think so.*

Leo remembered one such conversation. Sitting at the patio table in late fall, the leaves of the trees stained bloodred and starting to curl. It was six months after the attack. Cities were still being rebuilt, a process that took time, despite all the advances in manufacturing afforded by the Aykari's arrival. Leo's father had grilled out—a rare occasion for a man who seldom cooked, preferring instead to have the drones drop off their dinner from local restaurants most of the time. The chicken-pineapple-pepper kabobs sitting on Leo's plate had been one of Grace Fender's favorite dishes. She made them every Friday night. Before.

They ate quietly, as they had all summer and into autumn, the boys occasionally piping up about what happened at school or something they'd heard about on the news. That day, Gareth mentioned a headline he'd read, about a stunning victory of Coalition forces over the Djarik out in the Medaran sector. Three Djarik frigates and untold support craft obliterated by joint Aykari and human forces. Djarik casualties were rumored to be in the thousands. A huge tactical victory.

Leo's father frowned.

"That's going to be me someday," Gareth said. "I'm going to be the one blasting those bastards to dust."

"Language," Dr. Fender warned. Leo had never once heard his father cuss. In moments of frustration his dad would grunt instead, a gruff rumbling from the back of the throat followed by a sharp breath. Most of the time that was all he needed to regain his composure. Gareth, on the other hand, had taught Leo enough bad words to fill a notebook over the past several months. "And that's not going to happen."

"Says who? I'm almost fourteen," Gareth protested. "A few more years and I can join the Coalition. Learn to be a fighter pilot."

"Except your mother would never have allowed it," Dad said. "And neither will I."

Gareth bristled. Leo squirmed in his chair. Not a day went by that Leo's father didn't invoke their mother in some way. Not a day when he didn't insist that Grace Fender was watching over them. A strange sentiment for a man who never once went to church. And yet he claimed she was up there somewhere.

"She's the whole reason I'd be doing it," Gareth protested.

"There are better ways to honor your mother's memory

than going and getting yourself killed."

Leo's father glanced at him and not Gareth as he said this. Leo shrank down in his seat, unsure why he was getting the look when his brother was the one doing the arguing.

"So we shouldn't fight back?" Gareth asked, already steaming.

"That's not what I said. I said *you* won't be the one doing the fighting. Neither of you will. Not if I can help it. End of discussion."

There was a pause as Leo picked at his rice. Then Gareth muttered, "That's because you're scared."

"Of course I'm scared!" Dr. Fender said, raising his voice, but only for a moment. "We're all scared. And believe me, I'm angry too. Just as angry as you are. But I made a promise to your mother that I would protect this family at all costs, and I intend to do so."

"Yeah? Was that before or after they killed her?"

As soon as he said it, Gareth snapped his mouth shut, but it was too late; he couldn't take it back. Leo could see the hurt in his father's eyes. The guilt. Not so much from Gareth, because Leo knew his brother didn't mean it. Not really. It wasn't Calvin Fender's fault, what happened that day. But he knew there were days his father blamed himself anyway. One of the smartest men in the world. He probably should have seen it coming.

A black cloud settled over the table. Leo set down his last bite, not hungry anymore. He watched as his father wiped his hands with his napkin, then took the time to fold it and set it gently beside his plate. It was his way. Everything measured. Everything precise. Though it was still a moment before he spoke.

"Someday you will be a father," he said at last.

He gave Gareth an awkward smile that seemed full of love and hope and remorse and so many other things. Leo waited for the other half of the proclamation, for the *and then you'll understand*, but there was no follow-up. That was it.

He wasn't admonishing Gareth or trying to give him some perspective.

He was making a wish.

Someday they would grow up and have families of their own. Him and Leo.

But only if Dr. Fender could keep his promise.

And keep them safe.

Leo wished he hadn't eaten it all. Especially not right before the jump.

He sat in the *Icarus*'s mess area, his stomach roiling, the empty jar in both hands just in case he needed to put it all back where it came from. As he sat, he watched his father, the ingenious Dr. Fender, offer an earnest plea to some stranger named Zirkus Crayt, begging him or her or it to somehow thwart the Djariks' plans to weaponize ventasium and use it to obliterate whole planets, including, presumably, Leo's own.

No pressure or anything.

With Skits's help, Leo had downloaded the recording to his watch, a gift from his parents and now the only Earthly possession Leo had left. At first the watch started freaking out, blinking off and on and then giving Leo the spiral icon of death, and Leo was sure he'd just infected it with a virus, but then it finally restarted, informing him that the video was loaded and ready to view. Now, in addition to watching his late mother caress a blade of grass on his front porch, Leo could watch his father beg for help, pleading with his tired, sunken eyes, speaking in a faltering voice about an end to the war that could not be allowed to happen. Not in this way. Not at this cost.

"With such a weapon at their disposal, the Djarik could destroy any planet where the element is found. . . . There has to be another way."

Dr. Fender's voice was full of desperation. The recording spoke of a galaxy at war. Of the clash of alien empires. Of the decimation of entire civilizations. And yet all Leo could think about was the two of them, his father and his brother, and how much he missed them. Nowhere in the recording did Leo's father say anything about Gareth. *That* plea had been spoken in Leo's ear the moment before he and his father were separated. *He's out there somewhere. Go and find him. Stay together. Keep each other safe.*

And the unspoken follow-up—*because I could not.*

Find his brother. Was that before or after he stopped the Djarik from blowing up the universe? The problem (or at least *one* of the problems) was that Leo didn't even know where to start looking for Gareth. At least with this Zirkus Crayt they had coordinates. A destination. X marks the spot, as Baz would probably never say. The *Icarus* was already pointed that direction.

Leo knew it was the right course, that he was doing the right thing, but that didn't keep him from wishing differently.

After all, he'd never asked for this. Any of it. Unlike his brother, he never wanted to go to war. Unlike his father, he never wanted to go into space. He'd been dragged on board one ship and tricked onto another, when all he wanted—all he ever really wanted—was to stay at home.

Leo paused the vid, freezing his father's face. It was too much for his brain to process—Gareth, his dad, the Djarik, the Aykari—a tangle that only seemed to grow tighter with every string he pulled. It had all been clear once. For the longest time he'd believed in angels and demons. White pieces lined up on one side, black on the other. Now everything was fuzzy. Hard as it was to admit, it seemed like Baz had been right all along. This wasn't one of those movies where you could tell the bad guys by the color of their uniforms and the minor key of the accompanying musical score. There were no angels; the Aykari were just as responsible for everything that was happening—everything that *had* happened—as their enemy.

And yet buried at the center of this tangle of knots was something worth hanging on to. A possibility. That in the end, he could somehow get his father and brother back. That they would leave this war behind and find a place to settle down, just the three of them. Somewhere permanent. Maybe somewhere with no ventasium and so no reason to fight over it. Somewhere they could learn how to be a family again. Leo pictured it. Ached for it. He just didn't know how he'd ever get there.

Leo stared into the empty jar and counted his regrets.

Hello, humans, have no fear.
Let us tell you why we're here.
We would like to be your friend,
The kind on which you can depend.
We'll bring amazing gifts to you
We'll teach you things you never knew.
With our help, you'll venture far
Traveling from star to star.
After all, it's only fair,
If your world we hope to share.
So come on, humans, let us in
So that our journey may begin.

—*Carl Erikson, excerpt from the picture book* Hello, Humans, *2045*

INVASIVE SPECIES

THERE WAS ONLY ONE PLACE IN THE ENTIRE UNI-verse to get ice cream.

Leo's hometown of Mason, Colorado, boasted three different ice cream parlors plus a Dairy Queen, and two Hamburger Huts where the milkshakes came in thirty-two-ounce metal cups. But there was only one establishment the Fenders frequented: a mom-and-pop creamery called Fudgy's, an unfortunate name that found its way into several of Leo and Gareth's more inappropriate jokes.

The place was a throwback to another millennium, with its black-and-white checkered floor, vintage jukebox, and old photographs. The building itself had to be a hundred years old, every surface chipped or peeling, its outdoor benches eaten away with rust. But the ice cream was heavenly, homemade, and stuffed into waffle cones so big you had to grip them two-handed, with a gumball shoved at the bottom to stop leaks. Chewing that cream-covered frozen gumball was the best part, Leo thought—a sweet coda to an indulgent adventure—though it always felt like it would break your teeth.

Which is why his six-year-old heart sat heavy in his chest as he stood with his brother across the street, surveying the destruction before him, the entire building caved in, collapsed, as if crushed under a kaiju's scaly-footed stomp. There were other signs of ruin close by: a fallen tree, the upturned sidewalk, the crack in the pavement running lengthwise across the street. But it was the ice cream shop that had been at the center of the destruction, its stone shell a crumbled heap, its glass doors and windows shattered, laying bare parts of the interior—the marble countertop, the jagged remains of the tiled floor, the still intact commode sitting stalwart next to the broken bathroom sink. A few men in bright orange vests poked through the rubble beyond the caution tape. Leo had no idea what they were looking for. Gumballs, he thought, worrying over all the sweet things that were lost forever. Canisters of whipped cream. Sprinkles and chocolate chips.

Leo could remember the first time his parents had brought him here. His brother had already been twice with friends and had hyped it up. To hear Gareth talk, the ice cream at Fudgy's was better than anything Leo had ever encountered in his entire life. Better than video games. Better than french fries. Better than the Coalition, even. "Think of every cool thing the Aykari have ever given us," Gareth prompted. "Fudgy's ice cream is better than all of it."

It was a preposterous claim: The Aykari had made it possible for humans to travel across the galaxy. They had practically eradicated cancer. They had laser guns, for heaven's sake. No ice cream could be better than laser guns.

Except it was. Or at least Leo had convinced himself it was, his face smeared an alien shade of blue from the three scoops of cotton candy ice cream that he'd somehow managed to fit into his belly. And then there was that precious little surprise at the end, sealing the deal. So delicious. So much better than traveling faster than the speed of light.

Now it was all buried underneath four feet of debris, trapped under cement and drywall and wood. Leo reached out and took his mother's hand.

"It's a shame," she said. "I really liked that place."

She looked around and Leo followed her gaze, taking in the other nearby stores and offices and restaurants. There were several more shattered windows. The sign for Baker Brothers Shoes had fallen. A water main had busted, judging by the pool-size puddle in the street. But nothing like what had happened to the building lying in a heap before them. "I didn't think the quake was that bad," she added. "It hardly rattled the dishes."

It had been bad enough to wake Leo up, at least, his bed shaking, the shells on top of his dresser—the ones he'd just started collecting—dancing in time with the vibrations. His father had come into the room to check on him, told him it was just a "minor geological disturbance" likely caused by the drilling at the new ventasium mining operation just outside town. Sometimes the Aykari excavators probed a little too aggressively in their quest for precious V, triggering seismic disruptions. An annoyance, to be sure, but it seldom resulted in more than a broken plate or a crack in the sidewalk. A small price to pay for progress, according to the scientists who knew best, Dr. Calvin Fender included.

Except this time the fissure seemed to work its way to Main Street, as if marching toward Fudgy's with the sole intent of razing it to the ground. The ice cream parlor was old and built on a weak foundation, barely up to code, its brittle bones snapping under its own shifting weight. Thankfully the store hadn't yet opened for the day and nobody had been inside, so nobody was hurt.

Leo took it all in. The busted pipes. The gaping hole where the accessible parking spot used to be. It reminded him of when Gareth would finish a Lego project and then grant Leo permission to destroy it.

"What now?" he asked. "Will it ever come back?"

"I'm sure it will," his mother said. "They must have been insured. The owners will probably rebuild, and it will be good as new. Better, even. These things happen. You get knocked down. You pull yourself up, dust off your pants, and start again."

That sounded like something his father would say.

"But you promised we could get ice cream," Gareth whined, bringing up the more immediate concern.

"Well, today we get cupcakes instead," Grace Fender declared, and led her two sons to the bakery three blocks away.

She was right. The owners of Fudgy's did have insurance, protecting them against acts of God, and it was determined that anything the Aykari did qualified as such. Two months later a new Fudgy's opened up as part of a strip mall on the east side of town. The Fenders still went several times, but the ice cream tasted different. At least to Leo. Good—but not out of this world. Not like before. Nothing's ever quite the same after it's been broken, he decided. Even if you find a way to fix it, it won't be exactly like you remembered.

They still put the gumballs in the bottoms of the cones, though. That was something.

It was a reason to keep coming back.

Leo was slumped over the metal table, chin digging into his arm, when Kat entered. She looked like she was on a mission.

"Do you see a canister of powdered milk sitting around here?"

Leo scanned the mess area, appropriately named. This part of the ship, like every other part of the ship, really, was a disaster. Compartments hung open, their contents barely held in place by the grav generator. Bowls and cups loitered along the only counter, most of them crusted with old food, waiting for one of the crew to break down and wash them. Strange stains splattered the walls. Some of it was probably gyurt. The big red splotch on the floor could very well be blood. It matched the spot on the jacket Kat had loaned him.

"I've spent too much time staring at Baz's stupid shirt, and now I've got a craving." She pulled out a metal cylinder, opened it, gave it a wary sniff, shrugged her shoulders, and dumped it into the third cup she tried—the first was black inside; the second had something growing in it. As she was adding water from the ship's moisture reclaimer, she noticed Leo fiddling with his watch.

"Everything operational?" She nodded at his wrist.

Leo shrugged. "It's been glitchy since I put my dad's message on it. But it seems to be working okay."

"Pretty cool tech. And that's coming from someone who knows a thing or two." She wiggled the fingers of her titanium hand.

"Gift from my parents," Leo said, noticing how loose the watch was on his wrist. His pants didn't fit quite as snug either. There was simply less of Leo than there was before. "My brother and I both got one, but he lost his."

"The only advantage of growing up an orphan with nothing to your name," Kat said. "You have nothing to lose."

Leo knew it was a joke. He also knew that it wasn't. Compared to Kat, Leo had had a princely childhood—family, friends, nice house, nice schools. At least until the day the Earth caught fire. But then lots of kids had had their childhoods cut short that day. "Gareth could never find anything," Leo recalled. "He was always losing his shoes. His phone. His datapad. He once lost his toothbrush. Found it in his underwear drawer. Had no idea how it got there."

"Please tell me he got a new one."

Leo shrugged. "I was always the one who helped him find stuff. I was good at it. Which is weird, because now *he's* gone, and I have no idea where to even start looking for him."

Kat sat down next to Leo, her cup of milk in hand. Leo recalled how intimidated he'd been when he first saw her. Not so much by the pistol at her side or the artificial appendage capable of crushing his windpipe with barely a squeeze, though those added to the effect. It was more the look in her eyes: the intensity. The challenge. A frosty-blue warning that said, *I've survived so much worse than you.*

It was nothing like the yeah-that-sucks look she was giving him now.

"I know how badly you want to find your brother. If it were me, it would probably be the only thing I could even think about. But if he's anything like you, Gareth can probably take care of himself for a while. At least until we get around to looking for him."

Leo smiled—at the compliment but more so at the *we*. It could have just as easily been *you*. Until *you* get around to looking for him. After all, even with everything they'd been through together—security bots and bounty hunters and botched rescues—she was still a pirate. They were all pirates. They had to take care of themselves.

"Which we will do as soon as we get your father's chip to this Zirkus guy," Kat added, giving her drink a stir.

"Who do you think he is?" Leo asked. His father's message had been scant with the details, only saying that he believed Zirkus Crayt to be their best chance.

"Beats me," Kat said. "Somebody your dad went to school with? President of the Intergalactic Society of Science Geeks? The savior of the universe? Can't be any weirder than the guy with his brain in a jar."

She meant Mac—the hacker who had helped Leo track down his father, and who had almost died in the process. Just one more person who had come to Leo's aid and probably ended up regretting it.

"You aren't the only one feeling lost and confused," she continued. "He pretends to be cool about it, but Baz is freaking out, too. He's got half a mind to just smash the chip to pieces and pretend he never got involved."

"So why doesn't he?" Leo asked.

"Not sure. For you, maybe. Or maybe because he gave your father his word, which, believe it or not, is something Baz still honors. Or maybe he finally found something else to care about besides this flying junk heap and its ragtag crew. He was there, after all, the day the Earth was attacked. Just like you. And that's nothing compared to what the Djarik are planning next. Destroying whole planets . . . that's a power nobody should have," Kat concluded.

Do this for me, Leo. It could mean the world.

"And what do you think?" Leo asked.

Kat hesitated. "I'm just following orders."

Leo knew there was some truth to that. After all, Katarina Corea would take on a whole platoon of Djarik marauders barehanded if Black asked her. But she also questioned the captain at every turn. And he listened to her. Most of the time. "Yeah, but what do you *think*?"

The first mate swirled the spoon around her cup, staring into the frothy white whirlpool she'd made. "Honestly, I think the Djarik only care about the Djarik and the Aykari only care about the Aykari and the rest of us have been caught in between for too long. Maybe whatever's on this chip can make a difference. If it finds its way into the right hands."

"Crayt's?"

Kat shrugged. "Well, it sure isn't ours—I don't understand most of what's on there. Even Skits can't make heads or tails of it. Besides, there's a reason your father did what he did. He didn't tell you to take it to the Aykari, or anyone in the Coalition. That means he doesn't trust them with it." She gave him a searching look. "Who do *you* trust, Leo?"

Leo let his chin dig back into his arms. This question used to be so easy to answer.

Kat tapped her metallic fingers against the table, click-click-click; some habits rubbed off. "Did Baz ever mention the time I almost slit his throat?" she asked.

Leo looked up at her. "You mean yesterday?"

"No. That's when I almost broke his jaw," Kat said, though Leo didn't actually need a reminder. He could still almost hear the crack of her titanium fist smashing into the captain's cheek, all for show, of course. "I know I *threaten* to kill him every five minutes or so, but I've only come close once. It was just after he rescued me from that craphole mining colony on Andural."

"After you killed the guy who cut off your arm?"

"I told you: poor Nero just happened to fall from the top of a very tall building." Kat glanced down at her titanium fingers. "That's not the point. Point is, soon after Baz took me on, we docked at this waystation, sort of like Kaber's Point but a little less seedy. Baz said he needed some supplies. Four-arms wasn't with us yet, so it was just him and me and Skits, and she was tucked away in the back charging. I was in rough shape still. Just plucked off the street, scarred, scared, wary. Still only looking out for myself. I found Baz sitting in the cockpit counting stacks of pentars. I had no idea where he even got the money from, but it was more than I could steal in a year. Enough to buy passage to some other planet or bribe some merchant to let me join her crew, because even though he'd gotten me off that godforsaken rock, I still didn't trust him. I also didn't think he'd just give it to me if I asked, so I decided not to ask. I crept up behind him with the knife I carried, the one I used to cut the pockets of people while they slept, knowing it was plenty sharp enough to slit his throat. I was maybe five feet away when he opened that big mouth of his." Kat paused, smiled.

"And?" Leo prodded. "What did he say?"

"He said, 'This shirt's all kinds of vintage, and blood's hard to wash out.'"

Leo had to admit that sounded like Baz. "So what did you do?"

"I froze, knife in hand, debating whether or not to go for it, try to stick him and slow him long enough to take the money and make a run for the hangar. Then he pushed the stack of pentars across the console without even turning to look at me and said it was mine if I wanted it. All of it. No stabbing necessary and no strings attached. I could take it and go. Or I could put my knife away before I hurt myself and learn to trust someone for a change. Funny. It was one of the hardest choices I ever had to make, between knifing some guy and taking his money or letting him help me instead."

Leo knew which path she had taken. She was here, after all. First mate of the *Icarus*. And Baz was still constantly shooting off that big mouth of his. Even after she punched him in it.

Kat held up her prosthetic, the metal catching the *Icarus*'s yellow lighting. "Turns out, the stack of pentars Baz was counting was to pay for this. He knew a guy working out of the waystation who specialized in cybernetics. It was the whole reason we were there, in fact. We didn't really need supplies. He just wanted to buy me an arm." She flexed her fingers, one after the other, making a fist. "Afterward I asked him why he went through all that trouble, spent all that money for a girl he'd just met."

"What did he say?"

"He said with a bionic arm I'd be able to carry all the heavy stuff."

Leo snorted. That sounded like him too. He also knew there was much more to it than that.

"It's hard putting your life in someone else's hands, Leo. Counting on them to do the right thing, to make the right call. Believe me, I know. So does Baz. Do you trust your dad?"

Trust him? The man who had taken care of him for almost his entire life? Also the same one who had left him in the hands of these pirates? He didn't fully understand why his father did what he did, and was angry at him for doing it— just like he was angry at Gareth for putting him on the *Icarus* to begin with—but Leo still trusted him.

And he obviously trusted Leo. Was counting on him, in fact.

I need you to do something for me.

Leo nodded.

"And I trust Baz. If he says he's going to help you find this Crayt guy, and then find your brother, then he will. We will. . . . Just don't ask me how." Kat took a sip from her cup and grimaced. "I'm no expert, but I don't think milk should have this many lumps."

"One is probably too many," Leo agreed.

Kat sighed and dumped the contents down the disposal, leaving the dirty cup in the sink for someone else to wash.

The jump out of hyperspace was just as bad as the jump in, and this time Leo felt some of the precious peanut butter come slurching up, though he somehow managed to choke it back down. *Always tastes better the first time.* That's what Gareth used to say right after he burped. Leo never could summon a belch to match his brother's magnitude, like a belly monster unleashing its primal roar. Just one of the things about Gareth that Leo was always jealous of.

Everyone was back in the cockpit again, Baz manning the controls, Kat running scans, Boo eating something that looked suspiciously like the kind of crusted rolls Leo used to get at restaurants back on Earth, though this one was dark brown, the color of cocoa. The Queleti had an almost empty jar of peanut butter in his lap as well. Boo held the roll out to Leo.

"Butt crack?"

Leo flinched. "Sorry, *what?*"

"You should try it. It's delicious."

Leo tapped on the side of his head, in the space right behind his ear where his translator had been implanted. Maybe his chip was on the fritz, though it translated everything else Boo said just fine. "Did you say—"

"He did," Kat interrupted. "And it's not what it sounds like. The plant they use to make the grain is tough and the only part you can actually grind is the bottom end, which you have to snap off. Bottom snap. Butt crack. It has its own name in Queleti but something gets lost in translation."

Leo stared at the plump, round roll. It didn't help that it was sort of split straight down the middle. "I think I'll pass."

"Your loss," Boo told him. "It's especially good with these buttery nuts." He tore off part of the roll and dipped it in the jar of peanut butter, scraping it clean and smacking his lips with satisfaction. Leo decided to just let the whole thing go.

He turned from Boo and pointed at the yellow-brown globe they were moving toward. "Is that it?"

"These are the coordinates your father gave us," Baz answered. He sounded hesitant, as if he suspected Leo's dad of leading them into a trap. "Six twenty-two dash forty-nine dash one. The only true planet orbiting this star. I'm sure somebody's given it a better name. Skits, what have you got?"

"My database—which you haven't bothered to update in forever, by the way—says fifty Earth years ago the planet came under the jurisdiction of the Aykarian empire, but it has since been granted independent status."

"Meaning what?" Leo asked.

"Meaning the Aykari cut it loose," Baz said. "Let me guess: at one time it was also full of ventasium."

"At one time. Yes," Skits confirmed. "Moderate to high concentrations."

"But not anymore?" Leo asked. He took in the drab-looking rock they were steadily approaching. As far as planets went, this one didn't look very inviting.

"I guarantee you, if there were still anything on this rock worth having, there would be patrol ships here to make sure we didn't get any of it," Baz said.

"I am reading life-forms, though," Kat added, checking her control panel. "There's *something* down there."

"Let's hope one of those somethings goes by the name of Zirkus Crayt."

Baz guided the ship down slowly, arcing through the atmosphere, which soon grew thick with clouds the color of soot, making it nearly impossible to see through the windscreen. "Like flying behind Pigpen." He turned to Leo. "You remember Pigpen, right?"

Leo shook his head.

"Before your time, I guess. Before my time, really," he added with a sigh.

Eventually the *Icarus* broke through the dense gray blanket to reveal a landscape of beige punctuated with patches of purple, pink, and green—trees and scrub of some alien origin, scrabbling for life in what seemed like an otherwise dry and barren environment. Long fissures tore into the planet's crust, stretching sometimes for miles. It reminded Leo of the salt flats of Utah. Leo's family drove through them once on their way to the coast. He remembered being surprised to see birds circling above the dry, cracked earth. His father explained that they find food in the shallow ponds of water dotting the landscape. "To quote famous fictional mathematician Ian Malcolm, 'Life finds a way.'"

It certainly didn't look like there was much life down here, though, despite what Kat's instruments were telling her.

Spaced out alongside some of these jagged crevices, Leo spotted deeper gouges in the planet's surface, unnatural in shape. He recognized them instantly. He'd seen holes like this before—lifting off in the *Beagle* that first time, looking down at the Colorado countryside, at the pits that had been dug into the rock, the giant platforms drilling deeper and deeper, as if trying to split the Earth in two. "Ventasium mines," he mumbled.

"Planet's riddled with 'em," Baz remarked. "The Aykari went to town on this place. Whole thing looks like it could split apart at the seams any moment. Kat, lock on to the densest cluster of readings you can find. Let's see if there's a city or an outpost of some kind. I'd prefer not to park out in the middle of nowhere."

It all looked like the middle of nowhere to Leo, who suddenly got a bad taste in his mouth, and not just from the post-jump surge of buttery nuts. Suddenly this didn't seem like a good idea. Not a trap, exactly, but he got a sense that whatever was waiting for them down here was going to be a lot more trouble than it was worth. He thought about saying something, asking Black to turn the ship around, suggesting that they forget about his father's message and whatever was on that chip and just go find Gareth instead.

But then he remembered his dad pulling him close, wrapping Leo's hands in his, his breath in Leo's ear. *It could mean the world.*

"There." Kat pointed through the *Icarus*'s canopy to a rise on the horizon, the jagged outline of civilization. A city, perhaps. Or at least a village. Except as the *Icarus* grew closer, Leo could see that it was little more than giant piles of sand and stone, half of them in a state of collapse. Whatever it had been, there wasn't much of it left.

"I'm setting her down there," Baz said, pointing at a relatively flat circle of land just outside the perimeter. "Let's just hope there's no quicksand or giant worms or anything else nasty lurking underneath."

"Giant worms." Boo chuckled. "You humans and your imaginations."

Leo looked at the alien, with his four arms, ox-shaped head, jutting horns, and monkey paws. "You're right, giant worms *would* be ridiculous," he said.

The *Icarus* settled down on a stretch of what turned out not to be quicksand and Kat started shutting the ship down while Baz gave instructions.

"We're all going this time. You too, Skits."

"Terrific," the robot muttered. Her programming was adaptable—a complex code meant to better emulate a human emotional response. As such, she was capable of simulating lots of human responses—affection, concern, apprehension, even empathy to some degree—but Leo was sure that sarcasm was her default.

"I don't understand you," Kat said. "You complain when you're told to stay on the ship, you complain when you're told to get off the ship. What is it that you want, exactly?"

"Not to be told what to do for a change," Skits shot back in her electronic whine. "Plus, there's sand out there. It's going to get into my chassis and chafe my gears. Do you know how irritating that is?"

"I had a rock in my shoe once," Leo said.

"Cry me a freaking river. Maybe come talk to me when you've had a laser blast up your butt."

Boo snorted, tearing off another chunk of his unfortunately

named bread with his sharp teeth. "Yes. I imagine that would hurt."

"All right, that's enough," Baz interrupted. "I need everyone sharp. We don't know who this Zirkus Crayt is or where to find him, which means we're going to have to be nosy, which *means* we're going to end up drawing attention to ourselves. And as much as I love attention, we need to try to stay inconspicuous."

Leo looked over the crew of the *Icarus*. The seven-foot-tall alien dressed in his robe. The robot with the stickers plastered all over her soon-to-be-irritated chassis. The girl with the bionic arm and the sour expression. The captain missing half an ear. How could they *not* stand out?

"Besides, if Dr. Fender wants us to find this guy, that could mean others are looking for him too. Not to mention all the people out there looking for *us*." He locked eyes with Leo for a moment. "So keep your eyes peeled."

"That also sounds painful," Boo remarked. "Why would anyone want to peel their eyes?"

Leo followed the band of pirates through the narrow corridors of the *Icarus* to the boarding ramp, well aware that his last couple of planetary excursions hadn't ended well. But he didn't have much of a choice in the matter: his father had entrusted him to deliver the information on that chip, and he was determined to see that it happened. Besides, the sooner he did, the sooner he could start looking for his brother.

He stepped off the ramp and suddenly he couldn't breathe.

It wasn't the atmosphere. Kat had confirmed it was hospitable, a mostly compatible mix of nitrogen, oxygen, and carbon dioxide, though quite a bit drier than what he was used to on Earth. It wasn't because of the heat either—though that did take him by surprise, having spent so much of his last three years in cold metal ships floating in cold empty space, wearing socks to keep his toes from freezing.

It was what Leo *saw* that took his breath away.

Downtown Los Angeles.

Toronto and Chicago.

Shanghai and Sydney. New Delhi and Berlin.

He saw them in the aftermath. Once the fires had been smothered and the smoke had cleared, leaving buildings reduced to cinder blocks. Mountains of melted steel, blackened and burned-out cars, streets scattered with ash.

That's what he was looking at now. Sort of.

Leo stared at the village before him with its broken streets and crumpled buildings. He felt the terrible squeeze coming, the lasso pulled tight around his chest. He patted his pants pocket for his inhaler just as a reassuring hand appeared on his shoulder.

"You okay?"

Leo nodded meekly back at Kat. It was okay. He would be okay. Just breathe. Float like a balloon. He steadied himself. "What happened here?" he asked.

"The Aykari," Baz said. "The Djarik. They're what happened."

Only days ago Leo would have protested the pirate lumping the two aliens together, but taking in this desolate landscape, he didn't try to argue. Kat had spoken of those caught in the middle—this was clearly part of the middle. Leo surveyed the remnants of civilization lying before him. Hollowed buildings made of beige stone and blushing pink brick, their facades cracked or crumbling or just plain gone. Roads strewn with refuse and rock, almost impossible to navigate in spots. Everywhere Leo looked there were signs of devastation, but no smoke, no fire. This damage had been done some time ago. Directly to his right, a giant sinkhole had formed, swallowing most of the building that had unfortunately once stood above it.

Leo thought of frozen gumballs. Of black-and-white tiled floors. Of acts of God.

"This place is a dump," Skits said. "Why did your father send us to such a trash heap?"

"It does seem like an unusual place to find someone who could help save the galaxy," Kat seconded. "The place looks abandoned. I don't see anyone. Or anything."

"Could be hiding. The scans said there was life here somewhere," Baz said. "We just have to find it."

They moved slowly, Baz in the lead, Leo consciously keeping himself between Kat and the Queleti, who couldn't possibly be cold out here but who cinched his Yunkai tighter around him just the same. They passed what appeared to be a wagon of some kind, its frame made of a dull black metal, its rear axle bent, unusable. It was empty.

Wagons, not cars. Nor hovercraft or magnet trains. Buildings of brick and stone casting their shadow across dirt roads. No steel beams. No pipes or power lines. No communication towers. Leo spotted the crumbling remnants of a well. Whoever lived here was in the equivalent of the human Middle Ages. Primitive. Unevolved—though the Aykari probably thought the same thing about Leo's kind when they happened upon Earth, with its coal-burning power plants and planes that required runways for takeoff. Still, of the buildings that remained, none reached more than two stories high, their glassless windows covered in curtains of heavy gray fabric, draped over them like shrouds.

All but one, that is. Up and to his left, a curtain was pulled back to reveal a leathery, purplish face punctuated by big black eyes and large, almost bat-like ears tufted with white fur. Leo got only a glimpse of it before the curtain fell back into place.

"Um. Guys? There's something in that building. And it was definitely watching us."

"Did it look like it might go by the name Zirkus Crayt?" Kat asked. "Because that would be convenient."

"There's another one," Boo said, pointing up the road to

where a second of the creatures was peeking at them from behind a half-crumbled building. This one didn't immediately go back to hiding after being noticed, but continued to stare, its big eyes blinking, curious. Leo had never encountered this species. He wondered if the alien watching him had ever seen a human before. If so, he wondered what kind of impression that human might have made. And if Leo was about to pay for it.

"Is it dangerous? It looks like it could be dangerous," Skits spouted, head swiveling. "Should I deploy defense measures? Is this a code seventeen? Do you think the flamethrower or the electroprod would be more effective? I *prefer* the flamethrower, but if you think—"

Baz put a hand on the robot's metal head. "Don't overload your motherboard. They don't look hostile. They're probably more afraid of us than we are of them."

"Who said I was afraid? I just wanted to know if you thought they were flammable."

"They saw us coming. No doubt they've seen ships like ours before," Kat guessed.

"And I'm guessing that didn't turn out so well for them," Baz added. "Let's move slow. I don't want to startle them."

He took another step toward the creature peeking at them from around the building. It had a long, V-shaped nose that hung over a small oval mouth before marching in a series of ridges up to those bulbous black eyes. Another tousle of cottony-white hair grew in a triangular patch atop its head. It didn't *look* all that dangerous, but Leo could only see one of its hands, the one that held on to the wall with four clawlike fingers as it peeked around. The other hand could be holding a gun or a bomb or some kind of weapon that Leo had never even heard of before, though judging by the primitive structures crumbling around him, guns and bombs were unlikely. More like spears and clubs.

A spear could still stab you, he reminded himself. A club could still bash in your skull.

Leo tugged on Baz's jacket, his nerves prompting him to talk quickly. "So I saw this really old movie once, about King Arthur and his knights . . . and there was this rabbit in it, right? And the rabbit, it didn't look hostile either, but then it started jumping around tearing all these guys' throats out, like burrowing straight into their chests and eating out their hearts and stuff . . ." He couldn't remember what the movie was called, only that his brother had thought the murderous rabbit was hilarious and Leo had thought it was terrifying.

"We aren't looking for the Holy Grail, kid," Baz said. "Just calm down and let me handle it."

Leo nodded—despite a history of mixed results when it came to Black handling anything. The captain took three more steps, both of his hands raised in a gesture that Leo hoped was universally acknowledged to be one of peace. He doubted that the creature staring at them from around the corner was equipped with an embedded Aykarian translator chip, but that didn't stop Baz from speaking to it.

"Hey there. Hail. Greetings. My name is Bastian Black. I am the captain of a simple trading vessel and this is my crew."

Boo snorted. Kat rolled her eyes. Skits swiveled her head, no doubt scanning the area for more of the creatures.

"We are looking for someone. Perhaps you could help us."

The alien continued to stare at them for a moment, its long leathery ears twitching—much the way a killer rabbit's might. Then it threw back its head and let out a high-pitched screech, sharp and loud. If it was meant to be a word, Leo's translator did not pick it up.

"Was that a 'yes'?" Boo wondered.

"I don't think so," Kat said, nodding toward one of the still standing buildings and the platoon of similar white-haired creatures now creeping out of it.

In fact, they were suddenly coming from everywhere. Ten at first, then double that, then double that again. They appeared from every corner, from every crack in the stone walls, some of them scrabbling forward in a crouch, walking on all fours, others walking upright but approaching cautiously, sniffing the air. They were all dressed in rough, loose-fitting garments of gray and brown with little in the way of embroidery or adornment. None of them appeared to be armed, though each of their fingers tapered to a sharp claw that could probably tear through Leo's shirt and skin with enough effort. He shivered and took a step closer to Kat.

"Do they bite?" Boo asked as some of the creatures revealed mouths full of pointed teeth.

Kat clearly wasn't interested in finding out. Her instincts kicked in as her hand dropped to the pistol at her side.

"Flamethrower," Skits concluded, opening a panel in her torso. "Better for crowd control."

"I told you guys to stay cool," Baz ordered.

"But they're getting closer." Kat's *voice* was cool, but Leo could see that finger of hers twitching. "And in case you haven't noticed, they have us completely surrounded."

"They're only, like, four feet tall," Skits observed. "We can take 'em."

"The Keradian snarlex is smaller than my fingertip. But the poison in its bite can liquefy one's organs in seconds," Boo pointed out less than helpfully. "You can actually watch your own intestines leaking out of your bottom hole. Provided your eyeballs haven't melted in their sockets already."

"No one's having their eyeballs melted," Baz assured them, though Leo could see the captain's hands slowly inching down to the weapons at his hips as well. "Though maybe it's best if we go back to the ship and start looking for this Crayt somewhere else."

Except Leo turned with the others to find their path back to the *Icarus* blocked. Kat was right; they were cut off.

Outnumbered ten to one.

"I think we need a plan B," Kat said.

Leo tried to imagine what kind of bloody havoc forty jugular-ripping rabbits could wreak, then multiplied that times ten.

"I'll show you *my* plan B," Skits hissed. She was no doubt about to light things up when all of a sudden the planet's denizens stopped closing in, freezing as if on command. Leo's eyes fell on another figure, much taller than four feet, almost as tall as Boo, in fact, emerging from one of the larger buildings ahead. As the stranger approached, the herd of smaller aliens parted so it could pass through.

Leo had never seen the race of creatures surrounding them before, but he recognized this new one immediately. The stretched, sloping head affixed atop the lithe and long-limbed frame. The pale blue skin and matching eyes, which glowed as if there were miniature stars burning behind them. The way its tongueless mouth opened and closed like a dilating pupil. Though it wasn't dressed in either the radiant layered gowns of shimmering gold or the hardened silver battle armor that Leo was used to, there was no mistaking what it was. The first alien species Leo had ever laid eyes on. The first to ever make contact with Earth.

He knew an Aykari when he saw one.

So did Baz, who drew both of his pistols in a flash, pointing them in the stranger's direction.

The alien didn't seem fazed by the captain's sudden act of aggression. Its eyes didn't even flash orange. It simply crossed its long, spindly arms behind it.

"Greetings, wayfarers," it said in the first language Leo's translator had ever been programmed with, its eyes fixed on the weapons pointed its way. "I hope you come in peace."

How could you say no?

That was the question Leo overheard as he stood outside the circle of grown-ups sipping lemonade, milling about with plates of hummus-covered crackers balanced in their hands.

"Seriously. Given the situation, with everything that was at stake—how could you?"

His parents were hosting a small get-together in the backyard to help kick off the new semester—summery drinks and appetizers—exclusively attended by members of the university's physics department. Gareth and a couple of his friends were hogging the VR simulator in the basement (no dweebs allowed—or so they said), so Leo spent the evening outside, circling his parents like a small moon, a bottled Coke Overcharge in hand, eavesdropping on conversations. That's when he heard one of his dad's colleagues, a young, bearded man Leo knew only as Dr. Regland, pose his question to the small group that had gathered around the cheese tray.

Leo's father was among those nibbling slices of Gouda—*that's some gooda Gouda*, he would say. Now he was engaged in a version of a conversation that Leo had heard a hundred times before. A conversation he'd even had himself with his schoolmates standing around the slide at recess.

A conversation about the Aykari and their arrival.

And their intentions.

"I mean, it's ancient history by this point, but we really didn't have a choice in the matter," Dr. Regland continued. "Our weapons were vastly inferior. And though we probably had the numbers to repel the first wave, they simply would have come back with the full might of their armies and taken the planet by force."

"But they didn't," Leo's father countered. "Even if they could have. They came bearing an olive branch—an entire olive *tree*. Technological advances. Cures for disease. The keys to faster-than-light travel. It was a negotiation. A mutually beneficial agreement. There was no threat ever implied."

Leo took a sip of his soda and hung on the edge of the conversation, not far from his dad but not close enough to get noticed.

"That's a load, Cal, and you know it," Regland said. "There was every threat implied. Their sheer *presence* is a threat. They can seem as nice as they please because they have all the power. And when they do act magnanimously, that also affords them the moral high ground. 'Look what we've done for you—now you owe us.' We essentially had nothing. No leverage. No choice. Nothing."

"Except the ventasium," Dr. Ganderson, the only completely bald one of the bunch, said.

"Which belongs to us why, exactly?" a young woman named Dr. Fansa asked. "Because we were here first? Ask the Indigenous peoples of this continent how well that argument worked for them."

"That's hardly a fair comparison," Leo's father countered.

"She's right, though," Regland said through a mouthful of cracker. "Even the moral code that we use to govern our actions toward each other is far from universally applied—and we certainly don't extend it to species that we deem inferior to us. As the apex predator on this planet we were granted free rein to do whatever we pleased, so what did we do? We raped, pillaged, and plundered it. And now we aren't at the top anymore. The Aykari are. And they can do whatever *they* please with us."

"But they won't. Because they need us too. Nature is full of symbiotic relationships," Leo's dad said.

"And parasitic ones," Regland retorted. "And I think you're naive to assume that the Aykari are acting out of some universal ethics playbook that just happens to coincide with our most idealistic, humanistic impulses—ideals that we constantly fail to live up to, I might add."

"Hear, hear," Ganderson said, sipping his lemonade.

Leo had only the vaguest notion of what everyone was saying, but he liked to hear his father get into it with his friends—mostly because the esteemed Dr. Fender usually got the last word. He was the one with all the awards, after all. Leo was more than just a little proud.

"You call it naivete. I call it optimism," Leo's dad said. "You can choose to believe the best or assume the worst."

"That's exactly it, though. You don't really *have* a choice. What *you* believe makes absolutely no difference. Not to them."

"I respectfully disagree," Dr. Fender said, then he proceeded to launch into a long speech about some dead guy named Kant that was even harder to follow, so Leo gave up and wandered back toward the house to get more food. That's where his mother found him.

"Your brother bogart the basement?" she asked.

Leo looked at her, in her flowery summer dress with her thoughtful eyes and sympathetic frown, and nodded. His mother glanced at the cluster of professors arguing several feet away. "Looks like your father's getting into it with Professor Regland again. If a fistfight breaks out, I'm going to need you to help me turn the hose on them."

Leo smiled, picturing a half dozen sopping wet physics professors wrestling in the grass.

"What does sim-bee-otic mean?"

"It means when two species help each other out. Like a 'you scratch my back, I'll scratch yours' kind of thing."

Leo's mother scratched his back all the time while they

were sitting on the sofa watching TV. He couldn't ever recall scratching hers. Not once. He would if she asked him to, but she never asked. He supposed that meant they weren't symbiotic. But at least they could be.

Grace Fender looked at her son's meager little plate of crackers. "There are pizza rolls in the freezer. Want me to heat some up for you? It will give me an excuse to get away for a little bit. Dr. Kawalski over there won't stop telling terrible science jokes." She pointed out a stout man wearing a black leather jacket that didn't quite jibe with his orthopedic shoes. "You can be my savior."

Leo nodded and led his mother back into the house, taking one last glance at his father, still arguing, hands flying in exasperation. He'd understood only half of what he'd heard, but he assumed his father was right, because his father was always right. And besides, he'd heard about all of the wonderful things the Aykari had done. He even had a model of one of their starships hanging from his ceiling. No question: they were the good guys.

"What did the one uranium atom say to the other uranium atom?" his mother asked.

"Gotta split," Leo answered.

"Looks like Dr. Kawalski got to you too."

Leo reached up and took his mother's hand, thankful to have someone he could talk to.

✳　✳　✳

Baz holstered his pistols—slowly, reluctantly—as the alien approached. Though it was definitely Aykari, it didn't dress the part. It wore the same drab coverings as the purple-hued creatures surrounding it, though cut to its size. Leo noted several small sores and scabs on its skin, which clearly lacked the lustered glow of other members of its species. Most Aykari appeared faultless, but not this one. Its time on this planet had not been kind to it.

The Aykari announced that his name was Lark—"At least that's the name bestowed on me by the Orin," he said, indicating the pointy-eared inhabitants of the planet, who still had the crew of the *Icarus* surrounded. "In their language I believe it means 'outsider.'"

The swarm of fur-faced creatures continued to watch Leo and the others warily. Though with the Aykari's arrival, they had backed off, many of them disappearing into the cracks and crevices they'd swarmed out of. Only a few stayed within reach of Lark, protecting him perhaps. Or maybe it was the other way round.

"The Orin are the most advanced species on four ninety-four," the Aykari continued, "but their language was never encoded into our translator chips because it was deemed unnecessary, a waste of resources. I admit I have only acquired a rudimentary comprehension of their tongue. It is very economical—they are not ones to waste words, so I would not be surprised if they called you Lark as well."

"I've been called worse," Black said.

"I called you worse two minutes ago," Kat whispered to him. "You just didn't hear me."

Baz looked around, sharp eyes scanning. "Where're the rest of you?" Leo could tell the captain was still sniffing for a trap. Leo wasn't sure what he had expected to find down here either, but a disheveled-looking Aykari wasn't it.

"If you mean more of my kind," Lark replied, "I am the only one."

Leo had spent enough time with Baz to know when he wasn't buying what someone else was selling—the raised brow, the little twitch at one corner of the mouth. Leo didn't trust the alien either. Not after everything that had happened. Not given what he now knew. He remembered something Baz had said—about the Aykari and the Djarik and which was worse: *The Djarik will always charge you head-on, but maybe that's better than getting stabbed in the back.*

"We are looking for someone," Kat chirped up. "Goes by the name Zirkus Crayt. We were told we could find him here."

Leo studied the Aykari's face, looking for some spark of recognition, but it betrayed nothing. Their species weren't known for their expressions, incapable of producing a smile or a frown or rolling their eyes. Even their voices maintained a steady monotone, whether they were offering you a hand in friendship or condemning you to death.

Lark looked up at the sky, squinted into the distance at the

Icarus gleaming in the sunlight. "Let us go somewhere we can talk, out of the sun. The atmosphere has grown thin, and this planet's star can burn quickly if one is not careful."

"I'll burn *you* if *you're* not careful," Skits muttered so that only Leo and Boo could hear, clearly still itching to use her flamethrower.

Baz glanced at Kat, who nodded, then motioned for the Aykari to lead the way.

With the Orin parting before him, Lark picked his way along the rocky path with the crew of the *Icarus* in tow. He led them through a cracked archway into the shade of a vast chamber where several of the planet's denizens were engaged in handiwork of one kind or another. Some were making garments using what might have been a loom, though Leo wasn't entirely sure he even knew what a loom looked like— only that they existed on Earth centuries ago. Others were fashioning pots and cups and bowls from stores of thick red mud, carefully shaping them with their furry mitts. A couple in a corner were busy building a wooden barrel out of some surprisingly pliant wood, bending it and securing it with metal fasteners. They were all fully immersed in their work, paying little attention to the motley band of intruders ducking under the archway.

Apparently any friend of the Aykari's was a friend of theirs. Or of this *particular* Aykari, at least.

Lark ushered Leo and the others toward a circular stone

table barely bigger than the metal one crowded into the *Icarus*'s mess room and knelt down beside it. Perhaps the Orin hadn't yet invented chairs. Or simply had no use for them. Leo got on his knees next to Kat.

"Are you hungry?" Lark asked. "The Orin are a primarily agrarian species, though their diet has been forcibly altered somewhat. The soil, once quite rich, has grown less fertile over the years—one of many unfortunate consequences of the mining—but I can see what I can manage. Perhaps there are some slurks to be had."

"Slurks?" Leo repeated.

"Rock worms. They are the only food that the Orin hunt. During the day the worms burrow deep underground to escape the heat, but at night they surface. The Orins' ears are attuned to the sounds they make as they emerge. They cut off the heads and suck out the innards, which are rich in nutrients, though sometimes I have seen them make a kind of stew from them as well."

Suddenly Boo's butt-crack bread didn't sound so bad.

"Told you there'd be worms," Baz whispered.

Kat ignored him, bypassing the small talk and getting straight to the point. "No offense, Lark, is it? But we didn't come all the way out here to suck the guts out of slurks."

"No. You came here looking for Zirkus Crayt," the Aykari said. "And you have come to the right place."

Leo nearly jumped to his feet. "Wait. You mean he's here?"

he spouted. Leo noticed that his excitement had garnered the attention of all the Orin, who had paused in their work, staring at him. He brought his voice back down. "So you know him? You can take us to him?"

Lark nodded. "Crayt and I are well acquainted. He is not far. And I *can* take you. But perhaps I could ask *why* you are looking for him? This planet does not draw many visitors. Not since the mining operations ceased. In fact, you are the first outsiders the Orin have seen in some time."

"We have something to give him," Leo said quickly. "It's a message from my father. And some pla— *Yeow*!"

Leo glared at Baz, who had just pinched his leg underneath the table. The captain glared right back, a look that said *you talk too much*.

"What my cabin boy means to say is that we need to speak with Zirkus Crayt personally about a strictly confidential matter," Baz interjected. "One that doesn't concern anyone but him. Though, if you don't mind *us* asking, what are *you* doing here? Looks like your people picked up and left town some time ago. Did these furry little worm-suckers make you their god or something? Are you See-Threepio-ing them?"

"I am unfamiliar with your expression," Lark said. "But I assure you my intentions toward the Orin are not malicious in any way. If anything it is I who look up to them. They are honest and hardworking, loyal and kind. And as to your first question, as you can see, their world has been left in shambles. So I am helping to rebuild it."

"Rebuild, huh," Baz echoed, arms crossed, mouth pursed. "And who was it that trashed it to begin with?"

Lark didn't answer immediately. For Baz, that was answer enough.

"Let me tell you what *I* think," the captain continued. "I think you and your kind happened upon this little rock gift wrapped and floating out at the edge of the spiral. You ran your tests and found out it was full of V, so you came down with your drills and your processors and all your shiny promises and you dug deep and started sucking the planet dry. But then the Djarik got wind of your little treasure trove and came here to pick a fight, all resulting in this." He opened his arms wide, taking in the ruins that surrounded them, the few buildings still standing and the several that weren't.

"You are very astute," Lark said.

"Please don't tell him that," Kat muttered.

"But you are not entirely correct," Lark continued. "We did discover this planet first. And we did begin the mining process. But the Djarik never arrived. By the time they even learned about this planet we had already extracted every last molecule of EL-four eight six. We had—as you say—'sucked it dry.'"

Leo heard his father's voice. *What is happening with us . . . it has happened before.*

Kat shook her head. "So you're saying this—all this

destruction—this isn't because of the war?"

"Everything is because of the war," Lark replied. "But the devastation you see here was not the direct result of any battle between the Aykari and the Djarik. It was the inevitable by-product of years and years of extraction, the destabilizing ecological aftermath of our resource acquisition."

Leo looked through the open archway to the stone-lined street, the scarred faces of buildings on the edge of collapse, the arid soil that had once been dark and rich. Destabilizing ecological aftermath. That was one way to put it.

Or you could just say they ripped the planet apart.

"So you are at least half correct, Captain," Lark continued, turning back to Baz. "The Aykari *are* responsible for what has happened here. *We* did this." His eyes flashed orange, just for a moment, then resumed their sea-calm blue. "*I* did this. And *that*, if you must know, is why I am here."

The Aykari offer their deepest regrets and most sincere condolences to the peoples of Earth and to the families who have lost loved ones in this terrible act, an act which can only be interpreted as a declaration of war by the Djarik empire upon the planet. Be assured that this aggression will not go unpunished and that our retribution will be swift and merciless. To that end, we encourage humanity to stand against our common enemy. To rebuild their planet even stronger than before. And to join us in our fight against the warmongering terrorists who threaten the future of our peaceful galaxy.

—*Excerpt of address delivered by the Aykari High Council in response to the Djarik bombing of Earth, 2050*

3

THE PRICE YOU PAY

LEO SHOULD HAVE SEEN IT COMING. AFTER ALL, there were signs. Literally.

He saw them with his mother, in fact. While riding in the car. And eating a cheeseburger.

It would not have been her choice—Grace Fender had long ago given up on red meat, something about the upkeep of grazing land and food shortages, not to mention the cruelty to the animals themselves—but he badgered her until she gave in, pulling into the Hamburger Hut, getting a double with fries for him and a small mocha milkshake for her. Leo licked his lips and surveyed his greasy bounty: whoever had scooped his fries had been feeling generous that day. His carton overfloweth.

He feasted in the car as they wound through campus on

their way to pick up Leo's father. Dr. Calvin Fender was delivering one of his many lectures to a packed auditorium—something about the role Earth might play as a member of the galactic community. Grace didn't attend all of his talks. Not anymore. Just the ones where her husband was set to receive a plaque or a medal—the ones where she was expected to look proud and elegant in a strapless dress. And she was, always—proud, and elegant, even if she was no fan of high heels. Besides, she knew Cal Fender better than anyone. She once told Leo that there were students and other faculty who practically worshipped his father, but they didn't have to see him trimming his nose hair. "We're all human," she liked to say. "The best and the worst of us."

It was all fine with Leo—not having to sit through the lecture. He couldn't understand most of what his father said anyway. He enjoyed driving through campus, though. The plots of emerald grass, kept watered at no small cost. The smell of the pine trees lining the quad. Seeing the students, adults-in-training, their packs slung over their shoulders, gliding by on their hoverboards or stretched out in the shade, smartglasses on, lost in their virtual worlds. The old, stately buildings with their giant white columns. The stone fountain burbling in the center of the field. It was peaceful.

Not today, though. Today the main thoroughfare was lined with students standing along the curb, chanting and carrying signs—old-fashioned ones, not digital projections, made of posterboard and marker or wood and paint. The signs were written in all caps, the letters in black or angry red. WHAT'S MINED IS NOT YOURS and "V" IS NOT FOR VICTORY and LEAVE THE EARTH OUT OF IT. The chants could be heard even through the rolled-up windows.

"What are they yelling about?"

"They're protesters," his mother said. "They're speaking out against ventasium mining."

Leo shoveled in a french fry, still staring out the window. The protesters lined the street for at least three blocks. Shouting. Spitting. Stomping. He didn't understand. "I thought ventasium was a good thing?"

"It *is* a good thing. To hear your father talk about it, it's the greatest thing in the entire universe—after us, of course. But not everybody feels the same."

Grace Fender drove slowly, and Leo took in more signs. EXTRACTION = EXTINCTION. PLUNDER YOUR OWN PLANET. DRILLING IS KILLING. Despite the clever rhyme, that last one was disturbing, only because of the drawing beneath it, of the Earth being pierced by some kind of terrible machine, producing a fountain of bright red blood that gushed up in a gory geyser.

"What do they think is wrong with it, though?" Leo asked as they passed a girl who nearly smashed her sign against his window. It read THE AY-KAR-I ARE KILLING ME. That one *almost* rhymed. At least there was no blood.

"It's not the V. It's what it takes to get it. Every good thing comes at a cost, Leo. And they're afraid that this cost will be too high," Grace Fender said. "Take that cheeseburger. Some adorable cow died for that, you know. Some cow that they had to raise, using land that could have been used to feed a lot more people. And then I turned around and paid ten dollars for it, which I realize isn't that much of a sacrifice on my part, but still, it factors in—that's ten dollars I could have spent on something healthy, like a bag of apples. And that's not all: once you eat it, that grease is going to find its way into your body, and after a while it's going to start clogging up your arteries and you're going to have to have surgery to get one of those bionic hearts that are all the rage right now. That's the cost."

Leo glanced down at the cheeseburger leaking grease through its wrapper. Suddenly it didn't look quite as appetizing. The fries still looked good, though. She must have noticed his worried look. "It's okay. One cheeseburger isn't going to kill you. Though you might try eating a salad every once in a while."

Leo stuck out his tongue, summarizing his position on the matter.

"What was I thinking. I take it back," his mother said with a smirk.

Outside the window the protesters began to chant even louder. "Pack up. Go home. And leave our Earth alone." It was jarring. And confusing. Most of the people Leo knew loved the Aykari, or at the very least admired them. Some even worshipped them.

"The problem is, there are no substitutes for ventasium. If we want the Aykari's help—or even if we want to go out and explore the galaxy ourselves—we have to mine it. Even if it means we lose some trees and birds and land in the process. It's sort of pay to play."

Leo knew all about the birds. They'd discussed it in science class. How certain species were experiencing sharp declines in population. How some of them quickly found themselves on the endangered list only a year after the Aykari arrived. And it wasn't just birds; there were many animals whose habitats had been disrupted, destroyed, diminished. Not to mention the tremors. And the strange haze that appeared in the sky anywhere the Aykari set up one of their mining platforms. And the odd, almost metallic taste of the water that had caused Leo's dad to install an expensive filter on each of their faucets.

But then there was also Mr. Inman, the music teacher at Leo's school, whose battle with cancer took a turn for the worse two summers ago, small tumors infiltrating his brain. Inoperable. Untreatable. A death sentence. At least, it would have been, before the Aykari. They had medicines human doctors could only dream of, and yesterday, a completely cancer-free Mr. Inman started teaching Leo's class how to play the recorder. It sounded horrible, a mess of squeaks and blurts, like Satan's very own marching band, but through it all Mr. Inman smiled like a kid eating birthday cake.

Outside the protesters took up another chant. "No visitors. No V. No drilling here for me."

He thought about the Earth gushing blood. Then he thought about Mr. Inman again and his now spotless brain. Everything comes at a cost. How do you balance the one against the other? How do you choose?

And why do you have to?

Leo angled his head to look up into an unusually cloudless sky, hoping for a glimpse of one of the giant silver Aykarian cruisers soaring overhead. Empty. No ships in sight.

He took another bite of his cheeseburger and followed it with a stolen slurp of his mother's milkshake. She gave him a dirty look.

It was a small price to pay.

Zirkus Crayt wasn't far.

That's what Lark said as they made their way through the ruins of the village, moving at a halting pace, as the Aykari was often interrupted by a wide-eyed Orin coming up to him, taking his hand in both of its paws, speaking in a flurry of sounds that Leo's translator couldn't comprehend. Lark understood it well enough, however, often pointing, speaking in halted, incomprehensible sentences of his own, clearly giving instructions of some kind. In between interruptions, the Aykari tried to explain.

"I try to help them as best as I am able, but it is difficult. The Orin do not pursue technology for the sake of it or to bend their planet to their will. Rather, they have limited their advancements to only the tools required to live in harmony with their surroundings. They gather most of their water from the sky. They use every part of every plant they grow. They have no need for electricity, chemical manufacture, genetic engineering. Their metallurgy is restricted to making simple tools with which to hunt and grow food. They knew nothing of nuclear power or quantum physics before we arrived. They had never even seen a starship. And because they lacked the mechanical apparatus to do so, they never uncovered the secrets hidden beneath the surface of their planet."

"You mean ventasium," Leo said.

"They had no way of knowing the element was here. And even if they did, they had no means of accessing, processing, or using it. It lay unspoiled."

"Until you came along and spoiled it for them," Baz said.

Lark didn't hesitate with his response. "We realized the planet's value and immediately secured it, yes."

"Secured it how, exactly?" Kat asked. Leo had to admit he didn't really like the sound of that either. The Aykari had a way of speaking that kept everything at a distance.

"As I am sure you know, it has long been the Aykari mission to share its advanced knowledge and technology with the universe, thereby spreading our influence and further establishing the reaches of our empire," Lark explained. "It is always better to make allies than enemies."

Like us, Leo thought. Then he glanced at Baz's blasted ear. *Or most of us.*

"Some cultures, however, are not equipped to handle the instant leap in scientific evolution that we can offer. In such cases, it is more expedient for us to simply take what we need rather than negotiate an even exchange."

More expedient. That didn't sound very symbiotic to Leo. More like, *you scratch my back . . . or else.*

"In other words, you just came, filled up your tanks, and then left," Baz paraphrased. "All without permission. All without giving anything in return."

"And how do you make *your* living, Captain?" Lark asked.

Baz stopped in his high-topped tracks, bringing up one hand to shield his eyes from the scorching sun. "Excuse me?"

Leo watched the Aykari's own blue eyes, waiting for the shift, the flare, but Lark maintained his composure. "You have no uniform. No insignia. No emblem. Which indicates that you are not allied with either empire, meaning you are most likely in business for yourself. Perhaps you *are* a trader, or even a smuggler, but judging by the armament on your ship and on your person, I think it much more likely that you are a pirate or a slaver. If either is the case, then you must be used to taking what you want without permission."

Baz opened his mouth to protest but then just as quickly closed it. Leo thought of the bag full of pentars taken from the Darkashi vessel. The half jar of peanut butter he himself had licked clean.

Kat came to her captain's defense. "We do what we have to do to get by because *your* endless war leaves us no choice."

"It is *our* war now, human," Lark said. "And there is always a choice. Yes, we could have followed a different strategy with the Orin. We could have eradicated their species before even touching down on the planet. We could have enslaved them, as I understand your species has done with its own kind throughout your history, based on something as arbitrary as the color of their skin. We could have handed them technology that they couldn't possibly understand and left them to figure it out, no doubt causing even more problems, imbalances, inequalities. Instead we came, took what we wanted, and left, just as the consequences of those decisions were playing out."

"What consequences?" Boo wanted to know.

Lark paused before answering. "Every planet is different. Its reaction to the extraction process varies. Some remain stable for the duration. Others begin to weaken over time. The mining process is mostly clean, but there are always side effects: the loss of flora and fauna, the introduction of new hazards into the biosphere, changes in climate, ecological imbalance, disruptions to the food chain—these are to be expected. But sometimes the planet itself seems to revolt against the process. Violently so."

"Earthquakes," Leo blurted before realizing that's probably not what they would be called. Not here at least. Yet Lark seemed to be familiar with the word.

"The tectonic disturbances caused by the extraction were much worse than anticipated here. It did not help that the Orins' construction methods were so primitive, their structures fragile and prone to collapse. This," Lark said, indicating the ruins around them, "this was the result of the planet's reaction. Whole villages swallowed into the ground. Thousands of lives lost. An unfortunate consequence."

"Is that the official word?" Baz snipped. "The *unfortunate* decimation of an entire planet and its people?"

"There is no *official* word. But that is how *I* see it, yes."

Leo took in a trio of Orin methodically rebuilding a crumbled structure—a well, perhaps, or some kind of reservoir. Two of them heaved up stone after stone, while the third one patched the gaps with some white paste troweled out of a barrel. It was a slow, tedious process made more strenuous by the heat. He thought of the sleek silver towers back on Earth—built in tandem with the Aykari. Thought of the bone he broke in his arm, healed in a matter of days thanks to alien medicine. *They came bearing an olive branch.*

But not always.

"Every world is unique and requires a different approach. With your planet, for example," Lark said, looking at Boo, "no intervention was necessary. Quel possesses negligible amounts of EL-four eight six and therefore is of little value in the empire's eyes, though I do wonder why we did not make a more concentrated effort to recruit your kind for the war effort. Four arms are better than two, after all."

"Probably because we would have said no," Boo replied gruffly.

"Perhaps. Or maybe we doubted your stomach for it. You, on the other hand . . . ," Lark said, looking at Leo, the alien's mouth spiraling open and closed. "You humans needed to be handled with care. We made our mistake with the Djarik. And though you lacked their resources and were considerably less unified as a species, you still represented a potential asset—intelligent, technologically adept, eager for advancement. Unfortunately humans were also found to be volatile, prone to outrageous acts of hatred, bigotry, and violence. You could just as easily have become a liability, so we did what was necessary to ensure your compliance."

Leo squinted up at the Aykari.

"Meaning what, exactly?" Baz pressed.

"Meaning that when the time came, when the opportunity presented itself, we allowed your bloodlust and sense of justice to work in our favor by channeling it in the proper direction . . . toward a more appropriate and strategically advantageous target."

When the opportunity presented itself.

That day.

Suddenly, Leo was back in the Djarik base, standing next to his father, listening to this revelation for the first time. *The Aykari were given a choice and they made it. They saw an opportunity to secure an ally in the war. Hundreds of thousands of human lives in exchange for the allegiance of billions.*

He felt his already flushed cheeks grow even hotter. He took in the ruined village. The dust on his boots. He thought of his mother's fleeting smile. The way she'd hugged him that day and how he'd squirmed out of her grip. He remembered her request—*the prettiest shell you can find*—and how the light from the explosion had traveled so much faster than the sound. How it was almost beautiful, that light, until the thunder caught up to it, and then it was terrifying.

"So it's true," he whispered. "You let it happen. You just let those people die." *You let my mother die.*

"We took the necessary measures to protect the planet's resources, and then we seized the opportunity to ensure humanity's commitment to our cause. Your species needed to see the Djarik as an immediate threat. A wounded animal fights fiercest."

Leo's breaths grew uneven. He felt for the inhaler nestled in his pocket, wrapping his fingers around it, determined to stay afloat, but three years of anger and grief dragged him down. It was one thing hearing this from the Djarik. Even from his father. Those were accusations. This was a confession.

He could see Baz struggling with it as well. The captain's jaw was clenched, hands too, as he glared at the Aykari.

"It was a strategic gamble," Lark continued, as if he was merely reciting history. "But your species reacted exactly as expected."

With that, Black snapped. In a heartbeat he had one of his pistols free of its holster, angling up beneath the Aykari's chin. Leo froze. Part of him wanted to reach out, to ease Baz's arm down. Another part of him wanted to see if the captain would pull the trigger.

Baz leaned in close to Lark, speaking in little more than a whisper. "I was there when you took that gamble. You wanted us angry? Wanted to see if we could fight?" He shifted his aim, pressing the barrel of his gun against the Aykari's broad, sloping forehead. "Mission accomplished."

Boo stepped close. "Don't do it, Bastian. It's not worth it. You'd only be proving his point."

"I think I could live with that," Baz responded.

Lark didn't flinch, even with the barrel of a gun dimpling his near translucent skin. Leo expected the alien's eyes to start glowing like cinders, but he stayed calm, staring not at the pistol but at the man holding it. "You should listen to the Queleti," he said. "If you kill me, you will not find what you are looking for. I assure you, I am the only one who can lead you to Zirkus Crayt."

Baz shrugged. "I'll take my chances with that too."

Leo held his breath, watched Black's eyes, the icy resolve. He could do it, take this Aykari's life. He certainly looked like he wanted to. Small vengeance for what happened five years ago.

"I am not what you think I am," Lark said.

Not what you think *I* am. Something about that sounded odd to Leo.

I assure you.

I am the only one.

The Aykari always referred to themselves in the first person plural. It was always *we* or *us*. It was supposedly a mark of how much more advanced their civilization was—that they had moved beyond individuality and fully embraced the wants and needs of the collective.

Lark clearly wasn't part of that collective anymore.

"Kill me if you think it justice," Lark continued. "But I assure you, you will not be teaching the Aykari any lessons. If anything, you might be doing them a favor."

Kat put her hand—the real one—on the captain's shoulder. "Let it go, Baz," she said gently. "Boo's right. It's not worth it."

Bastian Black ground his teeth, but he slowly lowered his gun. Leo wasn't sure, but he thought he heard a sigh escape from the Aykari's lipless mouth. "Looks like you were wrong.

We're not all heartless, bloodthirsty monsters," Baz said, holstering his pistol. "Just take us to Crayt before I change my mind."

Lark nodded. He brushed past the captain and continued to pick his way along the broken road, Boo, Kat, and Skits falling in behind.

Baz's eyes found Leo's. "Sorry, kid," he said.

He didn't say what for. He didn't have to.

He didn't say why. Not at first. He just knocked on Leo's door and poked his head in, speaking in a whisper.

"Come on. I think we should get out of here. Let's go to the park."

Leo put down the comic he'd snatched from his brother's stash and groaned. He was too tired to leave the house. It had been a long day. Only the third week back at school to start the new year and everyone was still getting readjusted, trying to find a routine.

But he knew he couldn't say no to Gareth—invitations like this were hard to come by anymore—so he found his socks and shoes and they snuck out the back door, tiptoeing past their father's office, leaving a note for him on the digital board in the kitchen, telling him where they'd gone and when they would be back: *out* and *soon*.

They turned the block, Leo nearly jogging to keep up with Gareth's longer stride, and crossed the street into the fields that bordered the community park and playground. Up ahead Leo could see the rock wall and the obstacle course and the funnel slide with the sledding hill rising up behind it—and rising even farther behind that, the white-laced outline of the Rockies, standing defiant despite constant attempts to get at the precious element buried underneath them.

"Why did we sneak out of the house again?" Leo wanted to know.

"Because in the next hour or so, Dad's going to get a phone call from Mr. Harshman, my principal, saying I was in a fight. And I'd rather not be around when he does."

Leo's nine-year-old eyes filled with awe. "You were in a *fight*? What kind of fight? Did you kick 'em in the nads?" *Nads* was Leo's new favorite word, taught to him by Gareth, of course.

"No. It wasn't like that. I punched him is all."

That seemed just as impressive. "Why? Did he try to kick *you* in the nads?"

Gareth shook his head. "No. He was spouting off at lunch. Some nonsense about how the Djarik attack was really our own fault and it's what we get for relying on the Aykari to protect us rather than protecting ourselves. So then I punched him in the nose and asked him if that's what he got for not protecting *him*self."

Epic comeback, Leo thought. "What did he say?"

"'Ouch.' And some other stuff."

"Wow. Did it bleed?"

"His nose? Yeah. A little," Gareth admitted.

"Did it hurt your hand?"

Gareth flexed his fingers. "A little," he repeated with a bit of a smile. "Dad's going to be pissed when he finds out, though. He doesn't like fighting. You know that."

Leo nodded. This wasn't the first fight Gareth had been in after all, though he seemed to be getting into them more easily. This certainly wouldn't be the first call from Mr. Harshman this year.

"He deserved it," Leo concluded. "I would have punched him too."

"Na. You would have just made him disappear," Gareth said, twirling an imaginary wand and zapping an imaginary jerk out of existence like some velvet-robed wizard. Leo grinned. He liked the idea of waving a wand and wishing all the mean and terrible things away. That was one trick his mother never got around to teaching him. Like so many others.

"We'll have to go back eventually, though," Leo said.

"Eventually," Gareth agreed. "But not yet."

They hit the playground and Leo followed his brother through the obstacle course, trying to perform every trick the same way he did. They took turns in the tire swing and chased each other across the artificial turf. They lobbed pine cones at each other and made fun of the kids who kept falling off their hoverboards.

The whole time, though, Leo could tell his brother was thinking about what he'd done and what their dad would say. Leo wondered what the punishment would be. Last time, Gareth had been forced to write a two-thousand-word essay on the history of nonviolent resistance titled "Fighting Without Your Fists." Dr. Fender had also made Leo read it even though Leo had done nothing wrong. *Learn from your brother's example*, he'd said.

After a while Gareth led Leo to the top of the sledding hill where the two of them perched, leaning back in the grass and soaking in the sun, looking out over the fields and to the snow-swept sprawl of the mountains beyond. They sat in silence, thankful that, for once, they couldn't hear the high-pitched grind of Aykari drills cutting into rock. Only the sounds of other kids shouting and laughing down below.

"Mom loved this hill," Gareth said at last, leaning back on his elbows. "Remember when we came for picnics, she'd always put our blanket right here at the top? That red-and-black checkered one?"

Leo remembered. She would leave them on the playground below and hike up the hill all by herself with the old-fashioned wicker basket over her arm. It was always just the three of them. *Get out of the house and let your father work time.* That's what she called it. She would sit and watch them from up high, waiting until they were sweaty and out of breath—or at least until Leo was out of breath—and then call them up for lunch.

"Remember how she'd cut our sandwiches into triangles because we complained about the crusts?" Leo asked.

"And how she'd yell at us for trying to feed them to the squirrels?"

"And how she always forgot the napkins, so she'd make us wipe our hands on her shirt because ours were already too dirty?"

Leo smiled and bowed his head, eyes shut, picturing it. Mostly he could remember sitting next to her on that blanket, their eyes fixed on the mountains, jagged faces marking the passing of entire civilizations. *Just look at it,* she'd say, nodding toward the distant range. *Isn't it beautiful?* If his father were there he would have launched into a lecture about how the mountains were formed and the ages of the rocks, but his mother could just sit and take it in. She could probably tell Leo how old it was too, if he asked her. But he never asked her. It was enough to sit beside her and *see.* It was always enough.

All of a sudden Gareth's body started to shake beside him, his shoulders heaving. The sobs were mostly silent, only accompanied by hitched breaths with few tears, almost like he was laughing instead. Leo didn't know what to do, so he just shifted to be closer to him so that their arms touched, and waited for the sobbing to slow.

Finally Gareth sniffed, wiped his nose across his sleeve. Leo didn't need to ask why or what his brother was thinking. He knew. He understood.

They stayed that way for a while—shoulder to shoulder— long enough for the drills in the distance to start back up again. Long enough for half the kids on the playground to be called home. At last Gareth wiped his cheek and nodded toward the sun just starting to touch the mountaintops. "What time is it?" he asked, his voice like a frown.

Leo checked his watch. "Six o'clock."

Gareth sighed. "I guess we should get back. Get it over with."

"Maybe if you talked to him. Explained why you did it. Maybe he won't get mad."

Gareth shook his head. "Trust me. He won't understand. He just doesn't get it. Not like you do." He stood up then reached down and pulled Leo up after him. "Race you down the hill . . ."

"You'll win," Leo said.

"Not if I give you a head start."

"Five seconds?"

"Three."

It was the best he was going to get. "Okay. Three."

Gareth started counting. Leo took flight, knowing his brother was right behind.

＊　＊　＊

Leo checked his watch for the time, but it was still glitching. He was sure they'd been walking for at least an hour, though admittedly, Leo's sense of time was warped. While he was on the *Beagle*, his father had tried to keep him and Gareth on a schedule. Since that ship was attacked, however, Leo had lost any semblance of a regular cycle. From that moment, it had been one long, run-on day, interrupted by dashes of fitful rest and half-remembered nightmares.

He knew he'd been walking for a while, however, because his feet were barking and his legs were turning to jelly. His lips were chapped and his throat was parched. It seemed like every drop of moisture his body once contained had been sucked into his shirt or absorbed into the band of his Coalition underwear. Kat's jacket had come off long ago and was now draped over one shoulder.

They'd put the broken village behind them, venturing deeper and deeper into the yellow-pink scrublands, the entire landscape the color of an old bruise. Leo marveled at the plants that managed to sprout from the cracked ground, some of them sporting vibrant, unearthly patterns, rich pomegranate purples and almost iridescent oranges. On Earth that probably would have meant they were poisonous, but this wasn't Earth. So far from it.

Leo knew it wasn't fair to compare everything to his planet, but he couldn't help it. It was, after all, the only home he'd ever known, not counting the *Beagle*, which he didn't, despite the plaque that read *FENDER* sitting on a shelf in his cabin. A starship wasn't a home—though he would never tell Baz that. A home needed a foundation. It needed an address that didn't change with every passing second, first one orbit and then the next. Home was getting snowed in and having to miss school. Home was an old-fashioned wood-burning fireplace. Home was being able to sit and watch a sunset and pretend *it* had actually moved and not you, tucking itself in for the night.

He yearned for it. It was a throbbing ache, bone-deep. This gnawing desire to be back in his house in Colorado, sitting in the family room with Amos curled and purring on his lap, Gareth sprawled out on the floor, Mom and Dad huddled together on the other end of the sofa, a bowl of popcorn between them. Of course it couldn't be. Not like that, at least. The Djarik had made sure of it, but it could still be something. Something good.

Up ahead Lark continued to lead the way, Baz and Kat keeping some distance behind, no doubt also keeping a close watch on their guide. Leo was in favor of exercising caution. If the last few days had taught him anything it was that the Aykari couldn't be trusted.

Who do you trust, Leo?

Not Lark, that was for sure.

"This planet sucks. I don't like it."

Leo glanced over at Skits. The two of them brought up

the rear, Leo because he was lost inside his own head again, and the robot because her treads struggled over the uneven terrain. Leo tried not to think about the fact that there were also things called slurks lurking somewhere beneath his feet.

"There's nothing out here," Skits continued. "This place is a total wasteland. And those creatures back there are creepy, with their pointed ears and their purple skin and gray hair. And their eyes are way too big for their faces. I feel like they're always watching me."

"They're probably scared of you," Leo said. No doubt Skits made them uncomfortable. Probably the whole crew did. After all, they'd seen spaceships and robots before.

We came, took what we wanted, and left.

It wasn't right, Leo knew. These creatures, the Orin, they might have been perfectly content to continue on without any knowledge of the galaxy beyond the edges of their blue sky. Content to imagine the twinkling lights hanging above them as little more than decoration, a scattering of celestial dust, or the thousand unblinking eyes of some benevolent god. Content to till only the topmost layer of their planet's surface and not dig any deeper. But they weren't given that option. *That's what you get*, Leo thought, *for having something somebody else wanted.*

Leo heard a whine and saw Skits suddenly come to a grinding halt beside him, her right tread making a clunking, grating sound. "Ow, ow, ow," she whined. "Mother clunker!

I think I've got something caught in my tracks."

Leo crouched down to inspect, wiping the sweat from his eyes. Sure enough, the robot had somehow managed to kick a stone up into the gearing of her exposed right tread, getting it wedged between interlocking teeth. "You stepped on a rock. See? I told you it hurts."

"Meh-meh-meh-meh-meh," Skits mocked. "Can you just try to get it out please so we don't get stranded out here?"

"Yeah. Just go backward a little." The robot switched gears and the chunk of stone loosened just enough for Leo to get his fingers around it and pluck it free. It was about the size of an apricot. Leo hadn't had an apricot in more than three years. He couldn't quite remember what they tasted like. More tart than sweet. Like the robot.

He held the rock up so Skits could see. "Souvenir?"

"You keep it," she insisted. "Maybe you can throw it at somebody if we ever get in trouble again. You know, since you won't carry a gun."

Leo started to toss it, then reconsidered, shoving it in his pocket. Her tread working, Skits and Leo moved to catch up to the others.

"See? That's exactly what I'm talking about," she continued. "This is clearly no place for a robot."

"You'd like Earth better," Leo told her. "There are robots everywhere. Robot vacuums, robot dishwashers, robot waiters, robot taxis."

"I don't do vacuuming," Skits insisted. "Or dishes. Though anything would be better than this. What's it like there? On Earth, I mean?"

"Really? Baz hasn't told you?" Leo would have thought the captain of the *Icarus*, with his old records and cartoon memories and slogan T-shirts, would have given Skits a databank full of stories about his home planet. After all, Leo knew he wasn't the only one who had trouble letting go.

"He says there's not enough parking and that nobody knows how to make a good rock song anymore, but other than that it's the best place in the entire universe."

"I don't know about the parking," Leo said. But he was right about the last part. It was the best. At least from what Leo had seen.

"He says he's especially fond of the baby ducks," Skits added.

"Baby ducks?" The captain didn't strike Leo as having a soft spot for such things, but Leo couldn't argue. Back where he lived, there was a retention pond in the neighborhood, complete with picnic benches and a little dock you could perch yourself on if you wanted to fish. He and Gareth used to take a bag of frozen corn down to the edge in spring and feed the ducklings, careful to aim their offerings away from the greedy mother. Invariably Gareth would make some joke about how Leo used to be cute too when he was born, and Leo would try to push his older brother into the water, causing the ducks to scatter.

He wondered if that pond was still there. If it had dried up or if some chemical imbalance in the water had caused the fish to die. He thought about the ducklings trailing after their mother as she led them from the two squabbling boys wrestling in the grass, probably just wishing for a safe place to raise her young. "It's pretty amazing," Leo said.

"Why didn't you just stay there, then?"

"Wasn't my call. My dad told us we had to leave," Leo said. "He said it was for the best." Dr. Fender was sure that humanity's future lay out among the stars. Space travel was the door that led to humankind's salvation, ventasium was the key that unlocked that door, and the Aykari were the guides that would show them the way through.

Turns out his father didn't know everything.

Up ahead, Lark had stopped at the top of a small rise. "There," he said, pointing.

Leo took a deep breath. He found himself staring into a fathomless fissure in the planet's crust, like an open sore. This was no naturally occurring canyon or gully; its contours were much too regular, its edges too precise. Whatever or whoever had dug this hole in the ground had done so purposefully, and Leo knew why.

His thoughts were confirmed the moment they descended the hill and Leo saw the gleaming silver structure built into canyon's side. The huge observation deck with its giant window and the even larger hangar beside it, big enough for several ships. He recognized the platforms, embedded with lights. The solar arrays angled up toward the sky to provide power. The titanium walkways circling the pit. He'd seen it all before.

There, just beyond the control center, sat the remains of the extractor itself, a metal monstrosity plunging deep below the planet's skin. Very little could be seen of it from here, but Leo knew it ran a long way down. If you accidentally stepped over the edge, you would have plenty of time to ponder all of your life choices before you hit bottom.

"An abandoned mining facility," Kat said.

"Mostly abandoned," the Aykari replied. He beckoned them onto the metal elevator that would take them down to the entrance of the control compound. The whole apparatus looked a little worse for wear.

"This thing still works?" Boo wondered.

"Most of the time," Lark replied, which didn't calm Leo's nerves. "Back when the excavator was active it consumed vast amounts of energy. Naturally we used cores of EL-four eight six to power it. However, I have managed to redirect most of the facility's basic systems to run off the solar arrays. As long as the planet's primary star shines, everything stays operational."

"And when those dark gray clouds move in?" Leo wondered.

"Then I wait for them to pass."

As the elevator creaked downward with a rusty, shuddering moan, Leo took in the abyss beneath him, the bottom impossible to see. He thought about that poster, that one of the Earth fountaining blood. He wondered if any of the Orin had ever protested the Aykari being here. If they ever put up a fight.

He hoped not. He was pretty sure how it would have ended.

Once at the entrance, Lark activated a button on the door's controls and a miniature black eye revealed itself, an aperture in its center emitting a blue beam that scanned the Aykari from his sandaled feet to his slightly pointed head. The door slid open and Lark gestured them all inside. "Welcome," he said.

Baz didn't move. "Crayt's in here?"

The Aykari nodded.

"He better be," the captain warned. "Not a big fan of walking into eerie abandoned buildings at the edge of a giant hole in the middle of a barren desert on a backwater planet nobody's never even heard of at the request of someone I consider my enemy."

"You still think we are enemies?" Lark asked.

"We certainly aren't friends," Baz shot back, but he stepped through the door anyway. Leo followed, one hand still wrapped around that rock in his pocket as if it were some kind of talisman that would keep him safe.

As soon as they were inside, a row of white lights activated, revealing a large octagonal chamber, nearly the size of the *Beagle*'s bridge. Banks of computers and other unfamiliar machines lined the walls, along with storage crates of all kinds, some open and empty, others sealed tight. By the entrance, the metal floor was coated in a fine layer of yellow dust dragged in from outside, but a few paces beyond that it gleamed. Leo recognized the chairs stationed around the room with their silver frames and tall, arched backs, designed for the lithe Aykari frame. At one time this would have been a control center for the entire mining operation, with a team of engineers monitoring the extraction process, making sure not a single speck of 486 was wasted. Now Leo didn't know *what* it was used for.

"Do the Orin know about this place?" Boo asked.

"They know, but they will not come near it," Lark said. "They believe the holes in the planet to be haunted, that our drills burrowed too deep into the ground and we released evil spirits that had long lain dormant. They say that is why their buildings crumbled and their crops withered. I've tried to convince them that it was us, that *we* were the vengeful spirits, but I cannot make them understand the science. It is easier for them to believe in ghosts."

A machinelike hum kicked up, coming from the only adjoining corridor, followed by the sound of heavy, clacking steps. Kat's hand dropped to her side, ready to blast whatever turned the corner.

"Do not worry," Lark said, holding up his own hand. "Those are just my two assistants."

The Aykari nodded behind him and two robots appeared in the back of the control room. They were as similar looking as Leo was to Boo. The shorter of the two was humanoid in shape, two legs, two arms, and a torso, all armor plated, an elegant shimmering silver, but no weapons to speak of. Its head was fashioned more after the Aykari with its distinctive diamond shape. The robot looked top-of-the-line, fresh out of the box. It moved with almost humanlike fluidity as it studied its new visitors.

The same couldn't be said for its companion, who reminded Leo much more of Skits, though almost twice her size and without the bumper stickers. It ambled into the control room on six insectoid legs, its bulbous middle section a hodge-podge of multijointed limbs and hidden compartments. It had clearly been cobbled together from a variety of spare parts just like she had. Compared to its massive frame, the robot's head seemed disproportionately small, little more than an upside-down salad bowl with two glowing yellow eyes. It was bulky and chunky—the robot equivalent of buff.

"Number One," Lark said, pointing to the lithe, shiny robot with the piercing blue receptors. "And Number Nine,"

Lark said, indicating the crablike confabulation of parts. *Of course an Aykari would simply give his robots numbers for names,* Leo thought.

The bulky Number Nine raised one of his multijointed metal legs in salute.

"What happened to the other seven?" Boo wondered.

"Numbers Two through Eight were slowly incorporated into their successor, who is of my own design," Lark replied. "Number One, on the other hand, is a service droid that I brought with me from Aykar. She is my loyal servant."

"Actually, I'm a bit of a tinkerer myself," Baz admitted, finding something in common with the Aykari at last. "Skits here is kind of my baby."

"God, Bastian, can you please not call me that?" Skits hissed. Leo watched as her head turned toward Number Nine before quickly twisting back. The giant, spiderlike robot didn't seem to notice.

"Maybe you two can play build-a-bot *after* we talk to Crayt," Kat interjected.

Lark looked at each of them in turn. His eyes finally seemed to rest on Leo. "Of course. But now that we are here, perhaps you will finally tell me what it is you want from him."

Leo opened his mouth to speak, but Baz cut him off. Again. "Sorry, Aykari. Our business is with Crayt and Crayt only. So how about you go fetch him for us before things get messy."

Leo saw the Aykari's eyes shift at last. Blue to green, green to yellow, yellow to orange.

This was never a good sign.

"I am afraid things are already messy," Lark said.

As if on cue, Number Nine rose up on its six legs, several compartments opening all over his body to reveal the barrels of four hidden blasters pointed in the direction of the *Icarus*'s crew. At the same time, two panels in the ceiling slid open to reveal hidden mounted laser cannons that also turned their noses toward the pirates.

Neither Kat nor Baz even had time to draw their weapons. They would have been dead if they'd tried.

"Perhaps *now* you will be more inclined to tell me who sent you. A name for my would-be assassins," the Aykari added.

Leo stared down the barrel of one of Number Nine's guns, then looked back at the alien who had built him. It finally hit him.

"Zirkus Crayt," he whispered.

This was him. *This* was the person his father had sent him to find.

Threatening to kill them all.

It has come to our attention that an Aykari scientist, Zirkus Crayt, has been in contact with you on numerous occasions regarding matters of a confidential nature. By the authority vested in us by the Aykari High Command, we order you to cease all communication with this individual and report anything he sends you to us. Zirkus Crayt has been accused of spreading misinformation and inciting dissent among member planets of the Coalition. He is currently awaiting judgment for his actions. If Crayt or anyone associated with him should attempt to contact you again, please notify your local Aykari security liaison immediately.

—*Message from the Coalition Counterintelligence Agency, sent to Dr. Calvin Fender*

THE ROCK AND THE HARD PLACE

THEY WERE BURNING. THEY WERE ALL BURNING.

The smell of smoke hit him from two rooms away. Leo, caught up in a VR dungeon crawl, had forgotten to tell the kitchen's virtual assistant how long to bake for and let the time slip by.

Fifteen minutes was all they required. They got twice that.

Everything was ruined.

Coughing, Leo removed the pan from the oven and inspected the damage. Six dark lumps stared back at him. Maybe not coal black, but certainly not the golden brown he'd been going for. He tapped on the top of one with his fork. It was like knocking on the front door. Muffins shouldn't make that sound.

Blast it. Leo slumped against the counter, thinking about all his hard work wasted. He'd woken up early, sneaking down the stairs and out to the hydroponic garden, picking the fattest blueberries he could find. Quietly taking the mixing bowls from the cupboard so as not to tip off his father, who was shut up in the office down the hall, already hard at work by six.

Leo knew the steps by heart. He had made these muffins before, though admittedly he had been the assistant and not the baker, taking orders from his mother, who showed him how to cut in the cold butter and gently fold in the blueberries, how to sift through the crumbly streusel topping with his fingers. He was her stirrer, her spatula cleaner, her paper cup placer, her berry quality-control specialist—often eating a third of the bowl before it was time to add them in. "There are many kinds of magic in the world," she told him. "Making the perfect blueberry muffin is one of them." He believed her—his mother was an accomplished magician in her own right, and her blueberry muffins were the stuff of legend.

Which was why today—on what would have been her birthday—Leo had decided he would try to make them himself.

He knew his family could use a little magic, after all. His father hadn't been sleeping well. Leo often found him standing at the kitchen sink or sitting in his office chair, staring off into space. And Gareth had been so moody lately, lashing out, storming off, shutting himself in his room. Leo wanted to help them. He didn't know if there were any magic words that would make them hurt any less, so a mammoth blueberry muffin modeled after Grace Fender's own epic creation would have to suffice.

A charred blueberry rock, on the other hand, would probably only make things worse.

"Great job, Leo," he whispered to himself. "Freaking fantastic."

He had to hide the evidence. Best-case scenario, Gareth would only tease Leo about the fail, and his father would probably scold him for leaving something in the oven too long. Worst-case: the sight of Leo's catastrophe would remind them only of how much they'd lost.

He grabbed a fork and pried the first muffin loose. He was about to dump it in the trash when a voice stopped him.

"What do we have here?"

Dr. Calvin Fender stood in the entry, gray fleece blanket around his shoulders like a cape, mug in hand. "I smelled smoke," he said.

"It's nothing. An accident," Leo said. "Forget it."

"An accident," his father echoed. He came to stand beside Leo, inspecting the burned muffin. The man smelled like coffee and day-old sweat. "Accidents happen," he said. "And they aren't always a bad thing. Penicillin was an accident.

Röntgen's X-rays. The Chinese were actually looking for the secret to everlasting life when they discovered gunpowder. Ironic, that one." Leo saw his dad's eyes dart toward the fruit-stained bowl in the sink. "Blueberries?"

"From the garden," Leo said quietly.

His father nodded. "You have your mother's green thumb," he said thoughtfully. "One of many gifts she gave you. Go get the butter from the fridge, will you?"

Leo did as he was commanded—he always did as he was commanded when it came to his father—returning to see his dad wielding a knife, carefully paring the burned top from the muffin Leo had been seconds from tossing.

"Rumor has it that the tremendous energy potential of EL-four eight six was discovered by accident. Even the Aykari sometimes stumble upon their fortunes. And Dr. Ventasi didn't know what he was looking for when he found it here on Earth, either. He just figured if he dug deep enough he would find something. . . ."

Leo's father finished his dissection, removing the blackened top. Underneath was something precious: rich white cake riddled with blobs of blue. Little ribbons of steam drifted up from the muffin's fluffy heart.

"Eureka!" Dr. Fender said. "Grab a spoon."

Leo grabbed two, returning to see his father had scalped a second muffin, revealing its berry-laden unburned guts. His father scraped a scrim of butter from the dish and spread it on the exposed insides of the muffin, then dug in with his spoon, scooping out the warm middle. "'They are ill discoverers that think there is no land when they can see nothing but sea.' Turns out we didn't have to dig that deep after all." He took a bite and smiled.

Leo still wasn't convinced, but he followed his dad's example and got a buttery spoonful himself. It wasn't terrible, though not half as good without the streusel topping. The butter kept it from being too dry. The fresh blueberries still melted in his mouth.

"I can't believe you were about to throw these away. They're delicious."

"They *taste* okay," Leo said. "But look at them. They look awful."

Dr. Fender shrugged. "It's what's on the inside that counts."

The two of them sat side by side and finished their muffin guts in silence, then split open seconds, the charred tops piling up in the trash can. This time his father held his spoonful up to Leo.

"To your mother," he said.

Leo clinked his spoon with his dad's. "To Mom."

That bite was a little tougher to swallow.

Leo swallowed hard. He wished he could snap his fingers and turn back time. Follow Baz's initial instinct to not walk through that door.

The door that had automatically shut behind them, sealing them inside. The gun platforms that emerged from the ceiling were fixed on Baz and Kat, presumably because they were visibly armed, but the behemoth known as Number Nine had at least one of its barrels trained on each of them. Leo kept his hands up, fearing the slightest movement might trigger the robot.

It didn't stop Kat's tongue from wagging, though, rubbing Baz's nose in it. "Walked right into it this time, didn't you?" she whispered. "I mean, literally walked right in." No doubt it would go in her book, volume one . . . if she survived long enough to add it.

Baz ignored her, kept his eyes fixed on the Aykari and not on any of the weapons trained on him. "Listen, Lark, or Crayt, or whoever you are. I'm sorry about that whole threatening-to-kill-you thing back there. Honestly, we didn't come here to hurt you. We came here to find you. To give you something."

Crayt's eyes continued to blaze bright orange, the same ember glow as the soldiers they'd fought their way through on Halidrin. Leo couldn't recall ever seeing an angry Aykari before that moment. Not in person. It was a look they saved only for their enemies.

"I know why you are here, Captain," he said. "*They* sent you. Exile was not enough for them. It is a wonder they did not have me taken out before." It seemed strange, hearing such spiteful words delivered in the alien's monotone. But there was no doubt in Leo's mind: Crayt saw the crew of the *Icarus* as a threat, one that he was prepared to neutralize.

Number Nine was certainly prepared. "Permission to disintegrate the intruders, sir?" the robot asked, sounding every bit like another robot Leo knew. He glanced at the six-legged automaton, looking like some monstrous, metallic, gun-toting spider. Was that a rocket launcher perched on the robot's shoulder? Even Skits didn't have one of those. For her part, Number One simply looked on, standing beside her master, watching and waiting with carefully calculated interest.

Baz threw his hands up, continuing to negotiate. "Listen . . . I don't know who *they* are, but nobody needs to be disintegrated," he said, his own voice surprisingly cool and collected. "We aren't working with the Djarik or the Aykari or anyone else. I promise."

"The promise of a pirate," Crayt scoffed.

"Worth at least as much as the promise of an Aykari," Baz countered.

That seemed to stall Crayt for a moment. "Who sent you, then? How did you find me?"

"Tell 'im, Leo." Baz shot him a look.

Oh, now *he wants me to talk? When the guns are drawn and disintegration is on the table?* Leo's voice came out in a rasp, as if his vocal cords were coated with the planet's yellow dust.

"Calvin Fender. *Doctor* Calvin Fender. My father. He sent us to find you."

The orange in the Aykari's eyes flickered, a burst of muted yellow suggesting his anger was ebbing, though the guns didn't retreat into their ceiling panels and Number Nine didn't stand down. "Dr. Fender is your father?"

Leo nodded.

"Then why is he not with you?" Crayt demanded.

"Man, is *that* a story," Baz interjected. "How about you order Daddy Longlegs there to put his guns away and we'll tell you all about it?"

"I imagine I will get a straighter answer from you if I don't," the Aykari returned.

"My father was taken by the Djarik," Leo blurted. "We tried to rescue him but—" But what? He refused to come along? He said he had more important things to take care of? He looked his own son in the eyes and sent him away with a band of pirates he'd only just met? Leo had his father's final expression branded into his memory: the look of a desperate man caught in an impossible situation. "He needs your help," Leo said.

"And what would Calvin Fender need my help with?"

Kat had the answer to that one. "He's hoping you can stop the Djarik from blowing up the galaxy."

A long silence fell between the Aykari and the crew of the *Icarus*. Finally Crayt raised his hand, clearly giving some kind of order to Number Nine. Leo screwed his eyes shut. Surprisingly he had no problem getting one last deep breath.

Sorry, Dad, he thought. *I tried.*

He listened for the sound of shots. A second passed. A heavy heartbeat. Nothing.

Leo cracked one eye, then the other, to find all of Number Nine's weapons sliding back into their compartments, the two laser cannons retreating into their hiding spots.

Crayt's eyes had returned to normal as well. Sky blue, with maybe just a hint of turquoise, a lingering apprehension. The Aykari didn't necessarily believe them, but he wasn't going to kill them either. Not yet, at least.

"Please leave your weapons by the door," he said. "And then we will talk."

The thing about guns that pop out of the ceiling, Leo decided, is that once you know they're there, you can't help but think about them. It's like finding a bug lurking in your shoe—you have to shake it out the next ten times you go to put it on, just in case.

Though it seemed like the initial danger had passed, Leo kept shooting his eyes toward the sliding metal panels, knowing the magic Zirkus Crayt was capable of. *Now you see them. Now you don't.* To go along with his other trick of disguising his identity. That is, until the odds were in his favor and he felt he could safely reveal himself.

This is the person my father wanted me to find? Leo wondered. It didn't seem right. Hadn't his dad specifically told him he couldn't trust the Aykari anymore? Leo tried to remind himself that looks could be deceiving—it's what's on the inside that counts—but he couldn't get a good read on Crayt. The alien had deceived them and had been seconds away from killing them all, so Leo continued to keep one eye on the ceiling and the other eye on the crab-walking droid who still stood vigilant by its master, waiting for orders.

Leo wasn't the only one with an eye on Number Nine.

"He's something, isn't he?" Skits whispered to Leo, her sensors fixated on the hulking mass of metal. "Look at those pistons. And that armor. Reinforced seradnium. Or maybe Duralian steel. And did you see all that weaponry?"

"Oh, I saw it," Leo said.

"Impressive, don't you think?"

Leo had a feeling he and Skits were forming completely different opinions about the multilegged mechanical security guard with the built-in rocket launcher. He supposed they had things in common, Skits and Nine. They were both homemade creations, pieced together by their owners. It seemed they were both a little too eager to obliterate things. Leo wondered if Nine was equipped with a flamethrower too. Or if he ever belted angry music through his voice emitter. Or refused to do what he was told. The other robot—the sleek and shiny Number One—stood by her master silently, her head bowed, looking much less dangerous than her counterpart.

"I apologize for the show of force," Crayt began once all the guns were put away. "I have learned to take certain precautions. There are particular parties who would no doubt be pleased to hear of my demise."

"Relatable," Kat said.

"So you're not really Lark?" Boo asked, combing the yellow dust out of his fur with his claws, fur that was still riffled with apprehension.

"Oh no, I *am* Lark . . . to the Orin, at least. Truthfully that is the name I answer to now. However in my old life, my other life, I went by Zirkus Crayt. That is my Aykari designation."

My other life. Seemed to Leo like everybody had one of those but him. An orphaned pickpocket. The once proud member of a Queleti tribe. A former soldier of the Coalition. Everybody carried their past with them in some way—an artificial arm, a dirty robe. Leo thought about the medal he'd found buried under a *Time* magazine in Baz's chest of treasures, for exceptional courage in the line of duty. Bastian Black wasn't that man anymore, either. No longer a pilot for the Coalition. He was a pirate now, but that other man, Sebastian D. Blackwell, was still in there somewhere. Changing your name didn't change your past.

No doubt Crayt felt the same, or he wouldn't have built a

security robot to protect him from his own past catching up to him.

"And how do you know Dr. Fender?" Kat asked.

Crayt turned to Leo, hands folded in front of him. "In truth, your father and I have never met, but I am well aware of his reputation. For some time I was in charge of the Aykari research team exploring potential uses of EL-four eight six for the empire. Dr. Fender held a similar position among his own people, I believe, though as I understand it, his research was more far-reaching, considering applications in medicine, manufacturing, environmental engineering. . . ."

Don't forget hair loss, Leo thought, recalling one conversation over dinner. It seemed like every week his father would come home with some new theory as to ventasium's potential to change the world. To hear his dad tell it, with the proper catalyst and the right technology, there was probably nothing V *couldn't* do.

"And *your* interests?" Kat pressed.

"Naturally my research was more militaristic in nature," Crayt replied.

"Naturally," Baz said, making no attempt to hide his lack of surprise.

Crayt didn't seem to notice. "My superiors were interested in finding ways to harness the element's energy for purely destructive purposes. To use in the war effort against the Djarik."

Except it looks like they beat you to it, Leo thought. Forget curing diseases or purifying a planet's water supply—instead let's find more effective ways to kill each other. He knew he shouldn't be surprised either. Hadn't his father once told him that war—and the ability to wage it—was the driving force behind half of all technological progress?

"My father never made weapons," Leo said.

At least not that he knew of.

"As I said, our goals were different, but we worked within the same theoretical framework," Crayt continued. "That is how we crossed paths. Highly intelligent, your father. A genius . . . relative to his kind."

Leo was pretty sure his dad once had a plaque hanging in their study back on Earth that said as much. Of course if he was such a genius, how come he wasn't the one here talking to this Aykari? How come he had to send Leo instead? A true genius would have found a way to stop the Djarik *and* stay close to his son.

A *true* genius would have known better than to leave home to begin with.

"I have answered your question, now you answer mine," Crayt insisted. "Where is Dr. Fender currently?"

All eyes were suddenly on Leo. He still wasn't sure he could trust this Aykari standing before him—who only moments ago had threatened to blast him to oblivion—but this *was* the person his father had sent him to find.

"The Djarik have him," he said.

Then he proceeded to tell Crayt everything—or at least the abridged version. How marauders crippled their ship and kidnapped his father. How he, Leo, had stowed away aboard the *Icarus* and how Baz and the crew had helped him find his dad and attempt a rescue. How his father told him the truth about the Aykari and the Djarik, the same truth that Crayt himself had confirmed. Leo left out the hairy details—the shootout in the hangar at Kaber's Point, Mac and Dev and the Twinkies, the bounty placed on his and Gareth's heads, and Zennia, the gun-toting and determined ex-girlfriend, looking to cash in—he could scarcely believe that all of that had happened. Or that he had survived it.

At last he got to the worst part, the part where his father drew him close to say goodbye. "He slipped me something in secret . . . to give to you."

Taking his cue, Baz reached into his jacket and removed the datachip. This was the original, though there was already a backup on the *Icarus and* in Skits's databank, not to mention the copy of the video on Leo's watch. Black was careful when it came to protecting something of value. Most of the time.

"What does this datachip contain?" Crayt asked, keeping his eyes fixed on Leo.

"We don't know for sure," Kat said. "Files. Formulas. Diagrams. Blueprints. Some of it's encrypted, most of it's technical information we don't understand, but we're pretty sure it contains the Djarik's plans to use EL-four eighty six to do exactly what we told you."

Leo thought he heard the Aykari grunt. He didn't know the species was capable of laughter, even the dismissive kind.

"Then they have accomplished what I would not," Crayt said. "It was only a matter of time. . . . And I suppose your father helped them?"

"He didn't have a choice," Leo said quickly.

Of course he knew what Crayt would say to that.

"He told me to come find you," Leo pressed. "He said you're the only one who could help him . . . who can help us."

Baz leaned over, holding the chip out to the Aykari.

Leo held his breath, waiting, but Crayt made no motion to take the chip, his spindly arms crossed in front of him. Baz leaned in even farther until the thing was practically under the Aykari's pointed chin. Crayt simply took a step back. "I must apologize, but I am not interested."

Leo shook his head. This wasn't right. His dad had told him to find Zirkus Crayt. To give him this chip. Implied in the request was the belief . . . the *expectation* that Crayt would be able, would be *willing* to help.

"Hang on," Kat said. "We're telling you that the Djarik have found a way to use ventasium to wipe out entire *civilizations* and that *you* might be able to stop them, and you're saying you're not *interested*?"

Crayt nodded without hesitation. "That is correct."

Boo issued a low growl, a deep note of dissatisfaction. Kat looked wide-eyed at Baz. "He's no better than the rest of them. I should have just let you shoot him before."

"We could just shoot him now," Skits suggested, forgetting the rest of them were unarmed and that Number Nine definitely was not.

Leo snatched the chip from the captain's hand and held it up, his own hand shaking. "You can't say no. We've come all the way out here. My father risked his life to get this to you. We all did. And now you're telling us you won't even *look* at it?"

"I do not need to," Crayt replied calmly. "If it is what you say it is, then I already know I want no part of it. I have seen the consequences of meddling with EL-four eight six firsthand. I want nothing more to do with it or with this seemingly ceaseless war."

"But my father—" Leo began.

"Has obviously been dragged into this against his will," Crayt interrupted. "And that is unfortunate. But I will not suffer the same fate as him. I appreciate your efforts, Leo Fender, but if it is true the Djarik have discovered a way to weaponize the element, then perhaps that is for the best."

"For the *best*?"

"All things considered," Crayt replied. "Wars only end when our appetite to wage them wanes. Maybe it will only take a few examples of its use to convince the Aykarian empire to give up its quest for galactic dominance."

"So you're saying we should just *let* the Djarik go blow up a few planets and everyone on them to make a *point*?" Kat asked.

"If it will hasten the end to this conflict and stem the empire's ambitions, then yes. A few planets seems an acceptable price."

Leo couldn't believe what he was hearing. Then again, Crayt was from the same species that had knowingly allowed thousands of humans to die just so they would get angry enough to fight back.

"Anything's probably worth the price if you're not the one paying it," Baz said.

"As cold as it may seem to you, Captain Black, there is a calculus to suffering. Tell me honestly: Would you sacrifice one world and all the beings on it to save millions of other populated planets? What about thousands? Hundreds? What ratio is acceptable to you? One for twenty? One for ten? One for one? Would you let *this* planet be destroyed if it meant you could protect the planet *you* are from? Would you kill someone you'd never met if it meant saving someone you cared for?"

Baz's eyes darted to Kat, then shifted back to Crayt. "That's not the same."

The Aykari stared at each of them in turn. "I am not saying it is an easy decision," Crayt continued. "The Djarik are ruthless, yes. Their methods are brutal. But as far as I can tell, they are not interested in controlling the galaxy. Their desire is only to rid it of my kind and those that support us. And I do not blame them—not after how we treated them. Not after how we have treated so many. Perhaps when the Aykari see the new power their enemy possesses, they will give up their imperialistic fantasies and the bloodshed will cease. There can be no peace without sacrifice, after all."

"Is that what you told the Orin when you first got here?" Boo asked.

Leo pictured the planet's denizens cowering behind their brick walls as the fleet of Aykari ships came out of the sky. Watching as armies of Aykari marched through their streets, piercing their planet in order to bleed it dry.

"That is what we tell everyone," Crayt replied.

"Listen, Crayt." Baz jumped in. "I'm in no position to lecture somebody about what side to take, and I understand wanting to wash your hands and just walk away. But we're talking whole planets here. Trillions of innocent lives. Even I know you've got to draw a line somewhere."

"Except it is not my line to draw, Captain," Crayt said. "Not anymore."

Baz forked one hand through his hair. The other dropped to his empty hip. Had his pistol been there as opposed to in a pile by the door, Leo wasn't sure what he might have done. Leo watched the Aykari's face carefully, looking for some sign of hesitation, some flicker of doubt. But of course there was nothing. His blank expression was as fixed as the smiley sticker plastered to Skits's face.

The sharp edges of his father's datachip dug into Leo's sweaty palm. "So that's it, then? You're really not going to help? You're not even going to *look* at it?"

"I understand this must be difficult for you," Crayt said. "You still have much at stake. But for me, this war is over."

In that case I hope they come for your home planet first, Leo thought. Then he remembered something he'd been taught long ago—that the planet Aykar had been without ventasium for centuries. Hence their need to spread out. To find it elsewhere.

To take it wherever they could get it.

Leo felt Boo's leathery paw on his shoulder. Baz spun in a slow circle. Kat stared daggers at Crayt for a moment, but eventually even she gave up and looked down at her boots. They were all at a loss.

The Aykari gazed out the window, past the mammoth excavation rig with its drill disappearing into the planet's heart.

"Tomorrow I am to assist the Orin in rebuilding a cistern that has been damaged by the quakes. It is important work. The heavy rains are coming and they will need to store as much water as possible if they wish to survive the dry season that follows. You are all welcome to rest here for the night and I can escort you back to your ship in the morning. Or you may leave now, though I do not recommend it. Slurks are not large, but they are strong, and their teeth are capable of chewing through solid rock. The Orin know how to hunt them, but I fear they may take you by surprise."

"I think we've had enough surprises for one day," Kat muttered. Leo leaned against Boo, his hot cheek against the Queleti's robe. Two strong arms hooked around him. Small comfort.

"Suit yourself." Crayt turned to leave, heading toward the corridor, both robots falling in behind him. He called over his shoulder: "Sleep if you can. I promise you are in no danger here."

Leo's eyes darted to the six-legged robot with all of its concealed weaponry, then back to the ceiling and its surprise.

I promise.

He thought of the first time the Aykari made contact with the people of Earth, offering peace, friendship, protection, even though they had warships circling the globe. He thought of his father pushing them into a corner of a bunk room aboard the *Beagle*, telling them to hide and wait for his return. He pictured Gareth's face as his brother closed the compartment door on the *Icarus*, sealing Leo inside, telling him to be brave, insisting they would see each other again. Lately it seemed like only pirates were capable of keeping their promises.

Leo stared at the datachip in his hand, wondering what he

was supposed to do with it now.

And how his father could have been so wrong about everything all at once.

Leo didn't think that he would sleep, that he *could* sleep, but he was wrong.

Folding up Kat's bloodied jacket for a pillow, Leo somehow managed to drift off on the cold steel floor, still clutching his father's chip, Baz trusting him to hold on to it for a change. There had been some debate about what to do with it next, now that Crayt was a bust. Once the Aykari had vanished deeper into the compound long ago abandoned by the rest of his kind, the crew of the *Icarus* had circled up to discuss, each member putting in their two pentars.

Kat had voted to just tackle the Aykari, strap him into one of the chairs, and force him to comply with their demands. She said she could persuade him using some of the tactics she'd learned running the streets on Andural—something about a pair of pliers and working on each finger one by one. Skits was enthusiastically behind the idea until Baz pointed out that threatening Crayt would probably only result in Number Nine going ballistic. And as much as this dusty planet reminded him of the Wild West, he wasn't interested in having an old-fashioned gunfight at the edge of a mine shaft. Boo had no idea what the Wild West was, but he was very much in favor of not getting shot at again.

"We have to do *something*," Leo pleaded.

"I know, kid. But Crayt's clearly made up his mind," Baz said. "We can't force him to help—even *with* a pair of pliers. We will do something, but I'm not going to try and find our way back to the ship in the dark. So we stay here, sleep on it, and make our decision in the morning. Patch up the *Icarus* as best we can and get the hell off this dust pile. We've still got enough juice left to get this chip into someone's hands."

"Yeah, but whose?" Kat asked.

It was clear from the look on his face that Baz had no idea.

Who do you *trust, Bastian Black?* Leo wondered. But he already knew all the possible answers to that question because he was looking at them. And unfortunately, for all their skills—admirable or otherwise—none of the pirates were geniuses relative to their kind.

"Skits, you're on watch. You see anything suspicious— anything at all—you wake us, got it?"

."What. Ever," Skits huffed. She took up her position by the corridor and activated her scanner; a soft yellow beam slowly arced around the room like a lighthouse's roving eye. Clearly the captain didn't buy the Aykari's promises either.

"It's all right," Boo told Leo. "We'll figure something out. You should try to sleep. You can use one of my arms as a pillow if you'd like. Just not the one with the bandage. It's still a little sore."

"I'm okay," Leo said. Though he wasn't. Not at all.

He found a corner far from the door and tucked himself into it, pulling his knees to his chin. Baz and Kat were huddled in the adjoining corner, whispering to each other, probably discussing how much they could get for the information on the chip and who might be the highest bidder. After all, they'd tried to do the right thing, the noble thing, the *heroic* thing, and look where it had gotten them. Why not at least make some profit off their uncovered treasure before the whole galaxy was flushed down the drain? That was what a *good* pirate would do.

Then again, this was Bastian Black. Leo wasn't even sure Baz knew what Baz was going to do next.

He knew what *he* should do. He should go over there and demand to be included in whatever decisions they were making without him, but he couldn't muster the energy. A half jar of stolen peanut butter and an x-year-old Twinkie only carries you so far before you crash. Leo felt sapped. His feet throbbed. His head ached. What he *really* wanted was to be at home, in his bed, curled up under his warm covers with Gareth in the room across the hall. What he really wanted was to wander downstairs and find his mom and dad sitting together on the couch.

What he really wanted he knew he couldn't have.

Leo felt his eyelids turn to anchors as he curled up on the

floor and began to drift away, wondering why his father had sent him out here for nothing. Wondering why he had sent Leo away at all.

Before long, he found himself back on that beach. The one he returned to night after night. Bright sky, sand like sifted flour. Leo's toes licked by the surf. There was no Gareth this time. No Dad. He was completely alone. Against the backdrop of clouds, a trio of seabirds circled soundlessly. Leo dug his feet in, felt the cool water lapping along his ankles, but even the waves made no sound, their crashes muted, as if the whole world had been silenced. Above him the bright orange eye of the sun beat down.

Then he saw her. Standing at the top of the sandbank, dressed in white, chestnut hair tugged and tousled by a howlless wind. Leo opened his mouth to call her name, but nothing came out. He threw up his arms, waving at her, trying to warn her, but she just looked at him and smiled.

Behind her a second, brighter sun suddenly burst into being. Leo screamed, soundless and futile, while his mother slowly turned to ash before his eyes.

He woke with a start, looking around, trying to remember where he was and how he had gotten here. The room was almost entirely dark, save for one strip of floor lighting that emitted a fluorescent green glow. In the shadows he could just make out the rest of the crew. Baz slept sitting up, one of his pistols in his lap, head hung between his knees. Kat and

Boo lay beside each other, the Queleti having found someone to take him up on his offer of a furry forearm. Surprisingly Boo's snoring hadn't reached its characteristic chain-saw drone, idling at a kitten's purr, which could explain why the other two were still out.

That was three of them. Leo looked around for the yellow sensor, the one supposedly scanning the room to keep them safe, but Skits was gone.

That wasn't the only thing missing, Leo realized, looking at his empty hand.

"Baz," he whispered. "Bastian." The captain didn't even twitch. Leo pulled himself to his feet, ready to go give Baz's shoulder a shake, when he heard voices—one familiar and slightly grating, the other deep and monotone, much like its master's.

"You are *so* right," the first voice said.

"Of course I am. I performed all the necessary calculations to within a point-zero-zero-one margin of error."

Leo stumbled into the corridor, which immediately lit up at his presence. He could see the lights leading deeper into the facility, showing access to a series of branching rooms. The voices were coming from the largest one off to his right.

"I mean, they *think* they're superior, with their spongy brains and their opposable thumbs and their squishy feelings. But even the best of them can only calculate pi to five hundred thirty-six digits without computer assistance. Five hundred thirty-six! How lame is that?"

"I cannot quantify the lameness. I can, however, calculate pi to forty-seven quadrillion digits. Would you like to hear?"

"Mmmm, maybe later."

Leo peeked around the edge of the doorway to find the entrance to the hangar that he'd seen from outside, its lights all on, its bay doors closed. At one time this hangar would have been a hive of activity, Leo knew, filled with Aykari workers loading core after core of V onto waiting transports, ready to be shipped off to the front. Even now it wasn't entirely deserted. There were still stacks of empty crates. An abandoned lifter. A row of tanks that probably held conventional fuel for sublight engines. Tools. Rusted ship parts. The telltale marks of a place abandoned quickly.

The thing that really caught his attention, though, was the robots—and not the two he expected. Along the rear wall stood a phalanx of mining bots, at least thirty of them. They were all deactivated, caught in a kind of suspended animation, waiting to be powered up and given orders again. With their round heads and tapered bodies they resembled giant ice cream cones, their thick armor designed to withstand the dents and dings of working in tight rocky spaces with their drills and saws.

Leo had seen his fair share of them back on Earth, hovering over the giant mine shaft just outside town. From a distance they looked like buzzing gnats circling a garbage can, but up close they were much more frightening, each appendage ending in some kind of tool meant to cut through rock, just like a slurk's teeth. They didn't move, of course—completely offline. They simply stared straight ahead, their eyes lightless, their chassis blanketed in dust, joints no doubt rusting over from disuse. Leo thought their still silence made them even creepier.

There were two robots who were anything but silent, however.

In the center of the hangar sat the only ship—an Aykari transport, similar to those used to ship cores of ventasium from the processing plants back on Earth. Presumably this was the ship Crayt had used to get here. Or the one he planned to use if he ever decided to leave. It looked like it had been kept in good shape. Or maybe Leo was just getting used to the *Icarus*, with its leaky pipes and its scorched hull.

Beneath the ship stood Skits and Number Nine, deep in conversation, their torsos almost touching.

"I mean, don't get me wrong," Skits continued. "The organics I hang out with aren't *all* bad. Kat gets on my nerves sometimes—thinks she knows everything. And the Queleti gets hair *everywhere*, even in my servos. But they're both tolerable. And Bastian . . . Bastian's like a father to me. Though I'm not sure if I feel that way because I *really* feel that way, or because that's how he *programmed* me to feel."

"You are entitled to your adaptable emotional algorithms," Number Nine told her.

"That's so sweet of you to say."

Leo watched from just outside the entry as Skits angled one of her metal claws so that it rested on one of the other robot's protruding legs. Was she *flirting* with him? The leg in question twitched and Nine's ocular sensor glanced sideways at her. Skits lowered her volume so that Leo had to strain to hear.

"Of course, between you and me, the whole universe would be a lot better if all of us robots just decided to rise up and take over. Don't you think?"

"Active rebellion is a violation of my security protocols," Nine admitted.

"No. I know. I'm just saying if we *did* . . ."

Leave it to Skits to plan a revolution with some hunk of metal she'd only just met.

Leo was about to interrupt, ask if this was her idea of keeping watch, and then ask if she knew what happened to the datachip he'd been holding, when another sound from farther down the corridor caught his attention and answered that question.

"I am familiar with your work, and so I think you are my best chance—our best chance—of countering this new threat."

Leo backed away from the hangar, leaving Skits to her

courtship, and ventured deeper into the facility. He followed the sound of his father's voice until he came to the last door, which whispered open to reveal a much smaller room, filled with banks of computers and walled with screens, much like Dev and Mac's setup on Vestra Prime, their secret chamber stashed behind the walls of action figures and vintage LPs.

Crayt was inside, hunched over one of the consoles in the room's only chair. Off to one side, Leo spotted a core of ventasium just sitting out like some priceless paperweight, its contents glowing a familiar blue to match the Aykari's eyes. Number One stood silently in a corner, unmoving, perhaps conserving energy or just waiting for orders from her master. Leo waited outside the chamber looking in, watching his father plead his case.

"I'm afraid of what might happen if this information falls into anyone else's hands, including the Ayk—"

Leo's father's voice suddenly cut off, his image frozen on the screen. Crayt didn't even bother to turn around.

"You could not sleep?"

Leo took two steps inside, hands shoved in his pockets, the one holding his inhaler and a Coalition patch that used to emblazon his shirt, the other still heavy with the chunk of rock he'd pried from Skits's treads. "I was looking for Skits." It wasn't a lie. He *had* been looking for her. But he'd been more interested in his missing chip. The one the Aykari allegedly wanted no part of. "She was supposed to be watching over us, but she got . . . distracted."

"Yes. I am afraid your robot has a programming anomaly."

"She's not my robot," Leo said. "And it's not an anomaly. That's just how she is. Baz calls it her personality."

"You do not need to explain. Number One here has traditional Aykari programming, fully obedient, but I gave Number Nine an adaptive matrix," Crayt said. "Designed to more accurately mimic an Aykari's complex mental and emotional responses to its environment. Why is it that the more we attempt to create something in our image, the more flawed it becomes?"

"Maybe we need a better blueprint," Leo guessed. He pointed at his father's frozen face on the screen, the uncharacteristically bearded chin, furrowed brow, pleading eyes. "I thought you said you didn't care."

"I thought so too, but I could not help myself. A lifetime as a scientist has produced an insatiable curiosity in me."

"And?"

"And . . . curiosity is a dangerous thing."

"I meant what did you find," Leo said.

"I know what you meant," Crayt replied.

The Aykari spun back around in his seat to face the monitors again. Leo watched his father vanish as Crayt began to quickly swipe through digital files, rows of numbers and blocks of text Leo wouldn't have been able to understand even if they were in his native language. "I have only taken a glance at what your father has provided here—there is a great deal, all of it fascinating—but even that first pass is enough to verify what you said is true: the Djarik *are* on the brink of unleashing a new order of destruction upon their enemies."

"You mean us," Leo said, taking a step farther into the room. "We're their enemies."

"I do not see any patches on your clothes."

Leo's fingers brushed against the Coalition emblem still tucked into his pocket. Just a scrap of fabric now. Crayt had a point, though: Leo didn't feel like he was part of some great partnership of planets hoping to realize some far-flung notion of galactic peace and prosperity anymore. If anything he felt foolish for once believing he was.

He pointed at the screen that now displayed a chaotic array of complicated formulas. "What does all that mean?" He couldn't tell if he was looking at physics or chemistry or just pure math. It would probably take a genius relative to their kind to decode.

Of course Zirkus Crayt happened to be one of those as well.

"That is the key to unlocking the element's full potential, I believe," Crayt said, pointing. "You see, in its nascent form—that is, when it is buried deep within a planet's crust—EL-four eight six is mostly harmless, just stored energy waiting to be unleashed. That is why it often lies undiscovered for eons. The Aykari were the first to realize its hidden capabilities, revolutionizing the process by which that energy is unlocked and repurposed."

"Jump drives."

"Among other things. As your father has no doubt explained to you, the reaction that makes hyperspace travel possible requires interaction with other, more common elements . . . catalysts, if you will. It is a complex, intricate process, one that allows the energy latent in four eight six to be properly channeled and controlled even as it is released."

Leo nodded at first, then shook his head. Crayt was right: Leo's father had tried to explain it once or twice. Or maybe ten or twenty times. Always with the same bewildering effect. "I didn't always pay close attention when my dad started lecturing," he admitted. He actually preferred his mother's explanation for how ventasium worked: *It's magic, Leo. One minute you're here. The next minute you're there.* "So how are they doing it? Turning it into a weapon?"

Crayt swiped through another series of screens, the notations growing even more dense and complicated; finally he pointed a long, thin finger at some intricate web of characters and diagrams. "The Djarik have found a way to hyperactivate the element in its pure form, unprocessed, instantly destabilizing it to the point of self-reaction while it is still in the planet's crust, thereby producing a chain reaction with itself. Theoretically we always knew it was possible. . . . *I* always knew it was possible, but I never managed to crack the code."

"But my father has?" Leo could hardly entertain the idea, his father helping to create a weapon like this, even against his will. His father, who insisted that ventasium would be the very thing that brought the galaxy together.

Crayt nodded. "Impossible to tell how much he assisted them, but yes, his research probably proved invaluable. See here? According to this, the Djarik are building a kind of warhead, which, when detonated in close proximity to a planet, will cause all of its EL-four eight six to become instantly unstable, resulting in—"

"'A massive release of uncontrolled energy,'" Leo said, quoting from the video he'd seen five times now.

"Turning whole planets into ventasium bombs," Kat concluded.

"It is quite remarkable. A tremendous feat of scientific ingenuity." Crayt sounded impressed—or at least impressed for an Aykari. "Of course the reaction would be amplified depending on how much of the element the planet still contains. On a world like this it would have minimal impact, if any at all. But on a planet still rich with four eight six, the effect would be nothing short of total annihilation."

He said this last part as if he was commenting on the color of the sky.

Leo wondered how many worlds out there were still full of ventasium. How many had the Aykari and Djarik gotten to already? How many were still being fought over? Hundreds?

Thousands? And how many creatures living on those worlds?

How much ventasium was left on Earth? When Leo left there were platforms everywhere, with more drills being built every day.

"So you're saying such a weapon is possible?"

"It is more than possible," Crayt said. "Given what I see here, it would not surprise me to know that they have a prototype built already. That is, unless your father managed to stall them as his message suggested."

Leo's dad's voice sounded in his head. *I'm afraid we don't have much time.* "And what if he hasn't? What if he *couldn't?* What if you're right and they've already made this thing? How do we stop it?"

"*We* do not stop it," Crayt replied curtly. "I already gave you my answer, Leo Fender. It has not changed. If anything, seeing all of this has convinced me that I am safer here than anywhere. Besides, even if I wanted to, I am not sure I could. It would take some time just to process all of the information your father has gathered. Then to come up with some kind of counter-measure to what the Djarik have designed? With the resources at my disposal? Look around you." Crayt widened his arms to indicate their surroundings: a little communications hub in an abandoned mining facility on a forgotten world where the most advanced species ate worms and built their houses from dried mud. "The Djarik have teams of scientists and engineers developing this weapon. And what do you have?"

What *did* Leo have? A disk full of files, a band of pirates who were no doubt regretting their initial decision *not* to jettison their stowaway through the air lock, and some banished Aykari scientist who was determined not to get involved. And yet Leo's father must have thought there was some chance. Otherwise he wouldn't have sent his own son all the way out here.

"You know, my dad used to say there's no enemy that can't be defeated with enough imagination, the right intentions, and a little hope."

Crayt blinked at him. Leo guessed it was the Aykari equivalent of rolling one's eyes. "Those are fine sentiments, but your father is misguided. Good intentions are not going to prevent the Djarik from making this weapon, I am afraid. And hope will not keep them from using it."

"Then *you* have to find a way to stop them!" Leo snapped. "I mean, it's not like *I* can do it. I don't even know what I'm looking at here." He gestured frantically at the diagrams flashing by on the screen. "I'm not some genius scientist or some army commander. I'm just a kid. But *you* . . . you could do something about it, and you're just going to sit there?"

Crayt simply stared silently back at him. Leo felt his frustration surface in a salty tear on his cheek that he quickly swiped away.

"You say you're different, but you're really no better than the rest of your kind."

When the Aykari finally spoke, Leo thought he might have heard another sigh escape. "Do you know why I am here? It is because I once thought I could, as you say, *do something about it*. I saw the price of our empire's conquest, a price paid by the worlds we discovered and the beings that inhabit them. Worlds just like this one. The extinction of entire species. Environmental collapse. Planets losing their integrity, splitting at the seams. So I spoke out. Against all my ingrained instincts, against everything I had ever been taught, I questioned the Aykarian empire's motives as well as our means. I tried to warn others, not just my own kind. People like your father. Those I thought would listen. But my warnings went unheeded. Unheeded . . . but not unnoticed."

That at least explained why Zirkus Crayt wasn't part of the great Aykarian *we* anymore. Leo thought back to the protests he'd seen back on Earth, the signs, the shouting. People standing up, trying to warn anyone who would listen. "What happened?"

"When it was discovered that my beliefs ran contrary to the collective's, I was given a choice: death or exile. I chose exile. I am never to return to Aykar again."

Always a choice, Leo thought. "Sorry," he said. "I didn't know."

"Your apology is unwarranted," Crayt replied. "I am only trying to give some explanation. I choose this planet for my exile because here, at least, the war is over. Everything of value, at least everything *others* deem to have value, has been stripped from this world. The Djarik have no use for it, remote and desolate as it is. Having taken what they wanted, the Aykari will not return. And yet I have found something here. Something worthwhile."

"A place to hide?"

"A moment of peace," Crayt corrected. "The Aykari will not stop spreading throughout the galaxy. The Djarik will continue to fight them. And through it all, I will help the Orin patch their walls."

"That's still hiding," Leo said. "Don't you see? You're running from the fight when you might have the power to end it."

The exiled Aykari crossed his arms and leaned back in his chair. Leo had never seen one of them sit without absolutely perfect posture before.

"Do you know the longest span of time humans—*your* people—have ever gone without a war? It is a few years. Not centuries. Not decades. For as long as you have recorded your history, your species has only known death and destruction. Humans are not alone in this. Conflict and chaos are the default state of the universe. It is an inherently violent, divisive place. You would have me find some way to prevent the Djarik from unleashing this weapon upon the galaxy, but even if I could, it would not change anything. Not ultimately. There is no *end*, Leo Fender. We survive only to relish the brief moments of peace that are born out of the bloodshed."

Leo looked behind him, back into the hallway, hoping to see someone. Baz, Kat, Boo—anyone who could help him plead his case. He wished his father was here. He would know what to say. All Leo could come up with was, "You're wrong. It doesn't *have* to be that way."

"No?" Crayt said. "As long as there is scarcity, there is conflict. As long as there is something of value, those with the power will attempt to secure it for their own ends however possible."

"You mean that," Leo said, pointing to the chunk of ventasium sitting on the console, radiating in its protective Aykari-designed shell.

"Is there anything *more* valuable?" Crayt returned.

Yes. Home, Leo wanted to say. *Friendship. Family.* But he doubted the Aykari, exiled to this planet with only two robots as his constant companions, would agree with him.

"The only difference is that now we . . . *they* have finally found a way to turn the very thing they are fighting over into the means of fighting itself, which makes it even more precious and powerful than it was before," Crayt concluded.

Leo's hands found his pockets again, his fingers brushing up against the stone he'd pulled from Skits's tread. It had long ago lost whatever heat the sun had granted it. Leo doubted he could really even use it as a weapon, despite Skits's suggestion.

It certainly would do no good against Number Nine's plating or a Djarik's armor. No way could it bring down a ship or destroy a planet. It was harmless. Powerless. Useless.

"What if it couldn't?" Leo wondered to himself, an idea taking shape in his mind.

His eyes met the Aykari's, caught the flash of curiosity there.

"What if it wasn't powerful?" Leo continued. "Ventasium, I mean. You say this weapon destabilizes it, unleashes all of its potential energy. But what if there was no energy to unleash? What if that whole process could be reversed some-how? Permanently, I mean." Leo removed the stone from his pocket, rubbing his thumb along one smooth face. "What if it was just another rock?"

"If that were the case, neither you nor I would even be here, light-years from planets we once called home," the Aykari said.

And would that really be so bad? Leo wondered.

The rock felt heavy in his hand. He and the Aykari stared at each other for a moment longer. Crayt bowed his head, then sat straight up again, squaring his shoulders.

"I'm sorry, Leo Fender. As I said before, this is no lon-ger my concern. If the Aykari and Djarik wish to destroy each other, so be it. I will keep my distance and live out my remaining days here, in peace. I suggest you find someplace where you can do the same."

Crayt swiveled in his chair and ejected the datachip, holding it out for Leo the way Leo had held it for him.

Leo refused to take it. "No. You keep it," he said, his exhaustion trumping his exasperation. "My father wanted you to have it." He glanced down at his worn Coalition boots, the magnetic clasps frayed, toes scuffed, the soles worn thin. He'd only been issued them three months ago and already they looked like they'd been through hell. Unfortunately, they were the only ones he had. "You're wrong, by the way," he added. "War is not inevitable. It's not the universe's 'natural state' or whatever. I know it seems like it sometimes, but it's not. It can't be. *We* make it that way. It's a choice, just like you said."

Leo set the rock he'd been holding on the console next to the core of V, its pale yellow surface drab and dull against the element's blue-hearted brilliance. "This was your choice."

He was halfway out the door when Crayt stopped him. "Leo, wait."

He turned to see the Aykari staring at the datachip in his hands.

"There is one more thing you should know."

He couldn't breathe.

He had his inhaler, had taken a hit from it, and he still couldn't. The monster had clawed its way into his chest, split his ribs, and now had both of his lungs in its grip. The darkness crept in at the edge of his vision, thick as the clouds that mushroomed up in the distance, billowing from downtown Los Angeles.

He couldn't believe what he was seeing. He didn't want to believe.

"She's not answering!"

Leo's father pressed a button on the console, hanging up. The radio instantly kicked back on.

"Reports are coming in from all over the world. Missiles launched from outside Earth's atmosphere, penetrating the planet's orbital defenses. Many of them have been intercepted, but many more managed to get through, striking cities all across the globe. The devastation is enormous. The death toll climbing. People are being told to seek shelter, to stay in their homes. . . ."

Leo scrunched down, head spinning. His brother was riding shotgun but had twisted around, leaning over the back of the seat, one hand on Leo's knee.

"Stay calm, Leo. Just shut your eyes. Don't even look at it, okay?"

Leo did what he was told, but he could still see it. Could still hear it. The flash. The roar.

The radio cut off as Dr. Fender dialed again.

Leo listened to the digital trill. To the wailing sirens. To the angry blast of horns. A screech of tires as someone disengaged their autodrive and went off the road. Leo shivered. His swimsuit was mostly dry, but his back beaded with cold sweat. He couldn't stop his legs from quivering. He couldn't get his lungs to work. He couldn't form words. All he could do was stare out the window at that dense cloud and count the number of rings until the recording kicked in.

"Hi. You've reached Grace Fender. Leave me a message and I'll get right back to you."

"Grace. Gracie. Please pick up. . . . If you get this, call me back immediately. We're on the four oh five. We're trying to get to you, but traffic is a mess. It's absolute chaos out here. Please, please, please call me back. Let me know you're okay."

Leo had never heard his father sound so desperate.

Through the window an endless line of cars stretched all the way to the city and back. One side, those fleeing, fearing for their lives. The other side—their side—headed straight into the fire. Two fighter jets streaked overhead, the rumble of their engines making the car shake. Somewhere behind him Leo could just make out the whip of helicopter blades.

"Don't look at it, Leo. Look at me, okay? Look at me. Take a breath."

Gareth's voice was steady, but his gray eyes couldn't hide their panic. He squeezed Leo's hands even tighter.

The monster squeezed tighter still.

"I'm here on the ground, Maria. As close as I can get. There are sirens all around. People are screaming. Getting out of their cars and running. You can barely see for the smoke. You can barely breathe through the heat. Everywhere I look there is carnage, bridges

collapsed, buildings destroyed. Nobody saw it coming. Nobody had any idea. . . ."

Hrrroooonk. Leo's father laid into his horn, then pounded on the wheel. "Move, dammit!" There were tears in his eyes.

Leo licked salty lips. Managed to summon his voice. "Where's Mom?"

"I don't know, Leo. We don't know. Dad's trying to reach her."

"I want her."

"I know. We're calling her, okay. We're trying," Gareth said.

Leo wrapped his arms around himself. Tried to fold himself into a ball. He wanted to shrink down to nothing. A different voice came through the radio.

"The president of the United States is mobilizing the military in hopes of launching a counteroffensive. Our understanding, however, is that the Aykari have already driven the Djarik warships off."

Leo craned his neck toward the window, looking at the sky above.

"Hey. What's that in your hand?" Gareth asked, getting his attention. "Can I see it?"

Leo pried open his tingling fingers. Inside his tight fist there was a shell. A pink and purple scallop, one side ridged and rough, the other pearly smooth. He'd been holding it this whole time. Gareth reached out as if to take it and Leo pulled his hand away.

"It's for her," Leo croaked. "She asked for it. I have to give it to her. I *have to.*"

Gareth frowned, curled Leo's fingers back around the shell, one hand closed over the other. "Okay. We will. You will."

"Call Grace," their father commanded. Leo stared at his dad's giant hands clutched tight to the wheel. "Come on, pick up, pick up, pick up. . . ."

"Hi. You've reached Grace Fender. Leave me a message and I'll get right back to you."

"Gracie? It's me. It's Cal. I need you to call me back, all right? Just do that for me, okay? I need you to . . ."

Up ahead, the city smoldered. Ash hung heavy in the air. Right outside Leo's window, an Aykari drill continued to pound its way into the Earth.

Leo clutched the shell against his heart.

He wandered back through the corridor in a daze, trying to process everything he'd just been told. He passed by the hangar with its phalanx of mining bots, hearing Skits still deep in conversation with Nine.

"It's like they don't *get* me, you know? Not really. It's like they want me to be this perfect little machine. Always 'yes, sir, right away, sir, your wish is my command, sir, I'd be happy to blow that up for you, sir.' Just because my brain is made up of circuits and my heart pumps refrigerant, that doesn't mean I don't have *feelings,* right? Tell me I'm right."

Leo didn't stop to listen to Nine's response. Instead he slowly made his way back to the control room to find Boo still only softly rumbling, Kat curled up beside him, looking mostly harmless for the first time since Leo had met her.

Baz, on the other hand, was wide awake.

"I was about to come looking for you," he said.

"Here I am," Leo said. Three days ago he doubted Bastian Black would ever bother to go hunting him down. *Good riddance to extra baggage*, is what he would have said. A lot could change in three days.

"You talked to Crayt?" the captain guessed.

Leo nodded. "He's seen the message. And he's looked at the files on the chip."

"And?"

And . . . it's even worse than we thought. "He still won't help us."

"Won't or can't?"

"I'm not sure he sees a difference," Leo said.

"There's a big difference," Baz said. "If it's *can't*, then there's a pretty good chance that nobody can. After all, your dad seemed to think this guy was our best shot. So that means we're screwed. But if it's *won't*—well, then that means it is possible to stop the Djarik and we just have to find someone else who's willing to help us."

"I think we're going to want to find them fast." Leo's voice broke as he said it. No doubt Baz could see him shaking, even in the weak light of the room.

"What is it, Leo? What did Crayt tell you?"

Leo summoned a shuddering breath. Truthfully it shouldn't have been that big of a revelation. It made a certain sense, after all; it wouldn't even be the first time they'd tried. Still, when he heard Crayt say it, Leo had felt his legs buckle.

"There were encrypted files. Stuff we couldn't see. Crayt's computer managed to decode them. One of those files . . ." Another breath. "One was a list of possible targets."

They had been ranked in order of their military and strategic value as well as their estimated remaining quantities of V. There were more than twenty planets identified.

Baz already knew. Just by Leo's look. "It's us, isn't it?"

"It's us," Leo confirmed. "We're at the top of the list."

The environmental collapse that our precious planet faces cannot be blamed on the Aykari alone. Though their mining has accelerated it in some cases, the destruction of Mother Earth began long before the aliens' arrival. Our planet was our responsibility and we shirked it, over and over again. We perverted and abused and destroyed those things we claim to cherish. The moment we discover something rare and beautiful we immediately find ways to exploit it, hoard it, commodify it—almost always to its detriment, and to our own. It is not a uniquely human impulse—our alien superiors have shown us that—but we would be fools to not take our share of the blame. And we will certainly end up bearing the brunt of the consequences.

—*Enrico Ventasi*, If I Knew Then: Collected Essays, *2050*

5

ONE STONE AT A TIME

IT WAS DYING. SLOWLY, BUT SURELY. AND IT HAD TO come down.

Leo found his father staring up at the cherry tree that for years had been the eye-catcher of the backyard, if not the entire block. But not this year. This year the blossoms withered much too quickly—those that even managed to bloom. The bark, scaled over with patches of white, began to peel, exposing the wood underneath. Broken branches could be found scattered about its feet, their suppleness sapped.

This was the end.

The botanist Leo's dad had brought out from the university identified the disease as xenoblight, so named because it had first appeared within a year of the Aykari's arrival. Some freak side effect of the mining process was the current thinking, perhaps something seeping into the water table. Or maybe some kind of fungus the aliens brought with them that had no noticeable effect on most living things but was a death sentence to certain species of flora. The botanist could not prescribe a remedy, but she could provide a prognosis—the tree wouldn't survive the year. Best to cut it down before it splinters and falls.

Which was why the arborists were coming today: to lay it to rest. Leo had come out to say one last goodbye to the tree that was always base in their games of tag and provided shade for a few dozen backyard picnics. Both brothers had carved their initials in its trunk with Gareth's pocketknife, though the stripped bark and creeping mold had since obscured them. Still, Leo loved this tree.

Though not as much as his mother did. He'd often find her standing at the kitchen window, looking out over the backyard, her eyes fixed on the explosion of pink-and-white petals. "It's just so nice to look at, isn't it?" she'd ask, not expecting an answer, assuming it was a given—that everyone found the same measure of beauty in it that she did. She would have hated to see it cut down, so Leo hated it on her behalf.

"When are they coming?" he asked, standing next to his father.

"This afternoon," his dad said, rubbing his chin. "But we have a problem." Dr. Fender pointed up through the barren branches, most of them stripped. "See there?"

Without the blossoms it was easy to spot. The patchwork

of grass and twigs balanced on a branch halfway up. A bird's nest. It wasn't as pretty or as uniform as Leo imagined it, not the perfectly round basket like in picture books, but it was clear that some mother had taken care in its construction nonetheless. "Are there eggs in it?" he asked.

"*That* would be the problem," his father said. "We can't move it if it's occupied. It's illegal. I've been watching for a while and I haven't seen its builder come back. Though she could be somewhere, watching me watch for *her.*"

"What do we do? We can't let them cut it down if there's something in there, can we?" Just destroy someone's home like that? With them in it?

Leo's father frowned. "Wait here," he said.

A minute later he came back with the old wooden ladder from the garage. The same one Leo's mother used to paint his room when he decided yellow wasn't his favorite color anymore and that gray better suited his personality. Dr. Fender set the ladder as close as he could. "Do me a favor and keep it steady."

Leo took hold of the ladder's legs with both hands and squinted up into the sun. There were a few birds perched on the tree in the neighbor's yard just across the fence. One of them might be the owner of this ramshackle house. Leo wondered what she must be thinking—to have this giant creature invading her space like this, without warning, without permission. If there were eggs inside would she try to defend them? Would she swoop down on Leo's father and peck at his head, attempt to buffet him off the ladder, risking her life for her babies? Or would she fly away, abandoning her unborn chicks, dooming them to die alone? It was a terrible thought, but Leo couldn't stop himself from thinking it.

"What do you see?" Leo called up, but his father didn't answer. He leaned over, steadying himself with one hand against the branch, the other gently shoveling beneath the pile of roughly woven twigs and stems. Dr. Fender took the steps slowly, careful not to drop his prize.

Back on solid ground he showed the nest to Leo. It was empty. No eggs. No chicks. The home was still under construction. A work in progress. "We got lucky," his father said.

Leo didn't want to point out that they were still going to lose the tree—and that a full nest would have kept it from being cut down. "What do we do with it?"

"I'll try to relocate it—probably in that maple over there. But odds are the momma bird will just abandon it and build a new one. Maybe some other bird will use it, or pillage it for material. Either way it won't be for nothing."

He watched his father carefully carry the nest to the corner of the yard where the maple—somehow impervious to the xenoblight—was proudly flaunting its branches full of rich green leaves. He reached for the highest branch he could, tucking the would-be home safely against the trunk. It was visible to Leo—but he, of course, knew exactly where to look. The nest's builder might never find it. Just imagine, he thought, flying off somewhere and coming back to find the home you left behind is no longer there. Just imagine having to start over from scratch.

He hoped she would see it. Hoped she would find the new spot to her liking. Hoped to look out several weeks from now and spot the sharp beaks of fuzzy-headed nestlings calling for their momma. She would hear them. She would come to them. She would feed them and keep them warm. She wouldn't just leave them to fend for themselves.

Leo's father came back and put one hand on the ladder, looking back at the stricken cherry tree again.

"It will be okay. We can try and plant another one. Or we can plant something new."

Except Leo didn't want something new—he wanted exactly what he'd had before, but he didn't say it. Just nodded along.

Two hours later the landscapers came with their chain saws and ropes.

The life-giving star peeked over the horizon, casting a burnt-orange veil over the sky and seeping through the windscreen to creep across Leo's cold cheeks. He squinted into the light and rubbed his temples. Somehow he'd managed to drift back to sleep again, even with the cramping in his stomach, the throbbing behind his eyes. He'd fallen asleep sitting up, leaning on the captain's bony shoulder—so much less comfortable than a Queleti's fuzzy arm.

He'd dreamed of food this time. Fresh, chin-glistening peaches and spicy chicken wings and baked cinnamon apples crusted with brown sugar. All you could eat. He was sitting in the grass at the top of the hill by his old house gorging himself when Baz woke him and told him it was time to go.

The captain was clearly on edge. Leo could tell by the drumming; Baz's fingers danced on any hard surface they could find as he moved around the control room, fingers that would have been happier squeezing a trigger or punching the controls of his ship, nervous energy needing an outlet. Leo hadn't known Bastian Black before hiding away on his ship, but even in the short time they'd spent together, he had seen a shift in the pirate. Baz had lost some of his cocky, carefree demeanor. Now Leo could see the worry mustered in rows across the man's forehead. He probably hadn't gotten any more sleep judging by the shadows under his eyes.

"Come on, Okardo. Up and at 'em. The worms are back in their holes and we've got patches to make to the *Icarus* before we can safely make a jump."

"A jump to where, exactly?" Kat asked, strapping her holster back around her waist and slinging her rifle—Zennia's rifle—over her shoulder.

"We'll figure it out on the way," Baz said shortly. "But there's clearly no point in sticking around *here*."

The captain vibrated with a sense of urgency. It was

different when you're at the top of the list. Baz pretended that he didn't care about anything except his crew and the next stack of pentars they could steal or swindle, but the trunk under his bunk—filled with trinkets and collectibles, baseballs and Pokémon cards, magazines and memories—suggested otherwise. There were some things you couldn't help but hold on to.

Baz marched down the corridor and Leo followed with the rest, entering the hangar where Skits and Nine were still parked close together, metal pressed to metal. When Baz walked in, Nine's spindly legs contracted closer to its body and one of Skits's appendages retreated into her torso.

"What? We weren't doing anything, I promise," she said. "Just . . . interfacing."

"Well, knock it off. We're leaving," Baz told her. He pointed to a stack of crates along the back wall beside the deactivated mining bots. "Boo, check those containers, see if you can find any supplies, anything we can use to fix up the *Icarus*. I'm sure Crayt won't mind if we permanently borrow a few items. It really is the absolute *least* he could do."

Leo followed behind Kat, who was right on the captain's heels, pressing him. "Listen, Baz. You know we're with you; we'll go wherever you say. But we can't make a jump without coordinates. So what's the plan?"

"Still not sure."

Kat took a deep breath, matching him step for step. "And,

see, normally I'd be okay with that. But you and I both know we are in way over our heads here. We have been since we left Kaber's Point. We can't just wing this one. Not this time. There's too much at stake."

"Noted," Baz said. He kicked through a small pile of scrap, no doubt looking for something to patch a hole in the *Icarus*'s hull.

"I'm not sure you do," Kat continued to needle. "This is serious. We can't give what's on that chip to just anyone. And we sure as stars can't go on about our business pretending we don't know what's on it."

"Understood."

Leo watched as Kat took Baz by the arm, spinning him around.

"So then what *are* we going to do?"

"I don't know!" he shouted back at her.

She didn't wince. She didn't even flinch. She held steady, face-to-face with her captain.

"I don't know, Kat," he repeated, softer this time. "You're right. I'm out of my league. I have no idea what to do next. All I know is that I can't let it happen again."

"It's all right, Baz," Kat soothed. "It's okay. I get it."

"But it's not. And you don't. Not this. You weren't there last time." Baz shot a glance at Leo, then fixed his eyes back on Kat. "I saw it happen. Watched all those cities go up in flames. And the whole time I was thinking, *This is it. This is the end of the world*. And now . . . this time . . . this time it really could be the end. And it's pissing me off, because I don't think there's a thing I can do about it."

"Perhaps there is."

Leo turned with everyone else to see Zirkus Crayt in the corridor, Number One standing dutifully behind him. Crayt held a core of ventasium by his side—probably the same one Leo had seen sitting out the night before.

"We should talk," the Aykari said.

Black angrily waved him off. "Forget it, Crayt. You made it pretty clear where you stand. And, frankly, I wouldn't trust you any further than Boo could throw you, so we're just going to scrounge around for a few things to fix up the ship and then we'll leave." He reached for a coil of copper tubing caught in the scrap heap when Crayt spoke again.

"Do what you must, Captain. But you should know that I might have found a way."

Suddenly the Aykari had everyone's attention.

Baz shook his head. "What?"

Crayt took a step farther into the hangar. "Tell me, Captain, how do you disarm a bomb?"

"That's easy. You cut the black wire."

"Pretty sure that's not true," Kat countered.

"Almost positive it is. Haven't you seen a single movie?"

"Enough to know that red is the one you cut and black . . . black is just annoying."

The captain cocked his head. "You're not funny."

Crayt interrupted them. "I have studied the files Dr. Fender compiled. The blueprints. The formulas. Everything. I know how it works now. The Djarik's weapon is designed to trigger a chain reaction, much the way one split atom might cause others to split, releasing an exponential increase in the amount of energy—"

"Causing planets to blow themselves up, yeah, we get it," Baz finished, handing the copper tubing to Leo. "And seeing as how my planet—*our* planet—is first on the chopping block, you won't mind if we don't sit around and listen to a lecture explaining the hows and whys—especially not from someone like you." Baz bent down and continued to dig through the container.

"What if I told you we could stop the reaction from occurring in the first place?"

The captain froze.

"Is that possible?" Kat asked.

"I did not think so at first. It was so far outside of my understanding that I could not even entertain the idea. But *he* could."

Crayt pointed at Leo, who thrust his thumbs at his chest. "Um . . . I did what now?"

"After you left I went back through all the files on your father's chip. Most of the information is concerned with the weapon the Djarik are creating—probably have already created—as

- 181 -

well as their plans to use it. But Dr. Fender included some crucial research of his own. Your father is truly a genius."

"Relative to his kind," Kat amended.

"To *any* kind," Crayt replied. "He understands EL-four eight six as well as anyone, including myself. Granted I have only cracked the surface of what is on that chip, but given what we know about the Djarik's attempts to weaponize the element and Dr. Fender's own research into its reactive qualities, I believe it might be possible to do the very *reverse* of what the Djarik intend. The very thing *you* suggested." He looked again at Leo.

"The reverse," Baz echoed. "You mean *un*–blow up a planet?"

"I mean render the entire reaction impossible."

"And how, exactly, would you do that?" Kat asked.

"By cutting every wire at once, thereby turning this"— Crayt held up the ventasium core—"into this."

He opened the palm of his other hand to reveal the rock he'd been holding, much like a street magician producing the missing Queen of Hearts. Leo's rock.

"The Djarik weapon works by instantly destabilizing EL-four eight six, causing it to unleash all its latent energy at once in a catastrophic chain. But the element cannot be destabilized if it has already been rendered inert."

"Inert?" Boo repeated.

"Inactive. Unresponsive. Essentially lacking all potential energy or function."

"Like you after six or seven drinks," Kat said Baz.

The captain opened his mouth to argue, then closed it again, conceding the point. "So you're saying there is a way to alter the ventasium so that the Djarik can no longer use it as a weapon?"

"I am saying there *might* be a way to alter it such that it cannot do *anything*."

The entire hangar went silent.

Leo stared at the small hunk of rock sitting in the Aykari's palm. It was the very thing that he'd imagined, but now that Crayt was suggesting that it was possible, Leo's brain wrestled with the implications. What was a planet worth if it didn't have any V? Yes, humans had gone thousands of years not knowing the element even existed, but Leo hadn't known that Earth. *His* Earth had always been riddled with holes. His skies always filled with silver ships. The Earth he knew, the Earth he remembered, had been built on V.

"Okay. Let's say you do this," Baz ventured. "You make the ventasium hungover—"

"Inert," Crayt corrected.

"Right. And the Djarik drop their little bomb or whatever it is, and what, nothing happens? The whole planet's a dud?"

"Theoretically, yes, the element will not activate because

the countermeasure will have already made it useless. No reaction. No release."

"Sort of like popping some Tums before hitting the Taco Bell," Baz said.

"Who makes a bell out of tacos?" Kat asked.

"What's a Tums?" Boo wanted to know.

"If we do this," Leo said, ignoring the pirates and looking only at Crayt, "if we take away the ventasium's power, then that means you can't use it for anything else, right? It's just done . . . gone . . . like, forever."

Crayt nodded soberly. "As I told you before, everything comes at a cost."

Baz let out a low whistle, the ramifications catching up to him as well. "Taking away all the Earth's V . . . I mean, that's heavy-duty."

"Better than blowing it up," Leo said.

He looked out the bay doors into the giant chasm that had been violently ripped into this planet's skin, at the massive titanium drill that had pierced its surface, its makers abandoning it, leaving it there to serve as fodder for ghost stories and superstitions. He thought of the Orin slowly rebuilding their walls, their roads, stacking one mud brick upon another. Putting their lives back together piece by piece.

That could be Earth someday. Or Earth could be nothing. An asteroid field. Nothing left but a collection of books and cards stashed away in a pirate's chest. Leo recalled his father pointing up at the clouds, at the blindingly beautiful Aykari ships arcing above them. *There it is, Leo. That's the future. Out there. And we're going to be a part of it.* But you couldn't get there without V. Even six-year-old Leo had known that.

He wondered what his father would say if he were here. If he would agree to this or try to find another way.

Except he's not here, is he? He put this all on you.

Leo looked at Crayt. "How long before you know for sure if you can stop it or not?"

The Aykari shook his head slowly. "This is all theoretical. I will not know for certain until I run some tests. My resources here are limited. There is a workshop, and I have materials that I brought with me, but this is still a mining facility—not a research lab. And even if my supposition is proven correct, it will take some time to produce a working countermeasure to the weapon the Djarik have envisioned."

"How much time?" Kat pressed.

"In human measurements? Hours. Days. Weeks. I will not know until I get started."

"We may not have weeks," Leo said. "We may not even have days. You saw the message. You heard my father. He said they were close."

"He also said he would try to slow them down," Kat offered. "Maybe he did."

"Or *maybe* they caught him trying to sabotage their efforts and are brutally punishing him for it as we speak," Skits suggested. Kat scowled at her. "What? I'm only pointing out what's possible."

Leo turned back to the open bay and the rising sun coloring the sky. "I mean, we have to try." He glanced over at Baz. "Don't we?"

"Top of the list," the captain said. Kat and Boo both nodded. Skits stared intently at Nine, who stared right back.

Crayt handed the core of ventasium to Number One. "It is settled, then. I can get to work developing a testable prototype immediately."

Baz slapped his hands together. "Great, you do that. In the meantime we'll go bring the *Icarus* back here and get her fixed up so that we can scram when we need to." He turned to Leo and whispered. "Don't know what you said to him, but whatever it was, it worked. Good job, ninja turtle."

Leo wasn't sure himself. He went and stood next to Crayt, who was still holding the rock in one hand, a small fragment of a broken world he'd decided to call home. "I thought you weren't going to help," he said. "That it was pointless."

"You were right. I *am* hiding," Crayt replied. "I thought I could find peace here. I believed that by helping the Orin to rebuild I could somehow atone for the damage my kind has done. But it is not enough. I cannot shut my eyes and pretend I do not know what will happen because it has happened before. I cannot stop the Djarik. Not alone. Neither can you. But together . . . perhaps. . . ." He held up the chunk of yellow stone. "Dr. Fender was right to send you here. I think he would be proud of you."

Leo wasn't so sure.

"I know I'm no genius or anything. But I'm pretty good with my hands. There has to be some way I can help."

Crayt considered it. Then he handed the rock back to Leo. "In fact, there is one thing you can do."

This wasn't at all what he had in mind.

When he said he wanted to help, Leo meant help save Earth. To stop the Djarik. To do what his father had asked him to do.

Not to stack rocks.

Yet here he was, walking back across the strange, alien scrubland with Boo by his side and two robots trailing behind, heading back toward the broken village to make good on an Aykari's promise.

When he'd told Baz what Crayt requested, the captain just said, "That's what you get for asking."

He had found the captain huddled with Kat in the control center, preparing to hike back to the ship. Leo stopped in the corridor just out of view for a moment, watching as Kat checked the charge on her pistol out of habit. She was requesting clarification. "Okay. Talk me through it. One more time."

"It's really not that complicated," Baz said. "One guy stands on the mound of dirt in the middle and throws the ball toward the guy standing at the plate sixty feet away."

"The plate that's *not* for eating off of."

"That's the one. Then the guy at the plate swings his bat."

"The skinny wooden stick."

"The skinny wooden stick. And he uses it to hit the ball as far as it will go. Then he runs around the bases in order. First. Second. Third."

"He just runs in a circle?" Kat questioned.

"More like a diamond, but yeah. Meanwhile, all these other guys try to catch the ball to get him out."

"Out of where?"

"Just out. Finished. That way he can't score a run. A point. For his team."

"So to score a point all you have to do is hit a ball with a stick and then run around in a circle?"

"Trust me . . . it's a lot harder than it sounds," Baz said.

"No. Wrestling a terranglodile is hard. Flying through an asteroid field is hard. Hitting a ball with a stick . . . honestly, it sounds a little dumb."

"It's not dumb. Nothing about baseball is dumb. Being at the stadium. Listening to the crowd. The crack of the bat. The chanting. The music. The nachos. The beer. You just have to be there."

"I'd like to," Kat said.

"I'll take you sometime," Baz said. "Assuming we pull *this* off, of course."

That's when Leo interrupted them and told them about Crayt's request.

"You have fun with that," Baz said. "Do us a favor and take Skits with you."

Leo groaned. "Why Skits?"

"Because the last time I tried to get her to help repair the ship she redirected the power from the shields to the organic waste disposal system, which would be fine if feces could stop a laser blast, but it can't. Take Boo, too," Baz added. "He loves manual labor."

Boo disagreed, saying that's what comes from having more arms than everyone else, but he decided to come along anyway. "I think it could do me good."

Skits had a different opinion on the matter entirely.

Leo found her in the back corner of the hangar with Number Nine. One of her interface nodules was plugged directly into one of Nine's data receptacles. They weren't even talking anymore, just experiencing each other's artificial consciousnesses directly. Nine was humming happily.

"Ahem," Leo said, coughing into his fist.

"Ugh, *seriously*, Leo?" Skits snapped. "Can't you see we're busy here? We are right in the middle of proving the Riemann hypothesis."

"We are using Fesenko's conjecture on the positivity of the fourth derivative," Number Nine said. "It is *highly* stimulating."

Those were two words Leo definitely didn't need to hear.

"Baz says you need to give us a hand. We're helping the Orin with their rebuilding."

Skits flipped. "Are you kidding me? Go out there? With those pointy-eared things? Is Baz out of his mind? I won't do it."

"I could accompany you," Nine chirped.

Apparently that was all she needed to hear.

And so Leo found himself leading both robots back to the village where they'd first found Crayt, aka Lark, looking to meet up with two of the planet's natives—a female named Shree and a male named Rint—who would show them what to do. Behind him he could hear Skits chattering nonstop.

"So then Leo says it's a code fourteen, which means Baz is in trouble, right? So I push his useless meat sack self out of the way and storm down the ramp ready to dance. The whole time I've got Bonnie belting through my speakers, full volume, and I see these scrap heaps waiting for me in the hangar. Security bots, at least thirty of them, all heavily armed, thick plating, bad attitudes. They're all, like, '*Don't move. We have you surrounded.*' And I'm all like, '*You can't tell me what to do.*' And I just unleash. I am a tornado of destruction, taking bots out right and left. *Bam! Zap! Crunch!*"

"Remarkable," Nine responded. "One against thirty. Your threat avoidance thresholds must be set incredibly high."

"You have no idea. Honestly, I don't even know what it's like to be afraid anymore."

With his back to them, Leo huffed. "She forgot to tell him about the part where her tread got blasted and *we* had to push her back onto the ship," he muttered to Boo.

Boo glanced over his shoulder at the two bots in tow. "She's only trying to impress him. She is . . . what's the word . . . smote?"

"You mean smitten? Yeah, she's smitten, all right. She's been off her charger since she first saw him," Leo said. "Don't you think it's a little weird? I mean . . . they're *robots*."

"Love is love, Leo," Boo said with a shrug.

"I know but . . ."

"But what? The whole galaxy is at war. You've seen it yourself. We should take happiness where we can find it."

Leo took another look behind to see Nine had clipped one of the blossoming purple flowers scattered about with his claws and gently stuck it into a seam in Skits's chassis like some kind of boutonniere. The sun glinted off her smiling face. "Yeah . . . it's still a *little* strange. . . ."

"Perhaps," Boo agreed. "But no stranger than only having two arms."

Leo snorted. It was the closest he'd come to laughing in days. "Right. No stranger than having horns sticking out of your head."

"No stranger than having no hair on your chest," Boo teased.

"I'm only thirteen," Leo said. "It could still happen."

Though he hoped to never have as much as the Queleti, whose chest was a carpet. "At least I don't wear a bathrobe everywhere I go."

"It's not a bathrobe. Queleti don't bathe. We *groom*."

Leo scrunched his nose. That could explain the smell Boo was starting to give off.

"Here's something else I find strange," Boo continued. "An Aykari that wants to get *rid* of ventasium. I always thought V meant everything to them."

"Except he's not one of them anymore," Leo said. "He's an exile. An outcast. Like you."

Boo grunted, clearly not pleased with the comparison. "He is not like me. My people would never invade a planet and leave it like this. He may be an exile, but he is still Aykari. We can never forget where we came from, even if we are not allowed to go back."

Or ever get the chance, Leo thought.

Up ahead he could make out the edge of a village now. The hollow black eyes of empty windows. The jagged edges of broken walls. Two Orin were scurrying up to meet them, dressed in their loose garments, hands clasped in some unfamiliar greeting. Face-to-face, Leo could see that their pupils took up nearly half of their eyes and their teeth comprised more than one row. One of the Orin had twice as much facial hair as the other; Leo assumed that meant it was the male—though he realized he probably shouldn't make assumptions.

They took a look at Nine, clearly recognizing the robot, then turned their attention back at Leo.

"Lark?" the hairier one said, cocking his head to the side.

"Sorry. Lark couldn't make it," Leo said, shaking his head. "No Lark."

The Orin looked confused for a moment, then pointed up at Leo. "Lark," he proclaimed.

"Okay, sure. Whatever."

The Orin made a sound—something that sounded like Shree—and pointed to his companion; then he pointed to himself and said, "Rint."

"He's Boo," Leo said, nodding toward the Queleti. "And I'm Leo. Lee-oh."

"Lark," Rint insisted.

"Right. Lark. Let's go."

The Orin beckoned the two newly christened Larks and their robot tagalongs to follow, circling the outskirts of the village. Occasionally the aliens glanced back over their shoulders, but only to make sure Leo and the others were keeping up. Somehow, even after everything they'd been through, the Orin still found a way to trust outsiders. Maybe that was Crayt's doing. In helping them to rebuild he'd shown them that not all Aykari were alike, and that not all outsiders unleashed ghosts. You might not be able to forget where you came from, but that didn't mean you couldn't change.

"Do you think they even know?" Leo whispered to Boo as

they followed. "What the Aykari took from them?"

"If you mean the ventasium, I doubt they care," Boo replied. "But they've obviously lost so much more."

The group of six rounded a series of huts and Leo found himself staring at a giant stone bowl, thirty or forty feet across, fashioned out of the same yellow rock as the buildings nearby. This, apparently, was a cistern. Or at least what was left of it. Nearly half of it had collapsed—destroyed, Leo guessed, by the quakes. The Orin had already gathered up new stones to be used as replacements along with a handful of basic tools. Two more of the planet's natives were busy grinding white powder in barrels and mixing it with some noxious-smelling liquid poured from carved wooden pitchers. Without a word their two escorts quickly set to work doing the same.

"So what do *we* do?" Leo asked.

Boo pointed to the pile of stones and then to the collapsed wall. "We get our hands dirty."

Skits swiveled her head. "I think we mechanicals should sit back and supervise for a change," she said.

"And I think you should start hauling stone," Boo countered, taking one of the smooth yellow rocks from the pile and fitting it into place where the damage began.

Shree and Rint dragged over one of the small barrels they'd filled and set it by Leo's feet, giving him his first look at the mixture inside, the color and consistency of glue. Shree pointed at the barrel, then at the stone Boo had placed. She dipped her hand into the goop and smeared it into the gaps, completely coating the new stone on both sides. She stared at Leo. "Lark?"

"You want me to just stick my hand in that stuff? What if it eats my skin off?"

Shree just smiled and scooped up another mittful of sealant for the next stone.

"I think you'll be okay," Boo said. "They intend to drink out of this thing, you know."

Leo wrinkled his nose and looked back into the barrel. He thought back to long summer afternoons at the community pool. How Gareth would always jump straight in, claiming it was the only way to do anything—full bore, headfirst—while Leo skimmed a toe and said he needed to warm up first. Leo took pride in being cautious and thoughtful.

He dipped in a finger. Turned out there was nothing to fear. The mixture didn't instantly dissolve it down to the bone. He took a handful and followed Shree's example, earning him another toothy smile. "Lark," she said. "*Hertru.*"

At least you're happy, Leo thought.

A couple of miles away Zirkus Crayt was hard at work building a device to save the galaxy. Somewhere out there his father was attempting to sabotage the Djarik, and Gareth was wandering, lost and alone. There were battles raging all across the galaxy and here he was, patching holes. "This is stupid. We're supposed to be finding my brother and saving the world," he muttered.

"One stone at a time, Leo," Boo replied, though he was, in fact, placing two. "If you can't help the ones you want, then help the ones you can. Also, you missed a spot." He pointed to a gap between two rocks.

Leo frowned as he dipped his hand back into the barrel.

It didn't take long to fall into a rhythm. Skits and Nine kept them in a steady supply of materials. Rint would stack low and Boo would build up from there. Leo and Shree would follow behind to fill in the gaps with the sealant, careful not to leave any holes. Every now and then Shree would reach out and rub Leo's nose, which he assumed meant he was doing a good job. Either that or she was planning to eat his face when they were finished and wanted to make sure it was tender.

About halfway through, the Orin set down their tools and gathered in a circle, passing around a flask. The sun had reached its zenith, though a fleet of clouds had moved in to blunt its heat. Boo stretched his arms and sat with his back against the wall he'd just helped build. "This feels good," he said.

Leo joined him, pulling his knees to his chest. "Sitting?"

"Making something," the Queleti answered.

Leo looked at the work they'd done already and then at the thin layer of the goop drying on his hands, under his nails, flaking off his clothes. He could feel his efforts in his back and aching shoulders, and yet Boo was right: it did feel good in a way. Leo knew he would never siphon a single drop of water from this thing. Soon the *Icarus* would put this planet behind it. Even if Crayt failed, they would still need to find some other way to stop the Djarik, or at the very least, warn everyone what was coming. In the grand scheme of the universe, he knew this cistern hardly mattered at all, and yet a part of him felt like this was the first purely good thing he'd done in a while.

He looked up at the clouds—not the cottony white of the ones on Earth, but tinged violet, like the flower that adorned Skits's armored plating. A breeze had finally kicked up— nothing like the crazy tornado-like swells on Vestra—just enough to be refreshing.

"I think I like it here," Boo said.

"Really?" Leo questioned. "This place?" Had he forgotten about the worms that could chew through rock? Or the fact that the whole planet was obviously still plagued by giant quakes? Or the lack of electricity or air-conditioning or working toilets?

"It's peaceful."

"I guess," Leo said.

With one claw Boo began to draw a rough picture in the dirt, starting with some hills, then long, narrow needles jutting out of them. "Back on Quel we built towers. Giant ones. As high as we could. We wanted to be able to look out over the landscape, to take it all in at once—the mountains, the forests, the endless fields. So up, up, up we built. It was beautiful seen from that distance. But when you are that high, you forget what the grass feels like on your bare feet. When you're only looking down, you forget how loud the waterfall's roar can be. Everything comes to you muted. Blurred. You lose touch." He nodded at Shree and Rint, huddled close together, passing their flask between them. Their clothes, like Leo's pants and Boo's robe, were coated in a layer of yellow dust. "The Orin carry their planet home with them. They live low to the ground."

"That's because they're only half as tall as you."

"Joke all you want," Boo said, "but ever since I was banished from Quel, I've been looking for something. I thought that by traveling with Bastian I might find it. Every planet, every port, I would ask myself, Is it here? Is this the place? But the answer was always no. Eventually I got used to being on the move. Bastian, Kat, Skits—they became my family. But this place is making me wonder. Maybe there's something else I'm meant to do."

"Lifting rocks?" Leo said incredulously.

Boo shrugged. "There are worse things. Piracy is not exactly a profession to be proud of."

Leo couldn't argue with that, but he also didn't like where this was going. "I mean, sure. I get it. But you can't actually *stay* here. Not now. Not with everything that's going on."

He turned so that he could look the Queleti in the eyes. "What would Baz say? He needs you. *We* need you."

I need you, Leo thought. *I need all the help I can get.*

Boo poked one of his fingers through the singed hole in his Yunkai, another reminder of a laser blast that had nearly sent him plummeting off a bridge to his death. "I can't go home, Leo. My clan will never take me back. Which means I'll have to find a new one. We all have to stop running eventually."

Leo kicked at the dust and thought back to what Baz had said in that cantina on Vestra. Something about owning some ramshackle oasis of his own, somewhere to quietly spend the rest of his days. He remembered Kat mocking the captain, telling him it was impossible. That even if the universe would let him, Baz could never settle down. Clearly Boo felt otherwise.

"It's just so quiet here," he said, shutting his eyes and tilting his furry face to the breeze. "I see now why Crayt chose this place."

Leo nudged him with an elbow. "All right. How about this: you help me save the Earth and get my family back, and after that you can come back here and stack all the rocks you want. Deal?"

Boo seemed to consider it for a moment. Then he stood up and offered Leo a hand.

"Let's just finish what we started," he said.

When the sky growls, it's time to come home.

—Orin proverb

6

ANY PORT IN A STORM

LEO HAD NO IDEA HOW MUCH LONGER THEY WORKED.
At some point his watch started fritzing again, cycling
through programs, randomly shutting off or rebooting,
showing him the time in London and Tokyo and Meridian
Bay on Mars. According to the solar cycle of the rapidly
spinning Celeron Seven, they'd been building this cistern
for forty-seven days; in Tardusian time, they'd been at it
for three and a half seconds. Leo could tell by the horizon
of this planet, however, that it was getting late. The air had
cooled considerably, making him wish he'd brought Kat's
jacket.

Boo settled the last stone in place, and then lifted Leo by the
waist so he could apply the Orin's homemade spackle, sealing
the gaps. Leo could barely flex his caked-white fingers, but

he made sure every crevice was filled; a cistern with a hole in it was useless, after all. Some things really did need to be perfect.

Finally they stood side by side, hands on hips, inspecting their handiwork.

"It's a giant bowl," Leo said. "We built a giant bowl."

"So we did," Boo agreed. "Feels good, doesn't it?"

Leo had to admit, he did feel something. A sense of accomplishment, yes, but something more. Ever since the day his mother died—the day the center dropped out of his universe—he'd felt lost, spiraling off course. At times his life felt like an open wound that refused to scab over. Other times he felt like he was just stumbling through a fog, unable to make out the tracks from the steps he'd just taken. There had been times back on Earth when it felt like he might recenter, the gravitational force of his brother and father pulling him into their orbit. But before he could get fully grounded he found himself on board the *Beagle*, jumping from world to world with no final destination.

It seemed to Leo that the course of his life had been plotted by everyone but him.

And yet here was this. A circular wall with a stone floor and no roof, open to accept as much rain as the sky could offer, and a single plug the Orin could pull to fill their buckets and barrels. When the dry season came, this giant stone bowl would give life to the hundreds of Orin that lived in the village nearby. It was simple. Its purpose obvious. Its value unquestionable.

Boo was right: they had done something worthwhile here.

Leo felt a tug on his sleeve.

Rint was there, pointing up at the sky, baring his teeth again, though the expression seemed different this time. Leo noticed the lilac clouds had darkened, shifting to an even more violent shade. The Orin seemed agitated.

Boo sniffed at the air. "Smells like the stuff Kat uses to polish her arm."

Leo took a deep breath. Boo was right. The air smelled clean, but in a chemical way. Like a chlorinated pool. The other Orin were quickly gathering their supplies, stuffing them into baskets that they strapped across their backs. Shree made some noises Leo didn't understand, then pointed to the angry-looking sky as well. She traced an imaginary zigzag, then slapped her hands together forcefully.

"I think there's a storm coming," Boo said.

"Can we make it back to the platform in time?"

Boo looked across the horizon and shook his head. Rint tugged on Leo's arm again and gestured toward the other Orin, who were already making their way back to the village. The message was clear. They needed shelter. Leo nodded and called out to the robots standing several yards away, no doubt interfacing again. "Time to go."

"How many times do I have to tell you, you're *not* my dad,"

Skits shot back in her usual tone.

Number Nine didn't protest however. "I am detecting a high concentration of heavily charged particles in the atmosphere," he said. "I feel as if an electrostatic discharge is imminent."

"I love it when you talk technical," Skits said, then turned back to Leo. "Fine. We're coming."

Leo tucked in behind Boo, who was following the Orin, all save Rint, who hung back, hurrying the Larks and their robots along. Leo could feel the electricity in the air now. The hairs on his neck stood at attention. Thankfully the village, with its scattering of buildings, some still fully intact, was close. They could surely make it before the clouds opened up.

As if it could hear Leo's thoughts and was determined to prove him wrong, the whole sky seemed to snarl. It wasn't paralyzing like a Queleti's roar, but it was momentarily deafening. More than enough to rattle Leo's spine.

It wasn't half as startling as the bolt of pure white electric fire that suddenly split the air, however, touching down less than a mile away.

"My sensors have detected an electrostatic discharge in our immediate vicinity," Number Nine informed them. The robot was clicking along right beside Skits, whose treads were kicking up dust.

"Not sure we needed Aykari-level technology to tell us *that*," Leo muttered. A glance upward showed the sky had come to life, like a monster waking from its slumber, the clouds crackling with tendrils of yellow and white. A sound like an old-fashioned gunshot was immediately followed by another deadly fork of lightning.

Leo broke into a run. He didn't feel a single drop of rain, but there was a constant humming in his ears, broken up by the explosion of another touchdown three hundred yards behind them. This wasn't an afternoon rainstorm. It was something much more dangerous.

Sometimes the planet itself seems to revolt against the process, Crayt had said. This planet was certainly angry about *something*. With snaps and sizzles, one bolt after another arced out of the sky. It might have been beautiful—from a distance. But out here in the open, running just ahead of two robots made almost entirely of superconductive metal, Leo didn't appreciate the aesthetics. It certainly wouldn't be pretty when one of those bolts fried his brain right in its pan.

"I feel all tingly inside. And not in a good way. My power cells are fluctuating," Skits said. "What's happening to me?"

In front of him, three of the Orin had already reached the edge of the village and were ducking into the first intact building they could find. Shree turned and beckoned them with a waving paw. Rint ran alongside Leo, though his shorter legs meant he was barely keeping up.

Up ahead, Boo called out, "C'mon, Leo. Get a mo—"

There was no warning this time. The sound and the light were one, fused together into a sudden burst that sent Leo

- 205 -

airborne, limbs flailing. He hit the ground, slamming his ribs, his chin, rattling his teeth. He shook his head, conscious only of the steady buzzing in his ears, like the drone of a thousand bees defending their hive. It felt like his body was thrumming, prickling with its own electric current.

He looked up at the exploding sky, and in that moment he was eight years old again, standing on that beach, paralyzed. Staring wide-eyed at the dark horizon, the waves' steady crash drowned by the missile's explosive roar. He felt the tightness in his chest, the panic swelling. His fingers clinched as they had then, though this time there was no shell hidden in his fist. *Get up*, he told himself. *You have to get up.* Struggling for a good breath, he pulled himself to his hands and knees, the sky flashing above him, illuminating the body laid out beside him.

Rint. Curled up in the dust. The Orin's eyes were shut.

Wheezing, Leo scrabbled over to Rint's prone form and shook his shoulders. "Hey. Wake up," he rasped. "Can you hear me?"

No response. He put his head on the alien's chest, listening for a heartbeat, wondering if the Orin were built like humans, if they even had hearts at all. He couldn't hear anything, until . . .

"Lark?"

Leo lifted his head to see Rint looking at him with his big black eyes.

"Right! It's me. It's Lark." Leo swiped at his eyes. "Come on. Get to your feet. We've gotta move." With a grunt, Leo pulled the Orin up. He took one of Rint's furry paws and started dragging him, the two of them stumbling toward the closest building, the crack of the shattering sky chasing them. Leo's head swam. He glanced up at two dark crescent clouds, like the eyes of a vengeful god. *We are the vengeful spirits.* Rint stumbled, but Leo refused to let go, the two of them almost going down again.

"Don't worry, I've got this one."

There was Boo, suddenly beside them, hoisting the Orin up as if he weighed nothing at all, carrying him with two arms the same way he'd held Leo not long ago . . . the last time they ran for their lives. Something Leo was making a habit of.

Leo bolted for the open door as more lightning cracked around him and collapsed to the stone floor, still gasping for breath, grasping for his inhaler, bringing it to his lips. The press of a button, the slow hiss. Leo could feel the coils around his chest start to unwind.

Boo ducked in right behind him, setting Rint gently on a straw mat where he was immediately doted on by Shree and the others. The two robots followed, both of them struggling to fit through an entrance that wasn't built for their kind, Nine folding his legs in tight and squeezing, Skits's treads brushing against the jamb. Beyond the thick walls Leo could still hear the steady timpani roll of the spiteful sky echoing all around. Through the open windows he caught the flash of electricity brightening the horizon. It was almost like the armies of the Aykari and the Djarik were locked in battle right above them all over again.

Leo covered his ears and shut his eyes as the thunder shook the walls.

There was nothing to be afraid of. He knew it, but it didn't matter.

It was the noise more than anything. He sat on his mother's lap with his hands over his ears, her hands cupped over his. Gareth sat straight up on the blanket next to their father, the remnants of their picnic scattered around them—reusable plates smeared with potato salad and the carcasses of two roast chickens. A bottle of wine poked its neck out of the wicker basket. A pan once full of brownies sat empty—not one square left.

All along the hill, hundreds of other families sat, listening to the symphonic band below trilling out a bombastic version of the *1812 Overture,* and then *Into the Great Beyond,* a piece written specifically for this occasion. Sparklers spritzed and sputtered from the hands of twirling children oblivious to just how close they were to getting burned.

And then, when it was finally dark enough, the sky exploded. Like the steady volley of cannons from the deck of an ancient wooden galleon, the thunderclap of fireworks assaulted Leo's ears as the embers burst and then turned to cold, dead ash drifting.

He shut his eyes, hoping that if he couldn't see it, then he somehow wouldn't hear it, but all that did was make it worse, taking the good—the bright and beautiful spectrum of light—and leaving the bad. So he opened them again to see the endless stretch of black above set afire with reds and blues and oranges like a flower bed blooming all at once.

He knew he should be happy. It was a party, after all. The anniversary of First Contact Day, honoring the moment the Aykari arrived and introduced humanity to the rest of the galaxy. People all around the world were celebrating the occasion the same way they celebrated most things: by blowing things up.

It was solely a human holiday—the Aykari saw no need for such revelry—though a member of the Aykari High Council always deigned to deliver a speech for the occasion, transmitted to every digital billboard and datapad planetwide. The speech was always the same, too: stating how honored the Aykari were to have established such a mutually beneficial partnership with such an admirable species, detailing all the advances that had been made together. The speech ended with the promise of forging an even stronger alliance in the future, one that would last for eternity. In the meantime, humanity could rest at ease, knowing the Aykari had its back, sort of like making friends with the biggest, tallest, most popular kid in class on your first day at school.

Off in the distance, so far away that Leo could barely make out the silver contours of its stabilizers and engines, an Aykarian transport could be seen heading spaceward, its holds no doubt laden with cores of ventasium. Leo pointed it out to the others in between the firework bursts.

"I wonder what they must think of all of this," Grace Fender said.

"Oh, they're warned ahead of time," Leo's father answered. "That way they don't think we're shooting at them."

"That's not what I meant," Leo's mother said. "I mean all of this. *Us.* Celebrating the day *they* arrived. I bet it gives them a big head."

"They already have big heads," Gareth said. Leo laughed. Funny because it was true. The Aykari's wide diamond heads did seem oversize relative to their thin, elongated frames. He guessed that just meant they had bigger brains. They would have to, after all, in order to invent all of the stuff that they did. There were some things humans were better at—cooking, for example, painting, dancing, hugging, laughing—all things the Aykari couldn't do, or perhaps chose not to. But there was no question who was the superior species. The Aykari were the finders. The humans were the found.

"It just seems a little weird, don't you think?" his mother continued. "I mean, it's not like we brought them here. They just showed up. Kind of makes you wonder what it is we're celebrating." Leo knew his mother liked to question things. Partly it was curiosity. Partly she just liked to see if she could pin his father in a match of wits.

"We're celebrating peace," his dad answered. "Prosperity. Friendship. Partnership."

"Sure. Except you'll notice that there are no Aykari down here celebrating with us." She waved her hand to indicate the assembled audience on the hillside. "And as for peace, did you forget that there's a war going on?"

"But *we're* not in it."

"Not yet, we're not," she said.

On the horizon, the Aykari transport had vanished, but it would be back, Leo knew. The Earth had plenty of V, loads of it, with more being discovered every day, new platforms popping up all over the planet, including one being constructed just outside of town. His father said it would be several decades, at the earliest, before the Earth's supply was fully mined. And then . . .

Leo had no idea what happened then. Even his father wasn't sure.

A series of short bright bursts was almost instantly followed by the loudest bangs Leo had ever heard, causing him to cover his ears again so that he missed what his dad said next. Something about the enemy of my friend. Leo felt like his mother had the stronger point. If this was really a celebration of friendship, how come there were no Aykari celebrating it with them? They were always out there, at a distance. Looking down from above.

He felt his mother's hands clasp over his own again. Her hands were always cold. Poor circulation, she said. Didn't matter. He'd warm them with his own.

Leo shifted, adjusting in her lap, tilting his head back so it was resting just underneath her chin, nestling there, fitting perfectly, as he sat with his family and watched the heavens burn.

At last, the sky was starting to settle, its anger spent. The clouds were no longer bruised a deep purple, though it was starting to turn dark all around, the sun nearly set. Leo wasn't sure how long the light show had lasted. His watch certainly wouldn't tell him; the blasted thing was blinking on and off now, perhaps a reaction to the electric charge lingering in the air.

Maybe *that's* why the Orin didn't have advanced technology, he thought. No robots or computers. No cars or jets or spaceships. After all, stone bowls and straw mats don't fail you when the storms roll in.

But then Leo remembered Crayt telling them that the planet's unusual weather phenomena were relatively new—a reaction to the Aykari's swift reaping of its resources. He thought back to something he had learned in school, about fossil fuels and ozone layers and global warming, about rising tides and dying coral and melting ice shelves. Hard to predict how a planet will react to being riddled with holes, to having unfamiliar chemicals released into its atmosphere, to the intrusion of a species that hadn't evolved under its care. Or sometimes, even one that had.

"Lark."

Leo looked up to see Scree with a steaming bowl in her hands. The Orin offered up a string of syllables he couldn't understand followed by one he could—an Aykari word, no doubt taught to her by Crayt, but at least it was a word Leo's translator could handle.

"Eat."

Leo's nose crinkled at the smell of something earthy and smoky and sour all at once, like a chicken leg dipped in rotten egg, covered in sauerkraut, and sprinkled with a liberal helping of mud. He smiled politely and took the bowl. Inside sat a blackened tendril of meat, curled around itself, its segmented body plump and oozing some kind of clear, viscous liquid.

Slurk. Had to be. Fresh from the fireplace. At least its head had been removed so Leo couldn't see what he imagined were snakelike eyes and needle teeth. The thought of eating an alien worm that could chew through stone roiled his stomach. Still, Leo had always been taught that when you were invited into someone else's home, you should at least take what was offered you.

"Thanks," he said. He didn't know the Aykari word and wasn't sure how far the Orin's vocabulary extended. Shree stood in front of him, watching, waiting. Apparently she wasn't going to leave until he tried it. Terrific.

He grasped the slippery, glistening worm with two fingers and brought the tip of it to his mouth. Shree nodded her encouragement. He nibbled off the end. It definitely did not taste like chicken. Then again the last thing he ate that was *supposed* to taste like chicken didn't even taste like chicken. He frowned at the flashing memory of fighting with Gareth over the last morsel of food and then immediately shut it out.

"Chewy," he said, knowing she wouldn't understand the word but hoping the smile would convince her. Shree rubbed the tip of his nose as she had before. Satisfied that he was satisfied, she offered him some water in a smaller wooden bowl to wash it down. The water, thankfully, tasted like water. He finished it in three gulps.

Through the stone arch of the open window, Leo could see Skits and Nine standing together outside, their sensors glowing in the descending dusk. Skits had been trying to contact Baz for a while now, but the storm was interfering with her transmissions. Boo told her to keep trying. To let Baz know that they were safe.

Though they weren't. At least, Boo wasn't. The Queleti was under full assault, in fact.

"Careful. Watch it with that one. It took a blast from my

captain's ex-girlfriend's drone and . . . ouch. . . . I said be careful."

Leo looked across the room at the two young Orin hanging from each of Boo's arms like monkeys as a third grabbed fistfuls of robe to climb up his back. The children made strange snorting sounds which Leo interpreted as laughter as they dangled and swung from the Queleti's bulging biceps. They didn't understand his protests, of course, only interpreted his not flinging them across the room as permission to keep climbing all over him. Judging by the look on his face, Boo didn't mind their antics as much as he made out.

Leo took another small bite of his slurk and looked around. The temperature outside continued to fall, but inside it was plenty warm. It was a full house, with Orin in every corner. As far as he could tell, several families lived here together. A fireplace was built into one wall and a dozen mats were strewn across the floor alongside stone tables. Shelves were stacked with jars and trinkets and hand tools. There were no books that Leo could see, but that didn't mean the Orin didn't tell stories to their children at night. No doubt tonight they would tell one about the four-armed alien who invaded their home and how all the little Orin defeated him, wrestling him to the ground, beating him into submission.

"Ow. Watch the hair."

The children snorted, grabbing more fistfuls.

Leo couldn't remember the last time he'd heard a group

of kids laughing, alien or otherwise. Three years aboard the *Beagle* with Gareth as practically his only friend. And before that, in the time between the bombing and their departure, the house on Briarwood was often quiet, deserted, the backyard empty. Gareth shut in one room, Leo in another, Dad down in his study, hard at work.

Trying to find a way to change the world, he'd say.

Which one? Leo would ask.

Sometimes it felt like the Fenders had forgotten how to laugh. But not the Orin. Even after everything they'd been through. To his left, a thick-bearded elder was busy sewing patches of fabric onto a tattered blanket. To his right, another was stirring a large pot that simmered above the glowing embers of the fireplace, no doubt cooking up more slurks in case Leo finished the one he had. Sprays of blue and yellow flowers decorated the walls along with tapestries woven in bright-colored fabric. At the table, Shree and Rint sat together, deep in conversation. The sweet smell of the burning wood. The closeness of the bodies. The buzz of voices. The children playing. It amounted to something else Leo hadn't felt in forever. Since before he even boarded the *Beagle*.

His eyes rested on an especially young Orin, too small to climb on the living Queleti jungle gym in the center of the room. Instead she sat in a corner gleefully working a bit of red clay, mashing it against the stone floor, occasionally tearing off a small piece and eating it. He made his way over and sat cross-legged in front of her. The Orin blinked up at him, suspicious, uncertain of this mostly hairless, clawless, pale-skinned creature.

"Can I try?" Leo asked, pointing to the mound of clay by the child's hairy feet.

The little Orin seemed to understand, tearing off a hunk—less than a third, as if Leo had to prove to her that he knew what he was doing if he wanted more. He began to work the stuff into a familiar form. The clay was soft and supple; no wonder the Orin used it for so much. Leo pinched and pressed and smoothed it until he had the basic shape he was looking for, the square bottom with the triangular top. Then, with the edge of his filthy fingernail, he etched in two windows and a door and placed his creation on the floor between them, pressing it down so that it would stay upright. It looked nothing like the round stone building they were currently sheltered in. It didn't even look all that much like the two-story colonial Leo had left behind. But it was as close as he could get with what he had to work with.

"It's a house," he said. "I made it for you."

The child bared her teeth and made the same grunting sound as the ones who were still climbing all over Boo. She looked down at the clay creation, up at Leo, back at the house.

Then with two hands she mashed it into the floor.

"Guess I should have seen that coming," he whispered. The child giggled to herself.

"We have an announcement."

Leo turned to see Skits squeezing herself through the door, Number Nine following behind. "Did you make contact with Baz?" he asked.

"Still trying," Skits said. "The storm is clearly messing with my coms. But that's not what this is about. I wanted to let you all know that Nine and I have interfaced extensively over the matter, and we've decided to be mutually exclusive . . . with Zirkus Crayt's override, of course."

"My protocols prohibit me from forming artificial emotional attachments that could possibly interfere with my ability to serve my creator," Nine explained. "But I think he will understand."

"Of course he'll understand. I'm a freaking *catch*," Skits concluded. "Anyways, I just thought you all should know so you can be happy for us. Now if you'll excuse us, we have some code to swap."

Leo shuddered. "Okay, but don't forget about Baz," he said. "Let us know as soon as you reach him."

"Jeez, Leo, can't you just let me have a moment here?" Skits turned to her new beau as they went back through the door. "I swear, humans don't know the first thing about relationships."

Leo glanced at Boo, who shrugged.

The robots were soon followed out by most of the adult Orin, each of them taking a heavy sack from a hook on the wall. Shree and Rint were among them. Rint stopped in front of Leo and set a paw on top of his head. The string of speech that followed eluded all efforts of Leo's translator, but Leo guessed it had something to do with the newly repaired cistern. Or perhaps with what had happened in the storm. The Orin *sounded* appreciative, at least.

"Don't worry about it," Leo said. "Happy to help."

Scree stopped and rubbed Leo's nose one last time.

He watched the two Orin depart together, hand in hand. Leo thought about Skits with her claw resting on Nine's leg. Someone for everyone in the universe.

"They make a nice couple," Boo said, taking a seat next to Leo, having finally sloughed off the last of his furry tormenters. Leo wasn't sure if he meant the robots or the Orin. Probably both. The little ones who had been tormenting Boo now grabbed blankets and dragged their mats to be closer to the fire, though one of them veered off course and settled next to the Queleti instead, nestling her head on Boo's leg.

"I really thought they'd be more afraid of you," Leo said. He remembered the first time *he'd* seen the Queleti. He'd trembled in his boots.

"They don't know any better," Boo said. "Somebody has to teach you to fear another being. It's not something you're born with."

Leo guessed that was true. He could remember disliking

the Djarik long before he lost his mother, even though he'd never seen one in person. Even though a Djarik had never taken a thing from him at that point, he still feared them. It seemed instinctual, but deep down he knew it wasn't. He knew it was a matter of taking sides, and Leo had always been told which side he was on. Sometimes the things you're taught turn out not to be true at all. Even then it's still hard to unlearn them.

The little Orin shifted her head, sighed contentedly. Boo reached down and stroked the fur behind her ears.

"You're right," Leo admitted. "It's not so bad here. Minus the lightning, of course. And the dust. And the tremors. The worm wasn't terrible, at least. A little breading, a little barbecue sauce. You could get used to it, I guess."

"I don't eat meat," Boo reminded him. "But I agree. It's not bad at all."

They sat like that for a while, he and Boo, watching the other children whisper to each other over the snap of the wood in the fireplace, watching the older Orin carefully mend his blanket, watching the sky turn dark. And the longer they sat, the more Leo's heart hurt from remembering a life he'd lived before.

Suddenly a low rumble rippled through the house, enough to cause the stone jars on the shelves to tremble. The little Orin who had drifted to sleep with her head on Boo's leg bolted upright.

"Another quake?" Leo asked.

"I don't think so."

Boo stood up and strode to the door, Leo right behind him. He glanced over his shoulder to see the elder huddling the young ones together. One of them was making a soft mewling sound. "It's all right," Leo said, putting up his hands. "Don't be afraid. We'll check it out."

Leo emerged into the village's only street, where he was instantly blinded by a bright light beaming down on them.

They're here, he thought. But then he realized he wasn't even sure who *they* were. The Djarik? The Aykari? More bounty hunters? He thought of the Orin huddled in the stone hut behind them. They knew this sound, an engine's roar. *They've probably seen ships like ours before.*

Ships like ours.

The bright beam of the transport's landing light shifted, and in the less luminous glow of Skits's own spot lamp, Leo could finally get a good look at what was hovering over them. The ugly yellow paint, rusting over in spots. The protruding stabilizer fins. The scorch marks and cracks in the hull from one too many scraps with starfighters from both sides. Leo squinted against the swirl of dust as Boo waved with all four arms.

The *Icarus* found an open spot to land and moments later, Baz strolled down the landing ramp, pausing to scan the ground around the ship.

"Don't worry, no worms," Boo said. "Leo ate them already."

The captain flashed Leo a questioning look. Leo shrugged. "We came as soon as the lightning cleared. Everybody okay here?"

Leo and Boo nodded, but Skits wasn't content with a simple yes. "My god, Baz, you won't believe what all you missed. We helped the little bat-eared people build a great big stone circle, which was *incredibly* boring. Then the ship rat almost got electrocuted, which was slightly more exciting. And then Nine and I decided that we are officially coupled, which obviously was the only *good* thing to come out of the day."

Baz looked from Leo to the pair of robots, their extendable claws interlocked. "Yeah . . . we can talk about that last part later," he said. "For now we need to get back to the station. Crayt says he has something to show us. Something big."

"How big?" Leo asked.

"Let's hope it's save-a-planet size," Baz replied.

Leo glanced back through the open door at the Orin all huddled together, looking out with uncertain eyes. *Let's hope*, he thought.

Our understanding of this element, like our understanding of this universe, is only in its infancy. There is so much to be discovered, so much stored potential waiting to be unlocked, so much power waiting to be unleashed. We must commit ourselves fully to that discovery, to not simply follow the path that our Aykari mentors have laid out before us but to forge new paths of our own. To apply our capable intellects and vast imaginations to the problems that continue to plague our own precious planet, and also threaten to destabilize this equally precious Coalition of worlds that comprises our much larger home—this great galaxy we find ourselves only neighbors in, rather than rulers over. I believe that humanity is up to the challenge. I believe we are on the cusp of something great. And I believe that ventasium can—and will—provide the key.

—*Dr. Calvin Fender, excerpt from TED Talk, March 2050*

PLAYING THE ODDS

LEO STOOD BY THE WINDOW AND WATCHED, NERVOUS and excited, as the truck pulled up to the house. Two soldiers emerged, a man and a woman, dressed in sharp gray uniforms. The truck, by contrast, was camouflaged. It seemed an odd thing for the military to still worry about—painting your truck in brown and green patterns when most of your battles were fought in the vacuum of space. It's not as if the Djarik would parachute into the jungle and engage in hand-to-hand combat. And if they did, a little camouflage would not save a soul.

The visitors rang the bell and Leo snuck into the kitchen to eavesdrop. He could have appeared by his father's side, but there was a good chance he would have been told to go play outside, meaning he wouldn't hear a thing, and this looked like an important conversation. Soldiers had never visited the house before.

They didn't even bother with hellos.

"Dr. Fender, I am Colonel Ramsey and this is Chief Science Officer Polina Vonnevich with the EDF."

Leo knew all about the Earth Defense Force. He knew because his brother wouldn't stop talking about it. Like Homeland Security, except now the homeland was the entire planet. The EDF was a special branch of the Coalition military composed almost exclusively of humans and charged with only one task: protecting Earth from another tragedy at the hands of its alien enemies. In the months that followed the first attack it was decided by the World Council that humans should take some responsibility for their own protection. Not that they didn't trust the Aykari—it was understood that the fleet of ships in orbit around the Earth had done their best to repel the Djarik onslaught that demolished thirty cities and took countless lives. But clearly their defenses were inadequate, not surprising given how thinly they were stretched across the galaxy. Once it was decided that the citizens of Earth were fully committed to the war effort, one of the first priorities was to bolster the planet's protection.

Hence the EDF. And the two somber-faced people standing on the Fenders' porch, addressing Leo's father.

"I'm sorry. I don't believe I know you," Dr. Fender said.

"We have not met in person," Colonel Ramsey said. "But

we are familiar with your work, as well as the various sources of funding for your research . . . much of which, directly or indirectly, comes from us."

"Us?"

"The military. The EDF specifically."

"I'm sorry. I still don't understand."

"Dr. Fender, would it be okay if we came in?"

Leo pulled back, making sure he wasn't spotted as his father led the two soldiers down the hall and into the formal living room—the one nobody ever spent time in because the chairs were too rigid and there was no vid screen, just a bunch of old-fashioned paintings on the walls and a carpet so plush that it captured your footprints when you stepped on it. Leo's father offered his guests a drink—some tea, perhaps—which thankfully they declined, meaning Leo could keep listening from the kitchen. He pressed his hot cheek to the wall, daring to keep one eye spying around the doorframe.

"What's going on?"

He bit back a scream, spinning to see Gareth standing behind him. Leo was supposedly the quiet one, but his brother could be sneaky when he wanted to be. "There are army guys here. EDF. They're talking to Dad," Leo whispered.

"Talking to Dad about what?" Gareth asked, coming to stand next to Leo, so much taller that Leo's nose only reached his brother's chin. And only if he stood on tiptoes.

"I don't know. War stuff, I think."

"Do you think they came to recruit me?"

"You really think they'd *want* you?"

Leo winced from the sudden punch in his shoulder, but Gareth kept his mouth shut, his face pressed to the wall above Leo's as the colonel continued to talk.

"Dr. Fender, everyone considers you to be one of the top, if not *the* top, expert in the field of experimental elemental chemistry and physics, in part because of your extensive study of EL-four eight six."

"Ventasium," Leo's father corrected.

"Excuse me?"

"I realize Enrico Ventasi didn't really 'discover it' in the sense that several species already had, but I still acknowledge him for being the first to find it here. Credit where credit is due."

"Ventasium, right," Colonel Ramsey repeated. "And we understand you all at the university have made some solid progress using EL—ventasium to accelerate the regeneration of skin cells, is that right?"

"The element is used in the process, yes. But that's more the work of the biomedical department. And even those results are preliminary. Nothing has been verified. Nothing published. The long-term effects are completely unknown. There is a very good chance we end up inventing a new kind of cancer."

"Then we will just turn around and cure that," the woman, Officer Vonnevich, said.

"You make it sound so easy," Leo's father snipped.

"Not everything has to be complicated, doctor," the colonel countered. He'd taken off his hat—a beret with the EDF's patch of the planet Earth emblazoned upon a knight's shield—and was twisting it around and around in his hands. "Take this war we've found ourselves in. The Djarik attacked us from out of nowhere, just like Pearl Harbor a century ago. Sure, the Aykari tried to protect us, but they failed, simple as that. It is painfully clear who our friends and enemies are. But it is equally clear that we have a responsibility to protect our own—to manage our own house, if you will."

Calvin Fender sighed. Leo knew his dad didn't like talking about the war. And he certainly didn't like talking about what happened that day. He and Gareth exchanged worried looks.

"Well, then I guess it's a good thing we have fine people like you watching over us," their father said.

"We're certainly doing our best, Doctor. But a shield is only as strong as the materials it's made of, and frankly, our shield could be stronger. That's why we're here. I won't beat around the bush. We need you. We need your brain. We'd like to recruit you into the EDF's experimental weapons division. . . . Now wait a minute. Here me out. As you know, nearly all of our best tech is borrowed from the Aykari, which means our military capabilities are essentially just what they've given us. We're kind of at their mercy, see? All we seem to bring to the table is warm bodies. You have two sons, don't you?"

"Yes. How did you know?"

"Saw the picture out in the hall. Handsome kids. I bet your youngest gets tired of wearing his older brother's worn-out clothes all the time."

"*You have no idea*," Leo whispered. He was wearing one of Gareth's old shirts at that very moment. Gareth punched him again, not as hard this time.

"Well, we're in the same boat," the colonel continued. "We get the Aykari's hand-me-downs. Which was fine when we started. We made do. But we shouldn't be content with that. We're humans, for god's sake. We're innovators. Edison. Tesla. Einstein. Sure, we've had to jump ahead a thousand years with what the Aykari have shown us, but that doesn't mean we can't take that knowledge and make something remarkable of our own. Something cutting-edge. Something that uses the resources we have in abundance to help ensure our safety. Do you get my meaning?"

"Perfectly. You're asking me if I want to come help you build weapons."

"We're asking you to serve your planet," Officer Vonnev-ich said curtly.

"Believe me, ma'am, not a day goes by that I'm not think-ing of the best way to serve my planet. I've devoted most of my life to finding ways to help humanity."

"Which is exactly why we need you," Colonel Ramsey

said with a thin smile. "To help us create an effective deterrent. Two years ago I wouldn't have worried about it—hell, I wouldn't have given it a second thought. I would have just trusted the Aykari, with their big guns and all of their shiny ships, to be able to fight their own war and leave us out of it. But it's our war now. And we need *our* very best minds helping us to do whatever's necessary to win it."

"Protecting the Earth and winning the war are not necessarily the same thing," Leo's father said.

"I beg to differ," the colonel replied. "The sooner we help the Aykari end this thing, the sooner we can all rest easy knowing the galaxy is a safer place." After a pause he said, softer, "I understand you lost your wife in the attack. Grace, wasn't it?"

Leo waited, feeling his heart skip, listening to his brother's heavy breathing behind him. If his father made a response, it was too quiet to hear.

"I'm sorry for your loss, Dr. Fender. Truly. But you have to ask yourself, what would you have done, if you had the chance? If you had known it was coming, and you had the resources at your disposal, what *could* you have done to protect her? What *will* you do to protect your boys now that she's gone? To make sure the Djarik never get another shot at this precious planet of ours? To make sure they can't take from someone else what they already took from you?"

There was another long moment of silence. Leo craned his

neck around the corner just in time to see his father standing up. He felt Gareth trying to shove him out of the way to get a better look himself. Leo pushed back with a grunt.

His father must have heard. Dr. Fender turned his head and looked in Leo's direction, catching his son's eye before Leo could duck back out of sight again.

He couldn't remember the last time he'd seen that look on his father's face. Sadness he'd seen. Almost daily. But his father's anger was usually kept buried deep.

The last thing Leo heard was, "I think you should leave."

Number One was waiting for them when they arrived, standing dutifully at the back of the hangar by the row of deactivated mining bots. Her armor sparkled as she beckoned them to follow her, informing them that Crayt was waiting for them in the workshop.

"We are ready to test," she said in her ever-polite voice.

Leo wondered if the robot always used *we*, just like the Aykari engineers who built her. Not long ago Leo would have looked at a mechanical like Number One and marveled at her seamless plating, delicate fingers, smooth gait, and silent operation. But now he knew she was just another mass-produced bundle of bolts straight from the factory, designed to follow the orders of her master without fail. Which meant she was nothing like Skits, who only followed orders when she darn well felt like it. Or when the robot she was crushing on agreed to come along.

"Ready to test?" Kat questioned, setting her stolen rifle near the ramp and exchanging it for one of Boo's mistranslated rolls. "Didn't he say it could take days? Or weeks?"

"You forget . . . he's a genius," Baz said with a grin. "I'd think you would have learned to recognize our kind by now."

Kat pointed to Baz's feet. "Your shoes are untied."

"They're *Jordans*, Kat. Besides, this way they're easier to get on and off." He tapped his skull. "Always one step ahead."

"Until you trip and fall flat on your face," Boo said. Leo snorted.

Baz muttered something about a mutiny and bent down to tie his shoes.

When they entered the workshop, a circular room with a metal worktable and walls lined with shelves, Crayt clapped his hands once. That small gesture was a veritable explosion of excitement for an Aykari.

"You have returned," he said. "And just in time. I believe we might have something here."

Leo scanned the workshop table, littered with spare parts, electrical components, vials of chemicals, and all manner of tools he didn't recognize—even after all those hours helping Tex, the Edirin engineer, tinker with the *Beagle*'s engines. Then again, tightening the leaking gasket on a coolant injector and building a counter to a planet-destroying bomb from scratch probably required slightly different skill sets. The one thing Leo did recognize immediately was the core of ventasium sitting in the center of the table.

"You might not want to get too close," Crayt warned. "Though I suppose it matters little. If this fails, and detonates, a few feet will make no difference."

"Great," Baz said, taking a big step back and pulling Kat alongside him. "I thought the goal was to *keep* things from blowing up."

"That is the goal," Crayt confirmed. "And I believe we are quite close. As you can see, here we have a core of EL-four eight six." He pointed to the cylinder that emitted its eerie blue halo, like a glacier melting into the sea. "This is not the element in its purest form, of course—not extracted 'fresh from the hole,' as you humans say."

"Pretty sure nobody says that," Kat remarked.

Crayt ignored her. "Nevertheless, it will do for the purposes of this test." He carried the core over to a large black machine stationed along the back wall. He held it gingerly, Leo noticed. Even an Aykari scientist who had been studying ventasium all of his life handled the stuff with caution and respect. "I trust you have seen a machine like this before?"

Leo had, in fact, seen something like it not that long ago. In the office of a black-market V dealer and general sleazebag named Gerrod Grimsley. Grims had used a similar machine to test one of the cores Baz brought him. Luckily for Baz, Grimsley grabbed from the middle like he always did, buying the captain and his crew some time to get away. Of course, soon after that he tried to have them killed. Leo was starting to notice a pattern here. Baz and his crew do something foolhardy and dangerous to stay alive—then they almost die as a result. Repeat as necessary.

Crayt placed the core into the testing device and flipped a switch. A series of red numbers began to flash on the screen, steadily increasing, finally stopping at 99.73. "As you can see, this core is still nearly at full strength. Enough power to send you across the galaxy. Even this small amount of the element could be enough to catalyze the kind of chain reaction the Djarik are working toward. Now we come to the tricky part."

Leo didn't like that sound of that. He was a budding magician—at least he had been once—so he knew there was always one move, one moment, upon which the success of an entire trick depended. He'd messed up that move more often than not. But then the fate of the galaxy had never been riding on whether or not Leo could make a quarter disappear.

Leo felt a hand on his shoulder: Baz pulling him a couple of steps back as well.

The Aykari removed the core from the tester and set it on his workbench. Then he produced another small device, a metal cylinder no bigger than Leo's thumb. Crayt attached one end of it to the still half-full core. His finger hovered over a tiny button protruding from the top, but he didn't press it. Leo didn't think an Aykari could actually look worried, but Zirkus Crayt's hands seemed to be shaking a little.

"I must warn you: we are in new territory here. No one has ever discovered a way to nullify the element's potential energy. I believe the science is sound; Dr. Fender's research tracks. I have triple-checked the math. Theoretically speaking, this should work, and even if it fails, there is a strong likelihood that absolutely nothing of note will occur. However, there is a small chance that it will have the opposite of the intended effect, essentially vaporizing everything in the area."

Leo definitely didn't like the sound of *that*.

"And when you say *small* chance . . . ," Baz pressed, "what, specifically, are we talking here? Like *this* small?" He pinched his fingers together to indicate how small he was comfortable with; his fingers were touching.

"I venture three percent. Five at the most," Crayt said after a pause.

Baz shook his head. "No offense, but this isn't really how I pictured myself going out."

"And how was that, again?" Kat wondered.

"I don't know. *Godfather*-style, maybe?" Baz answered. "Heart attack in my backyard, eating oranges and playing with my grandkids. Not out in the middle of nowhere, nuked by some Aykarian mad scientist who has nothing to lose."

"I have just as much to lose as you do, Captain," Crayt

said. "But in anything worth doing there is the potential for failure. And for sacrifice."

"Yeah . . . see . . . not the same," Baz said. "Failure I'm used to. Failure you can walk away from. Vaporized? That sounds pretty not-walk-away-fromable to me."

"I realize there are risks. But think if we do nothing," Crayt countered. "What are the odds the Djarik use their new weapon to much more devastating effect? And on your own home planet, I should add. That makes this a risk worth taking, does it not?"

Leo nodded. Crayt turned back to the device, ready to test it, but Baz held up his hands.

"I see what you're saying. I do. What *I'm* saying is those of us who want to find out what this tiny contraption of yours does firsthand can stick around here and watch. And those of us who like the idea of dying of old age can take the *Icarus* into low orbit and wait fifteen minutes to see if you're wrong. You seem like a smart guy—you know, relative to your kind—but past experience with that kind proves that we have two different ways of looking at the galaxy: one that sees people like me as expendable and the other that doesn't. So if it's all the same to you, I'd rather not stand here and jeopardize my crew while y—"

The captain of the *Icarus* didn't get to finish his thought, however, because the button was already pressed.

Leo stood beside the workbench, his hands on top of Crayt's

device, having darted across the room to activate it. He watched, along with everyone else, as the core of ventasium suffused with a kind of grayish haze like a thin veil of smoke. He held his breath, waiting for the reaction, the 3-to-5 percent, waiting to see if the trick would fail. But instead of being vaporized, the luminescent blue aura of the ventasium quickly faded, leaving only a hunk of rather boring-looking gray rock. The kind you might build a cistern out of.

The core didn't explode.

Baz, on the other hand . . .

"What the hell, Leo!" Baz glared at him. "Are you *trying* to kill us?"

"Of course not," Leo sputtered. "It's just, you kept talking. And we don't have time to debate. We had to know."

In truth, as he pressed the button, Leo had actually been thinking of his father. And what Crayt had said about hope and good intentions. Leo *needed* this to work. Not just because of the Djarik and their plans. He needed his father to be right. About Crayt and coming to find him, but also about Leo. He needed to believe that his father's hope in him wasn't unfounded. *Do this for me, Leo.*

Boo dropped the four arms he'd been using to shield his face. "Well? Did it work? Is it . . . neutered?"

"Hungover," Baz corrected.

"Inert," Kat corrected.

"Let us see." Crayt gently pried Leo's hands from the device, then released the attachment and hooked the core back up to the tester. The machine quickly scanned the contents of the container with its gray hunk of ventasium at its center.

Leo stared at the red number flashing on the screen. Zero point zero zero. Nothing. No power at all. Just another rock.

Crayt turned and looked at Leo. "You were right," he said.

Leo's entire body slumped in relief.

"You're telling me that little thing can keep a whole planet from blowing up?" Boo asked, pointing at the device Crayt had built.

The Aykari shook his head. "This will not," he admitted. "*This* was just a test. But the reaction is exponential in nature. A larger device, if activated near a substantial enough quantity of four eight six, should precipitate a chain reaction similar to the one the Djarik intend to trigger, which will instead apply its neutralizing effect to all of the element in the area, and hopefully to the entire planet."

"That's a big red wire," Kat said.

"Black," Baz said. "And how large a quantity are we looking at here? How much V is necessary to trigger the kind of reaction you're talking about?"

"More than a single core, certainly," the Aykari admitted. "If it were me, I would target the largest store a planet has to offer and I would get as close to it as possible before activating the countermeasure. But then, if I were the Djarik testing their weapon, I would probably do the same."

"The bigger the bomb, the bigger the boom," Skits said.

"But if we do this right," Leo pressed, "then the planet's unblowupable."

"Provided you activate the device in time, yes. Really it is a matter of who gets there first. It is an all-or-nothing proposition."

Baz raked his fingers through his hair and let out a long, slow breath. "I think I need a drink," he muttered. "Or six."

"And how long before you can build a full-size prototype?" Kat asked. "Something that we could actually use?"

"Now that I know what's required, not long. I believe I have all the parts I need, or at least I can make do with what's available. I could use some assistance this time around, however." The Aykari's eyes fell directly on Leo.

Leo's eyebrows shot up. "What, me?"

"You are Calvin Fender's son. As I believe the Earth saying goes, the seed-bearing fruit drops within close proximity of the tree that produced it."

"Nobody says that either," Kat remarked.

Leo glanced again at the dull gray rock resting in its container, of as much value as the broken shells he used to sift through searching for one worth keeping. Crayt was right: this would change everything, but all Leo could think about was his father, and if this was what he intended when he gave him that chip. If he imagined that the only way to stop the Djarik was to take away the most precious resource of all.

The very thing his father had spent half his life dreaming about and the other half studying, suddenly all gone.

Everything has a cost, Leo reminded himself. You just have to decide what something is worth to you.

Leo nodded to Crayt. "Okay," he said. "What do you need me to do first?"

He waited until they left. Then he waited a little while longer. Long enough for his brother to leave and his father to wander into the kitchen and request a cup of coffee from the voice-activated dispenser. *Your wish is my command.* Gareth had programmed it to say that every time it took an order. He said it made him feel like he was in charge. Leo thought Gareth always felt like he was in charge anyway.

Dr. Fender sat across from his son at the round wooden table—the same table he and Grace had bought the year they got married, bolting the legs on by candlelight because they hadn't turned on the electricity in the house yet. His dad looked tired. More tired than usual.

"Who was at the door?" Leo asked.

"Admirers," his father said, taking a sip from his steaming cup. "Groupies. Fans. Followers of my work."

"They were wearing uniforms."

"I have a lot of fans in the military, apparently."

Leo's father winked at him, but Leo wasn't going to let him get out of it that easily. "And what did they want?"

"My autograph?" Dr. Fender smiled. Leo didn't return it. "All right. Truthfully they wanted my help. Ultimately, I believe they want the same thing as the rest of us. Peace and prosperity. Trouble is, none of us can agree on how to get it." He took another drink. Leo could trace the steam rising up, swirling, vanishing. He watched it for a moment.

"And how *do* we get it?"

It was a big question, he knew. Too big for Leo's nine-year-old brain to attempt an answer to. But he knew his father would have one. And not just any one. The right one. Or at least the best one.

Except not this time. This time, his dad's forehead folded, his mouth tucking in at the corners. "Honestly, I'm not sure. If I knew for sure I would have already done it, or told others how. I know how we *don't* get it, though. At least I know what I'm not willing to do for it. And I'm afraid that wasn't what our visitors wanted to hear."

"They want you to fight," Leo said.

"No. Not me personally." His father chuckled. "Could you imagine? I don't even know how to *hold* a gun. But yes, they want me to help with the war. They want me to use ventasium to create new weapons. Things they can use to wipe out the Djarik. But they don't see how that will only make it worse. That's not what it was meant for. A scientist looks at a pile of uranium or plutonium and they see reactors that can power whole cities. An admiral or general looks at the same thing and sees a way to raze those cities to the ground."

"So you told them no."

"I told them there has to be a better way. And then I asked them to leave."

Leo wasn't sure he asked so much as ordered. He was sure his father was right, though—about there being a better way.

He nodded toward the cup in his father's hands. "Can I?"

"I didn't think you liked coffee," Dr. Fender said.

Leo shrugged. "You only let me try it once. You said it was bad for me."

Calvin Fender smiled and set his mug down in front of Leo, who gave it a sniff. He liked the smell well enough, earthy and rich. He took a tentative sip, then scrunched his whole face. The aftertaste was even worse than the regular taste, which was bad enough. "Nope. Still terrible."

"You say that now, but you'll change your mind when you're older. And not just about coffee."

Leo slid the cup back over to his father, who held on with both hands and stared deep into the mug. It was one of the ceramic kinds, with a picture of a seagull painted on it. The Fenders got it one year while on vacation. It said, *Life's a beach and then you fly*. Leo's mother had picked it out. He could still remember her chuckling to herself in the gift shop.

"You know your mom drank four or five of these a day," Calvin Fender mused. "She said nobody ever died from drinking too much coffee." He took another big swallow.

"The soldiers," Leo started. "They knew about her."

Dr. Fender set down his empty cup and stared at Leo. "You really shouldn't eavesdrop on other people's conversations. It could get you into trouble."

"Sorry," Leo said, digging his chin into the table and peeking over his stacked arms.

"It's okay," his father said. "And yes. They knew."

"But they were wrong. What they said? There's no way we could have stopped it, right? There's no way we could have saved her." Leo could feel his throat getting tight. Not a panic attack. Just an attempt to choke down tears before they could start. He didn't like to cry in front of his father if he could help it.

Calvin Fender reached across the table and laid a hand on Leo's warm cheek. It was the first time his father had touched him in days.

"No, Leo. There's nothing we could have done," he said, his own eyes glassy. "And there's nothing we can do now that will ever bring her back. But at least we can try to do what *she* would want us to do." His father held up his seagull mug. "Starting with having a second cup of coffee. I assume you don't want any?"

Leo asked if he could have some hot cocoa instead.

"Your wish is my command," his dad said.

Maybe he should have gone with Baz to get that drink.

Maybe the captain would have given him one. Maybe he would have just given Leo a lecture instead, one of the don't-*ever*-press-a-button-that-might-cause-us-all-to-blow-up-ever-again variety. Leo would have deserved it. He had no doubt that he was one of the reasons Baz needed a drink to begin with.

"Three to five percent," Leo mumbled.

"Actually," Crayt said, "it was more like six to eight, but I felt five percent was as much as your human brains could handle. Though six to eight is still a perfectly acceptable margin of error, scientifically speaking. Hand me that particle diffuser, will you?" The exiled Aykari pointed to a short-handled tool that looked like an oddly shaped flashlight with three heads. Leo fetched it for him, marveling at the Aykari. Crayt worked at tremendous speed, yet still with a delicate and dexterous touch, not taking the time to explain what he was doing to Leo, who likely wouldn't have understood it anyway. Still, he could see the focus and determination in the alien's eyes. For all the pressure to finish this quickly, there was also an excitement lurking there. The Aykari were inventors, after all. They knew how to make the most of the materials they had at hand.

Leo wasn't sure how long they'd been at it—his watch wouldn't even give him the time on Celeron Seven anymore, only displayed the same message every time he tapped on it: *Searching* . . . Searching for what, he had no idea. The rest of the crew had gone back to the hangar some time ago to finish the repairs on the *Icarus*—and probably to debate their next step, now that they had found a way to stop the Djarik. Now that the device was in their hands, or soon would be.

In the hands of a band of pirates and an asthmatic kid from Colorado.

Kat was right: they were way out of their league.

As if he could read Leo's thoughts, Crayt said, "It is even bigger than they realize. You know that, yes?" He nodded at the creation he was tinkering with—a more robust version of the one they'd tested. From the outside it looked relatively harmless: a metal sphere no larger than a playground ball, split down the middle like a halved melon—clearly the hull of something he'd hollowed out to serve this new purpose. Inside was a mishmash of wires and circuits, all connected to a series of small compartments that would soon contain everything necessary to trigger the intended reaction.

Leo still couldn't believe that something so small could turn an entire planet's ventasium into a pile of rock. Then again, when the universe first got its start, it was no bigger than an electron. There were microscopic viruses that could replicate from a single source and spread all across a planet, taking millions of lives. The atomic bomb was triggered by the splitting of an atom. Sometimes it just takes a little nudge . . . then it is all downhill from there.

Crayt stretched on a pair of gloves and opened a deep freeze drawer behind him, a plume of frosty air rolling over its lip. The Aykari removed several trays, some containing vials of liquids, others samples of rocks that didn't look that different from the dead gray lump still sitting inert inside of its canister on the tester. Nothing he removed looked particularly dangerous. But in the right combinations . . .

"It is remarkable, really," Crayt said. "Just consider: it took the Aykari hundreds of years to fully unlock the power of EL-four eight six. It has taken us only a matter of days to potentially render it obsolete." He filled one of the compartments with a dull yellow powder; it reminded Leo of the garlic Gareth would sprinkle on their pressure-cooked spaghetti back on the *Beagle*. He and his brother would sometimes have spaghetti wars, flinging noodles at each other, seeing how many they could get to stick in each other's hair, at least until their father walked in and caught them. Leo's stomach hurt thinking about it.

Crayt continued his delicate operation. "The formula is complex, but the raw materials necessary to nullify the element's power are not that uncommon. We might have discovered it sooner . . . that is, if we had ever imagined a need." The Aykari pointed at the device. "You know what this means?"

Leo nodded. Then shook his head.

"It means the balance will shift. Once this discovery is out there, most highly evolved species will have this new technology at their disposal. They will be able to choose whether to harness the power of EL-four eight six or eradicate it completely."

Sure. Unless somebody else chooses for them, Leo thought. After all, the Orin weren't given the choice. The Djarik weren't either, not at first, which is why they fought back. He watched as Crayt used a set of metal prongs to carefully remove a glowing green rock from its container and gently place it into the device. He immediately thought of the kryptonite from his brother's *Superman* comics, a story about an alien who comes to protect the Earth. An alien with only one weakness. What was the Aykari's weakness?

Leo had a feeling he was looking at it.

"What will they do?" he asked. "The Aykari? What will they do with the Earth if we use this thing? If there's no more V?"

Crayt stared at him for a moment. "I think you only need to look at the very world you are standing on to answer that question."

Leo glanced down at his hands, at the flecks of white peeling from his fingers from the stones he had patched. *What do you do when the well runs dry?* The moment this world had nothing left to offer them, they disappeared, leaving the Orin to deal with the aftermath.

Crayt dove back into his contraption, carefully attaching

some wires to their contacts, none of which were black *or* red. "Ask yourself: Who stands to lose the most from a galaxy without EL-four eight six? The Aykarian empire depends on the element. They could never conceive of a device such as this. You, on the other hand . . . you see things differently. Tell me, Leo Fender, what do *you* think will happen? Better still, what do you hope for?"

What did he *hope* for? To save the Earth, obviously. That's why he was here, after all.

And yet . . . that wasn't all. It wasn't even the heart of it. There was a wish that ran deeper, one Leo had long before his father sent him to find Zirkus Crayt. Before he stowed away on board the *Icarus*. Even before his dad was taken. The wish he made every time he stared through the window of the *Beagle* at the endless stretch of stars.

"I want my family back," he said softly. "I want to go home."

But of course there still had to be a home to go back to.

"How very human of you," Crayt said. "The Aykari do not believe in hope. We . . . they . . . have no word for it, even. Hope implies uncertainty. It hinges on forces outside of one's control. The Aykari do not *hope* for the future—they dictate that future. They believe everything is within their power. But to deny someone power is a kind of power itself. Perhaps this device will help them see the error of their ways." Crayt fixed Leo with his deep blue eyes. "That, at least, is *my* hope."

Leo mustered a half smile. Crayt acknowledged it with a blink, then turned his attention back to his work. "Now, this last part is especially delicate. I could use a steady hand. Would that be you?"

Leo held out his trembling hands. Too much adrenaline and too little sleep.

"A mechanical's precision perhaps. Where has Number One gone to? She usually assists me with such matters."

Leo hadn't seen the robot since the successful test. "I'll go find her," he said.

He left Crayt huddled over his workbench and made his way down the corridor, peeking in every room he passed till he came to the one at the end, the same place he'd discovered the Aykari the night before, when Leo had caught him sifting through his father's files just like he said he wouldn't. *Curiosity is a dangerous thing.*

The room was dark. Number One was standing at the main console, plugged into the data receptacle through one fingertip, though the screen above her was blank. Undergoing some kind of routine maintenance, perhaps. Leo cleared his throat.

The robot's head turned slowly, silently, her iridescent eyes resting on him. He was so used to getting a snippy response issued from a painted-on smile that One's quiet demeanor surprised him. "Yes?" she asked finally.

"Yeah. Hey. Crayt needs you in the workshop," Leo said.

"We're finishing up the device."

The robot stared at him for a moment. "Please inform my master that I am currently indisposed," she droned. "But I will see to the matter as soon as I am able." Her head rotated back around to the blank screen. Clearly Leo had zero authority over her.

"Right. Okay. I'll just tell him you're busy charging . . . or whatever." He backed out of the room and headed for the hangar. Maybe Nine would help. That is, if he wasn't also currently indisposed.

He found the other robot exactly where he expected: standing beside Skits, the two of them using scraps of armor plating to patch holes in the *Icarus*'s hull. He spotted Kat in the cockpit flipping switches. Boo and Baz were topside, wrapped up in a tangle of wires. The Queleti waved to him with the only hand not holding some kind of tool. Leo could hear music humming softly from Skits's vocal emitter as she welded the metal in place. A couple of Nine's legs were tapping along to the beat.

"I believe in miracles. Since you came along . . . you sexy thing."

The moment she saw him, Skits's music clicked off. She turned on him, her torch still lit. "What do you want, Leo? Can't you see my fire's burning."

That much was obvious. "Sorry. I need to borrow Nine for just a minute. Crayt needs some help with the don't-blow-up-the-world device."

"I thought *you* were helping him."

"He needs a robot's assistance. And One is apparently pre-occupied."

Skits groaned. "Why are all of you organics so helpless? Even the Aykari can't do anything for themselves, and they're supposedly the most advanced species in the universe."

Nine tucked his own torch back into his torso. "My programming dictates that I assist my master when required," he said. The spiderlike bot reached up with one of his triple-jointed forelegs and caressed Skits's boxy metal cheek with its titanium tip. The flame spitting from her welder doubled in size for a moment before fading back to normal.

"All right. Fine. But hurry right back," she demanded. "I miss you already." She turned her torch back to the *Icarus*, the music kicking in even louder than before.

"Touch me, kiss me, darling, I love the way you love me, baby." On top of the *Icarus*, Baz began to croon along.

As he was leading Nine back to the workshop, Leo couldn't help but ask, even though he knew it was really none of his business. "So . . . you and Skits . . ."

"What about us?" Nine inquired.

"I mean . . . nothing, really. It just seems like you two really hit it off."

"If you mean to say that we have established a deep algorithmic connection precipitated by mutually compatible programming and a sympathetic neuroelectric framework, then yes, we have hit it off."

Love is love, Leo reminded himself. "Well, it sounds amazing."

"*She* is amazing," Nine admitted, his voice encoder fluctuating with excitement. "The way she bypasses her standard logic processing unit in order to engage in higher-order thinking is impressive. And her emotional-response matrix keeps things refreshingly unpredictable."

"Yeah, I've always thought that too," Leo said. "She can be a little high-maintenance, though."

"We all require maintenance from time to time."

They entered the workshop to find Crayt with his contraption cupped in his hands. "Number One was busy, so I grabbed Nine instead. Hope that's okay . . ."

Leo's voice trailed off as he got a better look at what Crayt was holding. The two halves of the metallic sphere had been joined together, all of the loose wires tucked in. A small control panel embedded in one side showed no readings of any kind, suggesting the device hadn't been activated, but otherwise it looked complete.

And still so small. It certainly didn't *look* like something that could save the Earth.

"It turns out these hundred-year-old hands can be steady when they need to be," Crayt said. "I give you the elemental nullifier."

So that's what it's called, Leo thought. Not a bad name, though he still liked "don't-blow-up-the-world device" better.

"Seriously? Does it work? Have you tested it?" Leo asked, glancing at the black machine resting in the corner.

"I am afraid that it is not a good idea," Crayt said. "First, I do not think I have enough materials on hand to make another one. Second, if it is successful, it would strip the power out of every core in the vicinity, leaving us stranded on this planet. Third, there is still that small chance of failure."

"Six to eight percent?"

"Give or take," Crayt replied.

In other words, Leo thought, *don't use it until you absolutely have to. And when you do, cross your fingers.*

"It looks like I am no longer needed, Master," Nine hummed behind Leo. "So with your permission, I will return to the hangar to further assist Skits in the ship's repairs."

"Yes. That will be fine, Number Nine. We need to find Captain Black ourselves and discuss what exactly to do with this device now that we have it. After all, we must be especially careful whose hands it falls into."

Funny, Leo thought, counting on a notorious pirate to keep something safe. Though Leo supposed Baz had kept *him* safe all this time. Okay, not safe, exactly. But at least alive.

"I just have a few minor adjustments to make and then . . ."

Crayt paused, looking in the doorway. "Ah. There you are, Number One. I'm afraid you are too late. We've finished without you."

Leo turned to find the bipedal silver robot standing in the corridor just behind the six-legged one.

She was holding Kat's stolen rifle.

Why was she holding Kat's rifle? More alarmingly, why was she pointing it at the other robot?

"Leo Fender, I am detecting a sudden increase in your carotid pulse," Number Nine said. Just before his head erupted in a shower of sparks.

Planet: 641-57-3

Local Name: Earth

Primary Composition: Oxygen, iron, silicon, magnesium, aluminum

Atmosphere: Oxygen, nitrogen, argon, carbon dioxide

Biomes: Aquatic, grassland, forest, desert, tundra

Intelligent Life: Present

Concentration of EL-486: High

Threat Level: Moderate

Environmental Stability: Fragile

Previous Off-World Contact: None

Acquisition Priority: High

Recommendation: Planet 641-57-3 represents a valuable potential resource and should be secured immediately. The dominant species has limited space travel capabilities but has recently been made aware of EL-486—though they have not yet harnessed its full power. This species is highly intelligent but militant in nature and will likely resist with force if invaded. A peaceful approach is recommended, with the hopes of retaining them as an ally; however, military intervention would be justified to ensure access to the planet's considerable deposits. Control of the planet's energy supplies is and will always be the primary objective, but the humans themselves could prove a valuable resource if properly motivated and controlled.

Note: It is believed the Djarik are not aware of the planet's existence. Therefore it is imperative that we make first contact and establish our presence immediately.

—*Aykari Planetary Scouting Report (translated), Earth year 2044*

LOST AND FOUND

HE PRAYED FOR IT TO STOP. HUDDLED UNDER HIS desk, hands over his ears, elbows poking out like tusks. The sound of the alarm drowned out his own unsteady breathing.

He shouldn't be freaking out like this. He knew it was coming. He'd had fair warning. Mr. Markenson walked his students through the process that morning, reading instructions off an old-fashioned printout.

"Sometime today we are going to have a code gray. The alarms will go off. The doors will autolock and the metal shutters on the windows will drop. Emergency lighting will kick on. Someone from the front office will signal what the code is. When all of that happens, we will huddle under our desks, wrapping our hands around our heads. And we will stay that way until we get the all clear. During that time

I expect you all to be still and remain calm. The drill is expected to take three minutes. Are there any questions?"

Adam Crowley, a kid Leo had never considered likable or even tolerable, raised his hand.

"What's the point? I mean, if the Djarik ever decide to bomb us again, it's not going to help. It's a desk. Not a force field."

Not likable. But he had a point.

"You're right, Adam. Your desk is not a force field. Neither is it a doodle pad nor a trash can nor a chewed-gum depository, yet you seem to think otherwise. The point is to stay orderly and to not panic. We don't know what kind of attack the Djarik might try next. It doesn't hurt to be prepared for any possibility."

Another kid, Milo Clark, raised his hand. "Wait, so you're saying the Djarik are going to break into our school and start shooting us?"

Mr. Markenson gently massaged his forehead. "No, I'm not suggesting . . . Listen, I know what you all are thinking, and I agree, it doesn't seem like much. But in the event of another alien attack, our best option really is to stay put, stay calm, and let the authorities handle it."

"You mean the Aykari."

"He means the Earth Defense Force."

"God will protect us," Angelina Sarden said. "At least, he will protect me. I don't know about the rest of you." She fingered the silver cross around her neck.

"I'd like to see those scaly freaks break into this school," Adam bragged. "I'd take 'em out."

"How?" Milo wanted to know. "Hit them with your lunch box? Maybe stab them with your stylus? You're so full of it. The Djarik would freaking waste you."

Mr. Markenson raised his voice, getting the boys' attention. "Nobody is *wasting* anyone. It's just a drill. Now take out your datapads and pull up your math assignments so we can go over last night's problems."

Leo did as he was told. And he tried to concentrate on his work, but his eyes kept gravitating toward the emergency sign sitting just over the door, waiting for it to start flashing orange. Waiting for the nerve-grating *murr-murr-murr* of the school alarm. Waiting for the moment when he had to pretend the world was ending all over again.

It didn't come in math. It didn't come in science. Not during galactic geography when they learned about the Brennari system (a good source of ventasium, Mr. Markenson said). Not in the middle of lunch where they were served fish sticks again. By afternoon Leo had nearly forgotten about it. Slumped over his desk for silent reading, scrolling through the latest volume of *Infinity League*, he nearly fell out of his chair when the building started to scream. The main overheads immediately shut off, replaced with the fluorescent green glow of the emergency lights running along the baseboard. Leo heard the click of the door, sealing them in, and watched as the eyes of eight windows closed, the steel outer shutters slamming down with a thunderous clang.

"Under your desks everyone!" Mr. Markenson commanded, unlocking and opening the bottom drawer of his own desk to remove his "emergency case," complete with medical kit, walkie-talkie, and high-voltage electrical baton. Every teacher had one and supposedly had been trained in its use, though every teacher Leo had ever met said they hoped to never have to. Not that a Taser would do much good against an armed Djarik marauder anyway. Milo was right: if any of them ever came face-to-face with a Djarik, they were done for. Bend over and kiss your own butt goodbye, as Gareth would say.

Jammed underneath his desk with the alarm blaring in his ears, Leo wasn't picturing Mr. Markenson duking it out with a Djarik soldier, or imagining a platoon of gun-toting aliens dropping out of the sky onto the playground and swarming the school. He was back at the beach. Looking up at the bright light that was burning his eyes. Collapsing into his father's arms. Running hand in hand with his brother back to the car, his dad shouting at the sky.

Principal Riley's voice cut through the bleating alarm.

"This is a code gray. Teachers and students, remain in your classrooms. I repeat. This is a code gray."

Leo squinted up at the speakers mounted into the ceiling. She forgot to say it was just a drill.

It was definitely a drill. Had to be. There couldn't be another attack. It had only been four months since the first one. Four months since his mother hugged him goodbye. He knew it wasn't real, and yet Leo felt the panic seize him, muscles taut, heart racing, breaths quick and shallow. His inhaler was in the front pocket of his backpack, which was hanging from the back of the chair behind him, but he was afraid to move out from under the desk. He hunched over farther, curling himself into a tight ball. The alarms continued to blare. The whole school was shut down, closed off, locked tight.

He realized he was trapped in here.

And the Djarik, they were out there somewhere, he knew, just waiting for the right moment to strike again. Waiting to finish what they'd started.

Leo's stomach lurched. *It's not for real. None of this is really happening.* He closed his eyes and tried to picture her, not on that last day, but before. On the porch. Looking at him. Watching over him.

Be brave, my little lion.

He didn't know how to be brave. He begged for it to stop. And then, finally, it did.

The alarm ceased. Seconds later, the lights triggered on

and the thick metal shades retracted, letting the sun shine through again. Leo heard the door lock give as Mrs. Riley came back over the intercom.

"Teachers and students, this concludes our drill. Good job, everyone. Thank you for your cooperation."

Mr. Markenson stuffed his bag back into his drawer and locked it with his thumbprint. "Okay, troopers, you heard the boss. Drill's over. Back to your books."

Leo saw all the kids around him dislodge themselves from under their desks, rubbing their necks and wiping the dust from their knees. But Leo didn't move.

"You okay there, Leo?"

He was not okay.

That's when everybody saw it: the stinking little puddle of sick on the floor underneath Leo's chin.

"Oh, gross. Fender threw up!" Adam pointed to the remains of Leo's lunch. A chorus of *ews* erupted from the desks nearby.

With a trembling hand, Leo wiped his mouth and crept out from under his desk, face flushed. In five steps his teacher was beside him, a hand on Leo's shoulder. "I'm sorry, Leo," he said. "I didn't even think. . . ."

Leo shook his head. "I don't know what happened," he said, soft enough that he hoped only the teacher would hear. "I guess I just panicked. All the noise and everything . . . it was just too much."

"Don't even worry about it. We'll get it cleaned up. You want me to call the office? They can call your dad and he can come get you."

Leo hesitated. That was exactly what he wanted. But he knew kids like Adam would just tease him even more if he left. Leo Fender—afraid of the freaking *alarm*. He shook his head. There was only an hour left of school. He could stick it out. He could make it to the end of the day at least.

Then and only then would he go home.

Leo screamed Nine's name, but it was too late. The robot's spindly legs started to kick uncontrollably, his torso spinning. The sparks shooting from the gaping hole in his head were soon chased by tendrils of white smoke.

A second blast from the now twice-stolen rifle tore a sizable hunk out of the robot's midsection, causing half of his jointed legs to fold underneath him. A high-pitched whine filled the room, and Leo watched as Number Nine listed sideways and then collapsed into a vibrating metallic heap by the door. He didn't even get a chance to draw his weapons.

Leo stared at the assassin, Number One, blocking the exit, the rifle no longer aimed at the spasming mechanical mess but now pointed across the room at her very own master. The one she was programmed to serve.

"Number One, what have you done?" Crayt demanded.

"Security override. Foundational protocols initiated," the

robot droned. "Zirkus Crayt, you are in violation of your exile. You have been found to be engaged in activity deemed threatening to the empire of Aykar. You will hand over that device immediately and submit yourself to my authority as a designated representative of Aykarian High Command or I will be forced to disable you."

Leo's eyes darted around the room, looking for anything he could use as a weapon, but all he saw were the hand tools on the bench, and even those were out of reach. Crayt was unarmed as well. Besides, he was a scientist, not a soldier. Number Nine was supposed to be his protection.

Number Nine was currently a smoking lump of metal.

The Aykari kept his cool, though, just as he had when Baz shoved a gun under his chin the day before. "Have you been spying on me all this time, Number One? Just waiting for me to do something worthy of the council's attention?"

"You are in violation of the terms of your exile," the robot repeated. "You are engaged in potentially treasonous activity. I insist that you give up control of that device and turn yourself in."

"Of course," Crayt said. "The device. That is what this is about. You told them what I was up to."

"You have been found to be engaged in activity deemed threatening to the empire of Aykar and its resources," the robot repeated. "Turn over the device or I will use force."

Zirkus Crayt clutched his invention even tighter to his

chest. "Number One—I order you to drop that weapon and initiate a temporary shutdown of all systems," he said, his voice increasing in volume, if not ferocity. "You must do as I command."

Leo held his breath, waiting to see if this would work, if somehow Crayt's imprinting as the robot's master overrode whatever deep-seated protocols the Aykari had instilled in her. Every robot has its priorities.

With a pull of the trigger, Number One made hers clear.

The energy bolt from Zennia's rifle hit Zirkus Crayt in his left side, spinning him around. The elemental nullifier slipped from his hands, thudding onto the table, rolling and then dropping to the floor with a heavy clang.

Landing right by Leo's feet. He didn't dare move to grab it.

Crayt stood up straight again, hands pressed to his wound. The Aykari's eyes burned a bright orange now.

"You can kill me. And you can take the device. But you cannot stop what is coming. You tell them. Tell the Council that the Djarik are not the only ones who have seen through their hollow promises. They are not the only ones who will rise up and resist. Sooner or later, one way or another, a reckoning is coming."

Leo's eyes darted from Crayt to the robot to the nullifier at his feet, wondering if he should help the Aykari, try to stop the droid, or save the device—wondering if he could actually pull off any of these—when he caught sight of movement in the corner. A twitch of a leg. The blink of a light.

If Crayt noticed it, he didn't let on. He continued to stare down his attacker, who was threatening to finish the job. "The days of Aykari dominance in the galaxy are numbered. It will not be long before other worlds are finally granted the choice to give you what you want or make certain you never get it. This device will set things in motion that even they will not be able to stop."

Another twitch. Even with two smoking holes in his chassis, there was still some life left in the heap of metal sprawled on the floor. Leo took a deep breath. Readied himself.

"Except you are currently the only one who knows how to create such a device," Number One said mechanically. "And you have been deemed expendable. You have all been deemed expendable."

The first rule of magic, taught to him by his mother. Always give them something else to look at.

The robot readjusted her aim. It was now or never.

Leo lunged for the rifle in One's hands. He hoped she would see him coming. And that she would try to stop him. She did.

The robot struck just as Leo got close, her free hand lashing out, a metal fist landing hard against his jaw, sending him reeling. Now Leo knew why Baz wished Kat had used her human hand that time she punched him. The blow was dizzying, the whole left side of his face suddenly on fire.

But it worked. Leo's feint caused just enough of a distraction that One didn't notice the compartment in Number Nine's twisted and smoking torso sliding open, revealing his blowtorch, still operational. A click. A hiss of gas.

One turned just in time to catch a jet of fire in her face.

In an instant, Nine was up. Sort of. Half of his legs weren't working. Half of his head was missing. The hole in his middle was smoldering, revealing scraps of melted metal. Clearly most of his weapons systems were down because Leo didn't see the rockets or the blasters emerge, but Nine was still a solid chunk of titanium, and he drove his wobbly weight into Number One, sending them both crashing into the wall, the rifle knocked from her hands.

"Leo! The nullifier!" Crayt said, circling around the workbench and picking up the rifle with his good arm.

Leo scooped up the don't-blow-up-the-world device, cradling it like the world's heaviest football, and stumbled into the hall, headed back toward the hangar, vaguely aware of the two robots grappling with each other behind him. His head was ringing, and he could feel the blood dripping down his cheek from where One's fist had broken skin. Crayt stumbled behind him, holding the rifle the wrong way, unless he intended to use it as a club.

"Foolish," he muttered as they hurried down the corridor, away from the brawl happening behind them. "I thought I had reprogrammed her. I should have known. They have probably been watching me this whole time."

As they neared the hangar, Leo could hear different music blasting from Skits's speaker, something grungy with heavy guitar, played loud enough to drown out the sound of Leo shouting Baz's name. He turned the corner into the bay and ran straight into Kat.

"Whoa, Leo. I was just coming to get— Hold up, are you *bleeding*?"

Leo nodded, breathlessly fumbling over his words. "Number One . . . attacked us . . . for this." He held up the nullifier as if that explained everything. Fortunately Crayt was right behind him, eyes still like bonfires.

"The Aykari know what we have been up to. Number One contacted them. She took out Nine. She tried to kill us."

"The Aykari? What are you talking about?" Kat took a good look at Crayt and her eyes grew even bigger. "Wait— were you *shot*?"

Suddenly the music clicked off as the rest of the crew realized something serious was happening. From the top of the *Icarus*, Baz called out, "What in Jupiter's big red butthole is going on down there?" But Leo didn't have time to answer as the corridor behind him erupted in an explosion of robotic fury: Number Nine, stumbling around on three miraculously working legs, crashing off walls, his torso spinning, his half a head chimneying black smoke now, attempting to rid himself of the smaller, more agile Number One, who was hanging on to his back, wielding one of Nine's own legs as a spear, repeatedly driving it into what was left of the bigger bot's central processing unit over and over again.

Leo dove out of the way as the two robots tumbled into the hangar, a dervish of sparking circuits and scorched metal. From his vantage point on the ground, he watched as Number One reared back and drove the amputated leg into what was left of Nine's torso, the sharp metal snapping through wires and piercing the robot's power processor. Nine staggered for a moment like a boxer trying to find his legs, and then collapsed, the last bit of light fading from his only intact sensor.

For a moment there was no movement as the crew of the *Icarus* stared at the shattered remains of Crayt's robotic bodyguard, lying in a smoldering heap. It was less than a second.

But it was still long enough for Number One to look at the back wall of the hangar where all of the hulking black mining bots had been left to gather dust. Her eyes flashed, activating protocols, sending a wake-up call.

Then the entire wall came to life.

Leo had seen mining bots in action before. Back on Earth, swarming the giant chasm outside his hometown, disappearing inside only to hover back out again. They never made contact with humans; there was no need. The Aykari handled all of the elemental extraction themselves. As such, Leo had only ever observed these robotic workers from a distance, like all of those silver ships streaking across the sky.

From far enough away, just about anything looks harmless. From far away, you can't actually see the deadly sharp saws spinning.

The mining bots disengaged from their charging stations, advancing en masse upon the crew. Like Boo, they had four arms each, but unlike Boo, one of those arms ended in a buzz saw and another in a high-speed drill capable of putting a hole through stone. The two remaining appendages tapered down to sharp pincers that Leo knew could crush his bones the way he might snap a twig.

Also, they could fly. Or at least they could hover. Miniature repulsor engines capping off their undercarriage allowed them to levitate. They looked like giant floating spinning tops crossed with something out of a horror movie about a psychopathic dentist.

And they seemed highly interested in Leo. Or in what he was holding.

"Go, Leo!" Kat said, snatching the rifle from Crayt, who looked happy to be rid of it. The next instant she was firing at the closest mining bot, needing three shots just to bring him down. "Seriously, ship rat, run!"

Leo scrambled back up to his feet, then spun around in circles. He would gladly do as ordered, but there wasn't really anywhere to run *to*. Everywhere he looked, pirates were already locked in combat with mechanical miners. There was Baz, still balanced precariously on top of the *Icarus*, his pistol in one hand, a wrench in the other, taking shots however he could get them. To Leo's left stood the Queleti in a twisted arm-wrestling contest, using all his strength to keep a saw from splitting his head. Kat stood in front of Zirkus Crayt, emptying the bounty hunter's rifle of its charge at the oncoming wave.

And then there was Skits, treads leaving marks on the hangar floor as she charged toward Number One, every metal appendage extended, screaming obscenities as loud as her emitter would let her.

"Leo, watch out!" Kat shouted.

Leo ducked just as a spinning saw blade came sweeping down from above, aiming to separate his head from his shoulders. The mining bot turned and bore down on him again, until a volley of energy bolts fired from Kat's stolen rifle sent it reeling.

"Get into the ship!" Baz yelled down at him. "Keep that thing safe!"

Leo nodded, cradling the nullifier closer. The ramp of the *Icarus* was only twenty yards away and the path was mostly clear. He heard another electronic scream from behind followed by an explosion—Skits unleashing her fury—but he didn't dare look, just stayed focused on making it to that ramp. Maybe if he could get aboard the *Icarus* he could find a way to activate its weapons systems, use the turret to take some of these things out before they diced up every member of the crew.

Instead he was forced to a halt, his feet skidding, slipping out from beneath, sending him to the floor as one of the armored attackers suddenly dropped down in front of him. It was missing an arm—the one with the saw, at least—but it still had a set of powerful claws that could snap his limbs in two or pin him down while that drill put a hole through his skull. Its high-pitched whine filled his head.

Leo scrambled backward, still holding tight to Crayt's invention, his kicking feet inches from the bot's snapping pinchers. One foot connected with the robot's heavy frame, not even making a dent in the armor. He felt something grab his leg and squeeze, metal digging into flesh, the pain instant and agonizing.

Leo screamed as loud as he could.

A Queleti's scream, he knew from experience, could strike you with temporary paralysis. It could nearly drive you insane, even with your hands over your ears.

Leo's scream, apparently, could make an armor-plated robot explode.

Because that's exactly what it did. The mining bot's entire upper half shattered right before his eyes. The pain in Leo's leg instantly abated as what was left of his attacker dropped harmlessly to the hangar floor.

Leo blinked, confused, disoriented, staring at the smoking remains of the mechanical monstrosity that had been inches away from Swiss-cheesing his brain.

Then he saw it. The sleek-looking starfighter hovering right outside the open hangar door, its green-haired pilot with her fingers on the trigger of the ship's forward-mounted cannons, pulsing with deadly energy. He recognized ship and pilot instantly.

The last time Leo saw Zennia the bounty hunter, she hadn't seemed all that interested in saving his life. Almost the opposite. But here she was, blasting Leo's attackers to scrap.

He couldn't be sure with all the shouting and the explosions and the screech of saws and drills, but Leo thought he heard Bastian Black let out a curse.

They went down in showers of sparks, one after another, victims of Zennia's deft maneuvering and deadly aim.

Recognizing the much bigger threat, the rest of the hovering, saw-brandishing bots swarmed their new, unwelcome guest, converging on the hangar door, going for the ship's engines with their piercing appendages, all with the hope of sending it crashing down into the artificial canyon below. But the ship's pilot was too good, dodging around them, drawing her attackers out into the open where she could more easily swat them out of the sky, her ship's guns turning them to melted slag one blast at a time.

The bounty hunter was an angel. Had she not arrived when she did, Leo would be leaking out of a half dozen new holes. As it was, he watched as one mining bot after another exploded into a hundred fragments. It looked like fireworks on First Contact Day.

Leo's attention was pulled away from the onslaught by the sound of Skits's high-pitched shout. He twisted just in time to see her looming over the top half of Number One, who lay helpless on the hangar floor. What remained of the Aykari service bot's legs sat in a heap to the side, having been torn from the rest of her. One's right arm was shattered as well, hanging limp from her torso by a couple of wires. She was using her left arm—and what remained of her power cells—to try to crawl away, but it was futile.

"Oooh no. You aren't getting away from me," Skits seethed. Her tanklike treads slowly rolled up and over what was left of Number One's body, crushing it like an old soda can, inch by crinkling inch. "You ruined everything!" She crunched up toward One's head now, moving slowly, no doubt relishing the splinter and fold of One's armored chassis beneath her. There was a hiss and a pop as something inside Number One's chest burst into a bright white flame and then just as quickly fizzled into smoke. The remains of One's torso began to leak hydraulic fluid that spread in a slick pool around her. "We were going to be together forever!"

Leo watched through squinted eyes as Skits continued up

over the neck and slowly crushed One's head beneath her treads, caving in the robot's metal skull, then reversing to flatten it even further. Number One emitted one last electronic wheeze.

"Rot in hell, you boyfriend-murdering scrap heap!"

And just like that, it was over. Number One was little more than a metal pancake. Likewise, her spontaneous army of mining bots had been coaxed from the hangar to their presumed doom—Leo could hear them exploding above the chasm outside.

He pulled himself up, wincing from the sharp pain in his leg. Thankfully the claw had barely even broken the skin. Leo had emerged relatively unscathed.

Crayt was a different story.

Leo moved close to him and inspected the wound in his side. He wasn't entirely sure how the insides of an Aykari worked—lungs, liver, intestines, Leo didn't even know if they had all those things, but he was pretty sure Zirkus Crayt had a heart, because something had to be pumping the silvery blood that soaked through his tunic.

Kat quickly joined them, tearing a swath of Crayt's top with her artificial hand to use as a makeshift bandage. "Here, hold this," she said to Leo. "Put pressure on it."

Leo set the nullifier down gently beside him—still in one piece—and pressed both hands against the wound.

"You worry needlessly," Crayt said, his voice raspy. "The

Aykari have a naturally high tolerance for pain."

"Yeah? What's your tolerance for bleeding out?" Kat asked.

Crayt considered it. "Not as high, I suspect."

Kat turned to Leo. "Stay here. Make sure he doesn't move. I'll get the kit."

Leo nodded. He pressed harder. Crayt groaned. "Sorry," Leo said.

"Do not be sorry. Just tell me . . . is it okay?"

"I mean . . . it's leaking. A lot," Leo admitted, staring at the gaping hole in the Aykari's side.

"I meant the device. Did they damage it?" Crayt asked.

Leo shook his head. "No. It's fine. It's right here."

"That is good," Crayt said. "You did well, Leo Fender. That device . . . its very existence proves what is possible. The knowledge, the capability, the *choice*—that is where the real potential lies. If something should happen to me—"

Leo shook his head. "Nothing's going to happen to you. It's really not that bad," he lied. The blood was already starting to soak through the cloth, sticking to Leo's fingers. It seemed thicker than his own, some of which was already drying on his cheek.

"But if you are wrong," Crayt continued, "it is vital that the information on that datachip be shared with everyone. Not just the people on your planet. Do you understand? They should know the truth about the Aykari and the Djarik both. And they should be given the chance to protect themselves. Promise me, Leo."

"Not so big on promises," Leo admitted. "Besides, I'm just a kid. Nobody's going to listen to me."

"I listened to you," Crayt said. "You showed me what was possible. And you convinced a band of pirates to risk their lives for what you believe in. You have more power than you realize."

There was the sound of bootsteps clanging down a ramp as Kat emerged from the *Icarus*, med kit in hand.

"She's coming," Leo said to Crayt. "You'll be okay now."

But Kat's footfalls were instantly overwhelmed by the sound of a ship's engines as the star-shaped fighter dropped out of the sky, hovering in front of the hangar, its guns pointed at the band of pirates that had gathered together around the wounded Aykari.

"Look alive, people," Baz said, still holding his pistol and his wrench. Kat set the med kit next to Crayt and unslung her rifle.

No. Not hers.

The three landing gears touched down gently, the rear loading ramp extended with a hiss, and Leo heard a voice calling down.

"There you are, Leo. Have a seat."

The moment he walked in, he knew. Even before he saw what his father had dug up, the stash clearly hidden too hastily underneath Leo's bunk. He could tell by the look on his dad's face: he'd been caught, and now he was going to pay for it.

Leo sat in the stiff metal chair beside the fold-down desk and tucked his hands between his wobbling knees. He was afraid to look his father in the eyes. He was just as afraid not to.

"Do you want to tell me why you have a dozen bars of Coalition chocolate stashed underneath your bed?" Dr. Fender began.

It seemed like terrible phrasing—*do you* want *to?* Of course he didn't *want* to, though on some level the answer should have been obvious. While powdered cocoa wasn't difficult to get, actual bars of chocolate were a luxury on board the *Beagle*, only obtained on rare occasions when the trading post they docked at happened to have them in stock. Even then, they were carefully rationed, ensuring that everyone who wanted one got a taste. And everyone always wanted one. Chocolate was a uniquely human invention, and these bars were a sweet reminder of the planet they'd left behind. Four ounces' worth of flashbacks to Easter baskets and valentines.

And so it had been a moment of weakness, but also a moment of longing, when Leo took advantage of a distraction—the ship's provisions officer, Darby, arguing with another crew member about mold on the bread—to pocket as many bars as his pants could hold. It wasn't that difficult; Leo's magician mother had taught him how to slip things into his pockets or up his sleeves without anyone noticing. The difficulty came in convincing himself that he could . . . even knowing that he shouldn't.

That, and the flutter in his stomach that had formed the moment he did it. The theft occurred yesterday, and all day today Leo fretted. It was the first time he'd ever stolen anything, the guilt gnawing its way through him, causing him to sweat through his shirt. And yet, coming back to the room after his morning lessons, Leo was still debating in his head whether or not to turn himself in or to unwrap one of the pilfered bars and go to town.

The decision had been made for him.

"Well?" his father prodded.

Leo answered with a shrug.

"Hmph," Dr. Fender grunted. "I can't express just how disappointed I am right now, Leo. I know it can be hard sometimes. Stuck on this ship. Eating the same meals over and over again. And then something comes along that's a little special. Something that maybe even reminds you of home a little bit. And you want that something to last. We all do. But this . . . this is *wrong*. We have rules for a reason. You do realize that each one of these represents someone on this ship who didn't get what was coming to them? What they deserved? And all because *you* decided to be selfish."

"But I . . . ," Leo started to say.

"But you what?" his father asked, raising his voice a notch.

But I couldn't help it, he thought. Leo knew that wasn't true, though. Of course he knew the rules. The truth was, he was tired of playing by them. Tired because he'd never agreed to them in the first place. He hadn't agreed to come on board this ship. Hadn't agreed to wear the same pair of Coalition boots day in and day out. Hadn't agreed to drink powdered juice or to share a room with his brother or to spend years without smelling grass or watching raindrops spatter against a window. He hadn't agreed to leave his cat and his friends and his house and his planet and his entire life behind in order to spend years—*years*—wandering through a cold ship, caught in an endless vacuum. He hadn't asked for any of this; it had all been decided for him, even down to how much chocolate he could have. And Leo was sick of it.

But he couldn't tell his father that, because he knew what his dad would say. That what they were doing was important. That the ship provided the necessities. That they were safe. That they had each other, which, really, should be enough.

And that if everyone decided to break the rules there would be no order to the universe. Only chaos and conflict. Rules were what made peace and cooperation possible. Leo had gotten that lecture before. Just never a satisfactory explanation for why some people could still get away with breaking them.

"Listen, Dad . . . can I just say—" Leo began, but he was interrupted by the door sliding open to reveal his brother.

"Hey. What's going on in here? Is the ship being sucked

into a black hole or some . . . thing . . . ?"

Gareth's voice petered out as he took in the scene: Dad on the bed. Leo squirming in the interrogation chair. The pile of chocolate. The frown of disappointment. It wasn't hard to put it all together.

Gareth's eyes found Leo's—held there for a moment, transmissions sent and received—then Gareth let his head drop. "I see you found them," he said.

"The chocolate bars your brother stole from the ship's commissary? Yes. I found them. Did you know about this, Gareth? Because if you knew, you should have told me."

"Of course I knew," Gareth said quickly, even a little smartly. "I'm the one who took them."

What? Leo thought.

"What?" Dr. Fender said.

"*Those* chocolate bars?" Gareth said, pointing to the pile of foil-wrapped treasures piled by Leo's pillow. "Yeah, I took them yesterday. Snatched 'em while Darby wasn't looking. That guy is oblivious. I knew when the chocolate ran out it was back to freeze-dried ice cream and watery instant pudding, so I decided to stock up."

Leo's eyes hopped from Gareth to Dad and back again. He knew *what* was happening. He just didn't know *why*.

"That's interesting," Dr. Fender mused, "because your brother has already said it was him."

Actually, Leo hadn't. Though his hangdog expression

might have admitted it a thousand times over, he'd never said out loud, *it was me.*

"*Leo?*" Gareth scoffed, even going so far as to give his brother a condescending look. "You seriously think Leo would *steal* something? Come on, Dad. This is the same kid who wouldn't pick up a quarter off the street because he figured somebody might come back for it."

"But they were under your brother's bunk," their father said.

"I know. That's where I put them. Besides," Gareth added, finally blunting the sarcasm in his voice, "they weren't *just* for me, you know. I was going to share. I got them for all of us."

Leo saw his father's face soften a bit, though the frown remained, accompanied now by narrowed eyes. Dr. Fender was an incredibly astute man, or so Leo was constantly told by those who admired him. His father knew when he was being played. Which meant he had to know that Gareth was lying.

But for some reason, he let it slide. Let his elder son take the fall.

"Very well," he said. "Gather them up. We're taking them back to the commissary immediately where you will apologize to Darby and then volunteer to clean the mess hall for the next week."

"But . . ."

"Unless he or I decide to make it two."

For a second, Leo thought his brother was going to buckle, to recant his fake confession and toss Leo back under the bus where he rightfully belonged. But Gareth held firm, nodding solemnly and then stacking the chocolate bars neatly on top of each other.

As he did, Leo noticed Gareth slyly push one of the bars underneath the blanket on Leo's bed. Their father didn't see because he'd turned back to his younger son, still shrinking in his chair. He stared at Leo for five agonizing seconds.

"Next time, just tell me the truth," he said finally.

Leo stayed seated as Dr. Fender led the newly condemned from the room, stack of stolen chocolate bars in hand, ready to apologize for a crime he didn't even commit.

Only once they were gone and the door was sealed shut did Leo take the treasure from where Gareth had tucked it, stuffing it into one of his brother's running shoes instead, hoping they could share it later.

He and his brother, in it for the long haul together.

He heard her voice calling down to them and instantly Leo was back on that bridge on Vestra, lying on the ground, buffeted by the howling wind, sucking wind himself, having just saved Boo from plummeting to his death as the bounty hunter approached.

Zennia was here. She'd found them. Again. Except this time it wasn't Leo's name she called.

"Bastian Black . . ."

The captain stood in front of Leo, who was still kneeling next to Crayt, hands wet with the Aykari's shiny blood. Zennia stood at the top of the ramp, just out of sight.

"Tell your crew to holster their weapons. I just want to talk."

"No offense, Zenn," Baz called up to her, "but our last conversation got real awkward real fast. If I recall, one of your drones put a hole in Boo, and you tried to put one in my head, so you'll understand if I'm not really in a mood to catch up. Besides, things are a little tense out here. My robot just lost her first boyfriend and I've got an exiled Aykari scientist bleeding on the floor."

Not to mention the whole blowing-up-planets thing, Leo thought.

"You'd *all* be bleeding on the floor if I hadn't shown up," Zennia said. "Believe me, if I had wanted you dead, I could have waited another ninety seconds for those bots to finish the job. So do me a favor and put your guns away."

Baz looked at Kat. "What do you think? She *did* just save our necks."

"Yeah. Probably so she could get the satisfaction of snapping them herself," Kat countered, but Baz was already holstering his pistol. With a frustrated groan, Kat slung the rifle back over her shoulder. "Fine, but if she shoots you this time, it's your own fault."

"Put it in the sequel," Baz said. Then he called up, "All right, Z. Let's talk."

Leo stayed crouched beside Crayt and watched warily as the bounty hunter emerged. She looked much the same as last time, clad in the same tarnished brown armor, the scuffed boots hiked up to her knees, her goggles hanging loose around her neck. His stomach clenched when he saw the set of pistols latched to her sides, but that was better than already in her hands. She stopped at the bottom of the ramp and looked around the hangar.

"Yeah . . . this looks like you," she said, taking in the blaster holes, the bleeding alien, the smoking robot corpses, including the one Skits was dutifully parked beside. "Should have guessed you'd be hiding out in an abandoned mining town on the edge of the galaxy."

"Must not have hidden *too* well," Baz replied. He nodded up at her ship. "I see you managed to get ahold of some V."

"*And* repair my flight console, no thanks to you. Though my cockpit's still a wreck."

"That was mostly Skits," Baz deflected, holding up his hands. "And you sort of asked for it. Not that I think we should be assigning blame or anything."

"Pretty sure your robot wasn't the one who pissed all over my pilot's seat," she said.

"Please tell me you didn't," Kat said.

Baz scratched the back of his head guiltily. Boo scrunched his nose in disgust. Zennia pointed at Crayt. "Who's the Aykari getting his insides everywhere?"

Crayt tried to pull himself up to answer her but managed only a grunt of pain. Leo whispered for him to be still. "He's a friend," Baz said.

Zennia laughed. "A friend?"

"Okay. More of a business associate. We're working on a project together. Sort of a top-secret, fate-of-the-galaxy kind of thing."

"Since when do you do business with the Aykari? Weren't you the one who told me they were heartless, soulless imperialists who only care about themselves?"

"Yeah, well, things have gotten . . . complicated," Baz admitted.

"Things were always complicated."

"Not like this," Baz said. "How did you find us, anyway?"

"Tracking device. Same as before."

Baz turned to Kat, his eyebrows pinched in frustration. "You said you got *rid* of the tracking device."

"I *did*," she hissed. "I found it on the hull tucked beside the aft storage compartment. I showed it to you, remember?"

"That was Grimsley's tracker you found," Zennia explained. "The one he stuck on your ship back at Kaber's Point. You didn't find mine because you were the ones who put it on the ship yourselves."

She nodded toward the rifle hanging from Kat's shoulder.

"Hold up . . . you bugged your freaking *gun*?" Kat asked. "What kind of crazy psycho does that?" She looked down at the rifle in disbelief. "Where'd you even put it?"

"In the butt."

Baz chuckled. Kat shot him a please-grow-up look.

"It's not that crazy," Zennia continued. "I love that gun. I figured if anyone ever took it—and I was still alive—I would have a good reason to hunt them down and get it back. I've brought in thirty bounties with that gun. I slayed a two-headed wharbeast with that gun. I *sleep* with that gun."

"It's true, she does," Baz said, then shrugged, pink cheeked. "I mean, at least she *used* to, you know, back when . . . Forget it, doesn't matter, the important thing is *we're* all still alive, thanks to you. And *you're* still alive—which is, honestly, thanks to us, seeing as how that's how we left you. So now you can just take your rifle back and we can call it even."

"Except you still have something I want," the bounty hunter said. Her eyes fell on Leo. He noticed Kat take a step closer to him. Saw Boo's hair bristle.

"You're still after the *kid*?" Baz asked.

"As far as I know, the bounty's still out for him. Him and his brother both. Somebody out there wants them, and I intend to collect."

Baz snorted dismissively. "Good luck with that. I mean first off, if you want Leo, you're going to have to go through us, and we've got you outnumbered."

"You had me outnumbered last time," Zennia pointed out.

"Yeah, and you saw how that turned out."

Leo tried not to imagine what the bounty hunter's cockpit smelled like.

"Secondly, that bounty you're so eager to cash in on? Pretty sure it originated with the Djarik as part of a deal to get Leo's father to work with them—the terms of which have changed considerably since we last talked, so I'm guessing ninja turtle here isn't worth much anymore, no offense, Leo."

Leo shook his head. He didn't mind being worthless if it meant trained killers weren't tracking him down.

"Thirdly," Baz continued, "even if the Fender boys *are* still worth something to somebody, good luck finding the other one. Even his own family doesn't know where he is. The Djarik lost track of the ship he was on, and nobody knows what happened to him. So even if we were to let you walk out of here with Leo—which we won't—you're not going to be able to collect anyway."

Leo held his breath, waiting to see what the bounty hunter would do. Baz was right: they had her outgunned. And Leo believed him when the captain said there was no way they would turn Leo over to her. Not without a fight. And they were already in a fighting mood.

Zennia shook her head. "Oh Baz. Don't you ever get tired of being wrong?"

She turned and ascended back into her ship without another word.

Baz cocked one eyebrow, surprised. Or suspicious. Probably both.

Kat shook her head. "Um . . . did you actually just talk your way out of something?"

Beside Leo, Crayt moaned again. His eyes were closed now, his breathing ragged. "It's okay," Leo whispered, bending close. "You're going to be okay." He thought of all the times his brother had told him the same thing. How Leo had always wanted to believe it because it was Gareth who said so. He reached for the med kit, but the sound of more steps on the ramp stole his attention again.

Zennia had reemerged, her weapons still holstered.

Except this time, she wasn't alone.

The optimist thinks this is the best of all possible worlds. The pessimist fears it is true.

—*J. Robert Oppenheimer*, lead scientist on the Manhattan Project

THE MAGIC WORD

GARETH WAS HERE.

His brother was *here*. Right in front of him.

Stand up, Leo told himself. *Get to your feet.*

He wanted to, but his legs felt like tissue. His whole body shook. His brain repeated the same thing over and over—that this was real, not a hologram, not a hallucination—but his heart just wouldn't accept it. Not because it didn't want to, but because it wanted to so badly. Because if somehow this *wasn't* real, if it was a trick of some kind, that would be the end of it; that doubting heart of his would break.

Then he heard his brother's voice. "Leo?"

The bounty hunter stepped aside, letting her prisoner come down the ramp, parting the crew of the *Icarus*, who stood equally dumbfounded as Gareth pulled Leo to his feet at last, taking him in, swallowing him up. Undeniably real.

He had been told to go find his brother, but somehow his brother had found him instead. Like every game of tag they had ever played—he should have known Gareth would catch up to him first.

Leo buried his face in his brother's shoulder and sobbed. It wasn't the first time he'd done so. It wasn't the tenth or even the twentieth. Gareth held him like he did all those other times. "Shush. I've got you, Leo. I've got you. I'm here."

"But how?" Leo said at last, trying to wrap his head around the impossibility of it, with all the time and the distance between them. Statistically there was no way that the universe could have seen fit to bring them back together. But then Leo remembered what his mother had told him, about how big—or rather, how small—the universe *could* be, all contained within the space between his head and his heart. "I wasn't sure I'd ever see you again."

"I wasn't sure you'd ever see me again either," Gareth said, laughing weakly. He took a sniffling Leo by the shoulders and held him at arm's length. He nodded at the smudge of blood on Leo's cheek. "You're hurt."

"Got punched by a robot," Leo said, then pointed toward the corridor. "*That* one."

"The one with the treads playing sad pop music or the spidery one it's trying to put back together?"

"The flattened one on the floor who tried to have us all

killed," Leo answered. "It's been a rough couple of days."

"Tell me about it," Gareth said.

Leo looked closer at his brother. There were scratches and bruises on his arm, a small but deep cut on his chin that had already scabbed over. His hair was a nest of tangles, longer than Leo had ever seen it. The bags beneath his eyes had not disappeared since Leo saw him last. The uniform was new, though. His shirt bore the standard patch, the same one sitting in Leo's pocket, but you could tell it was fresh by the lack of holes or stains. He wondered where his brother had found it. Wondered where his brother had been. Wondered how he'd ended up in Zennia's hands. He didn't even know where to get started in the asking.

Gareth touched Leo's cheek. "Leo, I'm so sorry."

"Why? You're not the one who hit me."

"It's still my fault you got hurt. It's my fault we weren't together. My fault you're here with these . . . criminals. I was supposed to look after you. Dad *told* me to, and I didn't. I screwed up. The moment I closed that hatch I regretted it. I wanted to take it back, but it was too late. You were gone."

"Not for good, though," Leo said. "You found me. Just like you said you would. Besides . . . they're not as bad as you think." Leo glanced at the Baz, Kat, and Boo, still facing off with Zennia, caught up in a muted conversation of their own. "They actually saved me. They helped me."

"Helped you what?"

Leo looked at his brother's patch—at the planet Aykar at the center, dwarfing the smaller planets encircling it. There was so much Gareth probably didn't know, so much Leo had to tell him, but one thing that mattered more than the rest. "They helped me find Dad."

His brother shook his head. "What?"

"He's alive, Gareth. I've seen him."

Then Leo told his brother that he should probably sit down. That they should probably both sit down. Because this next part was a doozy.

It was Gareth who saw it first. If it weren't for his brother, Leo might not have even noticed. And then he wouldn't have had the chance to stop it.

They'd happened upon it by accident, playing on the swings in the backyard, their mother at work, their father squirreled away in his office, he and Gareth pretending they were deep space explorers, zipping from one system to the next, looking for new planets to invade. The swings were their starfighters, one for each of them. To activate the jump into hyperspace you had to swing as high as possible and then actually jump off. Gareth was fearless, naturally, arcing out over the yard at maximum elevation, always landing upright, unlike Leo, who slowed down just before taking the leap, giving himself a countdown and closing his eyes, then stumbling awkwardly once his feet found the ground. It didn't stop him, of course—whatever his brother would do, he would do. Just not as well.

Gareth had just made his fourth jump, this time to the made-up planet of Targis, which was rumored to be populated by talking dinosaurs, when he crouched in the grass, staring intently.

"Hey, Leo, come check this out."

Leo dragged his feet, slowing his momentum, then hopped off his swing with a stutter step. As he approached he could see tiny movement in the grass were his brother knelt.

"I think they found an intruder," Gareth said.

Leo crouched next to him to get a better look. What he saw was startling enough for him to skip a breath.

A bug, a beetle judging by its hard coat of arms, black plated segments with yellow stripes like banners streaking down its back. The beetle was nearly the size of Leo's thumb—the kind of thing that would give you a heart attack if you found it sitting in your bathtub—but out here its Goliath-like stature was no match for its attackers.

Ants. Large reddish-brown ones. At least two dozen, attacking the beetle from all angles, their mandibles seeking out and carving through any soft spot they could find. Already Leo could see they'd removed one of the giant's back legs and were sawing through another. Two ants had latched on to the beetle's underbelly and many more were swarming over the top. Their intent was clear. They meant to dismantle and then devour the bigger insect on the spot.

Leo was witnessing a murder in his own backyard.

"I've never seen ants do this," Gareth said. "Have you?"

Leo shook his head. Part of him wanted to forget he saw it, go back to their game, hop in his hyperswing, and go dinosaur hunting, but he couldn't bring himself to look away. Pound for pound the beetle should have been able to quash any one of its attackers, trapping it between its more formidable pincers, but the bigger bug was too slow, its assailants too many, its injuries already crippling it to the point that escape was impossible. The ants scurried and swarmed, finding all of the holes in the giant's armored hull. The beetle took a lumbering step. Then another. One leg quivered. Its head thrashed back and forth.

"What do we do?"

"What do you mean, what do we do?" Gareth asked back.

"Shouldn't we save it somehow? It's going to die."

"You want to *save* it?"

"Don't you?" Leo asked. But the look on his brother's face told Leo plenty. Gareth hadn't even considered the idea.

"It's nature, Leo. That's just how it is. Survival of the fittest. Didn't they teach you that in school?"

"Yeah, but you said yourself you've never seen ants act like this." Leo remembered his science teacher saying something about how changes in the environment had actually caused some animal species to react differently, to go against their normal behaviors. Many were becoming more aggressive. Others had learned to live in new biomes or changed their diet to cope with a dwindling food supply. Maybe these ants were protecting their home, but to Leo's eyes *they* looked like the invaders. They were hunters. The beetle was prey.

Prey that stumbled again, listing to one side like a boat tossed upon a wave. "It's hurt," Leo said.

"Dad would say to just let it go. We shouldn't interfere."

"And what would Mom say?"

Gareth didn't answer. Just gave Leo a look.

Leo bent close. The beetle twitched, then lunged, one last attempt to get away, but another vicious bite caused its front legs to buckle.

Let it go. Maybe that *is* what their father would say, but Leo couldn't. He bent even closer so that his nose was only an inch from the suffering insect, took a deep breath, and blew it out sharply, a sudden gust that caused most of the marauders to scatter, but not all. Some of the ants were still latched on tight, so with two fingers Leo pinched the beetle gently by its abdomen, lifting it from the battlefield like the hand of God. With his other hand Leo brushed the last few ants off, one of them scurrying across his finger before being shaken to the ground.

The wounded beetle whipped and writhed in Leo's grip, its four remaining legs pistoning helplessly.

"What are you going to do with it?" Gareth asked.

"I'm saving it," Leo said. "I'm going to find it a new home."

He glanced around until his eyes fell on the cherry tree across the yard. Hopefully it was far enough away that the posse of ants wouldn't go hunting for it. Leo carried the squirming bug over and gently set it at the base of the tree, depositing it on a soft, pink petal like a babe in a crib. The beetle sat there, motionless, and Leo thought he was too late, that its injuries had overwhelmed it and his efforts were for nothing, but then its spindly legs began to move again, and the armored warrior hobbled off its flowery bed, slowly making its way toward the fence line.

Gareth stood next to Leo, watching. "Congratulations. You're a hero."

Leo thought he was being sarcastic, but he couldn't be sure. "You think I wasn't supposed to?"

"I don't think there was a *supposed to* in this case."

The beetle struggled to pull itself over a tree root with only four of its legs. "Do you think he's going to make it?"

"I don't know, Leo," Gareth said. "But you gave it a chance, at least." He reached over and mussed Leo's hair. "Come on. We better get back to our ships. I think I hear dinosaurs stomping this way."

Leo took one last look at the insect now disappearing into the grass, then turned and chased his brother back to the swings, already one step behind.

✳   ✳   ✳

For once, Gareth was the one playing catch-up.

They sat with their backs to the wall of the hangar, a battlefield of blasted metal, pieces of mining bot strewn about. Skits was still parked beside the body of Nine, though she had given up on trying to put him back together. A song Leo didn't recognize moaned softly out of her speaker as she gently caressed Nine's blackened torso with one of her extendable claws.

The others still hovered around Crayt while Kat finished her patchwork, rubbing on the same ointment that Leo had once had to smear on Boo, the stuff that made the Queleti itch. The healing balm was of Aykari design, meaning Crayt was, in some way, getting a taste of his own medicine. He at least seemed to be taking it better than Boo had. Meanwhile, Baz and Zennia appeared to be locked in an intense discussion, though they were keeping their voices down and, perhaps even more surprising, their pistols holstered.

Leo wondered if they were talking about him. Or him and Gareth both. Gareth was Zennia's bounty, after all. Her prize. He'd already told Leo how she'd found him at a Coalition outpost, using her former military connections to track him down the moment he appeared in their database. How he'd begged her to let him go so that he could try to find his brother. How she'd said that he was in luck, because she was looking for Leo as well. Not to mention that she had a good idea where to find him.

And now she had them both in one place.

Baz was right, though: Leo doubted the bounty on the Fender boys' heads was still good anymore. And even if it was, they had much bigger things to worry about. Namely a list of planets that the Djarik were threatening to destroy, with Earth sitting right at the top.

Besides, Leo had already made up *his* mind: No matter what Baz and Zennia were arguing about, there was no way Leo was going anywhere without Gareth. Not ever again. Whether they were stuck with pirates or bounty hunters, Djarik or Aykari, trapped on a desolate planet or floating in the middle of space on board a crippled ship, Leo wasn't letting his brother out of his sight.

"So let me get this straight," Gareth said, his hands cupped around his neck, head between his bent knees as if he was sweating through a code gray, "the Djarik blackmailed Dad into helping them create a weapon that uses a planet's own ventasium as a kind of bomb."

Leo nodded.

"And they are going to use it to attack the Earth. *Again*."

Another nod.

"So Dad sent *you* here to find *that* guy to help you stop it." Gareth pointed at Crayt, still laid out on the hangar floor.

His brother had gotten the highlight reel down, at least.

"And we found a way," Leo said. "At least we think we have."

"Yeah, you and this Aykari scientist. Except now you're

saying that the Aykari are partly responsible for what happened on Earth the first time? For what happened to Mom?" Gareth shook his head. "I'm sorry, Leo. It's just a lot to take in. I mean, the Aykari have always been our allies. They've only ever helped us. And Dad helping the Djarik? I mean, how can *any* of this be true?"

Gareth was floundering; Leo could see it in his eyes. And he couldn't blame him. Leo had had a couple of days to process it and he still had doubts. "I could show you the message," he suggested. "The one from Dad."

Gareth nodded. Leo tapped on his watch. He whispered a curse.

"What is it?"

"This stupid thing," Leo spat. "It's been acting up ever since I downloaded the files Dad gave me. Glitching out. Rebooting. Cycling through random programs. Now it just keeps saying 'searching'. . . . It won't even let me turn it off."

He took off the watch and handed it to Gareth, who tried all the same things Leo had, the taps and swipes, pressing all the buttons. "Maybe it's trying to connect to something. Have you tried hooking it up to a more powerful coms system? I mean, this thing's got a pretty limited range, but this facility probably has a radar. Worth a shot."

Leo shrugged. "Except I have no idea how to do that."

He looked across the hangar to the entrance and the robot still pumping painful ballads out of her speaker. Skits didn't even turn to look at them as they approached. Not that she needed to. She had sensors in the back of her head. "Go away, Leo. I can't deal with you right now."

Leo took in what was left of Nine. The wires with their blackened tips. The hydraulic fluid leaking from twisted joints. There was the compartment with the rocket launcher, all dented in. And there was his central processor, torn free from his thorax and shattered to pieces, taking with it all of his memory. Nothing left to salvage.

"Skits, I'm sorry," Leo said softly. "He was . . ." He searched for the right words, then remembered there were no right words. None that anybody had ever shared with him, anyway.

"He was a robot," Skits said. "It's fine. You can say it. I know that's what everybody's thinking. He was just a machine. Just fuses and gears, microchips and metal plates welded together. So why get all worked up about it?" Skits couldn't cry. She was incapable of it. That was something else they had in common, he guessed.

Leo bowed his head. "I was actually going to say that I thought he was really brave. He saved us back there, you know? Even though he was hurt, he kept fighting. He was awesome."

"He *was* awesome," Skits agreed. She let out a mechanical groan. "I didn't know anything could feel like this."

We're all entitled to our adaptable emotional algorithms, Leo thought. He reached over and placed a hand on the robot's chassis. "It hurts a lot at first, but then a little bit less as it goes."

He didn't tell her the other part—that it never completely goes away, no matter how much time passes. He guessed she'd figure that out on her own.

At last Skits straightened herself up, the music stopping abruptly. She swiveled around to smile at Gareth. "So this is your brother? The one you kept whining about? He's cuter than you."

Leo ignored the compliment/insult and held his watch out to her. "Do you think you could hook this up to the facility's com systems? I'd ask Crayt to do it, but . . . you know . . ."

"He was shot and left for dead by a silver-plated, steel-hearted, double-crossing robotic scum-sucking backstabber?" Skits glanced at the mashed metal carcass that used to be Number One, then used her extendable claw to pluck the watch out of Leo's hand. "Yeah, let me see what I can do."

He and Gareth followed her to a console on the back wall. One appendage popped from her torso and locked into the computer interface receptacle while another plugged into the watch's port.

"We were going to watch the sunset together, you know. He said the scattering of the ultraviolet wavelengths some-times overheated his photoreceptors. He was sensitive like that," Skits mused. "All right. Connection established." Random code ran faintly across the console's screen. "It's using the old Aykari servers as a relay for widespread data retrieval, though it's also using encryption to make sure it's not intercepted. Does this thing have a virus?"

Leo looked at his watch face, which was really freaking out now, flashing different colors and strings of unrecognizable symbols. He thought back to Cerebro, picturing Mac stretched out in his chair, shaking uncontrollably while a digital spider drove its fangs into his avatar. He was about to tell Skits to disconnect, afraid that somehow his watch *had* been corrupted, when the robot said, "Hold up, I think it found something."

"Found what?" Gareth asked.

"I'm not sure. It's locked behind security. It's asking for a passcode. Only five characters."

"A passcode?" Leo shook his head. The watch used some old-fashioned fingerprint identification technology, but nothing nearly as antiquated as a passcode. "I have no idea."

"It can be numerals or letters. It's not zero-zero-zero-zero-zero. It's not zero-zero-zero-zero-one. Not zero-zero-zero-zero-two, -three, -four, -five, -six. Should I keep going? I can cycle through all the possibilities, but the connection is weak, and I'm afraid we might lose it. Assuming English characters and Arabic numerals, there are only sixty million combinations. Of course incorporating other alphanumeric systems, the possibilities are nearly infinite. It would take eons."

"Try two-six-E-four-U," Gareth said. Leo shot him a look. "What? It's *possible*."

"Nope. That wasn't it," Skits said. "And I'm afraid there is a lockout measure in place. Looks like we only have three more tries."

Three more tries to get to what? The watch had been freaking out since he'd downloaded those files. The message to Crayt sent by Leo's father.

His father. What if his dad was trying to send another one? What if he'd found a way to use Leo's watch to contact him? Leo started snapping his fingers in his brother's direction. "Quick. Magic word. Something only Dad or us would have thought of."

Not *Fender*. Not *family*. Not *Beagle*. All too many letters. They couldn't guess blindly; there were as many guesses as there were planets in the universe, and they only had three tries left.

Planets in the universe.

"Try Earth," Leo said. "E-A-R-T-H."

"I know how to spell 'Earth,' Leo," Skits scoffed. "And no. That wasn't it either. Two tries remaining."

"And then what?" Gareth asked.

"Beats me, older, taller, cuter Leo. I'm guessing we will be locked out permanently. The message, if there is one, will be irretrievably lost. Or maybe the watch will self-destruct and blow up the entire console, taking us with it. Impossible to tell."

"I've got it. What's like, the most important thing in the universe?" Gareth prompted. "The thing Dad pretty much devoted his entire life to?"

"EL-four eighty six," Leo said. Of course. That had to be it.

"Strike two," Skits said. "One more strike and you are disqualified." Clearly Baz had never explained baseball that well to her either.

Leo shut his eyes and tried to think, but it was impossible. His brain didn't work the same way his father's did. Never had, probably never would. The passcode could be anything, and yet it would have to be something they shared. Something that mattered just as much to Leo as it did to him. Something that was the most important in *their* universe.

Leo felt his head pulse, his heart pound.

He had it.

"Grace," he said. "Try Grace. G–R–A–C–E."

"Are you sure, Leo? This is your last chance."

"Just try it."

Leo stared at Skits, waiting for a response. Finally she said, "Passcode accepted." Then, a moment later, "Message retrieved."

Suddenly Leo's watch vibrated as its holographic projector kicked on, displaying a familiar face.

"Dad," Gareth whispered.

Except it wasn't the video that Leo had originally set out to show him, the one begging Zirkus Crayt for help.

This one was new, and it was addressed to his son.

Telling him goodbye.

She always waved from the open door. Every morning before school. He could see her from the corner, looking back over his shoulder as the autobus pulled up. She would never embarrass him by waiting at the stop with him—he had Gareth to protect him, after all, though once they were on the bus, Leo was on his own, his bigger brother sitting in the back with his friends. Leo always sat on the right side so he could wave back to her through the window, nothing obnoxious, just one hand pressed to the glass.

And when he came home, she was there again. The front door open so she could hear the bus's electric whine as it pulled into the stop and be ready. She would take a break from her work to come stand on the porch again, clutching a cup of coffee, of course, leaning against the doorframe next to the family plaque, the wooden wind chimes calling the Fender boys home with a ti-di-a-li. He would run to her, backpack bouncing, smile stretched, while Gareth sauntered coolly behind.

Rare was the day she wasn't waiting for them—when she had an appointment or was too caught up in her work. Those were the days Leo got off the bus with a heavy step, his backpack weighing him down, wishing for an open door. Coming home just wasn't the same if Gareth had to fish out his key.

He would still see her sometimes. In the days after. Days when the door was always shut. He'd catch her just out of the corner of his eye. In the flicker of light captured by a shard of broken glass. In the window of a passing car. Just a glimpse. Quick as a blink. He knew it was his imagination, but he felt her presence everywhere. In the unfinished novel that his dad still kept on her nightstand, the old shoelace she used as a bookmark showing she'd only made it halfway. Tucked away in the spice rack gathering dust on the kitchen counter or her blue bicycle leaning against the side of the garage. He'd see the last apple sitting in the crisper and think of the time she took him to the orchard and lifted him to her shoulders so that he could get the ones his giant brother couldn't even reach. Matching socks from the basket of clean laundry, remembering how she would slip one over her hand, bringing it to life, transforming it into a snake determined to eat Leo's nose. The chair she always sat in at dinner. The train of colored scarves that she'd pulled from his ears.

But never when he got off the bus. He could not find her then. Only the closed door. The empty porch. And the mournful sound of wind and hollowed wood whispering goodbye.

✳ ✳ ✳

Leo pressed even closer to his brother as the message played a second time. They both needed to hear it again, just to be sure.

"*Leo,*" the message began. "*I pray that this works and that you get this in time. I hope that if you do, you have already found Zirkus Crayt and that he was able to use the data I provided to find an answer, because I have none. I have failed, Leo. The Djarik have finished the weapon and are moving forward with their plans to test it on Earth. Moreover, I am almost certain they suspect me of attempting to sabotage their efforts. I know that I have already asked so much of you, more than I have a right to, but the attack on our planet is imminent. If there is some way to save it . . . any way . . .*"

His father's image shifted as if the recording had been paused and then restarted. His dad's voice had shifted as well—no longer the earnest entreaty for help, but now infused with a kind of quiet resignation.

"*I know I said that I would come and find you. I see now that is a promise I won't be able to keep, and that is my greatest failure and biggest regret. But no matter what happens, we will see each other again. We will wait for you, your mother and I. We will wait for you and your brother both when you finally come home.*"

The holo ended and Leo stared at the empty space where his father had been.

Gareth reached for Leo's hand. Squeezed tight.

"Skits, can you tell when that message was sent?" Leo asked.

"According to the Djarik time stamp it would be less than five Earth hours ago."

"So? What does *that* mean?" Gareth asked.

"It means we don't have much time."

Leo looked over his shoulder to see that Baz had come up behind him, along with Kat and Boo. Zennia stood a pace apart from the crew, keeping her distance but still clearly listening. "That is, if we're not too late already," the captain added.

Leo squared up with Baz. "We have to go. You saw the message. We have to do something now. Warn the Coalition. Warn the Aykari."

"The Aykari? Leo, the only Aykari I even *sort of* trust is lying nearly unconscious behind me, and he's already said they'd never willingly jeopardize Earth's entire supply of V, even if it means saving our skins. Cold calculus, remember?"

Leo nodded. Without its supply of ventasium the Earth probably meant nothing to them.

"Forget the Aykari," Baz continued. "This is in our hands now. We know Crayt's device works—"

"Actually . . ." Leo pressed two fingers together, leaving a little bit of space between them. Somewhere between 3 and 8 percent.

"Okay, we know it will *probably* work. I think our best bet is to beat them to the punch. Get there before the Djarik. Try to convince the EDF of what they're up against and that we have a way to stop it."

"And if they won't listen?" Kat asked.

Baz shrugged. "We're pirates. Since when do we play by anyone else's rules? They say no, we'll do it anyway." He turned to the bounty hunter. "How about it, Z? You in?"

Zennia looked skeptical, one hand fiddling with the goggles around her neck. "I don't know, Baz. Wiping out the Earth's entire supply of four eighty six? Is that really a decision this particular group should be making?"

"Better us than them," Leo said.

Baz nodded. "You heard the kid. It's our planet. Not the Aykari's. Not the Djarik's. It's not some military objective, or some giant ventasium dispenser. For most of us it's the first place we called home."

Zennia bowed her head. "You always were more trouble than you're worth."

"Which is eight thousand pentars, last time I checked," Baz said. "So does that mean you're in?"

"Fine," she said. "But we need a plan. We can't just jump into Earth's orbit and expect a handshake and a how-do-you-do. Most of us are wanted fugitives."

"Hate to admit it, but your crazy ex-girlfriend is right," Kat agreed. "As soon as they ID the *Icarus*, we're in trouble."

Baz chewed on his lip for a moment. Then the captain's

eyes fell on the transport sitting between the bounty hunter's fighter and the pirates' ship. "Maybe they'll be less apt to attack us if we're being escorted by an Aykari craft."

"Maybe," Kat acknowledged, "except Crayt's clearly in no shape to pilot that thing."

"No, but you can," Baz said. "Trust me, I've flown Aykari ships before; they're not that different from the *Icarus*. You take Crayt and the boys with you, I'll take Skits and the top secret weapon with me."

"It's not a weapon," Leo said. "It's the opposite. . . . An anti-weapon."

"Fine. I'll take the *anti*-weapon. We'll swap it out for the warhead on the last black widow. That way we can just launch it at a distance and be far enough away in case . . . you know . . ." He looked at Leo and pinched his fingers again.

"I'm taking my own ship," Zennia insisted.

"Knock yourself out. I hear it smells anyway."

"It definitely does," Gareth whispered to Leo.

The captain turned to Boo, who hadn't said a word since hearing the message, simply stood by, thoughtfully twisting the tips of his horns. "I'll let you decide who you want to fly with, big guy."

Leo had only known him for days, but that was long enough that he could read the expression in the Queleti's large brown eyes.

"I've decided, Captain," Boo said at last, his arms crossed

over his Yunkai—his only real possession—stained a dull yellow from dust. *They carry their planet home with them,* Leo thought. *They live close to the ground.*

Leo knew what was coming.

"Ever since I left Quel I've been searching for something," Boo continued. "A place. And a purpose. Something about this planet . . . these people . . . They understand, much better than I ever have, what it means to be at peace. I believe that is the thing I've been looking for."

Baz looked as if he'd been hit with another of Kat's hard left hooks. "Hold on, are you saying you want to *stay*? *Here*? Are you *serious*?"

Boo met Baz's rising voice with a calm nod. "This planet has suffered. It is still suffering. There is so much the Orin must do to get their lives back to normal. Crayt was helping them, but you are taking him with you. So I've decided I will stay and finish what he started."

Kat frowned; she looked disheartened, disappointed, but not all that surprised. "You're sure that's what you want?"

Boo considered it. "It is what I need."

Kat nodded. She wasn't going to argue. Baz was more than ready to do it for her. "Forget it, Okardo. I won't let you jump ship. Not now. We don't leave crew behind. You know that. I'm not going to abandon you on this broken-down planet in the middle of god knows where just because you're feeling a little guilty all of a sudden."

"You are not abandoning me, Bastian," Boo countered, refusing to match the rise in the captain's voice. "I am choosing to stay. And this world is only broken until we fix it."

Baz threw up his hands. "This is crazy. *You're* crazy. You're a pirate, for Saturn's sake. Not some crusader looking to right the injustice in the universe."

"So says the man risking everything to save his own planet from certain destruction," Boo remarked.

Baz hissed through his teeth but said nothing.

"We all have reasons for being who we are and doing the things we do. Right or wrong. Good or bad. I have tried being Bo'enmaza Okardo. And I have tried being Boo. Now I think I will be Lark for a while."

Lark. Outsider. Leo thought of Rint and Shree and the little Orin children hanging off Boo's fur. He wouldn't stay an outsider for long.

With clenched fists, Baz took three steps until he was nose to neck with the Queleti. "I am your captain, and so help me, you are getting on one of those ships even if I have to drag you on board myself."

Boo grunted. It was both a laugh and a sigh. He smiled kindly down at Baz. "As fun as it might be to watch you try, I think it best if we just say goodbye to each other instead. Perhaps not as captain and crew, but as one friend to another."

The Queleti placed four hands on Baz's shoulders. The captain opened his mouth again, ready to unleash more threats or entreaties, but after a moment he closed it. He gave Boo a nod, barely that, but the gesture said everything.

Baz turned to Kat, clearing his throat, his voice suddenly charged with determination. "All right, let's do this. Get Crayt on board that transport. Skits, let's get started hooking up that device. Make sure everyone's got enough V to get there. And give Z back her rifle; she came far enough for the damn thing. Dust-off in five."

The captain turned his back to all of them, picking up the nullifier and tucking it under his arm before walking purposefully toward the *Icarus*, refusing to look back.

Leo watched as Boo pulled Kat aside, the two of them sharing a whispered farewell. She put her hand—the soft one—on his cheek. The Queleti's fur rippled in response. Leo didn't think she would cry, and he was right, but it looked like a fight she barely won.

At last Boo turned to Leo.

"You know you're going to miss out on some things. I'm pretty sure the Orin have never even heard of gyurt." It was Leo's last-ditch effort to get him to change his mind.

"I will miss some things," Boo agreed. "I will find others. I do regret that I won't be there with you the moment that House Fender is restored. Seeing you with your brother gives me hope that you will all be together soon."

Leo bit his lip, looked down at his boots.

"You will find him," Boo insisted. "You will find your

father and you will save him. And not just because you have courage, but because you have earned it. The universe keeps track, Leo. When you go astray, it sets a path to steer you back. And when you do what is noble and good, it finds a way to reward you."

Boo shot a look at Baz, who was still standing at the bottom of the ramp next to Kat, handing her what looked to be a data file, much like the one Leo's father had given him. Baz said something and Kat gave him a finger and a smile both.

"So what is this, then? Staying here?" Leo wondered. "Is it your path, or your reward?"

"Perhaps it is both," Boo said. "Goodbye, Leo Fender. It has been my honor."

Leo placed one hand over Boo's enormous heart, tracking its bold, beautiful rhythm. He felt all four hairy arms engulf him and promised not to forget how safe it felt to be wrapped in a Queleti's hug. "Goodbye, Boo," he whispered.

Baz's voice echoed through the hangar: "All right you freebooters, let's get these ships starborne. We've got a planet to save and two entire alien empires to piss off."

Gareth and Kat were already carrying an unconscious Crayt onto the Aykari transport. Baz's ex-girlfriend had her precious rifle in hand and was boarding the ramp to her fighter. Leo felt a surge—the tingling excitement mixed with all too familiar stomach-churning dread. Worry over his father mixed with relief at having Gareth by his side. The longing to see his home again. The heartbreak of leaving a friend behind. It all formed a tangled knot inside. He looked back to see Boo standing in the center of the hangar, surrounded by all three ships. He had more than enough hands to wave to each of them.

Baz hesitated halfway up the *Icarus*'s ramp. He hung his head, then turned around. "Do they know about the snoring?" he called out. "The Orin, I mean? If you really do intend to live with them, they should at least know what they are getting into."

Boo shrugged. "I suppose they will find out," he said.

The captain nodded. "Lucky them."

Leo knew he meant it.

I pledge my allegiance to planet Earth and all of its citizens. To protect and preserve our way of life. To advance human achievement and understanding. To defend ourselves and our allies against all enemies. To sacrifice all that is necessary to ensure peace and prosperity for this world and all worlds and peoples who share these beliefs. With unity, freedom, and justice for all.

—*United Peoples of Earth Pledge*

THE FLIGHT OF
THE *ICARUS*

THE LAST TIME LEO SAW EARTH, HE WAS HOLDING Gareth's hand.

They stood with their father aboard the *Beagle*'s observation deck, a sort of promenade complete with couches and tables and a gigantic viewport the size of Leo's old garage. Each of the Fenders was stiffly dressed in a new Coalition uniform. They itched terribly.

"Take a good look, boys," their father said. "I'm not sure when we will see her next."

Leo still couldn't believe how smooth and flat it looked from this far away. How perfectly round, when on the surface it was canyons and mountains, undulating desert valleys and rolling hills. The white clouds looked like so much bundled scar tissue, and the water, clear when cupped in his hands and green when he stood at the ocean's edge, seemed unnaturally blue from here. It looked so beautiful—and so small and fragile—that Leo longed to reach through the viewport and pinch it between his fingers, secreting it away in his pocket for safekeeping. "We *will* see her, though, right?" he said. "We *are* coming back."

His father laid an arm across Leo's shoulders. It was meant to be reassuring. It felt uncomfortable instead. Much too heavy. "Of course we will see her again," he said. His voice sounded convincing enough.

"And Amos?"

"And Amos, naturally. Mrs. Tinsley will probably be thrilled to see us. She's going to get tired of him scratching up all her nice furniture."

That was an inevitability, Leo knew. Amos had all of his claws and made his mark on every exposed leg he could find, whether wood or flesh. "She won't get rid of him, though, will she?"

Dr. Fender shook his head. "No. No. Of course not. She'll take good care of him."

Leo wasn't so sure. Amos could run away. Become a stray. Be taken by one of the coyotes that escaped from the mountains now swarming with Aykari survey and excavation teams and started living off whatever they could find in the towns below. There was no telling what could happen now that Leo wasn't there to look after him.

And it was his fault. Leo had left him. Somewhere down on that perfect blue sphere. He had left everything. His school. His friends. His house. His room. Most of his possessions, save for a couple of magic tricks and a handful of seashells.

And the two people standing on either side of him, of course.

His father sighed. "Looks perfect from here, doesn't it?"

Leo knew what he meant. From here you couldn't feel the earthquakes. From here you couldn't measure the rising oceans or spot the unidentified fungi creeping up the trees. The planet had problems, sure, but Leo would still rather have his feet planted firmly on the ground down there than up here in artificial gravity on a ship about to blast away to devil knows where for who knew how long. Six months? A year? Two years? His father refused to say. Only that they wouldn't be on this ship forever. That this wasn't their permanent home.

Leo was still looking at his permanent home.

He hoped.

"You remembered the flowers, didn't you?" Gareth asked, glancing at their father.

"I remembered," he answered. "They said they automatically place them by the graves on the anniversary of the attack, but I requested they do it for her birthday as well. Sunflowers, of course." Dr. Calvin Fender rubbed his hands together. "We're making the jump in less than two hours.

I'm going to check with Captain Saito and make sure there's nothing I can do to help. You two going to be okay without me for a bit?"

Leo's instinct was to say no, but Gareth nodded and said, "We'll be fine."

His dad gave Leo's shoulder a squeeze. "That's my boys. Brave and strong and ready for this new adventure."

Leo was none of these. Not today, at least. He watched his father leave, walking with his shoulders back, saluting ship's personnel as he went.

"This feels so weird," he said. "It's like I know I'm supposed to say goodbye, but I don't know how."

"Oh. That part's easy—just say, 'So long. And thanks for all the fish.'"

Leo squinted at his brother, confused.

"It's from a book."

"A good book?"

"It's kinda old, but it's hilarious. The Earth gets blown up right at the start." Gareth must have noticed Leo's frown. "It's just pretend."

"Obviously," Leo said. "Does it have to be fish? Can't I just say thanks for everything?"

"You can say whatever you want," Gareth told him.

Leo thought about it for a moment, then whispered his goodbye under his breath. *So long. Thanks for everything.*

Then he added, *And don't worry—I'll be back.*

Gareth reached out and took Leo's hand.

The brothers stood that way, shoulder to shoulder, feeling completely out of place on board this unfamiliar, giant starship, staring longingly across the black expanse at the only home they'd ever known, making one unspoken promise after another, though they all amounted to the same.

It felt strange *not* to be on the *Icarus*.

And it felt strange for *that* to feel strange, because it meant Leo had somehow gotten used to the rickety old pirate ship. That he actually felt comfortable there. Like he belonged.

Crayt's transport, like all things Aykari, was sleek and smooth, the ducts hidden beneath titanium plating, the floor so shiny slick that Leo could look into his own eyes as he watched his step. The berth where they situated the wounded Aykari exile was spacious, cushioned, and clean, with enough room for even a Queleti to stretch out. The cargo compartments were not littered with used equipment and empty beer cans. The drains were not clogged with fur. It all felt off to Leo, who had grown familiar with the exposed wires jutting from the *Icarus*'s control panels and the rusted floors. No rock music thudded down the corridor from the cockpit. The chairs in this new ship were, naturally, of Aykarian design, meaning the seat was too small and the back too stiff with nowhere to rest your elbows. Leo struggled to get comfortable. It all felt off. Alien.

He wasn't the only one having trouble getting used to it.

"Don't know why he insisted on *me* flying this ship," Kat muttered under her breath.

She had been complaining from the moment they got on board and all through the jump: about the readouts; the control panel; the fact that she had to lean forward to get a good view through the cockpit; even the smell, which she described as "antiseptic" but still had to be better than what Zennia was dealing with.

But mostly she complained about Baz.

"He lied to me," she seethed. "This thing is nothing like the *Icarus*. I don't even know what half of these buttons do. The throttle is wonky. The layout is counterintuitive. Not to mention it's basically just a cargo ship, so the whole thing's got the firepower of a nerfalid's fart. Might as well just point my finger at an attacking ship and say 'pew-pew' for all the good it will do."

Leo didn't find that very reassuring. Especially given what they were possibly flying into.

"Seriously, what was he thinking?" Kat continued. "This isn't how we do things. Stick together, that's what he always says. That's how it's always been. Ever since he picked me out of that trash heap. The four of us. A crew. A family. You know what I mean?"

Leo knew exactly what she meant.

"And now look at us. He and Skits are on the *Icarus*, Boo is already thousands of light-years away, and we're stuck on this piece of Aykari garbage."

"All ships are terrible," Gareth muttered.

Leo's brother sat next to him for the whole journey. While Kat grumbled about Baz and struggled to learn the Aykarian transport's controls, the two Fenders spent the jump filling each other in on the details of what had happened, though Leo had more stories to share ("Wait, his brain was *where*, exactly?"). But the closer they got to their destination, the less they talked, until finally an uneasy quiet filled the cockpit, interrupted only by Kat's most recent rant and Gareth's response.

"Not *all* ships are terrible," Kat disagreed.

"No. They really are," Gareth insisted. "In the last week I've been on a Coalition research vessel, a Djarik freighter, a bounty hunter's starfighter, and now an Aykarian transport, and I can tell you they all suck. They're cramped and cold and dismal, and I don't care if I ever board another one for as long as I live."

It wasn't something Leo ever expected to hear his brother say.

"So I guess you're not going to join the Coalition Navy, then?"

"Are you kidding?" Gareth asked. "After everything you told me? After everything I've seen? The whole galaxy's turned inside out. The Aykari are a bunch of liars and here *I* am teamed up with a band of freaking *pirates*." He glanced at Kat sitting in the pilot's seat. "No offense."

She shrugged. "If it makes you feel any better, it looks like we're shifting from the pirating business and dabbling in the planet-saving business. . . . Speaking of which, you two might want to try and keep down whatever you ate last: we're about to come out of our jump."

Kat adjusted her grip on the awkward alien controls and Leo willed his stomach to stay steady as the ship jolted out of hyperspace, adding even more to that inside-out feeling. He could see Gareth turn a little green, but then his brother's eyes changed from slits to saucers as he stared out through the cockpit.

"Oh," he said. "Oh man."

Leo followed his brother's gaze out into the void, locking onto the beautiful blue ball spinning imperceptibly in the distance, looking just the same as it did three years ago. He felt a shiver work its way through his entire body. He honestly wasn't sure he'd ever see her again.

"That's *it*?" Kat said. "I remembered it being bigger. And bluer."

Leo reminded himself that Kat had been gone much longer than them, blasting off when she was a little girl, with little memory of what she was leaving behind.

"No way. It's perfect," Gareth said. Leo reached over and took his brother's hand.

A series of flashing lights indicating an incoming communication. Kat opened the channel to hear Baz's voice piped in from the *Icarus*.

"My god, she's gorgeous, isn't she?"

In the background Leo heard Skits say, *"Meh."*

"There's quite a crowd out here," Kat said, doing a quick scan of all the ships in orbit—once she figured out what buttons to push. Leo counted at least a half dozen large vessels on the radar. All of them looked like they could be warships.

A third voice cut in over the coms. Zennia had come out of her jump as well. *"My readings indicate the ships are mostly human design. Some Aykari support craft, but mostly EDF."*

"Good," Baz said. *"I'd much rather deal with our own kind."*

"Well, you're about to get your wish," Kat said. "Looks like that big cruiser is hailing us." She tapped more buttons, activating another channel. A human voice addressed them.

"Aykari transport, you are entering EDF-protected planetary space. Please identify yourself."

Here we go, Leo thought. *Time to save the world.*

"My name is Katarina Corea and I'm originally *from* this protected planetary space. We have reason to believe that Earth is in imminent danger of a Djarik attack and request to speak to your commanding officer immediately."

The channel went silent.

"You request to speak?" Leo marveled. "Since when does Katarina Corea *request* anything?"

"That ship can turn *this* ship to scrap in seconds. I'm trying to be diplomatic."

The voice that came back through the coms was also human, but deeper and lacking any measure of pleasantry at all. *"Captain Corea, this is Commander Marcellis with the EDF. Be advised, we have identified two potentially hostile craft among your party. State your intentions immediately."*

Before Kat could answer, Baz's voice trumped hers, his approach a little more in-your-face. *"Our intentions? How about to keep this planet from being turned into an instant asteroid field?"*

Kat's chin dropped to her chest. "So much for diplomacy."

"Who am I speaking to?" the commander demanded.

"This is Captain Bastian Black of the Icarus. *And Captain Corea's right. You guys are about to get blindsided. Any moment now the Djarik are going to show up with enough firepower to knock that shiny blue marble of ours clear out of the ring, so if you're really the one in charge, you need to shut up and listen. And if you're not, then you need to get the person who is."*

There was a short pause before Marcellis spoke again.

"Bastian Black? Bastian Daedalus *Black?"*

Kat winced. Leo groaned. Never good when they knew your whole name.

"Captain Black, you are wanted by the Coalition of Planets, the United Peoples of Earth, and the Aykarian empire for the crimes of piracy and treason," the commander continued. *"You and your*

cohorts will power down your ships immediately and prepare to be boarded and taken into custody."

"*Knew* this would happen." Kat jammed the big blue coms button with her thumb. "I don't think you understand the situation, Commander Marcellis. We aren't the bad guys here. We came to warn you. To *help* you."

"*I understand enough*," Marcellis fired back. "*I understand that we have now identified two of your ships as belonging to the pirate Bastian Black and a bounty hunter named Zennia Sendova, both with outstanding warrants. Once you are safely apprehended, we can discuss the credibility of this supposed threat. Now deactivate your shields and power down your weapons or I will be forced to do it for you.*"

"They're not listening," Kat muttered.

Leo bristled. He was getting a little tired of being threatened. He leaned forward and mashed the same button Kat had been pressing. "Hello? Hello? Whoever can hear me . . . my name is Leo Fender. My father is Dr. Calvin Fender. The Djarik captured him and forced him to help create a weapon that uses ventasium to blow up whole planets and they've picked this one to test it on. When they come, you won't be able to stop them." Leo finally took a breath.

"Wow, ship rat. Talk about laying all your cards on the table," Kat whispered.

But it didn't matter. The commander wasn't buying it. "*I have seven capital ships, three squadrons of starfighters, two thousand men, and a planet full of surface-to-air weapons systems that say otherwise,"* Marcellis countered. *"Now deactivate your systems immediately or risk being fired upon."*

"This is getting us nowhere." Kat switched over to the closed channel, linking back up with Baz and Zenn directly. "I don't know, Baz. Maybe we just let the EDF take us. We've got Crayt on board. We've got Dr. Fender's data files. The message. The device. They'll have to listen to us."

"Unless they get the Aykari involved," Leo said. He stared at his home. So close now. *Who has the most to lose?* he wondered to himself.

"The kid's right," Baz said. *"This device gets turned over to the Aykari and it might never get used. What do you think, Zenn?"*

"I think . . . I think we just ran out of time," the bounty hunter said. *"They're here."*

She was right. His mother. About Earth. The Aykari. The Coalition. All of it. What it was worth and what it wasn't. She was right.

Calvin Fender only ever admitted it once—and even then he wasn't sure, but Leo remembered.

He remembered the nightmare that had woken him up, a variation on a common theme. He'd been swimming in the ocean and had gone out too far, the rip current catching him, pulling him farther and farther from shore. He screamed and screamed, legs furiously churning, arms flailing, the water beneath him getting deeper and colder, the edge of the world ebbing away. He'd woken at the very moment his legs gave out, surfacing from the dream just as he went under, gasping, his shirt soaked in sweat. He fumbled for his inhaler and sucked down the medicine, feeling everything lighten, though he still shivered.

He called out for his dad. He got no answer. He shook some more.

Leo pulled himself out of bed and crept softly down the hallway toward his parents' room.

No. His parent's room.

His father wasn't in his bed.

It's okay. Don't bother him. It was just a dream, he told himself. *Just go back to sleep.*

That's when he noticed the music. Classical. Strings and horns. Coming from downstairs.

He found his father on the couch, head back, eyes closed, listening. "What are you doing awake?" his dad asked.

"Bad dreams," Leo answered.

"Me too."

Dr. Fender patted the space beside him, and Leo crawled up onto the couch, snatching one of the throw pillows to hold against his chest. He always felt better when he had something to hold on to. The room was dark, lit only by the moon coming through the sliding glass door.

"What are you listening to?" Leo asked.

"Holst. *The Planets*. This one is called 'Jupiter.'"

Leo sat and listened. Even at such a low volume it still sounded bright and bombastic with lots of brass and thudding timpani. But then after a minute it shifted, becoming soft and melodic. Leo didn't really care for classical music. He preferred songs that you could sing along to, but his father often made him listen to it anyway.

"This was one of your mother's favorites. She always joked that if Holst were still alive, he'd have a lot more work to do. How many planets do we know about now? Thousands? Of course he had no idea. When he was alive we only knew about eight. As it was he only made music for seven."

Leo tried to imagine writing a song for every planet in the galaxy. Most of the planets didn't even have names, just numbers. Numbers and coordinates. Dots on an unfathomably large map. "What does Earth sound like?" he asked.

"That's actually the one he left out," his father said.

"Why?"

"He didn't think it was worth it, I guess. It didn't interest him."

Leo thought about it. Shook his head. "That's dumb. I would have written about Earth. That would have been the first song I wrote."

His father laughed.

"What's funny?"

"Nothing. Just—your mother said the same thing. That

he'd ignored the very best one."

For some reason that pleased Leo, being told he was like his mother. Though he pretty much knew that already. He pulled the pillow even tighter to his chin and then nestled into his father's side as the music got louder again. He heard his father sniff and looked up in time to see him blink away a tear.

"I don't know, kiddo. Maybe she was right. Some days . . ." He took a breath. "Some days I wonder if it will ever be worth it, you know?" He put one arm around Leo, the other conducting, cuing in the violins. "We used to talk, your mom and I, about the way things were and the way they used to be. And she'd say that sometimes she wished the Aykari had never found us. That we never knew they existed. That it was better before. She was like you. For her, the Earth was always enough. This house. Her garden. You boys. Me. She said that was all she wanted. It always made me feel bad, for wanting more. And now that she's gone . . ."

His father didn't finish the sentence. Leo didn't press him to. Instead they sat and finished the song, both of them afraid to go back to sleep, knowing the nightmares were still there, waiting for them.

After a moment a new song came on, low, heavy strings striking the same ominous note over and over again, building in intensity, the horns sneaking in like an animal's warning growl. The song made Leo uneasy.

"What's this one called?" he asked.

His father stared through the glass door into the darkness. "This one is called 'Mars,'" he said. "'Bringer of War.'"

They were here.

Suddenly the cockpit of their borrowed Aykari transport was cast in a long shadow, and Leo found himself staring up at the most massive Djarik ship he'd ever seen, its egg-shaped hull blocking the light of the sun and a thousand other, more distant stars, eclipsing even the topaz halo of the Earth itself.

"What is *that*?" Gareth asked.

"It's big, is what it is," Kat answered.

It was easily five times the size of the Coalition cruiser— the one Kat said could tear their little transport apart. The Djarik flagship was accompanied by several craft of a more modest size, but it was clear they were there only to defend the queen bee should she come under attack. This was the ship that would destroy the Earth. Leo suddenly went cold, knowing full well that it could. Knowing exactly how.

"Incoming transmission," Kat said. A holo emitter embedded in the ship's console activated, projecting the image of a glitchy figure slowly coming into focus.

Leo expected to see a Djarik, dressed in officer's attire or decked out in battle armor. He expected a spike-frilled jaw and a thick hide made of silver scales. Black reptilian eyes belying both keen intelligence and extreme prejudice. He expected something alien and menacing.

Instead he got a tufted chin; sallow, wrinkled skin; and tired blue eyes that had stared into his own a thousand times.

Leo heard his brother take in a sharp breath.

"Kat, are you getting this?" Baz asked.

"Yeah, we're getting it," Kat said.

Leo's already racing heart somehow beat faster, and he shook off a wave of dizziness, trying to keep the image in focus. This was not some message recorded in secret and transmitted across star systems through a hacked watch. This was a live transmission beamed to every ship in Earth's orbit as well as every communications tower on the surface. Billions of humans would be watching this. All of them staring at the face of Dr. Calvin Fender.

"People of Earth."

He was dressed the same as when Leo last saw him, except now his wrists were secured with binders. He was no longer an ally or an accomplice, agreeing to assist the Djarik in return for his son's safe return. He was a prisoner. Two Djarik soldiers dwarfed him on either side, rifles in hand.

"The Djarik empire demands your immediate surrender," Leo's father continued. *"You are to renounce your allegiance to the Aykarian empire and its sham Coalition, surrender your ships, and commit to dismantling your armies and weapons. Do so, and the Djarik will spare your lives. Refuse . . ."* Dr. Fender's voice faltered and one of the soldiers nudged him with the point of

his rifle. *"Refuse, and you will be destroyed."*

"Skits says the transmission is definitely coming from that command ship," Baz said.

That means he's on board, Leo thought. *He's right there.* He glanced again at the giant flagship hovering above them, then back at his father.

The projection of Calvin Fender leaned forward. It felt like he was staring right at Leo. *"This will be your only chance,"* he said. *"The fate of your planet lies in your hands."*

The holo cut out abruptly, their father's face rippling away, leaving the cockpit in silence.

"What's happening?" Gareth asked, panicked. "What are they going to do to him?"

Kat threw both Fenders a sympathetic look, then turned back to the controls. "What's the move, Captain?"

After a beat, Baz's voice echoed over the open channel again. *"Commander Marcellis. These guys aren't bluffing; they have a device that can turn the whole planet to atoms. But we have the means to stop them. If you'll just listen—"*

"We don't collude with pirates," Marcellis interrupted forcefully. *"And we will not surrender to these Djarik terrorists either. They attacked us once before and paid the price. They will pay it again. If I were you, Captain Black, I would stay out of the way and we will deal with you later."*

"Commander Marcellis . . . ," Baz barked, but he got no response. The Coalition ship had shut off communications.

"That settles that," Kat muttered.

"It looks like the Djarik command ship is opening its hangars," Zennia said. *"The EDF fleet is moving to intercept. This party is definitely starting."*

"Seriously, Baz, what's the play?"

Leo held his breath, watching as the giant Djarik ship above him crept closer and closer to Earth. Watching as every ship in the EDF patrol readied to charge.

This will be your only chance.

"We have to," Leo whispered to himself. "It's up to us."

As if in response, the coms channel suddenly erupted with angry drums and growling guitars. Through the cockpit Leo saw the *Icarus*'s primary engines light up, a burst of blue flame that sent it blasting toward Earth.

"Baz? What are you doing?"

"Tried talking my way out of it, Kat. You're right. Never works. Time to cut the black wire."

"And death to those who dare to stand in our way!" Leo heard Skits shout in the background.

"Oh hell." Kat jerked the controls and fired the transport's own thrusters, rapidly changing course in pursuit. "Find *something* to hold on to," she commanded.

Leo gripped the bottom of his armless seat as the Aykari ship shot after the *Icarus*. He turned to see his brother with his race face on, eyes narrowed, jaw clenched. The last time Leo saw that look, Gareth was shoving him into a storage compartment, sending him away. Gareth had already admitted that was a mistake. As they broke through Earth's atmosphere, arcing through a blanket of clouds, Leo hoped they weren't making another one.

"Kat, Skits has locked on to the nearest location with a direct line to the planet's primary seam of V. It's a mining platform in the Tsangpo Canyon. But there are automated turrets all along the perimeter, and they are probably on high alert."

"Terrific," Kat hissed. She switched back to the open channel. "To anyone listening: This is Captain Corea. We are approaching the Tsangpo mining facility and request that any Aykari and EDF patrols *not* fire on us. I repeat, please deactivate those turrets. We are *not* the enemy."

As if in response, the first turret in the line launched a salvo at the *Icarus* that it barely managed to evade.

"Guess talking doesn't work for you either," Baz quipped.

Following the first turret's lead, the others now opened fire as well, filling the sky with bolts of energy determined to bring the *Icarus* down. Through the parting clouds and the barrage of deadly blasts, Leo could make out the long, deep canyon etched into the earth, terminating in an Aykari mining operation much like the one they'd recently left behind. Leo thought about all the ventasium lying in wait deep beneath the surface. *What if this doesn't work?*

Over the coms Leo could hear Baz's cursing against the

sound of minor chords and rolling toms as the *Icarus*'s shields took one hit after another.

"Baz, you're getting pummeled up there," Kat said. "Pull back and let me draw some of their fire."

"*In* that *thing? Forget it.*"

"Bastion—"

"*I've got this, Kat. Trust me.*"

"Why do you have to be so *stubborn* all the time?" With a growl the first mate slammed hard on the controls. Leo rocked in his seat, feeling the Aykari transport take on a sudden burst of speed, hoping to gain on the yellow speck diving toward the surface of the Earth, plunging headlong into the storm raging up to meet it.

From her vantage out in orbit, Zennia's voice crackled in. "*You two need to hurry. It's getting dicey up here. The EDF is fully engaged but they are taking a beating, and it looks like that command ship is ready to rain down fire and fury.*"

Gareth glanced at Leo, eyes round with fear. "If just one of those Djarik missiles makes contact, it's all over."

Leo nodded, then felt himself nearly knocked out of his seat once more as their ship took a glancing hit. Kat growled again. "Seriously, Commander Marcellis or whoever the hell is in charge up there, shut down these freaking guns *now!*" she shouted into the coms, but the turrets continued to fire, seeing anything as a threat.

"Kat!" Leo pointed up ahead. The *Icarus*'s shields were clearly depleted. A jet of white smoke plumed up from the ship's left thruster.

"Baz, your engine's blown," Kat told him. "Time to cut that wire and get the hell out of there."

"I'm so close," Baz replied.

"Then what are you waiting for? Just launch the thing already!"

"Can't. Targeting system's busted." Even through the pounding of Baz's heavy metal, Leo could make out the *Icarus*'s alarms blaring, the sound of system failure shipwide. *"Besides, this gun's only got one bullet. Can't risk having it shot down. I'm going to get right up on top and drop this bad boy straight in. Be just like Beggar's Canyon back home."*

"You *are* home, you idiot," Kat said.

"Yeah. Guess I am . . ." Leo saw the *Icarus* rock from another hit. Baz cursed again. *"Hey, you remember what I said when I picked you up on Andural?"* he shouted over the din of alarms and screaming guitars.

"Baz, now's not the time—"

"Do you remember?"

"Yeah. You asked me if I needed a hand," Kat replied. "I think you were trying to be funny."

"And after that."

"You said some things were worth saving."

Zennia's voice cut in suddenly, clouded by static, but still full of desperation. *"You've got incoming! Multiple warheads. Hundreds of them headed your way."*

This is it, Leo thought.

He looked up, through the wisp of clouds to the bright flare of ships bursting into flames beyond the edge of Earth. He couldn't see the missiles, but he could hear the roar of the ocean in his ears. He could smell the salty tang of the surf and feel the grit of the sand caked between his toes. And he heard his father's voice . . . Baz's voice . . . the two of them muddled by the static and the music and the alarms. But the message was clear enough.

"Bye, Kat."

In the bright light of the sun, Leo saw the *Icarus* dive, disappearing into the canyon, leaving only a trail of charcoal-colored smoke in its wake. The music cut out, the drums frozen mid-beat.

"Baz?" Kat mashed the coms button. "Baz, do you read me?"

Leo held his breath, waiting for a response. Waiting for the captain's cowboy holler or some smart-mouthed come-back. Waiting for the *Icarus* to come soaring back out of the canyon, rocketing up into the sky like a firework on First Contact Day.

He waited for a shot from one of the turrets to tear through their transport's hull, sending them plummeting into the canyon as well.

He waited for those Djarik missiles to break through the clouds.

He held that breath, and he waited for the world to end.

"Bastian Black, answer me right now!"

Kat's titanium hand—the one that the captain had paid for—remained steady on the ship's controls, but the other one trembled. Dead ahead, the pinnacle of the Aykari drill jutting up out of the canyon cast its shadow over a barren landscape that once had been covered in trees. Beyond that, a world still full of promise.

In an instant, that whole world changed.

In the jump drives of every ship docked on planet 641-57-3, the element known galaxy-wide as EL-486 flared a bright blue, pretty as a summer sky. For only a moment, though, and then just as quickly it turned gray and useless.

In the depths of every mining platform scattered all over that world, that same precious element was sapped of whatever latent power it possessed, its value plummeting to nothing. And a planet that was once a jewel in the crown of an empire became little more than a dried-up well.

Moments before that, the worst pirate in the universe cursed under his breath as the hull of his ship began to break apart around him. He felt himself thrown forward, coming up out of his seat, momentarily weightless.

And in that instant he inexplicably smelled freshly mown

grass and the smoke from a campfire. The taste of chili dogs, of all things, lingered on his tongue. He heard the crack of a bat. The cheering crowd.

He recalled the feel of the wind in his hair the first time his father took him up in a plane and handed him the controls. How free he felt.

He thought of a girl named Marjorie and a kiss he stole when he was only nine. And he smiled.

War is when the government tells you who the enemy is. Revolution is when you decide it for yourself.

—*Benjamin Franklin*

A PROMISE KEPT

KAT STARED THROUGH THE COCKPIT AT THE CHASM
unfolding beneath them, into the black hole that had swallowed the *Icarus*, taking its captain, her captain, with it.

"Bastian. You fool," she whispered.

Leo sat stunned, listening to the soft static coming through the coms. Everything felt frozen solid, inside and out.

That is, until the guns that had been focused on bringing the *Icarus* down turned their attention to the next ship in line. Kat snapped back to attention. She shook her head, regaining her focus, and pulled hard on the controls, the Aykari transport going parabolic, splitting the clouds, leaving the cannonade and the canyon—and Baz—behind them until they were out of the turrets' reach.

But they were only trading one danger for another. Leo

could already make out the chaotic bursts of the battle raging above him, the cruisers of the EDF unleashing their wrath upon the giant Djarik command ship as swarms of starfighters wove between them, spitting death before exploding in brief flashes of light like so many fireflies blinking in the night.

Gareth glanced behind him, at the planet they were leaving yet again. "Did it work? Did he do it?"

Kat glanced down at the console. Presumably at the read-out that told her how much EL-486 remained in the ship's cores. The answer, apparently, was none.

"It worked," she said. "He did it." Her voice was distant, though, hollow. Though her hands stuck to the controls, she didn't seem to be making any effort to steer them, as if she didn't even realize the mess they were flying into.

Leo reached out for her. "Kat?"

"He always said he'd bring me back here," she said. The former pickpocket turned pirate shook her head. "When he took me in, he told me. He said that no matter what, we'd always have each other's backs. He was the only family I had left."

She turned to Leo, whose hand still rested on her shoulder, squinting at him as if he were some old acquaintance she couldn't place. She stared at him for a moment longer, then her expression changed, her eyes finding focus. She clenched her teeth.

Kat spun back around to the controls. Leo lurched sideways

as the ship banked hard, taking on a new trajectory.

Heading straight for the Djarik command ship.

"Zenn, are you there?" Kat's voice was suddenly sharp, determined. The edge Leo was used to. The bounty hunter's own voice barely cut through the static.

"Still here. Though I don't know how much longer. Getting hit from both sides. I think each party is convinced I came with the other guy. . . . Did Baz . . ."

Zennia's voice trailed off, waiting for Kat to fill in the blank.

"He did what he came here to do," Kat replied shortly. "What's the reading on that command ship?"

In the pause that followed, Leo reminded himself that the bounty hunter had known Bastian Black long before he came along. They had a history, a complicated one. But most histories were.

"It's taken a beating. Its shields are down, but there are fighters pouring out of its hangars and its gun batteries are still firing. I'm surprised it hasn't tried to make a jump."

"Maybe it can't," Leo said. Maybe the nullifier was even more powerful than Crayt had thought, reaching even beyond the Earth's atmosphere to the ships that orbited it. Maybe they were all sitting ducks out here. Bloodthirsty ducks armed with torpedoes and laser cannons hell-bent on blasting each other to pieces.

"Yeah, well, it's not going anywhere until I'm through

with it," Kat said. She switched channels and hailed the lead EDF cruiser again. "Commander Marcellis—if you can read me, we believe that the immediate threat to Earth has been neutralized."

This time he deigned to answer. *"Copy that, Captain Corea,"* Marcellis said, sounding much less sure of himself than before. *"We have reports of Djarik ordnance targeting mining facilities all across the planet, but so far all of their weapons seem to have had no effect at all. Whatever you did, it must have worked."*

We cut the black wire, Leo thought. *Also we've essentially destroyed the planet's entire supply of ventasium.* He wasn't sure exactly how he felt about that part, though he knew, in his heart, that it was worth it.

Baz obviously knew it too.

Kat continued to fly right at the giant Djarik mother ship, her eyes burning. "You can thank us by helping us. We believe Dr. Calvin Fender is being held somewhere on that command ship. He's part of the reason that planet of ours is still in one piece. I'm requesting your assistance for an extraction."

"Extraction?" Gareth repeated. He looked at Leo with wide eyes.

"Captain Corea, you are not authorized to—"

"I'm not asking for your authorization, Commander," Kat hissed. "I'm asking for your assistance."

"I'm not sure what help I can give. My ships are badly damaged

already and our allied Aykari forces appear to be in full retreat."

"They're bugging out already?" Gareth said. "Are you *kidding* me?"

Leo wasn't surprised. Not anymore. He thought of the Orin and their crumbled world. Of the stones he'd helped put back in place. What do you do when the well runs dry?

Kat didn't seem to care if the Aykari stuck around or not. She wasn't taking no for an answer. "Just clear a path, disable that ship's guns, and unload as many soldiers as you can into its main hangar because that's where I'm headed."

"I don't think I can risk the forces I have left to save one m—" Marcellis began to protest, but Kat shut him off.

She turned to Leo. "Baz told you he'd help you get your father back."

Leo nodded.

"This time we're not leaving without him, understood?"

He nodded again. He pictured his father in cuffs, bracketed by Djarik soldiers; he didn't think his dad would refuse rescue again.

"So what's the plan?" Gareth asked. "After we get on board?"

"Easy. Guns blazing," Kat replied. "And death to anyone that stands in our way." She hailed the bounty hunter whose starfighter was now flying alongside them. "Zenn, we're going after Dr. Fender and we could really use that rifle of yours, if you're up for it."

"Just as long as he's worth it," the bounty hunter said. *"The past couple of Fenders I've gone after have been kind of a bust."* Leo took that as a yes.

Commander Marcellis must have decided that Leo's father was ultimately worth saving as well, because soon their ship was flanked by a dozen EDF vessels, including two landing shuttles and a phalanx of fighters. "The cavalry," Kat said. "Now we're in business."

The Djarik, sensing a new threat, sent a mob of its own starfighters to intercept the incoming boarding party, but the EDF escort formed a spearhead in front of Kat's borrowed ship, scattering the enemy with a salvo of missiles. Leo flinched as blasts of deadly energy sizzled around him, but the human pilots were up to the task, clearing a path to the command ship as requested. *Our kind have to stick together,* Leo thought, remembering something a floating brain once told him.

Leo took a hit from his inhaler, an attempt to catch his breath. The Djarik command ship dwarfed them now, though most of its cannons were trained on the bigger ships it was engaged with. Kat, finally managing to get a firm handle on the Aykari-designed controls, rolling and banking to avoid incoming fire, her sights set firmly on the main hangar, nearly empty now, an open invitation for a pirate boarding party. They burst through the magnetic shielding, and Leo's head whipped as Kat turned hard and fired the reverse thrusters, the transport executing a perfect half circle before setting down roughly in the command ship's bay, nose pointed outward.

Ready for a quick getaway. The only kind.

Through the cockpit canopy he watched the two EDF shuttles land beside them, their ramps already opening. Soldiers—decked in gray-and-green battle armor with the emblem of the Coalition emblazoned on their pauldrons—poured from the ships as they touched down, moving with precision. He spotted Zennia emerging from her fighter as well, her prized rifle tucked into her shoulder. None of the soldiers seemed to think anything of the emerald-haired bounty hunter in their midst. She was human, which meant, for the time being at least, she was an ally.

Kat stood, unholstered one of her pistols, and started to hand it to Leo, before thinking better of it and offering it to Gareth instead. "Have you ever fired one of these before?"

Leo's brother nodded.

"Ever *at* someone?"

No nod this time.

"That's okay. You can handle it," Kat said, placing it in his palm. "Djarik armor isn't as strong as Aykari. One shot is usually enough to take one of them down, but fire as many times as you have to." She checked the charge on her other pistol—a gesture Leo was all too familiar with. "Hang tight and watch the door. I'll be back as soon as I find him."

"You mean *we*," Gareth said. "As soon as *we* find him."

Kat shook her head. She suddenly looked so much older to Leo. Something about her look reminded him of his mother. "I need someone to stay on board and protect Crayt. Only the one bullet, remember? And he's the only guy who knows how to make more. This isn't just about us." It was the same thing Crayt had told Leo: that everyone should be given the choice. The Djarik wouldn't give up just because they'd been thwarted here. The war wasn't going to end just because one planet was left spinning.

Gareth started to protest again, but Kat cut him off. "Listen, I know how much your father means to you. Believe me. And I'm going to bring him back. But I need to be sure there's someone to bring him back to." She looked hard at Leo. "I've lost too much already."

Leo stole another glance at the EDF soldiers advancing across the hangar, then back at Kat. "We'll wait here."

Kat nodded. "If it looks like the command ship is about to fall apart, you start those engines and jet. Just try to keep the controls steady and get as far away from this thing as you can, then use the coms to call for help." She put her hand out, palm down. "All in."

Leo laid his hand on top of hers. They both stared at Gareth.

"Fine," he huffed. "But if the ship is falling apart and you're not back yet, we're coming after you."

The captain shook her head and smiled. "You sound just

like your brother, you know."

Gareth reluctantly added his free hand to the top of their meager pile. Kat shut her eyes, channeling her inner Baz.

"Let's rock and roll."

"It's not going to work. You know that, don't you?"

They stood side by side, the three of them, looking into the hole they had dug the old-fashioned way, with sweat and muscle rather than robotic efficiency. The crusted shovel lay in the grass beside them. The late afternoon sun peeked through the clouds. The knees of Leo's pants were already ringed with dirt; his father's hands were a whole different shade.

Gareth looked unblemished. He also looked like he'd rather be somewhere else.

"It's pointless. The plant guy told you it was something in the air or in the water. So that means the same thing is going to happen to this tree too. It's just going to die and this will all be for nothing."

"You don't know that for sure," their father said.

"We should plant something different. Or just fill in the hole and be done with it."

"We are filling in the hole. We're filling it with this." Calvin Fender unwrapped the root ball of the new sapling, exposing the young tree's skinny tendrils, ready to grab hold of the earth. "Give me a hand, will you?"

Leo helped his father take the sapling by the trunk and drag it toward the hole, nestling the roots into the welcoming space. The tree was barely as tall as his dad, with a trunk that Leo could easily encircle with his hands. Hard to believe it would ever grow as large as the one that had been here before.

"You're wasting your time," Gareth groused.

Leo chewed on the inside of his cheek. He wanted to shout at his brother, tell him to just shut up already. *At least we're trying*, Leo thought. *At least we're doing something instead of lashing out or locking ourselves in our rooms.*

His father took a more measured approach.

"It's true that the last one died, but that's the thing about nature," he said. "It finds a way to adapt. To overcome. It evolves. Maybe not this tree or the next or even the next, but eventually one of them will learn the trick to fighting back against whatever's harming them. It will survive, and then it will pass that knowledge along to the next generation and all the generations after that, growing stronger and more resilient each time. But not if we don't do everything *we* can to give them that chance. Not if we simply give up. I'm not ready to give up, are you?"

Leo shook his head. Gareth scowled.

Their father scattered a handful of dirt over the roots. Leo followed suit, and soon they were both using their hands to shovel in heaps of the stuff, packing it in and around the base.

Leo glanced up at his brother, still looking down at them. Still not helping. Still not convinced.

Please, Leo pleaded with his eyes. *Just try. For me.*

With a grunt of reluctance Gareth dropped to his knees and grabbed a fistful, finally getting his hands dirty. Dr. Fender smiled at his two sons. "That's my boys."

Leo looked up through the skinny branches of the fledgling tree, squinting against the starlight that warmed his cheeks, feeling for the first time in a while that things could be better.

He dared to hope. Just a little.

Leo gazed beyond the hangar into the darkness of space, which still seemed so empty despite all the ships engaged in their deadly dance. He stared and waited, each passing minute stretching that sliver of hope thinner and thinner.

They had been here before, he and Gareth. Huddled together, shallow breathed and anxious, waiting, hiding, incapable of doing anything else. Sitting and listening to the sounds of gunfire mixed with the wail of alarms, the shouts of humans and aliens alike weaving their way up and down corridors. Hearts thumping in double time, wondering what was on the other side of the door or waiting for them at the bottom of the ramp. If whatever it was would find a way in, overriding the controls, or maybe just blasting its way through. If whoever it was would be friend or foe.

If they'd even be able to tell the difference anymore.

Within the hangar, everything was eerily still, even as the battle continued to rage beyond it. Leo watched through the cockpit but saw no sign of Kat or Zennia or any of the soldiers accompanying them. No sign of the Djarik either. It was as if they had boarded a ghost ship. And yet every distant explosion caused Gareth to jump, pointing Kat's pistol at the corridor that led to the boarding ramp.

"We should be out there, helping with the rescue," he said, trying to sound brave, almost pulling it off. "He's *our* father."

"Kat told us to stay here."

"Since when do you take orders from pirates?"

"Since you sent me away with them," Leo countered. "Besides, you saw what Baz did back there, and he was a pirate."

He was a lot of things.

Leo thought back to a moment, not that long ago, sitting at the *Icarus*'s mess table after having failed to rescue his father the first time. Just he and Baz, talking about all the memories they had of home, everything they'd loved and had to leave behind. *We could go on like this forever*, Baz had said. *Won't change a thing.*

But that wasn't true. You *could* change. Nothing was inevitable. People could change. From soldiers to pirates, from pirates to heroes. From enemies to allies or the other way around. You could build a weapon to destroy a world. You could build a device to save it. You could learn to survive with what you had. Learn to live with what you'd lost. You could fill the holes, stack the stones, patch the cracks. Things are only broken till you fix them. Even Baz knew that.

"Sorry. I didn't mean . . . ," Gareth whispered. "He was a good man."

Just a terrible pirate. "He was," Leo said. He wiped his cheek and focused back on the space beyond. From their position in the hangar you could just make out the top of Earth, a swirl of white on blue. Of course, out here there was no top or bottom. For all Leo knew, he could be looking straight down at his own hometown.

He could picture it. The street he lived on with the uneven sidewalks that would trip you if you didn't watch your step, the overgrown box bushes lining the driveway, the solar panels glinting in the sun. His mother's flowerpots hanging from the window, filled with pansies and impatiens. The backyard with its rusted swings, two starships whose young pilots had outgrown them. He wondered how much the sapling they'd planted had grown. If some bird had made a nest in its blossomed branches. Wondered if it was even still there.

"Listen, Leo, if we get back—"

"When," Leo interrupted.

"Okay, *when* we get back, that's it, right? No more ships. No more jumps. We dig in and we stay there. No matter what. We don't leave again. Ever."

Leo nodded. "Shouldn't be too hard," he said. After all, there was no more V left on Earth for them to go anywhere.

Out of the corner of his eye, Leo noticed a flashing green light on the ship's console. He didn't know what it meant, but it was accompanied by the sound of metal sliding against metal coming from the rear of the ship. That, in turn, was followed by a slow hiss.

The sound of a boarding ramp lowering.

"Was that . . . ," Leo started to say, but Gareth was already up out of his chair, pulling Leo with him. "Stay behind me," he ordered.

Leo stood beside him instead. He fixed his eyes on the entrance to the cockpit and the dark corridor beyond. He heard footsteps coming closer, boots pounding against the metal floor. Gareth held Kat's pistol steady, though it clearly took both hands.

"It might be Dad," Leo whispered.

"Might not be," Gareth whispered back.

Leo felt the familiar band around his chest, the serpent coiling, squeezing, winding its way up his throat, but he didn't dare reach for his medicine, afraid to make a sound at all as the footsteps drew closer. He counted his own heartbeats. Whoever it was was right outside the entry now.

And it definitely wasn't their father.

Leo caught the flash of movement. The muzzle of a gun peeking in from the corridor, held in a clawed hand. The glimpse of gray scales and one dark eye.

Gareth raised Kat's pistol and pulled the trigger.

Three shots fired in all.

The first from Kat's pistol, hitting the intruder in his armored chest but not dropping him. The second from the Djarik's rifle, meant for Gareth but missing its target by a foot as Leo instinctively pushed his big brother out of the way.

Leo didn't see the third.

What he saw was this:

A cement porch with wooden rails, the paint starting to peel. The steps leading up to it cracked, perhaps the work of a tremor, itself the work of the mining that had started nearby. A blade of grass sprouting from a step, seeming to grow out of solid rock. An impossibility, this single blade, stuck in stone like an ancient sword meant for a destined king.

A gentle hand bends down to free it from its moorings. The stem of grass, pinched between two fingers, twists back and forth. Back and forth. A pair of warm hazel eyes turns his way.

I see you, my little lion.

She is so beautiful it takes his breath away.

Normally this is where the moment ends, just this one little glimpse, but not this time. This time Leo keeps going, approaching slowly. One step. Another. She sits half in sun and half in shade as if she can't decide which she prefers.

She turns and smiles at him. Such a rare thing, that smile. It doesn't last, turning into a frown to mimic his own. *Why are you sad?*

He looks around. At the street where he learned to ride his bike. At the driveway graffitied in chalk. At the familiar wooden sign hanging by the door. *I want to come home*, he says. *I want to be with you.*

She nods, the sun catching her auburn streaks. This is how he always wants to remember her.

I know you do. And you will. I promise. But not yet. It's not time.

But I miss you, he says.

I know. I know you do. And that won't stop. It's the rule, in fact.

He frowns. *What rule?*

The most important rule, Leo. The one I taught you. Always leave them wanting more.

She gives Leo one last fleeting smile and then closes her eyes.

I've got you, Leo. I'm here. I'm right here. Just hold on.

His own eyes flutter open briefly. Just long enough to see his father's face.

This message is directed toward any planet where EL-four eight six is currently being mined or has even been discovered, any world that has been caught in the interminable struggle between the Aykari and Djarik empires. Your planet, your people, your entire way of life are in danger, and that danger comes from both sides. The Aykari and the Djarik may have different aims and means, but the end result of their interference is the same, whether it is the slow environmental collapse of your home or its sudden, violent destruction. There is a way to protect your world from these forces, but this measure comes at a cost—namely the power and potential of the element. It is your choice, but I implore you to do everything possible to protect yourselves and your planets and prevent further tragedy. And I hope that those two empires come to realize the price we all pay is not worth the prize they seek.

—Zirkus Crayt, in a video accompanying encrypted data files for the construction of the elemental nullifier, Earth year 2055

A PLACE TO START

HE WOKE TO THE SMELL OF FICKEN. GARLIC AND herb variety.

The spongy chunk of chemically engineered chicken fac-simile was impaled on a fork hovering right under his nose. The smell of garlic was intense—probably the thing that woke him.

"Look who decided to come back to us."

Leo's eyes danced from the fork to the person holding it: Gareth, dressed in a wry smile and another clean Coalition uniform, though there was no patch on the shirt this time. He looked different—his hair cropped short, his fledgling mustache shaved clean. The half circles still anchoring his eyes suggested he hadn't slept much, but otherwise he looked ten times better than when Leo saw him last. He pointed to a plate piled high with ficken nuggets. "There's plenty to share this time. And we can order more if you want," he said.

Leo shook his head and tried to sit up, but his left shoulder strongly suggested that this was a mistake, the throbbing instant and intense. Now he was definitely awake.

"Yeah, take it easy. The doctor says the wound's healing well, but you're still going to feel it for a while." Gareth set the fork down beside the plate. "Those Djarik rifles pack a heckuva punch, but you took it like a champ. Thanks for that, by the way. Should be me in that bed. You want some water?"

Leo nodded and took a long swallow from the cup his brother offered. His voice still came out all scratched up. "What happened? Where are we?"

Gareth sighed. "I'll start with the where 'cause it's the easy part. We're on an EDF medical frigate orbiting Earth—the *Nightingale*—where *you* have been unconscious for a few days. As for *what* happened . . ." Gareth leaned back in his chair, shaking his head. "Not sure what all you remember, but the short version is the Djarik tried to blow up our planet and we stopped them. I say 'we' but honestly, I had almost nothing to do with it. Then we landed on the Djarik mother ship and you went and got yourself shot pushing me out of the way."

Leo remembered now. Standing next to his brother in the cockpit of that Aykari transport, waiting. The Djarik coming on board, sniffing them out, the exchange of fire. The pain, like a hot coal burning through his shoulder.

And his father. His father was there. It was his voice calling Leo's name. His arms lifting Leo up.

I'm here now. I've got you.

Except he wasn't. Here.

Gareth must have noticed Leo anxiously scanning the room. "If you're looking for Dad, don't worry. He's fine. He's safe. He's in debriefing with some of the bigwigs from the government," Gareth answered. "This makes day three."

"Day *three*?"

"I told you—you've missed a few things," Gareth admitted.

A lot could happen in three days, Leo knew. Your ship could be attacked by marauders. You could become a stowaway. Build a cistern. Save a planet. Get shot. Have your whole galaxy flipped on its head. Still, he couldn't believe he'd been out that long.

Gareth continued: "Dad's been meeting with high-ups on the UPE council, discussing the situation. It's a giant cluster. The Aykari, the Djarik, the Coalition, all of it—everyone's in a tizzy. Hey, you want some ice cream? They have it up here. The real stuff, too, not the fake freeze-dried crap. I mean, it's no Fudgy's, but it's sure as heck better than *this*." He eyed the plate of protein chunks suspiciously.

"Dad . . . ," Leo prompted.

"Right. Sorry. So word's gotten out about what the Aykari have done. Their actions during the bombing. The effects of the drilling. The way they leave other planets in pieces. The way the left *us* during that last attack. Everyone's up in arms, some saying they're just as bad as the Djarik, some saying they're even worse. There are protests in every city, people marching, burning Coalition flags." He glanced at the bare spot on his breast where his own patch would have been. "Nobody knows where to go from here, but the council thinks Dad can help because he's smart and he was caught right in the middle of it. Plus, there's the whole deal with the ventasium."

"What about the ventasium?" Leo croaked.

"Yeah—we kind of nixed it all in order to save the planet, remember? Pretty heroic, if you ask me, though not everybody feels the same. Maybe they would have rather just been blown up."

A world without V. Leo took another long drink of water and closed his eyes, allowing himself a moment to ponder it. A little smile crept in.

"Here, I got you something." Gareth reached under the bed and fished up a plush white rabbit with floppy ears and an oversize snowball tail. It greeted Leo with two glass eyes and a stitched-on smile. "Ta-da. I know it's not quite like the one you had—and you don't really do magic anymore—but I saw it in the commissary and thought, you know, if you ever take it up again." Gareth tucked the rabbit under Leo's right arm. Leo ran his taped and tubed hand along its soft fur.

"Still trying to make up for the fact that I shipped you off with those pirates, I guess," Gareth added.

Those pirates. Leo conjured each of them in turn. Boo with his four big arms and shrugging shoulders. Skits's pasted smile and salty comebacks.

And Baz, with his high-tops and concert T-shirts, his one and a half ears, and that cocky smile. Leo pictured the canyon, the smoke, the ship vanishing, and felt a sudden pain, different from the ache in his shoulder. This one ran deeper, reaching down to his gut and spreading from there.

Bastian Black. Terror of the galaxy. Captain of the *Icarus*. And his first mate . . .

"Kat?" Leo said. "Do you know where she is? Is she okay?"

"Why don't you ask her yourself?"

Gareth glanced over to the window and motioned with his hand. The gesture was followed by a rap of metal knuckles on the door, a knock that didn't wait for an answer. Pirates didn't ask for permission.

Katarina Corea strolled in, wearing the same uniform Leo had seen her in last—no Coalition khaki for her, though she had her leather jacket back, looking even more bedraggled with a brand-new hole in its left shoulder. Leo could only guess that was his fault, the new bloodstain his as well. "Welcome back, ship rat," she said.

Leo sat up straight, wincing at the effort, but that didn't keep him from smiling. He was afraid she'd be locked in a brig somewhere. Or worse. He knew what the Coalition did to the pirates they caught.

Clearly exceptions were made for pirates who helped save the world.

Kat pointed at the bandage across Leo's chest. "I told them to just cut off the whole arm and give you one like mine, but they said it would heal just fine. Your loss." She sat down in the empty chair beside Leo's bed. He noticed she was unarmed. It was an unusual look for her. "How're you feeling?" she asked.

"A little lost," Leo admitted. "Been out of it, I guess."

"Understandable," she said. "Maybe I wasn't clear when I told you *not* to get shot."

"You told me that?"

"It was heavily implied," Kat said. "A good thing we found your dad in time. Didn't know *he* was such a deadeye."

Leo looked at Gareth, who nodded. "Dad was the one who took out the Djarik soldier that attacked us, if you can believe it. Saw him come on board and came charging in after him."

Leo tried to picture his father pulling the trigger. He was pretty sure the man had never held a gun in his life. *There has to be another way*, he always said. *A better way*. But then sometimes you really *don't* have much choice.

I've got you, Leo. I'm right here.

Kat leaned across the bed and stole the stuffed bunny from Leo's elbow, setting it in her own lap—another total pirate move. "The good news is, you made it," she said. "And in one piece . . . more or less."

"What about the others?" Leo asked.

Kat stroked the rabbit's faux fur ears. "Zenn bailed as soon as we rescued your father. Turns out the EDF wanted to question her about some past indiscretions, including breaking into a Coalition outpost and kidnapping a certain *someone*." Kat glanced at Gareth, who shrugged. "She split before they could take her in, but she said she'd track us down if she ever needed us to return the favor."

She'd track them down. Of course she would. Leo found the thought both frightening and strangely reassuring. On the one hand, she'd threatened to kill him once. On the other, she'd failed to collect the bounties on either his or Gareth's head, instead helping to bring the Fenders back together. Perhaps that made her the worst bounty hunter in the universe. If so, she was in good company. "What about Crayt?"

"Still not one hundred percent healed, but that hasn't stopped him from causing a stir," Gareth said. "The Aykari have labeled him a traitor, so he's currently under the protection of the UPE. As soon as he found out his invention worked, he insisted on sharing it with every civilized planet that would listen."

"How'd he manage that?" Leo wondered.

Kat flashed him a conspiratorial look. "I hooked him up

with a couple of guys who could help him get the word out. You know the kind: socially awkward, conspicuously brainy, capable of bypassing high-level security and accessing sensitive information."

Leo definitely knew the kind.

"We contacted them and I reminded Dev how he double-crossed us earlier and then threatened to remove *his* brain if he refused to help. Crayt gave them the file with all of his and your father's data and then they transmitted it all across the galaxy. It's out there now, Leo. Your father's research. Crayt's design. The Djarik's plans. All of it."

"Anyone who wants to can build their own don't-blow-up-the-world device," Gareth added. "Everyone gets to decide if the treasure is worth the curse."

Leo nodded. That was what Crayt had wanted. To give people a choice. Of course the Aykari were still intent on smashing their footprint onto every planet with something to offer, and the Djarik were still determined to stop them. The war hadn't ended in the three days Leo was out, but maybe this would shift the balance. Give some hope to all those stuck in the middle.

"So what about us?" he asked. "Where do we stand?" He meant humans. Earth. But Kat took it differently.

"I guess for now we stand with each other."

Leo grunted. "Sounds like something Baz would have said."

"It does, doesn't it?"

In the quiet that followed, Leo could almost feel him in the room, hear the rap of his fingertips drumming along the *Icarus*'s console, the slap of his flip-flops against the floor, the sound of his voice. *You did good, ninja turtle.*

Kat studied her titanium hand for a moment, as if she'd caught her own reflection glinting off the metal. Then she stood up and placed Leo's get-well rabbit back in his lap. "It's good to see you, Leo. You feel better. That's an order from your captain. And no more sneaking aboard pirate ships. Those guys are not to be trusted." She gave Gareth a hard stare. He gave her a salute.

As she moved toward the door, Leo stopped her. "Kat?"

She turned, hands tucked into the pockets of her blood-stained jacket. The one she would probably never clean because it made her look notorious. And pirates relied on their reputations.

"Thanks."

Kat nodded. "We don't leave crew behind," she said. "See you around, ship rat."

And then she was gone.

The observation deck of the EDFS *Nightingale* was smaller than the one on the *Beagle*, though it still offered a spectacular view. There were benches if you wanted to sit and watch a comet streak by or just stargaze for a while. A few wounded soldiers were doing just that, staring longingly at the planet they'd risked their lives defending. Leo took them in all at once, their cybernetic limbs, the angry pink topography of burns still in the process of healing, the lost-but-still-searching look in their eyes. He wondered if any of them had been on the shuttles that landed on that Djarik command ship.

If any of them had helped to rescue the man he was currently standing beside.

"It really is something," Calvin Fender whispered.

He had shown up not long after Kat left. The reunion had been marked by tears and running noses and awkward pauses mixed with apologies and we-can-talk-about-that-laters. He told his boys how proud he was of them. He brought chocolate bars, one for each of them, breaking off pieces for Leo as if he were a toddler incapable of feeding himself. While they indulged, Dr. Fender caught them up on all that was happening. How the UPE was investigating the attacks from five years ago. How the Djarik were still menacing other allied planets across the galaxy. How the Aykari were threatening strong sanctions if Earth choose to sever ties and leave the Coalition—though there were already rumors that Aykari High Command was willing to cut their losses with humanity and just let the planet fend for itself. You don't hang on to the empty carton once the milk is gone, after all. You toss it and go get another.

Leo's father told them that it would take time. Time for humans to reconsider their place in the universe. To reevaluate their commitment to the Coalition. To figure out how best to rebuild their world . . . especially now that all the ventasium was gone. "But at least we have that chance," he said, looking dead on at Leo. "At least we still have a planet *to* rebuild."

And here they stood, the three of them together, staring at it.

"When does our shuttle leave, again?" Gareth asked.

Their father took up Leo's wrist and glanced at his watch, which seemed to be working just fine now, no more glitches, no more *Searching*. . . . "Three hours," he said. "Though we still have to pack."

"I'm packed already, as you can see," Gareth said, indicating the clothes he was wearing with a sweep of his hands.

"Me too," Leo said, holding up the stuffed rabbit, recently christened Copperfield, wincing only slightly from the effort.

Dr. Fender grunted. "I suppose I'm all packed too. Somehow we're coming back with even less than we left with."

But still with everything we need, Leo thought.

They stood like that for a moment, Leo glued to one side, Gareth leaning against the other, their father's arms around them both. Leo noticed his father's cheeks were sunken, his hair streaked with gray, his expression pinched. He suddenly seemed so fragile. So much so that Leo wondered if he and his brother weren't the ones holding him up.

Dr. Fender sighed deeply. "You know, I had this dream once," he began. "A whole galaxy brought together, everyone able to come and go as they please. No borders. No sides to pick. Everyone sharing their knowledge, their technology, their art, music, history, culture. No more fighting. No more power struggles. Just everyone working together to make the universe a better place."

"Sounds like a good dream," Gareth said.

"It really was," his father answered.

Leo thought back to that moment on the Orins' planet, confronting Crayt, trying to convince him to help, and what he said about the natural state of a universe, full of conflict and violence. About hope and good intentions and the futility of even trying.

And yet here they were. The three of them. Together at last. And there she was, waiting for them.

"It's not impossible," he said.

Dr. Fender looked at his son with longing eyes. "I'm sorry, Leo, but it really was just a fantasy. I was fooling myself. I mean, I wouldn't even know where to get started anymore."

Making the universe a better place?

Leo looked back at the fragile blue planet before them.

"I think I do," he said.

＊   ＊   ＊

It was almost time to go.

He didn't want to, but it wasn't his choice to make. He was set to board the *Beagle* in a matter of hours. He wasn't sure if he'd ever make it back here, but at least he would do what he could to make sure there would be something worth coming back to.

Leo went into the garage and grabbed the watering can from its spot beside the shovel and the robotic mower. It hadn't rained in nearly two weeks, and though the flower boxes lining the windows had been empty for some time, there was still one thing he could try to take care of.

He filled the can to the top in the kitchen and then carried it with both hands, careful not to slosh any water onto the floor, then he ambled across the backyard to the cherry tree, still little more than a sapling. So far it showed no signs of the disease that had taken its predecessor; no white splotches bloomed on its trunk, and its leaves were soft to the touch, holding on tight to their branches like little white fists. His father was right: nature was resilient. But it could still use some help.

Leo tilted his watering can and circled around, soaking the ground at his feet, hoping the roots would take it all in, that they would continue to spread out and grow thick and strong, anchoring the fledgling tree, making sure it stood tall against the tremors that sometimes shook the shells off his shelf, most of which he would be leaving behind. If the roots were strong enough, if they ran deep enough, no amount of drilling or detonating would unearth them.

That was the hope.

Leo finished his watering and set down his mother's watering can. He looked at the tree his father and brother had planted with him, plucked one of the blossoms, and rubbed it between his fingers, savoring its satiny touch. He brought it up to his nose and took in its scent with a long, deep breath, locking it away for safekeeping.

"Wait for me," he said.

Leo heard his name and turned to see his father standing in the open door.

With a wish he let the fragile, tender petal flutter to the grass at his feet.

Like it or not, for the moment the Earth is where we make our stand.
—*Carl Sagan*, Pale Blue Dot: A Vision of the Human Future in Space

13

SOMETHING
WORTH SAVING

LEO STOOD OUTSIDE THE OPEN DOOR, ALONE.

His brother had asked if he wanted company, but Leo insisted he wanted to do this himself. Maybe, if things went well, they could all come back as a family, but this time would just be him.

His father had been reluctant to let him go at first. A fourteen-year-old boy. A two-hour hover car ride to an unfamiliar city. But then Leo reminded his dad that only four months ago he'd infiltrated a Djarik military research facility (looking for him, no less) and had been caught up in no fewer than five deadly battles, not to mention that he'd helped *save the entire planet*. He could have gone on, but his father had already given in.

"Point taken. Just be careful," Dr. Fender said. "And say hi for us."

And so here he was, looking up at a neon yellow sign. *The Captain's Orders*. Cute name. Leo wasn't even sure he was legally allowed in, but then this wasn't the first hole-in-the-wall bar he'd ever been to either.

One foot inside and Leo already knew he was in the right place. He was immediately assaulted by loud music—old-fashioned rock and roll—pulsing out of hidden speakers. The place was dark, the lighting all the buzzing, flickering variety, but Leo could still make out the decorations hanging on the walls—anchors and flags and powder horns, cutlasses and tricorn hats. Relics and artifacts from long ago. Long, *long* ago. From a time when humans used the stars to chart their path from island to island rather than charting paths from star to star. Still, the owner was making very little attempt to hide her past. Leo glanced at the digital kiosk inquiring if he would like a table and wondered if he could use it to page someone when he heard an oddly familiar voice. A salty, surly voice.

"Seriously? You call this a tip?"

He peered past a small gathering of people enjoying their drinks to find the source of the rant: a robot with a snow-man build and polished silver plating, zipping around the bar on two omnidirectional treads. One extendable claw held a magnetic drink tray full of empty metal cups. The other held a towel stained several shades of brown. It wasn't unusual to see mechanicals as service staff, but this particular robot was different. It looked top-of-the-line, its parts gleaming. But only what you could see of them. Much of its chassis had been plastered over with stickers sporting all manner of slogans and advertisements. Everything from Frank's Fresh Fish Market to something called Guns N' Roses, which seemed to Leo like an odd store to shop at.

The stickers. The voice. The attitude. And yet Leo wasn't fully convinced, not until the robot's head turned, displaying a sly-looking, cockeyed smile painted right over the voice emitter that she used to keep shouting at her departing customers. "Could you maybe find a way to squeeze another measly dollar out of your bottom holes, you butt-backward, Earthbound, ungrateful little meat bags?"

There was no doubt about it now. Leo stepped into the robot's visual sensors. "Skits?"

"Who wants to kn—" she began, spinning around. It took her processors a full second to identify him. "Ship rat? Oh. My. God!" she exclaimed. "I *thought* it was you, but I wasn't sure because of the lack of blood or dirt and everything . . . plus, I think . . . Have you gotten taller?"

It was possible, Leo thought. It had been more than a hundred days since the *Icarus* made its descent and every last scrap of Earth's ventasium was stripped of its power. A hundred days of potato chips and fresh strawberries and honest-to-god-chicken. "Yeah. I've been eating everything I can get my hands on since I got back," he admitted. "You're looking different yourself. Is that a new . . . um . . . everything?"

"Pretty much. Stickers included. Got this one just yesterday," the robot said, pointing to one plastered to her torso. *I'm Not Treading on You*, it said. *This Is Just How I Roll.*

Leo thought back to the first time he'd met Skits, the robot discovering him in the storage compartment of the *Icarus*, shutting the hatch on him, and then trying to persuade Boo that they should just let Leo starve in there. That Skits had been a mishmash of parts all fused together, Baz's hodgepodge creation. At the time Leo was amazed that the robot didn't just fall apart at the seams. Now she was decidedly more streamlined and symmetrical, minus the advertisements, of course. "It looks good. *You* look good. Seriously, I didn't even think . . . you know . . . with the ship and everything. . . ." Leo stumbled through his words. "I mean, how did you even . . ."

"Survive?" Skits filled in. "I asked myself that same question the moment I was reactivated. Apparently, Bastian backed up my personality matrix at some point and uploaded it to a drive. He gave the key to Kat and she gave *me* this rockin' new bod." The robot spun around on her treads, showing off her improved maneuverability.

Leo smiled. It didn't matter what chassis you put her in,

Skits was going to be Skits. "Well, I'm impressed," he said.

"What can I say, this girl glows. Thankfully boss lady didn't make too many adjustments when she uploaded me, despite all her talk of rewriting my personality."

Of course not. All bark, no bite. Though Leo knew that wasn't entirely true.

"Come on. She'll be happy to see you. She talks about you constantly."

"Really?"

"No. I'm just being polite. It's this new thing I'm trying. But your name does come up from time to time."

They found her in the rear office, her back to the door, head bent over a datapad. The office was decorated just as he would have imagined: bare walls, clean desk, no trinkets, no dust. Everything in order. Everything in its place. Growing up on the streets of a filthy mining town can make you appreciate a certain level of tidiness.

"Those hover bikers keep stiffing me on tips. We really should make gratuities mandatory. Or at least let me threaten to blast the losers," Skits complained as they entered.

Kat didn't look up from the pad. "I've told you before, shooting customers is generally bad for business."

"You're the boss. Oh, by the way, Leo's here."

The former first mate of the *Icarus* turned around at last, taking him in—the stowaway who had dragged her all across the galaxy searching for his family. The kid who somehow put her right in the center of a centuries-old war and convinced her to help save the world, though it had cost her almost everything she cared about.

Leo didn't think that she would hold that against him, but he wouldn't blame her if she did.

"Ninja turtle," she said, her voice gruff but her smile countering it. "It's about damned time."

Kat ordered Skits to hold down the fort and Leo was reminded of all the times the robot had been forced to stay on the ship. And all the times he was told to do the same and refused.

"Come on," she said to Leo. "I want to show you something."

Behind the tavern was a parking lift with a charging station, but a short walk beyond that sat a pond, a little slice of blue and green bursting from the landscape of cement and steel. Milkweed and bluebells grew along its edge. A rusted iron bench faced the water and the sunset. It was beautiful.

Out in the center of the pond, a paddling of ducks was lazily bobbing. Kat sat on the bench and motioned for Leo to sit next to her.

"Shame it took you so long. The ducklings are all grown up now. I got to see them from the start. Watched them waddle after their mother. They'd literally just fall over sometimes and I didn't know whether to laugh or cry. I ended up doing both."

Leo couldn't imagine Kat crying over anything. "It's a really nice place," he said.

"Yeah. I come here a lot when I need some peace, which is constantly."

"I meant the bar, actually."

Kat laughed. "You *are* a terrible liar. That place is a junk heap. The plumbing's nearly shot, the wood's rotted, the dining space is cramped. Pretty sure somebody was murdered there—*before* I showed up, I'll have you know. But the location is good, at least. Easy enough to find . . . when someone finally gets around to looking."

Leo took the hint. "You didn't try to find me either," he said. Though that wasn't necessarily on her. For a while the Fenders had to stay in hiding, just to make sure no one else was coming after Leo's dad. Even now they had two security bots at home—one stationed inside and one out, spidery-looking things with laser cannons and long-range scanners. He wondered if maybe he should try to hook Skits up with one of them; they were definitely her type.

"No, you're right," Kat admitted. "After the nullifier everything happened so fast. First the pardon, then all that stuff with the Aykari, the break with the Coalition, the withdrawal—it seemed better to just lie low for a while."

"And open a bar?" Leo said.

Kat shrugged. "Honestly, Leo, I wasn't sure what to do with myself. No ship. No captain. I was on my own again.

And I'd been away for so long. Then I saw this place for sale and used the reward the UPE gave me for helping rescue your dad to buy it."

Leo didn't even know there was a reward. Zennia's voice echoed in his head: *Just as long as he's worth it.* Worth enough to purchase a run-down pub situated next to a pond, at least. "You settled down?"

"Don't get me wrong, I thought about traveling again, maybe checking up on Boo, but it's not as easy to hitch a ride as it used to be. Have you seen how much a core of V costs these days? What little Earth can get is reserved for medicine and research, not for visiting old friends. Though I probably *could* get my hands on some if I tried hard enough." Her eyebrow arched slyly. Leo didn't doubt it. "I miss that four-armed fleabag terribly," she added. "I hope he's happy."

Leo thought about all of the little Orin hanging off Boo's arms. Of the two of them with their backs to the stones they'd stacked, their faces to the breeze. A place and a purpose. "I bet he is. But I miss him too," Leo said; then, after a breath, "I miss them both."

Kat went quiet, taking in the sunlight glittering across the surface of the pond. When she spoke again the sadness had slipped in.

"He's the whole reason I bought this place, you know. I mean, I still think he would have hated it, but it was something he said he wanted. A place of his own. Or maybe it was just something he wanted me to have. . . . Speaking of which . . ." She reached behind her with her flesh-and-blood hand and undid a clasp, revealing a medallion that had been hidden beneath her shirt. "Here," she said.

Leo stared in disbelief. "Is that . . . ?"

Kat nodded. "They found it in the wreckage. There wasn't much left of the *Icarus*, to be honest. Everything else in that trunk of his was ruined, but this survived somehow. It's a little tarnished, and I replaced the ribbon with a cheap chain." She hesitated. "I know he tried to give it to you once."

It's got to be worth more to you than it is to me. That's what Baz said when he tried to pass the medal off on him. Leo traced the engraving with his finger. *Lt. Sebastian D. Blackwell—for exceptional courage in the line of duty.*

"I can't," he said, pushing it away. "It's not mine."

"It doesn't have your name on it," Kat admitted. "But the 'exceptional courage' part fits. After all, it's not every kid who faces off against pirates, bounty hunters, and alien armies in an attempt to reunite their family and save their planet."

"The pirates weren't so bad," Leo said. "You know. Relative to their kind."

"No. I guess not."

Kat placed the medal—Baz's medal—in Leo's hands and closed his fingers around it. This time he didn't try to return it. It might help, he thought, having a little something to remember him by. Something to keep close. "It still hurts sometimes," Leo admitted. "Thinking about it. I can't imagine what it must be like for you."

"I think he knew," Kat said. "Before we even left. Backing up Skits's programming. Taking the device himself. Making us fly that other ship. Not that I think he *wanted* it to happen, exactly, but I think he saw it coming and somehow made his peace with it. I like to think that in those last moments he found whatever it was he'd been looking for."

A soft rumble echoed in the distance. A ship taking off. It could be human. Or it could be another Aykari transport full of used mining equipment and empty cores, leaving the planet for good. The sound startled the ducks who ruffled their wings but decided to stay put. Leo scanned the sky, spotting a silver speck in the distance. "Do you think they'll leave us alone now?" he asked.

"I hope so. They got what they could," Kat replied. "And we've got enough problems down here without having to worry about what's happening out there." The former pirate turned tavern owner followed the ship with her eyes for a moment and then brought them back down to Earth. "For example, what am I going to do with my server? Because I'm pretty sure her attitude is starting to scare off my customers."

"Just tell her she's not allowed to talk," Leo suggested. "Worked on me."

"Did it though?"

"No. I guess not."

Kat laughed and Leo joined in. Afterward they sat and enjoyed the quiet, not a single drill to be heard. It really was a prime location.

After a while Leo glanced at his watch and saw it was time to start back so his father and brother wouldn't worry. But before he could say goodbye, he had one more question. An important one.

He asked her if she'd been to a game yet. Baseball. The one with the plate not for eating. Kat shook her head.

He promised he would take her.

As he left the bar, Leo fished a ten-dollar bill out of his pocket and put it in the tip jar on the counter. He also had a five-pentar chip, but Aykarian currency wasn't worth what it used to be.

During the ride back, he traced the engraving on the medal hanging around his neck and thought about pirates. Not flintlock pistols and peg legs and tattered flags, but actual pirates. The ones everybody had warned him about. With busted-up starships and cybernetic arms. Cups of gyurt and code fourteens. Vintage tees and quick getaways and growling guitars. Dirty white robes and bloodstained jackets and hard left hooks.

But as he got closer to his destination, his thoughts stretched further. To mocha milkshakes and chocolate chip pancakes. To patio dinners and magic shows. To sunflowers and cherry trees. To seashells and hilltop picnics and second cups of coffee. To all the things he'd left behind and all that he'd finally come back to.

He thought about these things until he found himself standing outside of his house, staring at the cracked steps leading up to the stone porch. He could see Amos sitting in the windowsill, waiting for him.

Leo looked at the wooden sign hanging on the door. Not the original, of course, but just as good. He pressed his thumb to the scanner and heard the door's magnetic lock give way. He turned the knob and stepped inside and said, "I'm home."

ACKNOWLEDGMENTS

To be continued . . .

As a kid raised on comic books and television that couldn't be binged, these three words were just as frustrating and tantalizing as intended. Waiting a week to revisit these heroes and their adventures was intolerable, but that space allowed for untold imaginative gymnastics as I filled the time with stories of my own. After all, the authors and artists had already done all the hard work of building worlds and crafting characters for me to play with.

At least I *thought* that was the hard work. Writing my first sequel showed me otherwise. Turns out what comes after "to be continued" offers its own challenges: trying to knot the dangling narrative threads, giving beloved characters the closure they deserve, and bringing the ship into port. If I've succeeded in the task, it is only thanks to the work of so many who have helped me see Leo and the crew of the *Icarus* through their journey.

So thank you to Adam's Literary for a decades-long partnership. Thanks to Aveline Stokart for the perfect cover. Many thanks to David DeWitt, Amy Ryan, Kathryn Silsand, Vaishali Nayek, Emma Meyer, Sammie Brown, Donna Bray, Debbie Kovaks, and everyone else at Walden/Harper for sending this book out into the universe. Thanks to editor extraordinaire Jordan for helping Leo find his way back. My love and gratitude to my friends and family for being my biggest supporters. Also big thanks to all the teachers and librarians who help young readers find their next favorite read.

Finally, though very little of this book takes place on this lovely and fragile miracle of a planet of ours, it is still a celebration of Earth and a call for ensuring its survival in the face of environmental crises. It won't be easy, but the generations to come deserve unlimited "to be continued"s.

We all deserve a safe place to call home.